Writers in Lockdown

F. Jones, Ed.

ISBN: 9798655544482

DEDICATION

These stories are not about the coronavirus itself, but all were written in the days of the virus, when writers around the world were confined to their homes as part of 'lockdown'.

Tragedy can also be a time of inspiration. The most enduring example of which is the work that Shakespeare completed in home isolation from the Black Death in 1606: *King Lear*, *Antony & Cleopatra* and *Macbeth*. Between 1603 and 1616, pestilence closed England's theatres for 78 months altogether; how many plays would we not know without that tribulation?

It is a numbing feeling to read the daily update of losses from this plague which began, some say, with a single bat flapping about in China. Hopefully you have not lost someone. If you have, I hope you will find peace and opportunity among the ruins as life goes on.

Unrealistic as it is to define a pandemic's end date, all of the work in this collection, across a broad range of subjects and genres, was written between 23rd March and 20th June 2020, when we were all confined and anxious in the first months.

This book is dedicated to those who would not be beaten, who continued to turn out good work, who didn't go a bit peculiar and shave the cat.

CONTENTS

THE TROUT TICKLERS

An idyll by Kristýna Corres

A small and unremarkable child, who was always wrong in every way and usually being told off for it, parents were always right of course, picked her way through damp autumnal grass in her best pair of bed socks and dug into the soft slurries of kitchen waste with intrepid fingers which fetched and wiped and were soon back in her apron pocket with the prize of a crinkly stone that no one wanted. She wouldn't be allowed to keep the interesting stone, she knew that, so pushed it into a flower bed next to a brickwork scratch on the garden wall.

The drift of time is not easy for a child to measure, especially one with shame deeply ingrained under her fingernails, but one day, in between the arguments, banging of doors and rants that fruit from shops nowadays tasted of cloth and water, a bite of plastic shoes took her down to the bottom of the garden path where she slowed, blinked and could see the stone had sprouted through its lid of soil, strained and poked through a single viridian leaf.

Almost a lifetime later, or so it seemed to the young lady since that was all of life she remembered, the tree now lush and tall produced a gorgeously glowing example of a peach. Just one, so far, quite petite and very peachy, a weenie bit like she was. This wasn't surprising in itself, except to mention that for all these years her parents had been telling her that the wretched tree was a knee bracken.

This is her story.

'The trout is built from two substances – appetite and suspicion. Look, you're doing it all wrong.'

Stocky hadn't really encountered girls. At least, he'd seen the grown up versions, dressing elaborately for 'occasions', supervising strangers around the house and breathing jasmine in that rarefied layer of the world which streams three feet over children's heads. They discovered atmosphere in Switzerland and only used knives with cheese; or husbands. This one was different and it did something awesome. It spoke to boys.

He'd first noticed her from about a mile upstream, erratic as she appeared, standing in the middle of a clear, chalk-dashed stream almost as if she was shepherding it. With an Alice band and her dress pulled up, knotted to hold it clear of the water, she had knees. He'd never seen knees on a girl before, but supposed they needed to have them if they were going to stand on plinths. In a sermon-like doze of meditation, she stuck still for minutes on end, stooping and locked peering into the clear, shallow water as it coolly whisked over pebbles, around the chunkier cobbles and off across trailing weeds, swooning and swooshing down along the water meadows with its flotilla of leaves and away toward the town of Stockbridge.

The Test. There wasn't actually a test, not like in school, just a chalk-stream river but they called it The Test because that's where the high and mighty went fishing, when they needed to clear their minds, and he supposed they found it difficult, those statesmen and generals, to learn something new about the world at their age. Brown trout were the prize of these exotic, summer insects that came to visit the town; and the River Keeper didn't take to poachers, stuffing plenty of crusty rock salt into his cartridges.

'You have to stay still, very still', the damp girl told him. 'Don't lift your head because that's a giveaway.'

He did as he was instructed and copied the strange young lady's movements as she scrabbled slightly, then settled and planted her feet, good for the coming hour in that running tap of a stream. They both leant forward and let their hands enter the glass without a ripple. A sense washed over the boy that he couldn't believe he was doing this. Rivers were for watching, weren't they, not melding into?

'Your fingers get cold after a while, but don't let that get to you. Think about the sun warming your back and imagine being some place in the middle – and tell me if you see a kingfisher', she added.

'Okay', he answered. 'If I'm hunting trout, should I think like a trout?'

'Depends', she answered. 'If you hunt mushrooms, do you think like a mushroom?'

She was very patient. Stocky resisted the desire to tip his nose into the flash of water.

'Trout love to be tickled by weed under their bellies. What

you need to do is be the weed, understand? Hold your palms facing up, then curl your fingers and let the fish come to you.'

'Then what do I do?', he asked.

'Tickle them very lightly, from underneath, just a touch. They like it and then, if you're lucky, they go a bit sleepy. What's your name?', she asked him.

'Stocky.'

'My name's Fen. It's funny, you being called Stocky and living in Stockbridge, isn't it?'

'Closer to Houghton, actually.'

'That's why you came down from the top end of the river. When do you need to go back to the farm?'

'Not yet.'

There they craned for an hour or more in the rippling water, immersed in the tide-dance of light and fluidity that washed around and under and through them. Legs became stilts, became four in that mirror, silence was absolute until, at the very last, a large brown trout made Fen's inviting fingers its afternoon rest stop.

He watched her evident skill as gentle tickling lulled it to sleep, the patient weed-like stroking, wondering how many trout she'd taken in the last few years, smuggling them back to wherever she lived to what he imagined was the nefarious pleasure of her parents. 'Don't get caught, Fen, and if you do, tell them it was your first time and you did it for a dare. We'll tell you off like the very devil if a policeman brings you home but we won't really mean anything by it.' – Something like that anyway, for a protein tastier than all the tinned beans and instant blancmange at Co-op.

For eight or so minutes she tickled the trout, a voiceless interplay of pretending to be watery grasses, this subtle, soothing dance and behind it he perceived an iron nerve. This girl would never deviate, temper her resolve, weaken into temptation nor snatch too soon and lose what she and her loved ones needed. What he was watching was a rock, hunting.

A trance took Stocky, a living daydream of appreciation for this spring-soaked weirdling. Otherworldly she seemed in this reflected light, unimaginable that she could continue to exist anywhere but around those lazy days that yawned before the sultry storms of summer. If he ruined this for her he would simply die where he stood, a pillar of shame and clumsiness, so instead he forgot all about his own amateur efforts and waited for Fen to spring her chance. Fen of the Fenlands.

Pow! – a curtain of splashing, flashing, detonating water and up the mad thing lifted, a trout in all its thrashing strength, flying, railing, curling around itself and landing with a heavy thud on the riverbank.

A river flows so very far but never leaves home, a little like passed down stories. Stocky's grandfather had told him about the wartime enemy bomber that had lost its bearings in the night and ditched its ponderous load around here before it tail-turned home, loosing a stick of iron detonations which pock-marked deep craters in a half-mile string along the soft earth of the water meadows. This place seemed to attract bombshells.

To complete the elegant antic, Fen waded ashore and wrapped a soon-stunned fish in an inside-out mackintosh coat, then bundled it under the bushes.

'Aren't you going to go home?', he asked.

'You have to catch yours first. Let's see you try.'

For another twenty minutes he stood Stocky-stock still in the chalk stream, enjoying every moment of being with her. Something was happening to him, but all too soon that reverie was spoiled by the arrival of a swollen belly-finned fish. Fen raised her eyes in warning, which caused him worry at first but, looking down, he could see something had settled. A dark and slippery, very fishy, very real thing of a thing held its position with complicated fin dabbles which couldn't have been easy.

Petrified to move too fast or too soon, Stocky caressed his fingers beneath its belly, not even connecting with the surface at first, and then grew accustomed to the odd sensation of slither. After several minutes with both paws set underneath the trout, as any bear school would tell you, he flipped the fish out of the water like a bag of sand and straight into Fen's arms where, amazingly for a girl, she managed to hold onto it.

In those delighted and excited minutes, they picked their way out of the water to the sensation of barefoot on stones, collapsed and snoozed in the meadows for long hours before heading home. Although Stocky tried many times to see the fantastical girl again, his school and holiday schedule made it difficult. A few times he saw her with her parents in town or on her way to school where he couldn't just walk up, then they didn't have another chance like one that until years later.

It was after the great hurricane of 1986 that Stocky and Fen met again, when both had rushed to volunteer to help tug fallen deadwood out of the marshes. She still came down to the river sometimes on summer evenings, when home got too intense. Amongst the fallen alder trees that grew and fell freely on the banks and all the broken willows that would never now be cricket bats, Fen and Stocky got back together.

This isn't the end of her story, but here's something of his:

Seasons, decades came and went without ever changing the river. A bend or two bowed wider and rain played with the level of the stream but in those years and ever since, Stocky may have been described as being made from two substances; duty and appreciation. Appreciation verging on adoration for Fenella, but duty to his books.

You see, many years ago he had a forebear called Sir Robert Cotton, an unremarkable man except for the one thing he did which was remarkable. Sir Robert liked to read and it was he that put together the finest collection of early Anglo-Saxon manuscripts in all of history. Then, one desperate evening in 1731, a fork of summer lightning ignited his library and the fire which followed consumed some two hundred precious manuscripts. What wasn't saved was lost for all eternity, the literal shock of losing literature. Sir Robert, beyond consolation and against all reason, threw himself into the pyre of his house and passed beyond sight of his family and retainers. Then, in a burst of welcome rain, emerged choking, to kneel on the lawn with a handful of salvage.

One of the objects was charred, its cover singed beyond saving, but when opened in the aftermath was found to contain the one and only remaining copy of *Beowulf*, unique, intact, the poetic legend of the Geats ascendant. Not a scrap or fragment this, written for the East Saxon kings of Sutton Hoo, the royal court of the Wuffings at Rendlesham forest, the work that spoke to the Saxons of their ancient heritage in the faraway lands of Hrothgar in Sweden and Denmark.

Most people who have read it consider the story dark, rough, horrid and confusing, giving sparse credit that it is a translation and most of the original poetry and kennings are twisted. However, whatever that brutal and nearly lost work inspires in you or anyone else, it formed the first entry in the restoration of England's original public library (founded by an Act of Parliament, granted to Sir Robert Cotton in 1701), around which many other odds and ends such as Shakespeare's First Folio and the notes of the Venerable Bede were collected, then Newton's Principia arrived and the main bits and pieces by Jane Austen. Robert's life was a muddle, but his vision, alarmingly for some levels of society, had always been to put books into the hands of the public.

The cold water stream was carefully, respectfully being bothered again this morning, not by grownup poachers, with their muddied number plates and plunderous dragging sacks but by a few small children learning the nearly lost (and alluringly against-the-law) art of trout tickling. Apart from cupping a stickleback or two into a jam jar or sock, they hadn't seen much to interest them yet, but knew that when the weed was cut short for the summer season, the stream would be stocked and flush with booty.

The sun passed out from the last of the clouds and cast its lights and reflections across the water, tinting eddies, trickles, whirlpools and skin as if painting and strewing uncountable daisies. An elderly couple laid out their picnic on the rural bank and followed the scene as it played out in the water.

A child in glasses sat on the verge with his head deep in a book, bare feet left to trail forgotten in the flow. A handful of leaves spiralled and dipped through the shallows and swept past another boy with a stone in hand, raising the arm... but no, he couldn't throw and disturb the tight concentration of another.

A narrow bending stick of a girl stood statue still in the river. She'd found a nook inside the bend where the wash slowed, where she had willed herself invisible. A flight of light-green and yellow weeds had rooted there, a flowing carpet with occasional gaps, between which she had settled her fingers. Patience and skill in one so young, rolling through sights she could never share with us, communing with the living stream lest the daydream be broken.

Pow! – Up came a fish. 'Bravo' said the elderly man and the youngsters scattered. The girl stood in shock for a second, wide eyes snapped to another's dimension, then scooped up her trout and ran helter-skelter after the boys.

'We're not interested in reporting a crime', said Lady Stockbridge, later.

'My wife and I would be very grateful if you could tell us from the description who they might be. We weren't blessed with children ourselves and we wanted to pass something to...'

'To people like us', Fen interrupted.

The desk sergeant shuffled, unsure about the regularity of this, what with GDPR and everything.

'What were you thinking to give them?'

'Just some old books'

'and a bit of river.'

ADOPTION

by Dale E. Lehman

It didn't seem so awful, running beneath the crystalline skies in the calm after the storm. He was disobeying Mom, but he'd done it so often and always Dad laughed it off, which deflected her anger; but this night, he was wrong.

As the storm retreated north in the falling dark, the all-clear sounded. Len Vandermeullen was out of the door like a striking snake. He scampered through sodden gardens, kicking up mud, down the tree-dotted hill from the Secretary's Mansion to the open field inside the compound fence. He skidded to a halt, turned his eyes heavenward and pressed his new astrospecs against his face. His father had given him the device last month for his fourteenth birthday and he practiced with them on every clear night.

The stars had called Len since before he could read. He was quite the astronomer, so his science teachers said, knowing every constellation and bright star. Rising in the east, The Spacecraft swooped past Armstrong the Explorer; near the zenith, The Bearshark's gaping jaws roared; southward, The Silverbow Tree spread its branches from the horizon, its crown glittering with white, blue, orange and red stars. With his astrospecs, he sought out the unknown, stars too dim to have names, clusters that looked like tiny clouds, dark holes seemingly punched into the Universe by obscuring nebulae. Using eye movements and winks, he highlighted whatever caught his fancy and the astropecs served up delicious information: magnitudes, distances, ages, masses, sizes. He feasted on it all.

That was the danger Mom feared. Gorging himself on the cosmos, he missed what was closer to home. The storm, now far north, ablaze with lightning, sending thunder rumbling through the hills, could be followed by others. 'There's a reason', she had warned time and again, 'why the world is called Rudra.' She never explained, neither the name nor the reason, but Len knew storms. Weather fascinated him, too. Rudra's primary star and its distant secondary created complex patterns of differential heating, while its rapid rotation stirred the pot. Furious storms could ignite and swell in less than an hour. Sometimes they came in pairs, triplets even. When the warning klaxons sounded, you had but minutes to take shelter. The all-clear only meant the known danger had passed. The unknown could spring upon you minutes later.

Len didn't much care. Though Mom fretted, Dad relished and encouraged his enthusiasm for science and Dad *was* the planetary secretary, second in power to the governor. Mom had to listen to Dad, didn't she? Besides, Len could run. He'd timed the dash up the hill to the house and knew he could make it, should the warning ring out, before the first lightning seared the sky, before the first hurricane gust slapped his face.

Basically, Len thought, I'm invincible; and so he prowled the skies, searching out in awe.

Suddenly it was there near the zenith, a bright star he'd never seen before. The astrospecs didn't know it either, which made no sense. They could only tell him its brightness: magnitude two point three.

How could an object that bright not be in the database?

The device changed its mind. Magnitude two point two.

Two point one.

Two point zero.

It was brightening! Len whipped off the astrospecs and squinted, breath held, body rock steady. He compared the new star to familiar ones nearby – and yes, very slowly, almost imperceptibly, its light grew.

A minute passed, maybe two, maybe five, maybe five thousand. Why would a star brighten like that? Was it a supernova? Had he really discovered such a rare phenomenon in the very moment it happened? The star now blazed brighter than any other and then the impossible happened. It didn't just brighten, it grew, expanding from a scintillating point to a fat oval and then to irregular and boxy. Something was falling from space, not with a fireball flash that blazed and was gone, but controlled, deliberate.

A spacecraft!

Warning klaxons screamed. Len barely heard them but he knew today he wouldn't make it to the top of the hill. Whatever was happening, he couldn't escape. What did it mean, a spacecraft landing in the middle of the city, in the planetary government compound, almost atop Governor's Mansion?

I'm sorry, Mom, he heard himself whisper. I'm sorry!

A barrage of lighting erupted, not storm lightning but weapons fire from the descending ship and the world became a blaze of red engulfed in heat and smoke. Len dropped the astrospecs and ran. His legs ached as he powered up the hill through burning trees and slippery mud, running for the house, running for his life, running for his mother who appeared in the doorway, panic etched into her face, her arms stretched out as though she might reach him in spite of the distance.

Before he could get there, the ground heaved and the sky roared and the night swallowed him whole.

A hissing, squealing, like steam escaping an antique kettle. The choking smell of burned synthetics and molten metal. Len gagged. Something sharp gouged his left ribs. He rolled away to escape the skewer but pain followed. Voices in the distance cried and screamed and shouted, then he couldn't open his eyes for fear of what he might see.

Something crunched nearby, something heavy marching through rubble. Whatever it was stopped near his head. He kept still, knowing it wasn't a friend. He barely breathed, sensing he was being scrutinised by cold eyes and colder minds. He squeezed his eyes tight, hoping the invaders would leave. Then a hand touched his face and brushed something from his skin.

'Take him to Cranmore.' A woman's clear alto, strong, no-nonsense, both like and unlike Mom's.

'Just kill him', a ragged male voice said. 'He's half dead anyway.'

Len felt tears squeeze from his closed eyes. They stung. He couldn't even blink them away for fear of moving. He heard the crack of a hand striking a face, then he was lifted roughly and pain engulfed him. He nearly threw up but passed out instead.

'Took you long enough.' The voice was different, quiet, withered, like somebody's great-grandfather standing graveside moments before dropping in. The light was bright now, or brighter anyway, enough to make Len squint.

'Kids are supposed to be fast healers.'

Len blinked at the face that accompanied the voice. The man wasn't half as old as he sounded. His thinning hair was in disarray and his face was scarred and creased with lines, as though he had spent his whole life worrying over problems he could not solve. He was dressed in a threadbare gray coverall.

'Where...' Len's throat was dry.

'Oh', the man said. 'The eternal questions. Figures.'

Len coughed. He hadn't the strength to cover his mouth.

The man elaborated: 'Where the hell am I, how the hell did I get here and where the hell am I going?'

Len licked his lips, which were dry and cracked.

'Hospital. More or less.' The man lifted Len's arm and checked his pulse. 'Less than more, but you make do with what you have.' He dropped Len's wrist.

Len guessed the city hospital had been destroyed. This must be an emergency hospital. 'What happened?'

'Now that is a very big question. The Universe is thirteen billion years old, full of stuff happening and most of us are very small.' The man chuckled at his own humour.

'I mean...' Len licked his lips again. He wished for water but wasn't sure it was safe to ask.

'I know what you mean.' The man helped Len sit and passed him a translucent bottle with a tube protruding from the top. 'Sip slow.'

Len sipped. The liquid had a strange, soapy taste. He made a face.

'My favourite, too. I'm Cranmore, Doctor Cranmore, but we're neither formal nor proud here. Doctor is just one more job and hardly a glamorous one.' Cranmore put a hand on Len's shoulder, maybe to comfort him, maybe to test something, then helped Len lie back down. 'So you want to know what happened. You don't, really, but I'll tell you anyway. Your city was attacked and looted, so a lot of people died. I'm sorry.'

Len swallowed. What about Mom? What about Dad? He could barely think, much less speak about it.

'Be glad you met with fortune, boy. You could have died, too. Instead, you were rescued by one of the very few big people in the Universe.' Cranmore looked entirely serious as he folded his arms over his chest and stepped away. In his place, a woman came to Len's bedside.

His breath caught in his throat when he saw her. Her dark eyes pierced him. Her light brown hair, hanging in ringlets, framed a lean face, a face of authority, of command. She wasn't as tall as the doctor, yet in presence she was ten times his size.

'Name', she said. A demand, not a question.

He tried to push himself up but his head swam. He flopped back.

'I didn't say get up. I said, name.'

He didn't want to answer. He couldn't not. 'Len.'

'Leonard?'

'Just Len.'

The woman drew near, grasped his chin, turned his head to look him square in the eyes. To his astonishment, she smiled, if slightly. 'Len. Lenny. Welcome aboard.' She released him. Still commanding his eyes, she asked Cranmore, 'Prognosis?'

'He's fine. Skewered below the right rib cage, but reasonably shallow. No infection. Otherwise, just minor injuries. He should be fit for duty in two or three days.'

The woman nodded.

Len didn't understand. 'I want to go home. I want my parents.'

'I'm your mother', the woman said.

Panic engulfed him. Fighting dizziness, he sat. 'No you're not! I want to go home!'

The woman perched on the edge of the bed and ran a hand through his hair. Her touch wasn't harsh, but he didn't like it. He wanted her to leave.

'I know it's hard. Your home is gone, your parents dead. You're my son now. This is your home. You're one of us.' She stood.

'I don't even know who you are!' Len objected, as though that would make her vanish, bring his parents running, transport him home.

The woman's eyes swallowed him, swallowed the whole of the cosmos. One of the few big people of the universe Cranmore had called her. As Len looked into her eyes, he could believe there was none bigger.

'Everyone knows me', she said. 'I'm Anna Grande.' She waited just long enough to see recognition blossom in his shocked face, then she was gone.

Fear overtook Len. 'Oh, no.'

Cranmore cocked his head. 'Oh, no? God, Len, how many boys do you think get to call Anna Grande mother? It's an honour, one hell of an honour.'

'She's a pirate. A murderer!'

The doctor drew near. 'Sure', he whispered, 'and she's just like you.' He tousled Len's hair and smiled mischievously. 'Why do you think she saved you?'

The days passed in a blur. In his waking hours, Len longed for home and his parents and wished the nightmare would end. Sleeping, more nightmares invaded, half-remembered chases through fire and destruction from which he awoke in a cold sweat, but his strength returned quickly and before long Cranmore pronounced him fit for duty, whereupon he discovered it wasn't just an expression.

He was assigned a succession of jobs, mostly cleaning and minor repair work. He hated it. The jobs were dull and repetitive and in the service of the woman who had killed his parents. Rage and guilt filled him each time he recalled her ship, this ship, the Defiance, descending upon them. He should have realised, should have raised the alarm, should have saved everyone. Not that he could have, but his impotence made it worse.

Worst of all, he wasn't immune to the romanticism of Anna Grande, the unpredictable, the uncatchable, arch-nemesis of the Earth Security force, bane of the outer territories. Every boy filled with adventure-lust followed or fought her, every girl wanted to be her as she plundered through space, preying on cargo ships, transports, even military vessels, stealing and kidnapping at will. That had been the way of it throughout colonised space for twenty-four years Earth standard; but to meet her face to face, to be forced to join her crew...

He only escaped guilt and anger when helping Cranmore, who Len couldn't help but call Doctor despite the old man's protestations. Len couldn't see Cranmore as a pirate, not when he was so wise and kind, not surrounded by the trappings of medicine and science, primitive as they were.

Cranmore taught him everything, including how to access information from the ship's data stores, which proved as rich a library as any Len had ever known. Before long, the doctor even inducted him into the practice of medicine. A young woman came to the hospital with a nasty cut high on her left thigh, which she said she had received during battle training. Cranmore instructed Len in cleaning and sealing the wound. The woman was amused by Len's embarrassment and awkwardness, even when his clumsiness caused her pain but, in the end, Cranmore praised his work.

After their patient left, Len asked 'Where is she from?'

'Tria? She works in the galley most of the time.'

'I mean before she was here.'

Cranmore busied himself with sterilising the equipment and motioned Len to clean the surgical table. 'That's complicated.'

Len started scrubbing the surface. 'I guess I have time.'

'Short version, her parents were part of the original crew. They brought her along for the ride.'

'On a pirate ship?'

'What were they supposed to do? They couldn't leave her. She was only seven.'

That seemed wrong. Tria looked older.

Cranmore gave him a disappointed teacher look. 'Yes, Anna Grande has been on the loose for twenty-four years, but she gets around. Remember your Special Relativity, Len. Ship's time, she's only been plundering for fifteen years. Biologically, Tria is twenty-two.'

Len finished wiping down the table and tossed the cleaning cloth into the incinerator. A buzz signalled the reduction of the material to its constituent components. 'Why did her parents join the crew?'

'I already told you.' Clean-up done, Cranmore motioned Len out of the procedure room to the reception area, where an older woman was busy working a computer display embedded in a countertop. 'Watch this', he told Len quietly. He addressed the woman. 'Len wants to know why you came aboard, Falak.'

She turned. She had light brown skin, wrinkled and severe, but her voice was soft. 'That's complicated', she said, smiling curtly and turning back to her work.

'There you go', Cranmore said. 'Every story here is complicated and often too painful to voice. Just like yours. Why did you come aboard, Len?'

Len looked at his shoes and shrugged.

'Complicated', Cranmore agreed. 'Family always is.'

'You're not my family!' Len snapped. He turned away, embarrassed at having yelled at Cranmore. He ought to apologise, but he couldn't. He wouldn't. His family was dead and Cranmore had pledged his allegiance to their murderer. The doctor might has well have killed them with his scalpel.

Cranmore busied himself with a report on the computer display.

'Some of us', Falak said, still engaged in her work, voice still soft, 'joined in desperation. Some in anger. Some were conscripted. Some were born here. None are blood relatives of Anna Grande but we are her family. She has no other. Nor do we, any longer. She's our matriarch and we're all loyal to her.'

Len remembered Anna Grande's voice as she declared herself his mother. It wasn't harsh or cruel, but she had given him no choice. 'Why?' he asked.

Falak turned, eyes wide with incomprehension. 'Why? Because she's given us everything. It's right and proper to be grateful.' She turned back to her work and added, 'Besides, the alternative is death.'

Over his first two months aboard the Defiance, Len worked in every part of the ship, cleaning, repairing, operating, upgrading. His head crammed full of schematics and procedures, he could almost operate the vessel himself. Almost. He may be a quick study but there was so much to learn and each day he discovered something new. Boring tasks gave way to more interesting ones: propulsion, environment, computer operations. He felt a growing fascination for the ship but beneath that festered resentment, keeping him apart from the crew. They helped him and encouraged him to become one of them but he couldn't permit them too near, not when they gave allegiance to his parents' killer.

He was assisting the quartermaster, a thin, ragged man named Harlan Quinn, reviewing inventory records when

Anna Grande arrived and with a glance dismissed all but Len from her presence. Seated at a computer desk, he rose. She motioned him down and circled behind him, scrutinising him. He waited, barely breathing. If he'd had a weapon, he might have killed her, or tried to. Everyone knew you couldn't kill Anna Grande.

'Made yourself at home?' she asked.

Len didn't answer. This would never be his home.

'Don't pine, Lenny. You can't restore what's gone. This moment, right here, right now, is all you ever have.'

'Is that why you kill and steal? To get what you can right now?' The rebuke spilled out before he could catch it. He didn't care. Let her kill him. Death would be better than living under her rule.

Anna Grande neither answered nor struck him down. She rounded the desk, stopped opposite him and studied his eyes, a predator sizing up her prey. He couldn't look away. He resented her power over him even as he succumbed to it.

'I don't explain myself to anyone, Lenny. Not even you.'

'Because you're the Captain?'

'Because I'm Anna Grande. Remember that.'

'I can't forget it.' Len wished he could spit the words in her face. 'I can't ever forget what you did. Captain.'

Her face remained as impassive as stone. 'The others call me Captain. Not you.'

'What do I call you?'

'What did you call your mother?'

He lowered his eyes so she wouldn't see the hurt, but he couldn't keep it from his voice. 'Mom.'

'That's what you'll call me.'

He slammed his fist on the desk and sprang to his feet, shaking with rage. 'You killed my mother!'

Strangely, sympathy crept into Anna Grande's smoky eyes. 'No, Lenny. Not me.'

'I was there. I saw.'

'Rudra's planetary governor, a swindler named Harlow Cornwall, killed your parents.'

That couldn't be. He knew Harlow Cornwall. The governor had been his parents' friend and he'd always had a kind word for Len; and sometimes gifts.

'Sit down', Anna Grande told him, her voice unusually

gentle. Len sat. 'I kill and steal when I must but it's far easier to bargain. I had an agreement with Cornwall. He went back on his word. The fool should have known better.' She arched her eyebrows in query.

Len swallowed. Everyone knew you didn't double-cross Anna Grande.

'Had Cornwall been honest, your parents would be alive. A lot of people would be – and you'd still be on Rudra, gazing up at the stars.'

'How did you know...?'

'Cranmore mentioned your interests. You told him. Or he's psychic.'

He didn't remember telling Cranmore but the doctor certainly knew Len's interests.

'Now you're sailing the stars', Anna Grande added. 'I'd say you've traded up. So...' She stretched out her hand and for the first time Len noticed she was holding something. It looked like his lost astrospecs but more sleek, more elegant, with lenses that could be raised and lowered. He took the device and examined it.

'Infospecs', she explained. 'Keyed to Defiance's network. I've given you read access to everything. Behave yourself and someday I may give you control.'

'Everything?' He'd heard about this tech. Infospecs were used to operate industrial processes, transports, military vessels. With them, you could manage solar power collection, navigate spacecraft, plan and execute battles. With access to her entire network, Len might gather enough information to destroy her. Why would she give him such power?

'How old are you, Lenny? Fifteen?'

'Fourteen.'

'Why do you think I'm here?'

He could only repeat what he'd heard. 'I guess that's complicated.'

Humour brightened her eyes and she laughed like a girl, but the transformation unwound as quickly as it had come. 'You know how old I was when I got my first ship?'

Len didn't. The stories didn't say. Anna Grande was a titan sprung full-formed from the ether. She could be a billion years old for all he knew.

'Eighteen', she said, 'and scared stiff. I didn't ask for it. It was there when I needed it. So I took it and I've been Anna Grande ever since.'

'Weren't you always?'

'I was a different Anna Grande then. Tragedy changes us, sometimes for the better, sometimes for the worse. It will change you, Lenny, whether you like it or not.'

He put on the infospecs. The display came to life, edging the view of his surroundings with dozens of symbols he didn't understand.

'You'll be working with the navigation team for the next few months. Once you've mastered it, I'll put you on weaponry.'

Suddenly light-headed, he flipped up the lenses. 'You want me to fight?' He remembered treating the wound on Tria's leg.

'You'll get hand-to-hand training eventually but this is special, Lenny. Not everyone learns ship's weaponry.'

Anger resurfaced. 'I'm not a pirate. I'm not fighting for you.'

Anna Grande faced him, unruffled but no longer with sympathy. She stood, a barrier between past and present, refusing him access to what he'd lost, offering him a future he was sure to loath. When she spoke, her voice was matter-of-fact.

'You'll do as I say.'

He looked away, jaw locked, eyes ablaze.

'Right?'

He wanted to say no, but he felt tired and wanted her gone. 'Yes', he muttered.

'Yes what?'

What might she do to force him to say it? He almost didn't care but he said it nonetheless, just to be rid of her. 'Yes, Mom.'

When he finally looked back, he was alone.

Navigation proved harder than any subject Len had ever studied. On Rudra, navigation systems were built into everything and did all the work. 'Space ain't like that', Kayla Stetson told him his first day on the job. 'You got lots of unknowns out there, lots of gravity bumps and ruts to throw you off course.'

She was nineteen, lean, strong, intense, with hair like the summer sun. Len found sitting beside her unsettling. All he could think of was her. She knew it, too and smirked whenever his thoughts strayed too far from work; but she never said a word, neither to encourage nor discourage his attention – and gradually he learned the subject.

'It's an art', Kayla explained as they worked out the course to their next destination, a tiny mining colony on the edge of some remote solar system Len had never heard of, a place called Yellowknife. 'It's what you know plus what you guess plus what you feel. You've got the computer, but that's just a start. You gotta second guess it – and the Universe.'

Len watched her porcelain fingers work the desktop display. He only half understood her actions and knew she expected questions but he couldn't think of any. He could only watch her delicate movements.

She nudged the computer's recommended line to create a new path. 'Know why I did that?' she asked.

'Uh.'

She smirked again. 'A recent slow collision between two minor planets created a contact binary. The gravity well's here now. The charts don't show it yet. How'd I know?'

'Uh.'

'Talked to the port on Yellowknife. Navigation's contacts as well as computers. What you know plus who you know.'

Len wanted to impress Kayla with an insightful question but the only one that came to mind was nothing to do with navigation. 'Why are we going there?'

'Supplies. Hydrogen for the engines, mostly. They extract it from the ice. Captain has a deal with them and we get it cheap.'

In exchange for their lives, probably. Anna Grande said deals were easier than killing but threats must make negotiations shorter.

Kayla gave him a funny look. Had she guessed his thoughts? If so, she didn't let on. 'We monitor and correct our flight path *en-route*. You've got a lot of variables to track. Unknown objects, unexpected variations in the interstellar medium, variable engine output...'

She went on and on, but Len's mind was no longer on the

lesson or his teacher. He was thinking of revenge.

When his shift ended, Len sequestered himself in his bunk with his infospecs. Privacy didn't exist on Defiance. Only Anna Grande had private quarters. Her officers were quartered together apart from the crew, who were assigned bunks in two large, cramped compartments. Families bunked together but otherwise men, women and children were intermixed in each compartment. He quickly learned you didn't pay attention to what others were doing, but Len couldn't shake the embarrassed feeling that everyone watched him undressing, dressing and sleeping.

At least with the infospecs on he could pretend the place was deserted. Hidden behind them, he studied the communications systems and learned their operation. Intraship calls proved easy and largely unsecured but intership communication required security clearance. Although he couldn't send such messages, he found protocols for contacting thousands of base and planetary administrative, corporate and private organisations, even Earth Security. Some of these could only be used by the Captain and her most senior officers. Not surprisingly, Earth Security protocols were among them.

Without clearance, Len had no hope of directly contacting ES and little chance of making indirect contact. Disheartened, he flipped aimlessly through the remaining information, seeing not the words but his mother desperately reaching for him. When finally she slipped back into memory, he was staring at the answer.

Emergency signals.

The topic proved large, consisting of contingency after contingency and the appropriate channels for requesting emergency assistance in each case. Most required security clearance but one special case did not: a general distress call. Only to be used in the direst of emergencies – misuse was grounds for execution – such a call could be sent by anyone in case cleared personnel were all dead.

Len flipped up the lenses and wondered if he could transmit that call without being seen.

Eight days out from Yellowknife, Fate handed him an

opportunity, or the most he would probably get, when Kayla called him to the control centre, a small, cramped pit in the heart of the ship aglow with computer displays embedded into the walls. 'Bring your infospecs', she reminded him, although he was never without them. He found her standing like a marble goddess, intent upon the screens, her eyes obscured by her own infospecs. Len donned his and was instantly overwhelmed by a storm of information: objects, distances, socio-political data. A green line indicated their projected course. A blue line trailed back along their actual course to date.

He and Kayla were alone. The control centre's staffing varied by situation. At its busiest, it would be crowded with navigation, flight, environment and weaponry crew. At other times, it could stand empty.

'Let's review our approach', Kayla said.

He wondered how she knew he'd arrived, but then he realised she was annotated on his infospecs. He winked at the icon floating by her head and was presented with her name, age, height, weight and job assignments.

She started talking before he could explore further. She led him through planetary approach, orbital injection and descent. She pointed out issues with the existing plot and, while not letting him adjust anything, asked for his recommendations. She praised his good calls and corrected his bad ones. Once she laughed and said, 'That's double zero for sure!'

'Double zero?'

'You crashed us, bud.'

Len bit his lip in embarrassment.

'No worries. Guess how many times I double zeroed my first time out?'

He shrugged.

'Fourteen. My mentor said sixteen but he was wrong.'

The lesson continued. Descent proved more tedious than the rest combined and Len's mind drifted. He studied the control centre instead, soaking up every detail his infospecs provided: panel layouts, control procedures, available virtual interfaces. When he discovered a small communications console tucked in a corner, he examined it in detail. The emergency beacon was there, a red circle protected by a translucent cover. It could be operated manually or virtually. Instructions related how to record a distress message, how to virtually remove the cover with a blink and activate the beacon with another.

Len hesitated. He couldn't do it without Kayla knowing and he was pretty sure of her loyalties. If he did this, his life would be forfeit.

Just as his parents' lives had been.

'Hey', Kayla said, 'You listening?'

Was it right to follow them into oblivion? He wanted justice. Revenge. What would they tell him to do?

She snapped her fingers in his face. 'Control to Len, Control to Len. Come in, Len!'

He drew a breath. 'Sorry.'

'What's wrong?'

'Nothing. Just, there's a lot of stuff here.'

'Don't let it distract you. Not on final approach. That's double zero for sure.' She smiled, her eyes mischievous.

'Sorry', he repeated, but his mind was no longer on the work. Would his parents want him to sacrifice himself? What had Kayla's parents wanted? Where they part of the crew? If not, what had happened to them?

'How long have you been here?' he asked.

She flipped up her infospecs and cocked her head, confused. 'Since I was twelve. Why?'

'How did it happen?'

She didn't answer.

Len flipped up his lenses, too. 'Complicated. I know. Did you have a choice?'

She shrugged.

'Why do you stay?'

Kayla approached so close he could feel her breath. He flushed with embarrassment. 'Nowhere else to go. This is my family now. So're you.'

'Some family. When we get to Yellowknife, what happens? Do people die? People like our parents?'

She drew back and shook her head. 'I told you, Captain has a deal with them.'

Suddenly angry, he snapped, 'Like what? Hand it over and nobody gets killed? That's almost as bad!'

'Of course not! It's a fair deal.'

He turned away. How could she expect him to believe that? How could she believe it? This was a pirate ship!

'Damn, Len, you got a lot to learn.' She took him by the shoulders and turned him around. She held on as she spoke. 'We protect places like Yellowknife. They don't stand a chance without us. Without Anna Grande, Alexander Padgett would own it and he sure would kill to get it.'

'Who?'

Kayla flipped down his lenses. 'Look him up.'

He did. Padgett proved to be Earth Security's second most wanted pirate, more ruthless than Anna Grande, less cunning. Although rivals, the two had sometimes formed brief alliances. As with everything in the world of piracy, their relationship proved complicated.

He looked up Yellowknife, too. Although small, it played a key role in rim colonisation as the most remote supply outpost capable of significant output. Farther out, settlements remained small, barely self-sufficient and of interest to none but explorers and renegades. Earth Security had been hard-pressed to provide adequate protection so far from home, which left those territories vulnerable to piracy. Ironically, Anna Grande offered stability and had been generally welcomed by the inhabitants, vexing Earth Security.

'I don't understand', Len muttered.

Kayla flipped up his lenses and leaned close again. 'That's one simple thing', she said. 'Captain hates Earth.'

'Why?'

'They killed her family. Swooped down from the skies one day and...' Kayla gestured an explosion.

Len stared at her. He heard Cranmore's voice in his head: 'She's just like you.' Had Anna Grande seen herself in that frightened, broken boy lying in the rubble?

'There was a war', Kayla explained. 'People died. I lost my home and Anna Grande found me. I'm here 'cause I asked to be and she said, 'Welcome aboard."

She flipped down Len's infospecs and then her own. 'Enough syrup. Back to school, kid.'

Len studied the navigation display. 'Yeah', he murmured. 'Back to school.'

BLOOD CURSE

by Perry Lake

1. Zoltan.

On a stormy night at Castle Dracula, high in the Transylvanian Alps, the recently arisen Countess Báthory Erzsébet of Ecséd railed to the heavens that thundered over her head.

'I am denied my vengeance! My enemies go unpunished! What benefit is there in immortality if it leaves me impotent to have done my will?'

Vlad Țepeș merely observed the storm. No peasant would dare step forth from his wattle hut on a night like this and no window would be left open. There would be nothing for them this night but for how many nights thereafter?

Already he had too many fanged mouths to feed. He knew he needed Erzsébet, even before he turned her, but here also were Faust and Gretchen, Anna Darvulia and the twisted Katarzyna. If greatly starved, the Undead will go dormant, lifeless. True, they can be revived from that state... but when? Certainly they would be defenceless against their enemies; and if Vlad had anything these days, it was enemies.

He was just debating whom to send into exile, and where, when the Countess Báthory spoke again. 'Vlad, I want revenge against King Matthias, the Palatine Thurzó, the magistrate, Kaspar Wolkenstein and that preacher, Ponikenusz. How might thee grant my desires?'

'I might not', he replied succinctly. 'Thy revenge is warranted but it is not in my plans. I have need of thee in my campaign against Jhiang Shi in the east. I will have thee seek out and take new blood from the east to sire those blood-bound to thee as thou art unto me. With such an army, I would wrest the gold mask from the face of that easterner.'

The Countess Báthory may not have heard all that Vlad said, for she responded only to the first part.

'Thou willst allow me no revenge? I cannot believe this, for never hast thou foresworn thine!'

'I would not foreswear thine either, Erzsébet, but my need is the greater. If thou wouldst have thy revenge on these men, thou must do so by proxy.'

So, over the next year, Erzsébet consulted Dr Faust and Darvulia. Acting on their sage advice, she acquired a new entourage of witches, hoping their magicks and potions might gain her the revenge she desired. First, she insisted that each of them drink of her blood, that they would be blood-bound to her. Then she bade these witches curse her enemies.

Their spells had no result. Györgi Thurzó was a devout Catholic, with a small chapel in his house where he and his family said prayers daily, entreating for divine protection. The King of Hungary and Father Ponikenusz, who had vexed her so much, although Protestants, were equally devout.

Erzsébet soon knew she must expand her options but a common cutthroat could never make his way into the King's palace. Who could? Lady Erzsébet smiled to herself, then she went to Vlad and presented to him a new plan for revenge.

'Sire, I have a retainer for whom such challenges are but trifles', she said. 'I intend to call Zoltan Windischer to me. He is a man who is not a man but a wolf and thus has not the strictures of a man.'

'Impossible', Vlad said. 'Windischer is not blood-bound to thee.'

Erzsébet laughed. 'Oh, but he is. I saw to it that he fed from me.'

'Didst thou? My, thou dost have surprises, but thee will still have no power over him. Thou wert then but a thrall thyself. One thrall cannot bind another.'

'Twon't hurt to try.'

With a faint nod, Vlad conceded to her logic. 'As thou wisheth.'

Zoltan Windischer stood at the base of Castle Dracula, looking up at the crumbling towers and jagged parapets. Every night for the last week he'd heard her calling in his mind. He'd felt her in his blood. He could no more refuse her call than he could refuse gravity.

He climbed the seven hundred steps and found upon entering the gates a smaller castle than he supposed from looking at it from below. It was narrow, as was the summit, designed more for a daunting appearance than actual military value. Might the same be said of its master?

The Countess Báthory stood within, tall and imperious, perhaps taller than she stood in life. She did not smell the same to him – she smelled of death and decay, faint though that scent was. She smirked at him.

'Thou come in good time, Zoltan', she said. 'Thou may do honour to us.'

He knew what she meant. He hated to bow to any nobleman, let alone a noblewoman, but it felt as though a great stone hung from his neck; yet still he did not fall to his knees.

'We are pleased to have thee once more in our retinue, Zoltan. Yet we feel thy resistance. Wouldst thou break our bond?'

Windischer looked to the gate, hoping to spring away and run, but a man stood there blocking his way. It was the same darksome nobleman who had been in her retinue before. He was trapped.

'No... my lady.'

The vampire countess regarded him for a moment.

'Very well. We've a task for thee. Thou shall be our instrument of vengeance, after our witches and their spells have failed us', the countess said, as she petted Windischer's dark hair. 'Our Lord Dracula will not allow us to endanger our self and his plans with so slight a matter as our vengeance. This then will be thy duty. Though I may have another duty for thee, in the meantime.'

Not a fortnight later, Windischer found himself once more in Hungary, in the streets of Buda. In the day, he found the fine house, for all the townsfolk knew of it. This was the house of the King's palatine, Lord Thurzó. House? It was a mansion of brick, scant less than a castle, surrounded by a large garden and this surrounded by a short stone wall all about.

At midnight, it was not a man who sought entrance but a wolf. Wary of any gate, even had it been open, the wolf leapt to the top of the outer wall and there stopped, waited, watched and listened.

Satisfied that no ear heard his entry, he dropped to the floor inside and loped around the mansion, searching for an open window on the ground floor. The house was no castle and there were windows aplenty but none was open.

He made his way around a corner to the back, where he spotted a door, illuminated by a single hanging lantern left burning. Again he halted, sniffed and listened. He smelled men but none were in sight. He approached stealthily...

Without warning, the door opened from within, flooding the courtyard with more light. A man stood there, wearing gilded armour, gnawing on a piece of bread and holding a bowl with a spoon. The man stopped, his eyes enlarging as he beheld the large wolf.

The wolf tensed to lunge... then heard other voices from within.

' Miklós, you forgot your wine.'

Miklós had no concern for wine. He dropped his food, stumbling over his own feet as he turned and yelled for the others to come.

'A wolf! There is a wolf out here! Hurry or it will eat me!'

There were too many men-at-arms, the wolf knew. He turned tail and ran for the wall. Behind him, he heard more and more voices, confused and disbelieving, but one of them did believe what he saw. As the wolf leapt for the wall, an arrow struck him in his left thigh. A yelp issued unbidden from his throat. As he struggled to keep from falling backwards, a second arrow hit him, inches from the first.

A wolf pulled itself over the parapet; a naked man landed on the ground, with two arrows still in his thigh. Windischer half ran, half limped away from the House of Thurzó. If any saw him that night, whatever else they thought, they knew he was no wolf.

After failing to kill Györgi Thurzó, Windischer knew his future was bleak. Even with his enhanced ability to heal, he was sore wounded and travelled slow. That gave him time to think, to divine his future. He liked not what he saw, knowing the countess's capacity for the torture of those who angered her. He decided to run away, maybe to France, maybe to Russia, but far, far away.

That night, he felt the countess in his mind, searching, digging into his secrets – and suddenly, he felt her rage as she found something she didn't like.

Windischer ran the next day, though still he was not fully healed. He ran through the fields and swam the river and climbed the hills and in the forest he watched the sun setting. As the sun set, the countess was in his blood, in his mind, and as the countess's mind once more merged with his own, Windischer left the forest and descended the hills, swam back over the river and ran through the fields, moving ever closer to the she-fiend who called him.

After weeks of this back and forth travel, Windischer gave up and let himself be pulled back to the house of the living dead in Transylvania. When he limped back into the court of Castle Dracula, Erzsébet was not happy.

'Failure is unacceptable, Zoltan.'

Trembling, Windischer cowered before the unholy thing in the form of a woman. He began to speak, to beg, but he was interrupted by another.

'Ye wolf-man is wild and powerful, Beth', said the witch Darvulia, no longer deferring to Erzsébet by her title, as the blood of Dracula had made them sisters. 'But never did I say he was fit to slay kings or princes.'

'Then who can?' asked the countess.

'I've curses and malefica better suited to fell the mightiest oak', Darvulia replied. 'I can send these curses, if ye but give me charge over y'r witches. I can teach them and harness their powers.'

As the witches had proved no value to her thus far, Erzsébet agreed with a nod. Then she turned her attention to Windischer once more. Vlad and Darvulia looked on.

'As for thee, Zoltan, we would have thee healed of thy wounds and we would make the bond betwixt us redoubled, for we sense our blood-bond has grown weak and see thy defiance growing like thy wick.'

Windischer's eyes shifted left and right, looking for escape. Already Vlad and Darvulia had him flanked. He but blinked once and the countess stood before him, rolling back the sleeve of her embroidered gown. She stroked his face tenderly with the back of her hand. Against his will, he felt his manhood rise to her touch.

Her smile stretched, revealing fangs like a wolf's, like his own. A look of confusion crossed Windischer's face but this was supplanted by horror as he saw the countess open her chemise. A long, sharp nail slid long her bosom, leaving a thin red line. The line thickened. A single drop of blood slowly traced the rounded white flesh.

Windischer shook his head, even as he tried to back away, only to discover that Dracula and Darvulia held him in place. This was madness, Windischer knew, madness of the sort that had gripped his father and left him a ravening beast. Madness and evil, everything unnatural!

Countess Báthory pushed her trickling bosom before his mouth. He tensed his muscles, trying to pull away.

'Drink, Zoltan', commanded the countess. 'Drink of our blood that we might dwell within thee forever. Drink, that we might be joined.'

Erzsébet took Windischer's hair in her hand. She forced his head to her bosom. Once more, Windischer lapped her undead blood. At once, he began to change. No longer did he stand as a man, but as a wolf, resting its paws on her shoulders for balance. Or so it seemed to any not Undead. In truth, there was never a physical transformation; so deeply does the lycanthrope believe that he projects an illusion to all who live; but the countess was no longer alive.

Without control, with all his control given over to her, he ejaculated upon her crimson gown. She laughed.

2. Judge Wolkenstein.

The Wolkenstein family of Gratz were known to Vlad. Vlad's father, his biological father that is, attended the Scholomance with Oswald Wolkenstein and together they learned great secrets. Wolkenstein retained such secrets that made him a master composer and a skilled diplomat. Vlad II learned how to kill.

The current Judge Wolkenstein was of a cadet branch of the family and little in the way of musical skill had passed down to him. However, Kaspar was accounted a learned youth and gained favour in the court of the Lord Palatine. For his skill in law, he was made a travelling magistrate.

Kaspar Wolkenstein had tried the servants of the Countess Báthory and sent them to the headsman. For this, the undead countess had decreed he and all his family must perish.

Soon, very soon after his second draught of the countess's blood, Windischer healed. He felt stronger, perhaps stronger than ever in his life. Once more he travelled, first north, over the Carpathians, then across the Transylvanian plains, then turning west into Hungary and on to Austria. A travelling magistrate had quite the territory to cover in the days of the empire, it seemed.

At last, Windischer found himself in Gratz. A day of spending his mistress's coins in the taverns bought him the information he needed. He now knew where Judge Wolkenstein dwelt. He had but to wait until dark.

By night, Windischer returned to the street, but walking not as a man. Now he was, to all intents and purposes, a wolf, for any who saw him. The wolf could not and would not, enter through the front door. Doors were kept locked and possibly guarded. As a wolf, he had an innate wariness of anything that might be a trap. Instead, the beast circled around the rows of houses, searching for some means of ingress.

Shortly he found a low fence several houses away. This he leapt over in a single bound. He was in a garden, but the wrong garden. The houses here nearly formed a castle, sharing a common interior, although separated by fences of stone or wood. As none of these fences were very high, the wolf simply leaped over one, another and another, until he came to the garden he desired – the largest of all those in this block. This was the garden of the House of Wolkenstein.

He approached the door. It was unlocked but he had no way of knowing that and no hands – he believed – to lift the latch; but the night was warm and a window was open. Through this he leapt.

It was but a soft thump that Kaspar Wolkenstein heard when he knew his maids had gone to bed hours ago. His wife lay beside him as he read. Could little Erich be up and about?

Wolkenstein got up, put on his slippers and went out to see. He passed down the hall and looked in on his son. The boy lay slumbering, his golden locks clearly visible in the moonlight. Now a different thought came to Wolkenstein's mind. He returned to his bed chamber and retrieved his rapier, as Ilsa raised her head.

'Kaspar?' she asked. 'What is it?'

'Shh, probably nothing. The house settling, but I want to be sure.'

He turned and walked through the darkened hall once more, this time slower and more quiet, with his sword held out before him. He came to the top of the stairs and looked down. He thought he saw a shadow, moving like a dog. It was gone before he could confirm anything.

He descended the step, even slower. At the landing was a niche that held a lantern and flint. He ignored these and instead took down from the wall an iron shield that bore the colours of the cadet branch of his family. Wearing it on his left arm, he continued down the steps.

The rooms were dark but he could still make out the walls, the furnishings. Nothing was out of place... save for a pair of yellow eyes and pointed ears looking over his writing desk.

He barely gasped before the beast leaped over the desk and landed in the centre of the drawing room. Wolkenstein instinctively charged the wolf – he may have been a magistrate, but he had noble blood and he had not forgotten how to handle a sword and shield. Defending himself with the shield, he sought to thrust his rapier into the wolf's heart... but all Judge Wolkenstein's training was against two-legged foes. Like many a man before him, he was ill-suited to fight a creature so low to the ground. The wolf darted to the side and his thrust missed, the sword hitting only the wooden floor.

The wolf had plenty of instinct and skill against clumsy, two-legged foes. He dived in, even lower, and managed to get under the shield. His jaws clamped down on the man's ankle and instantly twisted. Wolkenstein went down with a cry.

The wolf released the shredded flesh of the ankle and lunged for the man's throat. Wolkenstein deflected the lunging wolf with his shield. From the steps, he heard the screams of his wife and maids.

The wolf got around the shield once more, his fangs finding

purchase in Wolkenstein's side. It was a quick bite, not intending to take flesh, but simply make his prey lose blood and weaken.

The wound may have done so but Wolkenstein was not without fight yet. He slashed with his sword and caught the beast across the face, opening a shallow wound. The wolf yelped and recoiled. Then the room was alight with lamps. The wolf saw he was outnumbered and would soon be surrounded. He turned to flee.

Using the last of his waning strength, Kaspar Wolkenstein drove his rapier deep into the wolf's belly. The wolf yelped louder, clawed at the floor to gain traction and pulled himself off the blade. The beast hobbled quickly to the kitchen, climbed the table and hauled himself out the window. He wanted to run, to make his escape in the hills and forests beyond the city – and what then? He'd failed the vampire countess not once but twice. His doom was sealed.

On the dawn after the attack, Ilsa Wolkenstein tended to her husband's wounds, staunching the bleeding, as a maid brought a fresh bowl of water. Earlier, Ilsa sent a maid to fetch the curate that he might say the final rites. No doubt the preacher would need to be awakened and dress, so it might be an hour before he arrived.

Ilsa wondered if Kaspar would last that long. His skin was hot to the touch and the application of damp rags did little to soothe his fever. He could not speak and she was unsure if he was awake. From time to time his eyes opened but he did not turn to her when she spoke. She realised he could not hear her. If he saw her, he did not know who, or what, she was.

The curate entered the room sooner than she expected. He gasped as he saw the bloodied man whom he'd known for years.

'Thank the Lord you are here, Reverend', said Frau Wolkenstein. 'Please pray for him. He will need it, for the Countess Báthory laid curses on his head ere she died.'

The curate did so, whilst Ilsa kneeled and clutched little Erich to her, pressing his small hands together in supplication. Together with their servants, they all prayed.

Kaspar lingered in delirium and fever throughout the day

and by night he hovered near death. The curate was summoned again and after he prayed and spoke the prayer for the dead, he told Mrs Wolkenstein to prepare for the worst.

In the morning, Kaspar awoke, still weak, still with a mild fever, but even that would pass in some hours. He was able to take soup for his dinner and appeared in good spirits. Ilsa told him what had transpired.

Curiously, it was a man they found in the Wolkenstein garden. It was a man that was hauled to the city gaol and bound over for trial.

'And it will be a man that will be strangled in the city square for the crime of lycanthropy', Frau Wolkenstein accurately predicted. 'May his body be burned to ashes!'

Kaspar Wolkenstein nodded in agreement. His wife clutched his hand, smiled and proclaimed his recovery a miracle. Delicately she embraced him.

On the morning that followed, Kaspar rose from his bed, dressed and walked about the garden, despite his attentive wife's protestations.

He laughed and said, 'My Ilsa, you would make a babe of me. I'm a bit stiff but I have recovered. No doubt my injuries looked worse than they were.'

He clutched her close and whispered, so that little Erich might not hear, and told her precisely what portion of him was stiff at that moment. Frau Wolkenstein blushed, then giggled.

That night, Kaspar Wolkenstein made great use of that stiffness, to his wife's delight.

Not four weeks later, after the ashes of Zoltan Windischer had long since blown away, a fully healed Kaspar Wolkenstein felt a pang of pain at dusk. It seemed like a cramp at first, then a fever, for his face was flushed with heat, but it spread throughout his body.

Ilsa noticed at once. 'Kaspar? Are you ill?'

Kaspar retrieved a handkerchief from his sleeve and mopped his face. 'I think... maybe I am.'

Ilsa was at his side, her arm around him, helping him to the stairs ere he realised it. 'You must lay down. I'll have Cook make you some broth. Here, mind the steps.'

Even in his distress, Kaspar chuckled. 'Woman, you treat me as an old man. It's most likely something she dropped in that stew that vexes me.'

Ilsa smiled back as they climbed the stairs. She soon laid him to bed, fussed over him a bit until he shooed her away, then went back down to find the cook.

It was Cook's night off. No matter, Ilsa thought. If she couldn't manage a bit of broth, she was hardly a wife at all. She took down a pot and filled it halfway with water, then set it by the fire. She unwrapped a slice of leftover ham from the cheesecloth and started cutting it into pieces.

The knife dropped from her hands as she heard her husband's cry of anguish. She lifted the front of her skirt, ran to the steps and all but flew up them. She stopped, seeing her young son standing at the bedchamber door, looking in, his face ashen, his eyes wide with fear.

'Erich!'

She ran to the boy and pushed him away. She looked within. There, Kaspar Wolkenstein kneeled on the floor, doubled over, his hand gripping the bedpost, yet too stricken to pull himself up. Ilsa went to him, put her hands on him.

'Kaspar!'

He rose his face instantly, angrily. Ilsa gasped and pulled back. It was not him, not her Kaspar – but it was! No! Yes – but changed, somehow.

He snarled at her. She pulled away. Then she looked at his hand, bathed in the light of the full moon. His hand, the hand that had written legal briefs, had caressed her and their son lovingly, was now darkened, hairy with claws, the hand of a beast. She screamed but Kaspar howled with delight.

Kaspar Wolkenstein awoke the next morning in the woods, having no idea how he had got there. He found himself without his doublet or shoes, his shirt and hose shredded. Even more disconcerting was the dried blood on his hands.

Making his way home, he found the front door open. He called, but no one answered and the servants had fled.

He found bloody smudges, like unclear footprints, leading out. He rushed upstairs, horrid, unclean images flashing in his mind.

Seconds later, he collapsed, kneeling over his wife's horribly mutilated corpse. He wailed and sobbed for an hour and then he prayed to Heaven that a bolt from the blue might strike him dead. Kaspar was not that lucky. For soon after, he found his son's body.

Kaspar's days as a magistrate had ended. His nights as a murderous beast had just begun. There was now a new kind of monster in the world, a new form of werewolf, with no control over his transformation, upon whom a lupine nature was forced, carried by a vampiric infection and enhanced by the light of the moon.

As his life as a Wolkenstein had ended, it was only fitting that he escape and take on a new name, that of Wolfenstein.

'My curses be more trustworthy than y'r wolf-man's bite, milady', said Darvulia, a year later. 'Thurzó is dead.'

'He is dead', Erzsébet conceded. 'Yet I think he passed in his own time, rather than by any curse of thine.'

'Believe as ye wish, Beth.'

Countess Báthory wrapped her arm around Anna and looked out from the tower of Castle Dracula. She saw only the mountains and valleys below, yet she sensed something.
'There is something new in the night, Anna. I sense that Zoltan is dead, yet likewise I sense something of him still lives. I am unsure if it is to my liking or not. I must find this thing, that I might know.'

THE HOSPITALLER

by Mike Sherer

'HEY!! YOU! YEAH YOU!'

Jerry Mack looked around to see who was hollering. He located a man standing at the edge of a narrow slice of city green space, staring at him. As soon as their eyes met, the man looked away. In filthy clothes and unkempt demeanour, he looked like some homeless guy. He was probably wanting money, Jerry thought. Dismissing the bum, Jerry turned back.

'HEY!!!'

Jerry span back around toward the screamer with a curse on his lips, but the curse never left his mouth. There was a tremendous crash behind him. Jerry reflexively crouched and span around to look. A minivan had T-boned a car. The two interlocked vehicles slid down the street before his eyes and the passing breeze they made peppered his face with hot debris; then they crashed into another car. Screams all around, as some people ran to help while most whipped out their phones to capture the moment.

Jerry did neither. He was a statue. Frozen on the street corner at the intersection where the accident had happened, his stunned mind scrambled for comprehension. He had been standing on that street corner waiting for the 'little walking guy' light to replace the open hand when the homeless man had yelled at him. Jerry checked the walk light. The little guy was still on the screen, so if he hadn't paused to look back at the screamer, Jerry would have stepped out onto the crosswalk when the walk light had signalled he could – and been crushed between the minivan running the red light and the car lawfully moving in the middle of the intersection.

Jerry looked back at the homeless man but he couldn't find him. The scene was a madhouse of people mobbing the crash site with their phones. Jerry waded through the onrushing crowd away from the street and into green spaces. Free of the maddened throng, he scanned the open area. The homeless guy was hobbling away from the wreck and, luckily for Jerry, he was injured in some fashion that kept him from moving particularly fast. Jerry dashed after him.

He ran up in front of the tramp, who turned out to be

surprisingly young, blocking his path. 'Why did you yell at me?'

The guy dodged around him and continued hobbling.

Jerry grabbed him, so the guy jerked his arm, but Jerry was way stronger. He tightened his grip. 'Were you warning me?'

The guy finally met Jerry's gaze. 'What do you want?'

'What did you want? You yelled at me.'

'Let me go or I'll get the police.'

'Fine. Let's go. I know where a bunch of them are hanging out right now.' Jerry tugged him toward the crash scene.

'No!'

Jerry stopped tugging.

'I don't have time.'

Jerry released his arm and looked him over. 'Looks to me like you've got nothing but time.'

'There's somewhere I need to be.' The guy resumed, hobbling down the sidewalk.

Jerry matched his stride, without the hobble. 'My name's Jerry.' Not getting a reply, he continued, 'If you don't tell me your name, I'll have to guess. Is it Asshole?'

He glared at Jerry without breaking stride. 'You'd call me a name like that after...' He looked away.

'After you saved my life? Is that what you started to say?' The man at his side stared straight ahead. 'You're right. I shouldn't do that. How about Angel? Are you an angel?'

At last, a reaction. The corners of the man's compressed lips ticked up just a little. 'No. Just a saint.'

Jerry laughed. 'Now we're getting somewhere. Which saint am I speaking to?'

The corners of his lips drooped back down. 'I really don't have time for this.'

'I didn't, either, a few minutes ago. I was rushing to a job interview, that I was late for... which I don't give a damn about anymore. Why worry about a stupid job I probably wouldn't like anyway when I should be dead right now?'

'Buy me lunch.'

'I'll be happy to. What would you like?'

'For you to leave me alone for fifteen minutes. Then we'll eat and talk.'

'Promise?'

'Know the Pike Alley Bar? Three blocks from here?'

'No.' Jerry pulled out his phone. 'But I can find it.'

'Fifteen minutes. Half-hour at the most. I'll be there.'

Jerry stopped and watched the saint hobble on down the sidewalk.

'His name is Julian.'

Jerry turned to find a young woman dressed for a run by his side. 'Okay. Who is he?'

She smiled. 'A local character.'

Jerry looked around. 'He's homeless?'

'No, he's got a little apartment down here somewhere.' She started to walk away. 'Come on, I'll show you where Pike Alley is... unless you still want to make that job interview?'

Jerry walked alongside her. 'No, I don't. Seems like I was fated not to do it, one way or the other.'

'So you believe in fate?'

'Not really. What was that about him being a saint?'

'You're not Catholic, are you?'

'I am nothing but glad to be alive, right now.'

The young woman laughed. 'So you've never heard of Saint Julian the Hospitaller?' Jerry shook his head. 'I don't blame you. There are over ten-thousand Catholic saints and Julian is kind of obscure. He murdered his parents.'

'Are you talking about Julian in the flesh or Saint Julian?'

'Both.'

'Saint Julian murdered his parents and they made him a saint?'

'It's complicated but Julian's, our Julian's, mother died in childbirth and his father was so grief-stricken he killed himself.'

'That's not murder.'

'Tell Julian that. He was raised in a Catholic orphanage and was probably perfectly normal; until he started having visions. That's when he changed his name to Julian.'

'So he is a loony.'

'Loony enough to save your life.'

'You saw what happened?'

'Not really. I just put it together. The wreck, Julian being here, you chasing after him.'

'How does that add up to him saving my life?'

'I didn't give you the last figure in my equation. Julian

saved my life, too. He's sworn to help others, as a Hospitaller.'

'What does that even mean?'

'It's another name for the Order of St John, holy knights who protected pilgrims on the road to Jerusalem. They set up free public hospitals centuries ago, in the crusades.'

Turning a corner, Pike Alley Bar came into view. 'Here we are. Now if Julian shows up.'

Jerry escorted the young woman inside. 'Do you think he'll stand me up?'

'He won't mean to. But Julian gets distracted easily.'

They sat at a table in the small neighbourhood bar and ordered drinks. Whilst waiting for them to arrive, Jerry learned Helen's name; and that he should donate money to Julian. 'Why would I do that? I've offered to buy him lunch.'

'He needs money. Julian can't hold a job, not with the life he leads. The parish gives him some money for food and helps with his rent.'

'Why do they do that?'

'To support his good works.'

Their drinks arrived. Jerry hardly noticed. 'Which are?'

'He helps all those who need it.' Jerry didn't blink. 'Other than that, I'd rather Julian explain it to you.'

Jerry took a long slug of his beer then leaned back with a smile. 'This is starting to sound like a scam you two are running on me.'

'I could be talking to a corpse right now.' Jerry's smile faltered while Helen took a slug. 'You could be, too. I was out for a run one day and I'd gone a little too far when it was starting to rain. I was exhausted and getting wet, so decided to take a short cut back to my condo. I started to turn down this alley which I would normally never have set foot in, then Julian yelled at me not to go in there. You saw what he looks like. With this crazy homeless-looking guy yelling at me in the pouring rain, I stayed out of that alley. Next day I learned a young couple had been robbed and murdered in that very alley not long after I had started to jog in there.'

'So why didn't he warn that couple, like he warned you?'

'He told me he did, when I finally located him, but he said not everyone listens.' The waitress returned to their table. 'The chili cheese fries are good. They'll add jalapeños if you want.'

Three drinks, a large helping of chili cheese fries with jalapeños and an hour later, Julian had still not shown up. 'I guess he got distracted', Jerry said, motioning to the waitress to settle up his tab.

'Julian might have had another vision and gone off to save another life.' Jerry looked askance. 'Jerry, come on, if we were scamming you he would have shown up.' Helen stood. 'Besides, aren't you glad he acted on the vision he had of you?'

Jerry shrugged. 'Can't argue with that.' He paid the bill and they walked out. Helen gave him her phone number then walked off. Jerry remained outside the bar for a few more moments, still hoping Julian would show.

After another fifteen minutes, Jerry gave up. He walked back to the crash site to see the street corner swarming with police and the intersection closed. That meant there had been fatalities. Jerry smiled, as he wasn't one of them.

Jerry set off for the garage where his car was parked. Passing an alley, at the far end he saw a man huddled up on the pavement against the side of a building. Was that Julian? Jerry laughed as he started off down the alley. The unlikely saint had probably been distracted by a bottle of booze. 'Hey. Saint Julian. You missed a good meal.' There was no response. He's probably passed out, Jerry thought.

As he neared, Jerry didn't see a bottle. What he did see was Julian's blood-soaked shirt. Jerry rushed up to him. 'Julian!' Still no response. Jerry squatted down to peer into his face. His eyes were closed, his expression slack, but he was breathing, barely. Jerry yanked out his phone and dialled nine-one-one.

While Jerry was reporting his situation, Julian's eyes cracked opened and he attempted to speak. Jerry finished the call then leaned in close. 'What was that, Julian?'

'I didn't foresee my own death.'

'You're not dead yet. An ambulance is coming.'

'It doesn't matter. Come here.' Julian attempted to raise his arms. Jerry leaned into him. Julian rested his arms on him, the action was too weak to be considered a hug and attempted to pull him close. There was a lot of blood and as Jerry leaned into him his shirt was soon as soaked as Julian's.

'What happened?' Jerry asked.

'This alley', Julian croaked. 'Where I met Helen. Killers

were waiting. For me. Said no more interference.'

Sirens sounded in the distance. 'They're coming, Julian. Hang on.' Julian muttered something. Jerry leaned an ear in close to his lips. 'What was that?'

Julian gasped a final breath into Jerry's ear, 'It's up to you, now', then fell still.

Jerry leaned away. He was soaked in Julian's blood and he could still feel Julian's breath in his ear.

An ambulance pulled up at the end of the alley with lights flashing. Jerry stood and backed away as EMPs hurried down.

Several days later, Jerry was taking a walk through his own neighbourhood. Still without a job, he had plenty of time for walks.

He approached a young girl, five or so, playing in her front yard just as a van pulled up before her. The sliding door flew open and a man jumped out and grabbed the child. He jumped back in, holding her, the door slammed shut and the van sped away.

Jerry pulled out his phone as he ran into the street to get the license number but the van vanished before he could. Jerry looked back to the yard where the young girl had been playing and... she was still there, playing. What the hell? Jerry stared at her, unable to comprehend.

Until... he saw that same van turn down the street toward him. Jerry stepped out onto the thoroughfare where he could be seen plainly and glared at the driver as the van crept by. The driver met his gaze and drove on down the street without stopping. Jerry snapped a picture with his phone as the van cruised away down the street, then the vehicle turned the corner and disappeared. Jerry looked back to the young girl, who was still playing in her front yard.

Jerry smiled. So this is what it's like to be the Hospitaller, St. Julian. Jerry waved at the young girl and then forwarded the photo he had taken to the police.

MAD LANGUAGE BROADCASTING

by Adam Corres

'Cob, you're a plum'.

'Sorry, what was that Thomas?'

'A total, absolute... stone less... come and look at this.'

Cob sighed and rose from the sofa as his flatmate basked in the irradiant glow of a laptop, where he was usually to be found when he wasn't being dragged against his will into the harsh daylight of Swansea campus.

'You told me, right, that the angelic Brynn...'

'I think you settled on the unutterably foxy, body and soul-wrenching Brynn', Cob corrected. 'She seems fairly normal to me'.

'Doesn't matter. The point I'm trying to get across, to beat into your addled brain substance is that you said it would put me in Brynn's good books if I recommended that translation job.'

'Which she got', added Cob. 'She needed paying work and you got it for her. Well done.'

Thomas nutted his forehead into the keyboard with mid-range force carefully calculated to cause no real damage.

'Right, yes, which she did get, obviously you prat, because she's the only Gaelic Erse translation student at the university, but look here duck-wit.'

'I don't know what your problem is. She's a very organised person, so if you set her off in the right direction she does it all herself. I have no idea why she wanted to work with me in her group project but I'm not complaining' Cob added, picking his way around the clutter of the flat rather than doing anything about it.

'Did she get a really good grip on your wrist and pull?' asked Thomas.

'She did that, yes. I got the feeling she only came up to Swansea University because she'd sprained all the available wrists in her village.'

The screen was bright and its appearance hardly forbidding, so Cob began to suspect that Thomas's problem could be somehow connected to some of the words written on it. 'Monthly broadcast viewing figures from the British Audience Research Board', ran the header. Cob focussed down to try and make sense of the problem as a seething Thomas prodded his most helpful finger at the passage which currently troubled him.

'*Brush up your Erse*. BBC ALBA, Scottish Gaelic-language digital free-to-air television; Descriptor: minor regional languages; Category: public information; Format: 30 minute broadcast production; Slot: late night; Viewing figures: 0.'

'Zero, Cob. Bloody zero. Last month there were more people sat on screen than watching the programme!'

'So?'

'What do you mean, so? What is this 'so' of which you speak? She's going to lose her job and hate me for wasting her time! You're a pillock, Cob!'

Thomas shook the dust out of his hair as his thoughts turned to the ever-present allure of instant noodles. 'It doesn't matter, Thomas. They get paid anyway.'

It was more or less at this point that Thomas realised it's no fun being the only person on the planet who has any common sense. He nodded into the keyboard once more, this time making enough of a dent to disconnect the internet.

'Look, mate', said Cob, brightening up the lives of those around him, 'minor language programming is all supported by grants. Some of the funding comes from the Cultural Board, some from the Diversity Council, some from the regional governments and the rest from the national broadcaster. They are obliged to support minority culture or it will expire and they'll be the ones who face the blame, in Parliament, see, where their money comes from. They can't be found to starve one culture or mother tongue at the expense of another, so it doesn't matter a jot that no one's watching. It's only important that the programmes are *made available*.'

With an expression that said there were a couple of dozen questions he would like to ask but he couldn't think of any of them right now, Thomas digested this fresh information and stood awhile in thought. He knew that some things took on new meaning with hindsight. For example, he had always been exceptionally good at camouflage as a small boy, when his parents would play a game where he'd win a special medal if they didn't see him all day. Thomas began to see that this might be another perfectly normal paranormal phenomenon. He also knew in his heart that any obvious example of byzantine stupidity didn't mean it wasn't also reality. 'Bugger', he concluded, dispensing with the philosophical metaphysics.

'What's the problem? You still get to sniff around Brynn, so why's that face hanging off you? You look dour as a pile of ironing. I know what this is – it's hereditary, isn't it? Just like that documentary *Akhenaten and the 18th Dynasty*. You've got an 18th Dynasty face and you think that's going to put her off. Come on, cheer up and have an almond Cornetto.'

Thomas shifted uneasily, like a lottery winner without the ticket. 'My grandfather, see, spoke a Celtic tongue which he wanted to teach to me but I wasn't interested at the time. He died, the last native speaker, standing on one leg, putting his socks on at the top of the stairs. That's a common cause of death in my family. Sometimes it's tights, sometimes a beekeeping outfit, or socks is the most common, but always, invariably we die changing clothes at the top of the stairs. Anyway, he went into the great 'oot' without ever explaining the language. Once he told me he wanted to pass on a great treasure, then he said where it was in his daft language so I never did find anything, digging dirty holes all over the garden. It was our cultural heritage and now we've lost it.'

'We, is it?', Cob chided. 'Thomas Thomas appropriates for his-self a sense of ethnic belonging. You'll be making ruddy coracles next.'

'Well I didn't think it was important at the time. There's no point in speaking a language that no one else knows because they'll ask you what it means in English and when you answer in English, that cuts out the middle man. I couldn't have guessed there'd be any genuine money in it. Why are you staring? It's disconcerting.'

'I was just thinking, what if it isn't gone?', Cob speculated.

'It wouldn't be much use us digging him up!' replied Thomas.

'No, what I mean is, who apart from us would know that the language is dead, that it wasn't passed along?', Cob ventured. 'It would be your word against theirs, about your own private conversations with your grandfather, right?'

Thomas considered this entirely radical possibility. 'So, what you're saying is, we could make it all up for a laugh?'

'Well...?'

The bus began to draw away, leaving Thomas alone on the kerb. The sound of a press-button bell stabbed insistently until the bus stopped again a few yards up to eject Cob, who was finishing an unhurried crisp packet.

The pair walked over the path toward a private car park which had a van in it marked 'Security', but both could see they were blocked by flower bed landscaping. Thomas stopped but Cob sprung straight over the flower bed, leaving footprints in the loose soil. Thomas looked up to check no one was watching and picked a tentative path across, at which point Cob inflated his empty crisp packet and banged it loud against his hand.

After a brief circumnavigation to find the front entrance of an imposing office building, they found a sign showing this to be to be the headquarters of a television channel.

In the flourishing adventure of life, many things run smoothly but few flow as smooth as the ink when you're signing your own death warrant. In this case, the document was a contract with S4C, to provide content for the Welsh regional channel. The 02:00 slot was something they'd been struggling to fill for years and this proposal presumably appealed to the broadcaster as heaven-sent diversification. The fact the language was incomprehensible authenticated why so few people spoke it. Proving impractical to prepare a contract in Wenghley dialect, which no lawyer could attest to, S4C provided one in Welsh and English, crossing their corporate digits that no offence would be taken.

The first broadcast attuned to Thomas and Cob's unspoken plans (and they'd invented a new letter). Wenghley was ready.

'Bleth plithy rhodwin, co na-corrog doppa-roob?'
'Carrottyhap. Tebewin ic, nanumptie. Plos dandwell carragoch.'

'Howpudwey, plagwe lemaft rop.'
'Lefmat rop. Lefmat, nah lemaft. Plom.'

'Prove to me that isn't a legitimate language', Thomas challenged Cob privately after the display, keying a digital PIN into the S4C back-office site to check viewing figures. Cob grabbed his shoulders and craned over, their eyes widening in triumph.

'Two! Two stupid viewers, probably drunk – and that's five hundred and fifty squids in our back pocket!'

'Less tax, Thomas, and insurance contributions. Being conditioned by the circulation of money is the same bad joke everyone falls for.'

'Pish. We're on easy street if we can keep this rubbish going. Look, once upon a time a Greek fellow tugged on the end of a chain...'

'Here we go.'

'... and on that was a great big anchor and caught up on it was an enormous sucker and stuck to the sucker was the planet Earth and when the bloke pulled, the whole planet landed on his head and the moral of the story is don't mess with the system.'

'I'm just being cautious', Cob worried. 'Ok, let's look at the basics. The trouble with talking like an elf is no one in our neck of the woods does it. "Sweet the rain's new fall", "mine is the starlight", "gently unwinds the florid sun down to its lover the sea". See? It doesn't roll well to the Silurian ear, which is adapted to a more... chip-based dialogue.'

'Not some Mediterranean ninny with leaves growing out of his head.' Thomas pondered. 'You're saying our language shouldn't be sung or barked, but should sound practical?'

'Yes, now you're getting the hang of it.'

'Plos dandwell carragoch – keep it sensible?'

'Exactly! I can't describe it but there's still a sense of discord to what you're doing. It sounds to me like a bit of a duck-call for fantasy kingdoms.'

Unbeknownst to the lads, the President of the National University of Wales Student Union was even now circulating a link to her followers to claim the green shoots of regional fight-back. She was angsty, she was tipsy and unashamedly nationalistic. 'Ragonwie vah! Plos dandwell crotch!', she signed it; and none of 1,600 recipients could bring themselves to disagree with her sentiment.

From the third or fourth broadcast, the viewing figures climbed steadily as students, at first in Wales and then wider, made Thomas and Cob's show required viewing. In bedrooms and sitting rooms, perched on the stairs, with phones at parties and going home on late-night busses, eyes followed their every mewling, keening sentence with bemusement, all the time nurturing the belief that they had found something wonderfully weird on the planet that was known only to them.

It wasn't more than a fortnight later, when all seemed to be going so well, that S4C forwarded a bundle of homework.

'Cob, there's even a petition here.'

'What does it say?'

'How should I know? It's written in our daft language. Rodhwy platt bloh tifflin...'

'This one's asking what Mohlbut means. You can answer that because I'm pretty sure you bloody said it.'

'This letter says they remember the dialect from when they were children.'

Cob joined the read-through session as Thomas handed over another, rather serious four-page letter. The gravity of their guilt took shape.

'This pedantic sod is some kind of linguistic code breaker who's listed all these nouns and adjectives, calculated 'way points' of our sentences and appended 47 grammatical questions. He wants a lexicon and primer! What are we going to do, Cob?'

'I always ask myself, what would Dracula have done?'

'That's so helpful, but two wrongs don't make a right.'

'You're correct there. Let's make it best out of three.'

Sometime later...

'I've got to the bottom of why we can't get hold of Brynn.'

'Why's that?'

'It's Graham's number.'

According to the rulebook of eternal verities, opportunity knocks and doors open, others closing unseen as the whale-shark of time soars past, to mix abstract metaphors. On this particular challenging Wednesday, the door of the collaborators' flat swung apart for a certain Brynn, a slight young woman with an unnerving ability to look through people as if thoughts were as visible as wardrobe. Combined with slender legs of exactly the type that cause so much distress in the oil-rich nations, the effect was unnerving to young men. Cob wondered how long she'd been outside and whether she'd heard them practicing idiocy.

'Ah, great, The... it's Brynn' said Thomas, unable to reach the door before Cob had offered to relieve her of her sun-bleached netball anorak. Netball was an alien world to Cob but he'd been to a basketball match once and sat close to the action, which sounded like stamping on a row of finches.

'He calls you 'The' Brynn' advised Cob in magnanimous fashion, 'to wave aside any suggestion that there might be others. Oh great, you brought the snacks.'

Brynn, nonplussed but lacking any factual way to put her finger on the problem, entered the flat and unpacked her haul. Her eyes were adjusting to the decade-old light in this place and the room beyond, which Cob noticed.

'Ah right. I expect that's the look you want for your kitchen.'

'Close', replied Brynn. 'That's the look I want for everybody else's kitchen to make my kitchen look fucking spectacular.'

'Hey. I said 'takeaway' and you brought cakes. Cakes aren't fast food.'

Thomas wasn't going to be part of Cob's insurrection. 'They can be. Merrrriinggggue. Scone. See?'

'That's playing with language. A good sign, considering', Cob responded. 'How much do I owe you?'

'I'm sorry, Brynn. My flatmate cares very deeply about his greasy kebabs', interjected Thomas.

'Well of course' said Cob, 'I'm not the kind of guy who'll lunge into a takeaway and grab just anything.'

'Did you steal these pub glasses? They're not very clean' Brynn asked them, picking up on lurid details around her.

'We paid for the drinks. No one said the glasses weren't

included.'

Cob prayed she would never want to meet them at their local pub, remembering the discreet health and safety signs such as the one in the gents urinals: "The tiles are very slippery here so please be careful when you are pissing on the floor."

Thomas drew Cob's attention to some ice cream wafer clinging to the upper slopes of his pocket, which Cob collected and dissolved in brief meditation. Appropriating this moment of silence, Thomas got to the point:

'What we'd like you to do, Brynn, is advise us on improving our uh-podcast, if you wouldn't mind seeing some footage? The premise is that my grandfather was the last native speaker of the old Celtic Wenghley dialect and he taught it to me before he passed away and I've been recording it so the language doesn't die the death.' Brynn took a seat and Thomas pressed play on the keyboard.

The image was of a functional table and chairs, which Thomas and Cob merrily infested. A bogroll facsimile of a quaint countryside sign-post was placed on the table between them. Without any introduction in English, they shifted directly into conversation in a sylphlike tongue with an occasional hark-back to ragged growling, accumulating in an syncopated effect unencountered by civilised ears. Thomas randomly pointed and appeared to enquire:

'Quo-lar-garry soyn naddy most?'

'Surrun most, quoin bedgry. Spearpon bedwee towtosh' replied Cob, signalling an adjusted direction.

'Co boblan g-dam' acknowledged Thomas, with a thankful wave.

A smiling 'Bobla g-dam tiddy ee' appeared to end the exchange on screen, as the film was paused and Thomas turned to Brynn for approval.

'Bullshit', she said, sitting back. 'That isn't a Celtic language.'

Cob bridled. Biting Hoola Hoops off his fingers didn't seem the same now there were only about seven in a packet. Sorry, what was going on? The boys exchanged glances and sensed they had to let her in on it.

'Quite right', admitted Thomas, 'Cob made it up.'

'Hey!'

'...and now it's a bit of a cult, with numbers growing daily.'

'You did a podcast of this?', Brynn enquired with the incredulous eyebrows of a coroner known to the Thomas family.

'Not a podcast, not as such. More of a full national broadcast – but it's all fine because we have the 2am slot on digital S4C Wales and nobody's watching.'

Brynn appraised Thomas Thomas with the cold, enquiring eyes of a coroner called out to the bottom of the Thomas family staircase *again*.

'Your hairstyle looks even better when you see the back of it.' Silence. 'Oh, no I'm sorry, I didn't mean it like that.' Elaborating would be a waste of effort, Thomas realised, as there were only so many black eyes one can gather. 'What I want to know is, how would we make it authentic, as far as we possibly can? What does a language look like as a bare-bones system? We can pay you as our confidential consultant.'

'In real money, not in kebabs or bourbon biscuits?' Brynn asserted to a barrage of nodding.

'We need a pamphlet. Something we can post back to people who send in questions.'

'Alright', confirmed Brynn, 'five hundred in real money and I'm not putting my name on it.'

'Pleasure doing business with you.'

Within weeks, things were back on track for Cob and Thomas. The boys were developing easy-handed confidence, applying subtle humour, sometimes hamming it up and inventing even more improbable set-pieces to talk gibberish from. The classic episode where one of them dressed up as a cosmonaut and conversed with blob-life on Mars threatened to go viral, then really did when some fan replayed it on the big screen at the World Science Fiction Convention in Tokyo.

The viewing figures became dangerously robust, sometimes assembling an audience which outpaced longstanding cheap daytime programming like *Tat in the Attic, Venerable Café Crustaceans, Packed Lunches for Train Journeys, Famous Cakes & Their Consequences* and BBC Manchester's evergreen *Lenny's Wallpapering Nightmares*.

Questions trickled in by letter and email, in answer to which Brynn's rather smart pamphlets were dispatched. Thomas regretted postage outlay, content instead to email a file without ever asking to see the paper version. A summer passed in creative bliss until the letters turned tricky.

'Thomas?'

'Yes, Cob. Give me a moment, won't you. I'm scribbling down an idea – and we're low on custard creams.'

'Thomas, you should read this first. People are trying to learn Wenghley and claiming that what we say on screen doesn't match the printed matter we're sending them!'

'We're wrong and proud then, like a vlogger's haircut.'

'Seriously...'

'Bung us a pamphlet', said Thomas, which Cob obligingly slung at him. Thomas caught it awkwardly and stared disbelieving at the chunky wedge of paper now weighing on his fingers.

'This isn't a pamphlet! It's a bloody novella! There must be fifty thousand words in this'. He flicked through. 'Oh no, not good, not good at all. She's done her job too well! She's codified the language, created a translated vocabulary of eight, nine hundred, a thousand words, there's grammar structure, everything. Faupgharosty!'

'Is that a swear word?', asked Cob.

'It will be one day, if I mention it enough. Do you know what all this means?', he said, waving the letters.

'A problem?'

'Yes. Now we're going to have to learn Brynn's damned language.'

As a pair of typical students, Cob and Thomas weren't used to learning except in the early morning before an examination, in which circumstance they soaked up knowledge and tea in equal proportion with an intensity that would have spun the owlish head of Minerva.

'How's progress?', asked Brynn, when she dropped in to see them.

'Hot as Einstein's chalk, actually. Pull up a tripod.'

'I'd rather not', replied Brynn, 'there's something

biological stuck to it.' She pulled up a sofa instead, walking it across the carpet in three minutes of grating effort. 'You really should vacuum under your shitty furniture.'

They learned and Brynn coached. They learned stuff like this:

1. It's really easy to remember new words if you associate something utterly absurd with them. It has to be surreal or exaggerated because human memory filters out boring things as unimportant and conversely latches onto unique images. For example, the Wenghley word for happiness is listed as 'acglamwich'. If you picture in your mind for twenty seconds someone taking a bite of a giant clam shell between two slices of bread, spitting teeth and rejoicing like all of their happy dreams have come true, the meaning of the word will be stuck in your mind forever.

2. Memory is like a storage room with the lights gone out. When a torch picks out one object/memory, it also illuminates the memories connected around it. If you recall one node memory, you get back the whole batch.

Brynn's eyelids dropped and something fizzed through the ether. A completely black space had cut itself out of Brynn's unconscious mind, leaving a lighter image of herself standing in it.

'These two really are the greatest challenge of my life', the phantasm informed us.

3. It is easier to remember information lyrically, like a song where the pattern reminds you of the order in which words appear next.

The boys were flagging a little and Brynn sensed she needed to get through that little urge to drop kick these two hopeless clomps into the sun.

4. Most languages have male and female words, which sounds like a hardship but if the noun is feminine, the ending should be feminine to agree with it. In Wenghley, feminine endings

were all 'a' except when using the female adjectives 'ma-sence' or 'breet' (chosen by Brynn), as opposed to the common male variation 't', as in 'divat'.

The Universe fizzed and adjusted beyond consciousness again but this time only Cob occupied the plane of darkness. 'Life is weird', he informed us. 'Did you know gnats are just a millimetre long, live six weeks, go through four larval stages, grow six heads and when they get too big they change their bottoms for new ones? I'm sorry; my web-search went very badly wrong.'

5. When you have an adjective and a noun together, like 'a busy bee' in English, in Wenghley the words are said the other way around. When asking a question, 'is the bee busy?', that is done in a higher tone of voice, so information is carried using more bandwidth on the intonation scale.

After 4 hours, Brynn soon looked like she'd had a bit too much of it, whatever it was, but wasn't one to get distraught.

6. There are always exceptions to language rules, which is a handy excuse when you get it wrong, and you can pronounce a dead language any way you like because... who's to say?

'Brilliant!', responded Thomas.

7. Female plurals add an 's', whereas male plurals often tail away with an 'oglch'.

Another neat black square pierced the subconscious dimension, this time featuring only the ethereal form of a startled Thomas.
    'Wow! So this is where I keep my emotional intelligence.' His face turned around the void space in wonder. 'There's certainly a lot of room.'
    Thomas winked out of existence and Brynn slotted into the black realm, claiming it and talking as if directly to camera.
    'Sometimes, talented linguistic students, charmed and

impressed by all the hours you're putting in to learn their prototype language, just want you to ask them out. A solitary young lady who's combed her hair and gone without biscuits to stay in shape since freshers' week shouldn't have to sit next to you on your bed and nuzzle. Honestly Thomas, pull your finger out and send your mate off for a long walk.'

The learning session had reached a natural conclusion, so Cob and Thomas were leaving. Cob was first out but Thomas was slower, thanking Brynn.

'Do you want to hang around for another mug of tea?', she enquired of him.

'I really shouldn't', Thomas answered. 'Too much caffeine does terrible things to my insides.'

Thomas turned to pass Brynn's door and completed two full steps before a ladylike hand extended through the gap, took a firm grip of Thomas's wrist and pulled hard, lifting him clear off his feet and back in.

At around a smidge after ten o'clock, Thomas, looking flushed and dazed, found himself returning home. Cob happened to meet him at the front door, holding a letter.

'You took your time.'

'Oh, hello Cob. I learned so much today, it's incredible!'

'You did, did you? I learned something more: If you pull the wool over the Regional TV Channel's eyes, you're off the air immediately and find yourself in court.'

'Oh, right', said Thomas, accepting the letter, then he laughed to himself as if enjoying some private joke.

'Why are you doing that?'

'This may be a calamity, Cob, but I do not see a reason why it should also be serious.'

Cob regarded him warily. 'You've only gone and lost it.'

The dappled sunshine of a slippery Spring spread its noontide benevolence across pavements and parks, rooftops and sparrows, cabs and cabesses, until the thoroughfares and public spaces of the grey old town sparkled and burned off their spent carpet of dewdrops. In this steaming light and a jaunty mood, Thomas smiled at a rainbow and contributed a rare something toward the burden of a homeless man's maintenance. Waking from a pleasant amble of daydream thought, never too far away from a certain someone special, he raised his eyes to a monolithic building and wondered for a moment what on earth he was supposed to be doing there.

The County Court seemed a lovely old historical place to Thomas; bitter, twisted, a knackered Regency building with architectural extravagances that you don't see today because people don't like them. Its ivy-scaled facade and heavy, intimidating steps which ran up the front past a carving of Sisyphus put visitors under immediate pressure to break down and admit to everything, even when only there to deliver the milk. Ah respect, the common word for fear. In fact, the architect was so good, the story went, that most of his labourers were transported to Australia on general principles long before it could be finished.

Thomas had never been in the justice system before, although he did have a wayward cousin who once made a drainpipe periscope and leant over the window sill of his flat to peek through the window upstairs. When an officer arrived to arrest him, his defence had been that he "wanted to see if they were normal". He fell down the stairs in '94.

It wasn't long before Cob headed in to complete the line-up image on the wanted poster. Thomas managed a whispered aside: 'I've been eating vegetables *in the morning*. What the hell is wrong with me?' Before Cob could reply, Brynn closed on them like a frigate from a tree-lined path that ran around the back of the building – a place where the finest legal minds of five generations had hid in breaks to demolish their cheese 'n' onion sarnies.

'Are you ok, Cob?

'I don't know. My lead weights feel like limbs.'

Thomas wasn't listening. He was tuned into a different melody as the light sloped over Brynn's left shoulder and post-boxed her eyes in the manner recommended by early cinematographers. Brynn wasn't feeling her usual self either. He may be an idiot, she thought, but he's a *very well educated* idiot.

A movie played out of focus... and her hazel eyes looked bigger now, a jig of colours and he was about to fall into them like a Hockney when the reverie was broken.

As if by magic, their solicitor appeared, popping out from behind a Doric column. Hauling Team Wenghley inside, he would have preferred to do so by their collars. Drawing lines through all the standard defences, the lawyer resolved not to appear so much for the defendants as for the fee. A winning team? Hardly. Two fools up for contractual fraud and their 'expert witness'. He literally didn't speak their language.

'If you attempt to run away', the solicitor informed them, you will be treated as felons, enemies of the Crown.'

'Why would an *objet d'art* have enemies?', wondered Thomas.

'It's an English concept.'

The gallery thronged like a cockfight, which hadn't happened since the mass adultery case of 1864, a false-accusation scandal cynically designed to draw attention away from the clotted cream taxes that had so angered the valleys. Whippings ensued.

Much of the crowd revealed themselves to be fellow students, by their faculty scarves and their rowdy demeanour. Two held aloft a cardboard sign which read 'We Speak Wenghlish!' and beneath 'Gitty-ta Stoddy Goch Wenghley, you sods'.

'All rise. This court is now in session.' The judge wandered in, sat down and told everyone to be seated. Despite support, the case itself was soon progressing inexorably against the defendants. Quite a lot happened next but to save you wandering off we shall only tune into the important bits:

Thomas took the stand – and luckily there were already gouges in the wood which perfectly fitted his fingernails.

'I put it to you that this language was not spoken historically.'

'You're right there, I grant you that. You're a sharp one', Thomas conceded. The prosecutor flinched at this unusually helpful reply, saving him several hours of technical analysis. He began to like this defendant on a human level but would have to overcome that impulse for now and go for the throat.

'Your fraud is revealed! What do you expect will happen next, now everyone can see you are incompetent and talentless?'

Thomas considered his options. 'I don't know. I'll probably go into teaching.' Realistically, he knew he could always work in his cousin's business, pumping out ships' lavatory tanks (The Poop Deck, Port Talbot, Owain Thomas, prop.).

'You stated in this contract that you would supply training in a spoken language.'

'Ah yes', responded Thomas. 'That is something we agreed to do for the television.'

'So you admit', the prosecutor pressed, that you took payment under false pretences for a service which you could not provide, thus breaching contract?'

'Actually, no', replied Thomas sheepishly.

'In the negative sense, or did you mean you know?'

'With respect, people have learned the Wenghley language, so it has become as real as any other. Brynn and I and my mate Cob speak it, as do quite a few of the viewers. It is a minority Celtic language, but qualifies, and training was provided. I don't think I'm wrong.'

'Prebath forminty didmoch na-divat! Pucklewockers!' called a supporter from the gallery. Judicial process was asserted as heckler was removed to the cold baths without further incident.

'English is spoken in this court!' said the prosecutor.

'Also Latin and even some French nomenclature, on occasion', the judge corrected.

The prosecutor hadn't foreseen Thomas's defence and recognised he might have a challenge on his hands after all. The bumpkin wasn't finished:

'It's the old story of the carrot and the egg, isn't it? It's usually one thing after another, but sometimes it's the other way around. What about Linear B? Have you heard of Arthur Evans, the local boy who discovered that? The Minoans spoke it three thousand years ago and only left their records in pictograms, so no one speaks it now. The last local language speaker on the Isle of Man died with without passing that on, like my grandfather did for his dialect and that was that. They are still languages, even though no one alive knows them or speaks them today. If those qualify and our language doesn't, even though we have plenty of living speakers using it and they have none, I mean, where's the sense? If you only accept truth if it remains static at an arbitrarily chosen point in time, you can't question any of the world's truisms: bodies are at rest, jokes make you laugh and eating green things is good for you. Some jokes aren't funny. Some green plants and compounds can finish you off.'

'On the date of the contractual agreement, was this language current?', Thomas was pressed to answer.

'On the date of the agreement, we contracted to provide a living language to a television audience, which we have now done to the audience's satisfaction.'

Time edged by in a haze of uncharitable questions. Cob had formed the opinion over the course of the day that the prosecutor wasn't entirely impartial. 'That's just the judge', Brynn told him. 'Oh, okay.' The sun changed position and a buttercup beam streamed through the window and picked out Cob's nose. Then so did Cob.

Thomas heard 'The Judge will now' something 'the verdict' before it all became too much and he shamefully fainted.

'This court is adjourned', announced the Bailiff. 'All rise'.

'What happened?', asked Thomas, waking up.

'It was amazing. The judge delivered the verdict in our language and then in English. Here you go – I got the judge to sign Brynn's pamphlet for you. Jump like crazy mate – we won!'

Thomas's head span and merrigoed again until Brynn noticed and ripped him away with a kiss. 'Let's get ourselves a bungalow.'

When he'd recovered and they all stepped outside, Thomas shot a sudden smile at Cob and threw the pamphlet so high in the sky it became a star.

RN40

by Magnus Stanke

'Anybody awake?'

Drew's question tore me out of my reverie and I opened my eyes. The dark, featureless landscape we were driving through made it hard to gauge how fast we were going; could have been 30 or 70. It's hard in daytime and pretty much impossible at night. It certainly felt fast. Excessively so, perhaps. Anyway, I'd dozed off or had been hallucinating – extreme altitude will do that to you – and I was grateful to be torn out of my dreams. It's no fun being mauled by indigenous zombies even if they're imaginary.

Instinctively, I looked at the screen of my mobile. No signal of course, only my screen saver, a stunning picture of a lake surrounded by snow-covered mountains from down in Patagonia where we'd set out a couple of weeks ago. 'Yeah, I'm up', I said, and 'Why did you turn the radio off? I never fall asleep when the radio's playing.'

'I didn't. It just kinda zoned out, uh, a while back', Drew said.

Poor Drew. Driving on Ruta Nacional quarenta – that's Route 40 for you and me – Argentina's longest highway which runs from the southern tip of the country all the way to its border with Bolivia some 5,200 km farther north, is no picnic, especially at night when your two road-trip companions are off in slumber land, rocked to sleep by potholes so deep even the fabulous suspension of this South Korean three-row SUV can't deny. For long, long stretches there are virtually no landmarks on either side of the road and of course there are no street lights this high up in the Andes, or rather, in the Pre-Cordillera, where the few godforsaken dusty towns that do exist are set back from the road so far you don't have to worry about slowing down whilst passing through them. If not for speed bumps and rain ditches you could set your cruise control and keep going all night. What little traffic there is...

'Fuck!' That was Drew yelling.

There was a dull bang, not mega-loud, but loud enough to

wake me up for good. For an instant I glimpsed a strange face. Wait. What?

'What just happened, Drew? You hit something?' I must have spoken louder than intended.

Tony stirred on the back row and said, without opening his eyes, 'We hit the jackpot? Hmm, is that the pong of money?'

He was right. A peculiar smell had spread in the car, although until he mentioned it I hadn't noticed anything. With my next intake of breath an unpleasant, musky stench flooded my nostrils, the kind wild animals emit to mark the boundaries of their territory.

'That thing. It came out of nowhere. It's not my fault.' Drew sounded defiant.

'What was it?' I said.

Drew whispered, 'Fuck do I know.'

Tony was coming into his own. 'No jackpot, eh? Che, what time is it?'

I glanced at my watch. 'Just gone midnight.'

I must have slept something like two hours. Two hours and the road was still climbing. How was that possible? I'd studied the maps before we set out today. We should have left the lofty bits of Route 40 hours ago. Did Drew take a wrong turn somewhere? He must have. Well, with me asleep I couldn't blame him and I didn't. Even now I don't.

'Is this one of your infamous shortcuts?' Tony's voice sounded far away. He laid spread out all over the back row, his face turned towards the rear windshield behind him. 'Che, look. The night's so clear. The stars, amazing. But... there! On the road, behind us. Stop. We hit someone?'

My blood froze. Tony had said 'someone', not 'something'. How he managed to make out any details by the light of the stars I still don't understand.

Drew prolonged my rising agony by not answering Tony's question right away. While the unrequited words lingered in the air, my mind conjured up all kinds of movie-induced nightmare images – poor, creepy kids, Japanese girls with long black hair, avenging Indians, victims of vicious bullying on a rampage of vengeance against some hapless, carefree Alpha kids like us – wealthy, white millennials whose only guilt is having been born into prosperity...

At last Drew's voice burst through my unhealthy stream of thought. 'Some kind of animal. A rabbit or something, I think.'

Tony was still looking out. 'Yeah? Well, whatever it is, it's still moving. It's not dead, your would-be road kill. Stop already.'

Before I could say, 'What do you want to stop for? Some mouth-to-mouth?', Drew hit the brakes. The SUV went into a tailspin which wasn't the way it was supposed to react on a pebble road. When it finally did stop we'd gone a little off the track and I felt Drew's accusing eyes on me, as though this was somehow my fault. 'What?'

'It came out of nowhere, bro. The road, this fucking dirt track, was all clear. Empty. You saw yourself. Then, suddenly, those eyes. Boom.' Drew demonstrated the impact by slapping his hands together.

In the hope of getting the smell out of my airways I climbed out of the car and filled my lungs with night air. Up here, breathing's a drag. There's so little oxygen around that even the smallest physical activity can leave you breathless. Since crossing the 3,000 m line I'd been feeling a severe pressure on my head, my lungs and my mind. To ease the symptoms of altitude sickness, take the edge off the peaks, so to speak, we'd been chewing coca leaves like cows chew the cud. It's okay. Coca doesn't buzz you like its more famous, powdery white relative and, anyway, we'd run out of leaves hours ago.

Anyway. I made sure to raise my head slowly. Tony had been right, the night sky was awesome. I'd never seen the Milky Way lit up so brightly, so brilliantly. Drew joined me and together we stared at the spectacle above us. Awesome or not, the sky didn't offer up any solutions. There was no roadmap to the nearest vet and we were hardly likely to mercy-kill the miserable creature – most likely a fox, a ferret or a Patagonian Mara – with our bare hands.

As Tony crawled out the car the spell began to dissipate. 'I think it's dead. It stopped moving. Come on.'

Without uttering another word he started towards the small bundle in the road behind us.

Was it really dead? It bothered me. All of it. I didn't like the way Drew'd braked, I didn't like the way we'd stopped and I didn't like the way our headlights now shone into the nothingness in front of the car. Something was decidedly, unfathomably wrong.

'You comin', Kev?' Drew said.

'Catch you right up', I answered.

I didn't want to stay at the car, alone. I wanted to go with them but my legs didn't obey me, as though they knew better. So I watched my friends shuffle off down the road without me. Two hundred yards doesn't sound like much but, like I said, at this altitude every step's a chore.

I just shouldn't have fallen asleep, earlier, I mean. Technically, by virtue of riding shotgun, all navigation today had been my job, so although I hadn't done the actual driving I felt partially responsible for our predicament. To make matters worse I couldn't even work out our current location because my phone still wasn't picking up any signal.

When I started digging in the boot it was mainly to give my hands something tangible to do. Idle hands do the Devil's work, as the old saying goes, but it wasn't as straightforward as all that. Last week Tony had broken the little light that comes on when you open the lid of the boot so I had to rummage in darkness. I was looking for my head torch – last spring I'd been on a sport climbing course and I'd brought the strap-on gadget along on our trip. It had to be somewhere in the...

That's when my fingers touched the gun.

A gun? Must be Tony's. Drew can be a nutcase but even he's not mad enough to bring a firearm on a plane into a foreign country and it certainly wasn't mine. Was the gun loaded? 'Course it was. Why else bring it?

I didn't bother to yell. I could see my friends about halfway down the road by the light of their mobiles, which they were using as flashlights. Right then, the thing moved. My eyes had adjusted to the darkness and the Milky Way did the rest. The dark bundle shifted. It wasn't dead, not completely. Drew and Tony noticed something, too. They stopped in their tracks and crouched defensively.

'Guys. Can you tell what it is?' I don't think they heard me. My voice was halfway stuck in my throat.

By then the movement had ceased and Drew and Tony

continued.

I wasn't sure what to do next.

At last I had an idea and as such it was so ingenious it almost cost me my life. Nobody had looked at the front of the car. In the centre of the bumper there was a winch with a big, sturdy rope. The hook at the end of the rope was tied to the left edge of the bumper. Perhaps caught in the rope or the hook I'd find some trace of the animal, some fur to tell me whether it'd be safe to approach. What if Tony was right? If it was 'someone' rather than an animal, what then? I remembered the Indian I'd seen before, a Diaguita or Guarani or whatever tribe the locals up here belong to. I pictured the face clearer now, with more detail. Weather-beaten it was, with deep, leathery furrows, eyes downcast and shielded by an oversized straw hat – you know what I mean. Bloodshot, piercing eyes; harmless in daylight but scary as hell at the side of a road in the middle of the night. What if we'd trodden on sacred ground or something? Who knows how many inscrutable laws we might have unwittingly violated just by being here? I mean, maybe we should have stopped at one of the Gauchito Gil roadside altars that dotted the landscape. We could have easily left a handful of pesos or a few cigarettes or a bottle of beer. What if Drew navigated onto one of their graveyards, desecrating it sideways and then some; and now their spirits had caught up with us?

I wiped my hand over my eyes to chase away the harrowing thoughts. Focus. I needed to focus. At last I found my head torch and I almost clicked it on with the beam pointing at me. It would have been a huge mistake. The bright light would have flooded my dilated pupils and I'd have been practically blinded. There'd be a right time for the torch, but this wasn't it so I slipped the straps over my head where they were designed to go.

Drew and Tony had nearly arrived. "Wait! Let me look at the bumper first", I wanted to say but it was pointless. All I could do was hurry, which I did and I almost stepped into the immense void that opened up before the heavy SUV. We'd been ever so lucky. The front wheels rested right on the edge of a huge drop. Another yard and we'd have plunged into the sheer emptiness below. I know it's practically bottomless because I did switch on the head torch and looked over the edge, very carefully, afraid the loose topsoil under my feet would give. Besides a ledge about five meters down, there were no features, just a big void full of empty.

Totally spooked, I turned towards my friends. 'Guys, I...'

The musky smell was back and simultaneously I heard snarling. The former wafted over from where Drew and Tony had presumably reached the road kill and the latter was neither human nor animal. It wasn't anything from this world. It was the scariest fucking sound I ever heard in my life.

'Drew! Tony! I'm coming!' I said and started in their direction.

As I said, at this altitude it's impossible to move very fast for any amount of time. The body needs more oxygen than the air supplies. I knew this but I ran anyway and predictably I didn't get very far. My lungs forced me to stop, screaming for air. I turned my torch on and moved my head, but the beam didn't reach far enough. For an instant I saw a brief flash, a reflection like when headlights hit the back of a cat's eye. I blinked and it was gone. When I clicked off the head torch I saw nothing at all.

Dread filled me while I listened. There was a growling, gnashing, grumbling and it got worse. Footfall in the gravel. Before I knew it I had pulled the gun and was wielding it blindly in search for a target. 'Drew, Tony. I'm here. Get down!'

Something or someone was coming at me. It might have been my friends. I might have been their best hope, but it might have been the thing. All I could do was wait, breathe and hope my pupils would dilate in a hurry.

So I waited.

It was the longest six seconds of my life. Gradually I made out movement ahead of me, coming closer. Dark spots at first. My breathing normalised and I was tempted to call out again. I didn't though. It would have been reckless. I needed every ounce of oxygen. Even the lifting my arm, the pointing of the gun, took its toll.

The image that presented itself to me gradually was bad, unspeakably bad. Drew was on the ground, was being...

devoured by two, no, three figures. I'm not kidding and I'm not making this shit up. My best mate. I couldn't tell if the attackers were kneeling people or crouching animals. Tony was still alive then, running up the road. They were behind him, too, he was stumbling, out of breath and out of luck. They caught up fast. I wanted to shoot but I couldn't get a clear shot, not at that distance. My finger caressed the trigger –

An idea.

I raised the barrel and fired in the air. I had to buy time, for Tony, at least. My eyes stayed on him and the report ripped through the night and echoed off somewhere in the distance while the flash from the nuzzle illuminated the scene for the fraction of a second. That's how I knew it was too late for Tony, too. His pursuers lunged through the air and brought him down to the ground. The sound was excruciating and I knew there wasn't a thing I could do to help. It'd be me next. What to do? I couldn't drive away. Drew never leaves keys in the ignition. It's an old habit of his.

I stuck the gun and the flashlight into my belt and made for the car. My subconscious had come up with a plan and my body obeyed without any conscious thought on my part.

Next thing I knew, I'd grabbed the end of the rope from the winch in the bumper, tied it around my waist and was abseiling onto the ledge below the car I'd spotted earlier, with astonishing dexterity. The sport climbing course last spring was money well spent! I just stepped over the fucking edge as though I did this every day, not a moment's hesitation. Meanwhile the hellish beasts were catching up – I can't think of a better way to describe them. I never got a really good look at them and I hope I never will.

Since then I've been on a ledge, my safe haven, writing this down for... for posterity, I guess, just in case. For now I seem to be alright here. It's been an hour or so and they're still up there but at least they can't follow me down. I can hear them from time to time. Awful sounds. If they're feline or canine by nature, their paws can't hold onto a rope. I reckon if I can make it through the night they'll go back to whatever hellhole they spend the daytime in and I can climb back up. I'll get the car keys, pack up whatever's left of my two friends (God!) and drive to safety. Fuck! I mean, what the fuck just happened?

It must be about one o'clock or half past. That means it'll get light in five hours or so. I'll sit down now and try to get some rest. If I fall asleep I mustn't roll over the edge. The gun's next to me and it's getting a bit nippy.

'Anybody awake?'

SHIT! That's Drew's voice and it's coming from somewhere up there where the beasts are. How can he? I saw him die, didn't I? I've got to stop writing to find out what's...

Police files, Province of Jujuy, 10.10.2019. Classified. Redacted.

Re: The discovery of the lifeless bodies of three white males (Kevin Aldon Kreuzer, Brit. nat, dob 11.03.1995, Andrew White, US nat. dob 28.02.95 and Antonio Quartz de la Sierra, Argen. nat, dob 01.01.94) off RN 40 on unnumbered dirt track commencing at KM xxxxx by Officer Gonzales, badge number xxxxx.

All three deaths occurred as the presumed result of xxxxx exposure following xxxxx road accident. Relatives have been informed that due to injuries sustained and, due to ensuing fire, corpses have been badly charred. The gun recovered from the scene has been deemed irrelevant to the cause of deaths. Due to recent unexplained occurrences on this section of road suggest xxxxx until further notice.

Signed, xxxxx.

OBERBOOTSMANN BECKER

by Stephen Mills

Smoke, thick and black and full of noxious oil, choked Franz as he came-to. Water lapped at his chin. He was lying face down, legs canted at an extreme angle behind, his head clamped in an invisible vice of painful pressure and with the iron tang of blood coating his mouth. Machines thrummed somewhere in the deep dark, the incessant humming of oil-fired boilers drowned out by screams of dying men. Flames, every sailor's enemy, cast a malevolent glow to push back sullenly at the hideous dark.

Franz's heart seized in his chest with stark realisation. He tried to scramble up, to stand and escape the cries of his dying shipmates, yet he only managed to push himself to one side with his good hand. Where is my left arm? he thought in panic. The shell had exploded with no warning, not the least notice or alarm and his world had gone dark in an instant.

Now?

Now, men were either fighting for their lives or else fighting the corpses for room. Seawater flooded his nose, its level rising slowly in the confined space of the ruined battery. The wretched seaman rolled onto his back and used his right arm to feel for its twin, but it came away empty. Not fully empty, really, for he held a chunk of sticky meat where his left arm used to be, its thick liquid coating his fingers. Head swimming, he leaned forward and vomited, tears stinging his cheeks as his chest heaved. No alarms sounded, no lights or commands. The only noises which reached Franz's ears were the groans and screams of the mortally wounded and the flames which had found purchase on combustibles elsewhere.

'Get up, Matrose Bauer', a gruff voice called from the dark. 'Get up! It does no good to die here.'

Franz choked back tears, the acid tang of bile burning his throat. 'My arm, Oberbootsmann Becker', he groaned.

'What of it?'

'It's gone.'

'How about the rest of you, do you want to lose that, too?'

Franz shook his head. 'No.'

'Take off your belt, Matrose Bauer.'

The seaman did as he was told, though finding purchase with his right hand proved difficult. Seawater rose a little higher, the ship's deck dipping to a noticeable list. Franz lost his balance and stuck his remaining hand out, then screamed as he grabbed a man's shoulder. It did not move. Bile rose again, but Franz choked it down. Morose flames flickered nearby, the angry light illuminating the corpse's face. Ernst Miller, Franz realised in horror.

'Stop screaming, Matrose', the salty chief barked. 'Take off your god-damned belt and tie it around your arm.'

Franz bit his lip, adjusted his body, then reached to his waist with a trembling hand. The oily water had made the metal buckle slick, but he worked in the dark to loosen its loop, then pulled the end of the belt free. Grunting with the effort and biting his lip against pain, he slowly managed to pull the belt from his trouser loops.

'Hurry', the old Chief grunted.

'I'm trying, Oberbootsmann!' Franz had fallen backward in exhaustion. His head swam from blood loss and shock.

'There is no try, Matrose', the veteran scolded his junior sailor. 'There is only to do, or to die and, unless you want to die, then I suggest you get to doing.'

Franz did not bother to answer. Biting back groans, he tried to loop the belt around the stump of his left arm but it fell and he dropped the belt into filthy water.

'Again, damn it! You are too young for hell, Matrose Bauer. Do it again!'

Fear gripped his chest. I don't want to die, he thought.

'Lay back, son. On the ladder, so you're above the water.'

Franz did as he was told. The ladder's treads, what were called stairs on land, were cold metal and slick with blood and oil.

'Good. Now, put the belt through the buckle and into the stay. Keep calm, damn it.'

The seaman followed his chief's instructions. He worked the belt's end through the buckle and pulled it back on itself through the fabric loop.

'Slide it up on your arm.'

A wave of nausea rolled over Franz, his young face white with fear.

'Concentrate, boy. Listen to my voice, focus on what I'm telling you.'

Franz nodded. He was a farm boy, a peasant from the Bavarian hinterland, the sum total of his experience at sea coming in the few short months he had been in the Kaiserliche Marine. When the Serbians executed Archduke Ferdinand, the whole country had risen in a patriotic furore. They were young then, he and his brothers, but as soon as Franz had come of age he answered the call to arms. Franz's mother had cried but his stern old father was bursting with pride. It had seemed so long ago now, as he lay in the fouled and oily seawater, surrounded by thick smoke, licking flames and the diminishing cries of his shipmates. So long ago, but not even a whole season had passed since their battlecruiser had thrown off the mooring lines to steam away into the North Sea, a wolf among sheep.

Now, that wolf had been horribly wounded by English wolfhounds. Only five hours prior, Franz and his shipmates had been on deck, smoking cigarettes and making lewd jokes about the terrible things they would do to the wives of their British adversaries. 'Mary won't be walking right, not when I'm done with her', Matrose Schmidt boasted, eliciting jeers from his closest friends.

'Mary won't even know if anything has happened to her, Gerhard!' Miller had shouted, his pinkie finger waggling.

'Poor Mary would be bored, Schmidt. Let a real man have her', Franz had laughed. Common insults amongst the three of them, best mates from training all the way to the fleet, but now Ernst Miller and Gerhard Schmidt were in the burning black, the cramped, dying space now nearly silent of men's pleas.

Franz began crying again. Not for him, but for his family and friends, those closest to him who he would not see again.

Not unless he hurried.

He was weak, though. He was weak and nauseous, beginning to feel tired and his hand barely managed to slip the belt over the stump of his leaking arm.

'Stop snivelling, Matrose!' the chief barked.

'Yes, Oberbootsmann. Where are you?' Franz asked sharply, a sob lodged in his throat. He looked around, but couldn't see anything in the oppressive dark and greasy smoke.

The seaman fumbled with the belt until it was looped around the meaty stump of his arm and pulled tight. Franz screamed against the stabbing, searing pain, but the fabric's webbing squeezed what was left of the mangled flesh until blood stopped leaking from its severed vessels.

'Cinch it tight, Matrose!' the Chief barked angrily. 'Cinch it if you don't want to die!'

'Help me, Oberbootsmann!' Franz cried, then he pulled tighter, an anguished cry escaping his clamped lips and the belt slipped momentarily, but he finally managed to get it tight, then tucked the loose end under his armpit where its additional bulk helped to further stem the flow of blood.

More cries rose up in the darkness, far fewer than before. One of them was a shrill voice, the voice of a man who'd just escaped boyhood; and it was a voice that Bauer knew well.

'Gerhard!' Franz screamed. An unintelligible answer, brief and pained. 'Gerhard!' Franz screamed again, his voice rising to a shriek. 'Gerhard, come to me! Come to my voice, it's Franz!'

Bauer strained his ears to listen to the sullen darkness. Groaning from somewhere, a few cries, but none were shrill.

'Gerhard!' Franz shrieked again, but now his cries were answered by silence. Bauer tried to cry, he tried to weep for his friend, but nothing came out. Not a tear, now, for his tears were spent. Exhausted, in pain and with a swimming head, Franz slipped into unconsciousness on the precariously tilting deck plates.

Wildflowers dotted the hillsides around a little alpine farm. It certainly was not much but Herr Bauer was immensely proud. His family had been serfs, peasants toiling under the heavy boot of landowners, but Herr Bauer, through hard work and guile, had managed to get a little plot of land to call his own. There, where the Bavarian Alps met lush fields amongst rolling hills, he raised a family.

Herr Bauer was also proud of Franz. His little boy, with a streak of blonde hair and a mischievous grin perpetually stretched across his freckled face, who had grown into a tall and handsome man. Of course, Herr Bauer was concerned about the war. So many went off and never came back and if, by God's fortune, they did return, most of them held scars, whether or not they were visible.

His boy, though, was joining the Kaiserliche Marine, the navy of the German Empire. If Franz went to war, then it would be on the seas and his chances of coming home alive and whole were much better than being blown to bits on the front. Herr Bauer breathed a sigh of relief. The sun was up and though he had let Franz sleep in a little, it was time for him to go. As the old man peeked through the bedroom's door, he nearly didn't wake his son. If he awoke, then he would leave, which was a nearly unbearable pain for Herr Bauer to bear. Franz was a man now, just so, but laying asleep in bed he looked like the little blonde-haired boy with the mischievous grin.

'Franz', he said, his creaking voice a touch above a whisper. 'Franz, it's time to go. Wake up, son. Wake up!'

'Wake up!' the Oberbootsmann's voice rasped through oily blackness. 'Wake up, Matrose Bauer! Wake up!'

Franz twitched, his eyes snapping open at Becker's admonishment. 'I'm awake, Oberbootsmann', the seaman mumbled.

'You must get out, boy. Up the ladder!'

Franz rolled onto his stomach, his missing arm a mass of burning fire. The pain was no longer excruciating and, though a dull ache drummed through his body and the stump felt as if it were aflame, its debilitating agony had faded into a horrid memory. The seaman used his remaining hand to grasp at the stairs and kicked with his feet. Too worn and weary to stand, the long minutes ticked away as he worked painstakingly up the metal treads of the battle cruiser's ladder-well. Up he went, tread by slippery tread and the ship began to list more.

'Hurry, god damn it, hurry if you don't want to die!' the coarse old seaman cursed at Franz. He pushed with his toes, inches at a time, grunting against the pain as he reached out with raw fingers to grab the next ladder tread. His hand slipped once, the nail on his ring finger catching in the ladder's tread to tear painfully back. The Matrose grimaced against this newly searing pain, tasted oil and blood as he took hold of the nail with his teeth to give it a good yank before resuming the upward crawl towards freedom, towards life. Time and again, Franz pushed, pulled, then pushed and pulled, until he reached the top of the ladder-well. Pausing to catch his breath, the caustic smoke was thicker here and he began to cough.

'It's no time for a smoke-break, Matrose Bauer. Move your ass', the Oberbootsmann cried, but Franz had once again fallen unconscious.

Battlecruiser Lützow was a sight to behold for an ignorant farm boy. She was new, she was massive and she was deadly. Freshly minted Matrose Franz Bauer looked upon her with awe. Great cannon turrets sat proudly fore and aft and her superstructure was studded with a smaller guns, some two dozen in all, with her twin masts standing tall and proud. A floating fortress, a leviathan to take the fight to the hated English, yet even the mighty Lützow was dwarfed by the grotesquely large dreadnoughts of the North Sea fleet!

Bauer gawked at the ships and marvelled at the smells of the sea: salt air, a faint fishiness on the breeze, the reek of oily exhaust as the ship's boilers built steam. Gulls swooped and cawed in their never-ending search for scraps of herring and oyster which the Kaiserliche Marine sailors would toss in the air, a boyish game to while away what little dead time they had.

Soon we will sail, Franz thought, soon we will hunt.

On this day, Matrose Bauer, seaman of the mighty Kaiserliche Marine, was a warrior of the sea. Until, that is, Oberbootsmann Becker opened the maw which lay hidden within a mass of gray-brown beard, a burning cigarette perched precariously on the cliff of his lower lip. He barked at the sailors fresh out of training, knowing that all they had been taught were the simplest of skills, the lessons in drill and seamanship barely enough to keep them alive even on the mildest of days; and so he would drive them hard over these next months. The seamen in his charge would hate him, they would hate their lives, but Oberbootsmann Becker would do it out of a fatherly love. Yes, they were young and unsalted and if they lived, if they grew into true men of the sea – then, years later, they would remember his lessons and they would pound those trials into their freshly minted seamen, even long after Becker was gone.

So, opening his great big mouth to split that great big beard, Oberbootsmann Becker barked at the boys to move their asses, because Kapitän Harder would not delay sailing for some unblooded, saltless, gawk-faced young seamen.

'Move your ass!' Oberbootsmann Becker screamed. Franz woke for a second time. He was so weak, so tired, he just wanted to close his eyes and go to sleep, so he laid his head down again, weak coughs failing to expel the noxious smoke from the young seaman's burning lungs.

'Do not give up on me, Matrose Bauer. Do not give up on your family, do not give up on your Kaiser!'

Franz lifted his head, willing heavy eyelids open. Weak light from the flames filtered through thick black smoke. There, just in front of him, the heavy steel door loomed, a portal to heaven. Franz sobbed once, from pain and relief, then willed himself forward, forcing his way the few metres to the door and, as his energy waned, the old salty chief barked at him once more.

'Matrose Bauer, you are almost there! Do not give up on me now, son. Pull yourself forward, that's it! You have an iron will within you, Bauer. Fight through the pain! Ignore the devil that is telling you to sleep, he only wants you to join him in hell. Fight, Bauer! Fight!'

Franz forced himself to his knees and grabbed the door's handle, absurd waves of relief pouring over his tortured body. He had made it, salvation now lay between him and an inch of steel and Bauer could nearly taste the fresh salt air on his tongue. He braced his knees against the bulkhead and pulled, pulled with every tortured muscle in his body.

The door didn't budge.

With a sob, Matrose Bauer realised the door was sealed, a dozen dogs thrown to make the battery water tight. He slunk to the deck without bothering to cough the greasy smoke from his lungs, his good shoulder pressed against the door as if willing it to be thrown open. What for? he thought in defeat, I am sealed in, I do not even have a dogging wrench and there are worse places to die than with my friends.

So close to freedom, so close to life, yet left wanting for a piece of pipe to undog the door, Matrose Franz Bauer mindlessly tapped at the steel with his knuckles. Faint, nearly imperceptible, he tap tap tapped on the metal door and once again fell out of consciousness.

Oberbootsmann Becker, gunnery chief of Lützow's forward-most battery of 30 centimetre guns, was proud of his crew, proud of the boys, but mostly he was proud to be the gunnery chief of such a deadly machine. Each battery held two of the gigantic barrels, each barrel capable of hurling nine-hundred pounds of hell over eighteen kilometres – and the Oberbootsmann was given the honour of leading the boys of battery number one.

Becker was, by nature and by training, gruff and uncompromising. Complacency led to laziness and laziness led to casualties, so his men drilled and drilled and when they were too tired to continue, he drilled them more. The English won't wait for you sons-a-bitches to be rested, he yelled during the drills, a cigarette waggling with every breath, they won't wait and neither will I!

Matrose Bauer feared and worshipped the Oberbootsmann. He was the chief and he was a hard man, but he loved them, every one of the men of battery number one. Such a fatherly instinct was plain to Franz, who had seen the same hardness and love on his own father's face and Becker had taken the place of Herr Bauer in Franz's eyes. If anyone would see him home safe, Oberbootsmann Becker would. Franz was sure of it.

Clear night air poured into the battery, a sudden charge of salt air causing Franz to cough violently. Smoke roiled from the open door and Bauer fell backward, collapsing onto the sea-washed deck of the Lützow. Shocked into consciousness, Franz rolled onto his back and panted, with his tortured lungs pulling in gobs of sea air until he began to retch. Sailors, his shipmates, surrounded him, a cacophony of 'he's alive' and 'we've got one!' filling the night sky.

Hands pulled at the seaman, Franz's shipmates frantically hauling him to a lifeboat. 'The Oberbootsmann!' Franz yelled in horror. 'Oberbootsmann Becker is in the battery!' Franz fought against the very hands which offered salvation. 'Oberbootsmann Becker, he's still in there, get him!'

Ignoring his cries, they dragged Franz into the lifeboat as he struggled. 'Someone get Becker, someone get Oberbootsmann Becker!' Matrose Bauer sobbed and then the little craft dropped into the sea.

The Lützow was dying, its stern beginning to rise in the air. Rough hands pulled away from Franz only to be replaced by the taut face of Oberleutnant zur See Wolf, Franz's gunnery officer. He was young but his eyes betrayed a newfound age, the look of a man who had cheated death. 'Oberbootsmann Becker is dead, son', the officer said flatly.

'He isn't!' Franz swore in anger. 'He helped me live!'

Wolf shook his head sombrely. 'I'm telling you, he's dead. Oberbootsmann Becker was killed in the first salvo.'

Bauer began to cry, fevered sobs wracking his body. 'He led me to the door, sir. Becker led me to the door. I'm alive because of him.'

'Listen to me, Matrose Bauer', the officer said, his eyes boring holes into Franz's soul. 'Becker was standing next to me when the first shell hit. I saw him die, Seaman. Oberbootsmann Becker is dead.'

German Naval Ranks of World War I.

Kapitän: Captain.
Oberleutnant zur See: Lieutenant.
Oberbootsmann: Chief Petty Officer.
Matrose: Seaman.

LOCKDOWN HERO

by Jenny Torniainen

'Mum, can I play games on your phone?'

'Have you finished all your schoolwork, Danny?'

'No.'

Not exactly true. On top of regular lessons, Mrs Vincent sends through stupid activities — complete a gratitude journal, help around the house, do a kind deed. Schoolwork online is boring, even more boring than real school and that's saying something.

Mum squidges the mop against the bucket. 'Well, go into the garden and play then. You're in my way.'

Ever since she lost her job selling houses, Danny's mum's new hobby, besides nagging about schoolwork, is cleaning. Dad's more fun, but for the last two days he's been upstairs on his computer. He doesn't even come down for meals and Mum sleeps on the sofa, like they've had a row.

'I don't like the garden.' The old house in Benfleet had a big garden with places to hide and a tree with a swing on it. This new garden isn't even a garden, just concrete slabs with nasty weeds that look like aliens growing from its cracks.

'Do you ever stop whinging, Danny?'

'But I'm bored! I want to go out-out. Can't we go to Basildon or go into the country park? Even Tesco's would be something.'

'Danny, it's only been a week. Move love, I want to get behind there.'

It isn't fair. His friends have brothers and sisters. David has his grandad, who talks about the old days non-stop, but even that's something. Then he has an idea. 'Mum?'

'What now, Danny?'

'Do you think the old lady next door is okay on her own?'

Mum sprays some bleach. Squirt, squirt. 'Why don't you write her a letter and ask?'

Letters are a waste of paper. 'Can't I just call or text her?'

'I don't know her number and a letter is nicer, more personal.'

Danny goes upstairs, stamping his feet. Thump, thump. The computer is on in his bedroom and the curtains are closed. Each day, his teacher sends more stuff, mountains of homework. At school, lessons where they got to use the computers were the most fun but now Danny can't be bothered. Don't the teachers see that it's pointless trying to make kids work?

Danny checks to see what's happening on Fortnite. David and Batu have invited him to a game. Since lockdown, he can play whenever he wants. Funny how the fun things seem less fun when you can do them whenever.

At eight o'clock the clapping starts. Clark joins in by woofing. Mum's explained they're clapping to say thank you to the doctors and nurses because they are heroes, which sounds a bit silly, as Danny doesn't think the doctors and nurses will hear. He joins in anyway because it's fun to see neighbours' heads poking out of their windows.

His room overlooks the yard and down below is the badminton net Dad put up using old tights. Danny sticks his head right out to see if the old lady joins in. Her house isn't even next door, it's just one big house that has been cut in two and given two doors. The only time he hears her make any noise is at six o'clock with the BBC news which she turns up really loud. Mum reckons she's a bit deaf.

Danny leans out a bit further. He can see other houses with their cut-in-half gardens. 'Pssst!'

If she's deaf, she won't hear that, especially with all the clapping.

He runs back downstairs. Mum's washing up the dishes.

'Mum?'

'What now?'

'What's the old lady called? The one next door.'

'I don't know, Danny. Go and brush your teeth.'

At night, he can't sleep for thinking how bored he would be if he was on his own like that old lady. Worse than bored. Then: what if she's got the virus and is sick and alone? What if she's dead and no one's realised?

The following morning, he tidies his desk. There. That'll make Mum happy. Under a pile of books is the worksheet his teacher set for homework. Childhood During the Second World War. Why do adults love to talk about the war so much? He checks his messages. 'Danny, I'm still waiting for your homework. Please, can you let me know how you're getting on?', Mrs Vincent has written. There's a ton of new work. Words everywhere, videos, worksheets, true or false questions, quizzes. It's not fair having all this work to do. Why can't teachers give everyone a break?

The date on the history homework was last week. Oops.

He tears a page out of his maths notebook. Anything to avoid doing homework.

'Dear Lady next door,

I'm Danny. I'm ten, but I will be eleven next month. Mum said to write you a letter to check you are okay. I heard Covid is bad for old people. I hope you are not too bored or lonely in lockdown. Today me and my friends sent each other selfies of us pulling faces then I played badmington on my own, but Clark (our dog) ate the shuttercock (sp?). I need to do schoolwork but I would rather play on my computer.

That's all for now.

Danny from next door.'

He takes the letter downstairs to show Mum but she isn't there. Through the front room window, there's a movement. What's she doing in the car?

When she comes back in, her face is all splodgy.

'Did the interview go badly, Mum?'

Before Dad started hiding in his room, Danny heard him and Mum practising for her interview next Tuesday. Danny asked what that meant and Mum said it was a bit like an exam but you have to speak.

'Everything's cancelled, Danny.' Mum blew her nose then went to the bathroom to wash her hands.

'Can't they do it online like we do school?'

'No one is buying houses at the moment, Danny. They don't need people.'

He wants to ask why Dad doesn't come downstairs, but her face says this isn't the right moment. He shows her the letter. 'How do I get it to her?'

'Post it through her letterbox, silly. Are you keeping on top of your homework?'

Danny's already slipped out of the front door.

'When do you think she'll reply?' It's spaghetti on toast again; the worst. Food during lockdown is almost as boring as online school.

'She might not reply. She's very old. Have you washed your hands, Danny?'

He nods.

'With soap?'

'Can I go and ring her doorbell so she knows there's a letter?'

'You leave her be, Danny. Are you up to date with your schoolwork?'

Danny nods. It's almost true. Sort of.

Clark goes bonkers the next day, yapping and wagging his tail at the door. He is bored of lockdown too.

'Danny, there's a letter for you.'

He's downstairs in an instant. The envelope is heavy. He opens it and unfolds the thick paper inside. 'I can't read it. The writing's all weird.'

Mum puts down her cloth and washes her hands. She frowns a bit, then points at the spidery squiggles:

'Dear Danny,

I was thrilled to receive your lovely letter today and I do hope you are not too anxious.

This is really an extraordinary historical moment to be living through and I can honestly say that in all my ninety-one years, I have never seen anything like it. The world around us is changing so fast. I remember seeing similar changes as a child when I was your age living through the Second World War, although this is about the only comparison I can make between that time and this.

I have a niece and nephew but they are grown up and live

a long way away so they can't come and visit. Ever since I received that letter from the government telling me to stay at home because I was a vulnerable person, they refuse to come and visit. I told them to come over anyway; what do I care if I fall off my perch at this ripe old age? It seems they are too worried about the risks a visit might have on my health.

Your message really made my day. I can't say I know what a selfie is. There are lots of things that I find I don't know, especially with all those thingamabobs and gadgets you have these days.

Sorry my handwriting is hard to read. These old hands aren't what they once were.

Eileen (from next door).'

Mum hands him the letter. 'How nice of you to do that, Danny.'

'Do you have some proper writing paper, Mum?'

Mum picks up the cloth again. 'I don't think you should keep pestering her. She's very frail. All those uneven flagstones, I worry she'll take a tumble on the way to our letterbox.'

'What if I told her she doesn't have to? She could leave letters for me on her doorstep.'

Mum shakes her head. 'She said it herself, it's hard for her to write back.'

'But Mum!'

'Danny! Go and get on with your work. I got an email today saying that you should have work to keep you busy for three hours a day, at least.'

This is pointless. He goes upstairs and knocks on Mum and Dad's bedroom door. 'It's me, Dad!'

There's coughing, a big whooping sound, then a raspy voice. 'Danny, I'm on a conference call. Not right now.' The door doesn't open.

'Do we have any writing paper?' Why doesn't he come out? It's been three days now.

'Try the bureau.'

Back in his room, Danny puts on his facemask and rubber gloves and pulls out a sheet. Basildon Bond — what a funny name for paper, like James Bond but from Basildon. He writes:

'Dear Eileen,

I liked your letter. I'm getting better at reading your funny squiggly handwriting.

Sorry mine's messy too. Rubber gloves are hard to write in. I put them on so you don't need to worry (even though you said you don't mind if you get sick). I don't think I'm sick. Before we left school, they told us that kids can have the virus and not know about it. I think my Dad is sick because he's not left his room since Tuesday. I'm not worried. Mum said that it's only bad if you're very old and Dad's not that old really.

Clark did a poop today and some bits of the shuttercock came out. It was gross.

Today was our first proper day of online school. It's even worse than normal school because Mum's stricter than my teacher Mrs Vincent and there's no football with friends at playtime.

For dinner we had Birds Eye cod that comes in bags with yucky white sauce and peas. Mum says we need to clean out the freezer. She said it was past its sell-by but that's because it's frozen so it won't matter.

A selfie is a picture you take of yourself by turning the screen of your phone around.

That's about all I have to tell you.

Danny.

PS. If you want to reply, you can leave your letter on your doorstep.'

He creeps down while Mum's mopping the kitchen with the radio on, runs next door and slides it through her letterbox. Although he has nothing much to tell her, he writes another two letters that day. Mostly just boring stuff.

At midday the next day, Clark goes crazy at the door.

'Who's that?' Mum calls from the kitchen.

'It's a — um it's a leaflet. Um pizzas.'

'A leaflet? Put it in the bin and wash your hands immediately.'

He runs upstairs, going via the bathroom to run the tap so Mum doesn't bug him.

'Dear Danny,

Three letters in one day!

I am sorry to hear about your Dad but I'm sure he will be fine. He's young, fit and healthy. I hope you are not too worried.

I don't have a mobile telephone, let alone one which can take photographs. I am amazed to learn that you do lessons using the interweb. As I said in my last letter, not only with all these computing machines, but also in terms of the world we live in, the changes we are seeing are really quite remarkable.

It's funny how reality can sometimes overtake fiction. The enemy you face now doesn't even have arms and legs like ours did. It's hard to understand and often it seems like it's not fair because it's not what we've chosen. I hope that you find inspiration in those who surround you, Danny. There are so many people in this world who are working their socks off to make sure that life can continue as much as possible.

When I was your age, I went through something similar when many schools closed. It was my time to step up, I suppose. I was fortunate enough that my lessons continued. Our teacher, Mr Browne was the oldest person I had ever seen — although I imagine he'd look like a spring chicken in comparison to me now — and he taught us in a church crypt.

Love, Eileen.'

He re-reads the letter, especially the bit where she says: often it seems like it's not fair because it's not what we've chosen. What a strange thing to say. She says lots of funny things, actually. He looks up the word crypt: An underground room beneath a church, then writes back asking her why her school was done underground.

Three days later she replies.

'Did I mention that I was the same age as you are now when World War Two started? I lived in South West London. During the Blitz, many nights we slept in the underground stations as they were the safest place. I remember feeling very afraid, as I am sure you are now, but we kept our spirits up. I recall singing 'We'll Meet Again' long into the night. It felt so good to sing.

One lady, her name was Ethel, took me under her wing. I saw her in a supermarket in Gravesend many years later. Of course, she didn't recognise me, but I went over and thanked her for taking care of me. These acts of kindness are everywhere today as well. It's truly remarkable the lengths some people will go to for others.

Looking back at it, I suppose that living through the war was my history, that was my time. I can only imagine the efforts your lovely teachers are going to in order to ensure they can keep education alive and meaningful for you.'

He sends more letters, telling Eileen how online school is going and asking more stuff about the war. When she replies, sometimes he doesn't open the letters immediately. It's fun to wait a bit.

'We had rationing cards back then for meat, butter, cheese, sugar and eggs. Clothes and books were also rationed. We grew vegetables in the garden and knitted scarves for the soldiers. It wasn't much, but at the time it felt like I was doing something important to help.'

Mum's on her hands and knees, deep-cleaning the bathroom.

'What does rationing mean, Mum?'

'It goes back to the war, when there wasn't enough food or basic items to go around.'

'A bit like toilet roll now?'

'Something like that. Why all these questions? You're not bothering that old lady, are you?'

In the next letter, he wants to know, what did you do if you needed to pee in the night? The only time he ever went to London, the underground smelt like the inside of a stinky old pencil-case. He didn't see any toilets.

That night in bed, he can't sleep. He reads Eileen's letter again and he's glad he doesn't have to do school in a crypt.

A day goes past. Eileen doesn't reply. What if the question about peeing offended her? Danny writes another letter to apologise. Three more days go by. At night, he creeps down and listens to the news. They're talking about whether the disease is mutating. Mum switches the channel to a documentary about how people in India are coping with the coronavirus. There is a little boy, he's very thin and talks funny. There are words in English at the bottom of the screen. "Sometimes people come and distribute food. I have no idea who they are, but it's very little. We only get to eat once in two to three days."

That night, he dreams about the thin little boy, then in his dream, Mum turns into a zombie from *The Walking Dead* and gets all bitey and attacks Dad, then eats the boy. Eileen tries to stop her but she's too slow and weak compared to Mum. Danny never told Mum that he played that video game with Batu's older brother Alex. He wasn't scared by it then.

'Do you know what's happened to Eileen, the lady next door?' He prods at his soggy cornflakes.

'I told you not to pester her. Eat your breakfast, Danny.'

'I'm not hungry.'

He goes upstairs to play Fortnite but keeps getting killed.

Two more days. No letter from Eileen and Dad hasn't come out of his room.

'Mum, is Dad sick?'

'Just a bit of a cold. He's very busy with work.'

Danny's tummy hurts and he thinks about that poor boy on the news.

Mum comes over and puts an arm around him. 'Dad's fine. He'll be alright soon. It's just a precaution, okay? You can go and talk to him through the door.'

Danny goes upstairs and taps on the door. 'Dad?' There's a rumble then footsteps.

'Yes, son?' The door doesn't open.

'Are you okay?'

'Much better.' Dad's voice is still croaky but he sounds brighter.

'I miss you.'

'Me too.'

'Dad, I'm worried about the lady next door.'

Dad goes silent for a bit. 'Danny, an ambulance came by last night. I think she might be in hospital.'

The ache in his tummy is worse, like when he drinks too much Ribena in one go.

He asks if they can go and visit her but Mum says it's not safe in hospitals.

'Your school emailed me this morning. What's this about you handing in history homework late? Your teacher says you haven't been online for two whole days.'

His chin wobbles. The tears come from nowhere, tickling his face.

'Danny love, are you okay?'

It's not little tears. He's sobbing like a silly little baby. Mum wraps him up in her arms. 'I'm sorry love. I've got a lot on my mind too.' She kisses his head.

'Can't you call and see if she's okay?'

'Hospital staff are run off their feet. Besides, she's not a relative, so I've got no right to ask for information about her. Tell you what, why don't you write her a get well soon card and post it to the hospital? The postman can deliver it.'

Danny turns to go back upstairs.

'Danny,' she calls out. He turns. 'The homework. I'm trusting you to get on with it. I'm here to help if you need me. Okay?'

Danny nods.

He writes a long letter and posts it that day. Over the next three weeks, he writes fifteen more letters including a long one where he asks some questions about life in the war; but actually, he's looked a lot of that stuff up. It's kind of cool to learn what children went through. It's also very sad. A lot sadder than what is happening right now, if he's honest. Danny doesn't mention to Eileen about falling behind with homework. He promises to himself to work extra hard so that when she's better he can tell her and she'll be proud.

Mum says that the postman will be charging overtime, whatever that means.

On the fourteenth day, Mum calls him downstairs.

'Danny, we need to talk.' Her face is creased like an old shirt. He hopes it's not about homework again. He's been trying harder, but his brain keeps thinking about other things.

'It's about Eileen,' Mum says, once he's sat down. 'It's been two weeks, Danny. It doesn't look good. She was old and very frail. You need to prepare yourself.'

Danny feels like it's him who's swallowed the shuttercock.

A letter arrives and Clark goes wild, yapping and whining.

He rushes downstairs. Mum's already at the door with an envelope in her hand. Her face looks funny.

She pats the sofa beside her. 'It's from the Enaychess. Sit down.'

'What's the Enaychess?'

'The National Health Service. The people we clap at eight o'clock. Maybe they want to ask you to stop pestering them with all those letters.'

'But why?'

'Oh Danny!' Mum strokes his hair and he knows what that means.

A tear runs down to the tip of his nose. 'Can you open it?'

Dad comes downstairs. He looks older. He gives Danny a big hug and swings him around like usual Dad, then sits on the other side of him and Mum and says 'What you did for that old lady was the nicest thing, son. You'll always know that she felt less alone because of you.'

Mum unfolds the piece of paper.

It isn't a letter, but a black and white printed photo of the old lady from next door in a chair. She is smiling a big wrinkly smile. Her face looks like a balloon that's run out of puff. In the picture, she's holding a piece of paper with a message on it:

'Dear Danny, The nurse helped me take my first selfie. I'm much better and that virus didn't get me this time! They say I'll be home to celebrate VE Day.'

Danny smiles a big smile and wipes away the tears. 'What's VE Day?'

'The day when we celebrate the end of the Second World War. Gosh, it must be the 75th Anniversary this year.'

'Mum, can I make a special welcome home sign for Eileen and hang it in our window?'

'She would love that, I'm sure. I'll help you if you like.'

'But don't you have lots of things to do?'

'This is more important.' Mum squeezes Danny close.

That afternoon, Danny submits his history project on World War Two and, in the evening, he tells Mum and Dad how Mrs Vincent gave him 90%, then he thanks Mum for the dinner of beans and waffles.

'My pleasure, love.'

On the eighth of May the ambulance brings Eileen home. There are balloons and signs all over the driveway. There's no way she could miss it. After drying up, he stands at his bedroom window. That afternoon, there's a special three o'clock clapping for all the heroes. He claps Mum for her cooking and cleaning, Dad who works so hard and isn't sick anymore, Mrs Vincent for all the online work, whoever it was who brought that little boy food and he claps the war veterans Eileen told him about in her letters, but most of all he claps the doctors and nurses who saved Eileen and brought her home.

Someone in the house across the way starts singing with a wobbly voice and soon more people join in.

'What are they singing, Mum?'

'It's a song called *We'll Meet Again*.'

Danny nods. 'Oh yes, I know this one.'

Once the singing's done, he goes up to his room and finishes the rest of his homework then goes to play Fortnite with Batu and David and wins. Being a lockdown hero really isn't so tough after all.

THE 7TH DIMENSION

by Paul Sloop

'Whaddya think?' my wife asked, her tone clearly signalling that she was thinking *let's do this*.

I was not convinced. We'd been on this hike for nearly two hours and were standing in a small, wooden cabin, her looking at me with eager, hopeful eyes. She saw an adventure on the horizon but I was not so sure.

We'd already had a bit of an adventure on this hike. Not long ago we stumbled upon a field of the brightest and most colourful flowers either of us had ever seen. We'd been following the trail designated on our map when we came upon a little-used footpath heading off into the woods. It was unmarked and uncharted. We could see the path led into a heavily-wooded area before twisting out of sight, then curiosity got the best of us.

'Let's check this out', my wife said.

'Sure', I replied, just as intrigued as she.

It was obvious it wasn't an official trail but we hadn't seen anybody else for some time, so we were willing to risk it. We followed the path into the woods until we reached a dead-end. It was there that we came upon the field of flowers. There was a sign at that end of the path that read 'Dimagenanthia Meadow: Never underestimate a bright little flower for little may you know of its incredible power.' We were both transfixed by the sea of brilliantly-coloured flowers we found before us. They were like nothing we had ever seen. Their petals were a fluorescent hot pink and each flower had seven violet anthers encircling a dazzling aqua blue stigma rising from the centre.

'What are those?' my wife gasped.

'You're asking me? I don't know if I could accurately identify anything beyond roses, carnations and maybe daisies and it'd be iffy on the daisies.' Then, pointing at the sign, 'Uh, maybe their called Dimagenanthias?'

'Yeah', she replied in a trance-like whisper.

'They're incredible. I've never seen anything like them', I added.

'Yes', she whispered again, barely acknowledging.

'Hey, maybe we should head back to the main trail?'

'Let's check these out first.' She seemed to come back to me.

'Sure', I responded, feeling just as curious.

Together we stepped into an ocean of fluorescent colours that rose just above our knees. As we waded ever deeper into the field of flowers, we noticed their filaments were a bluish-green, more blue than green, though not as bright nor as blue as their fluorescent aqua-coloured stigmas.

'Their stems are blue! Have you ever seen anything like this?' I asked in astonishment.

'No, but they're so beautiful', my wife replied as she reached out and plucked one from the ground. As she did so, a small puff of pollen floated off the flower and into the air. Then I picked one too for closer inspection.

'This is probably the most beautiful flower I've ever seen.' I whispered, further mesmerised by the exotic-looking flower.

'Agreed', my wife replied. We both picked a few more. Each time we did so, a small puff of pollen filled the air and slowly drifted away.

'Should we head back?' I finally asked.

'Yeah', she whispered.

Then she turned to face me and I started laughing.

'You're sparkling!' I said.

'What?'

'You're sparkling. You look like you've got glitter all over you.'

Then she finally glanced at me and in surprise replied 'So have you!'

We were both coated with a glittery dust of sparkling pink and purple flecks. We realised this must be the pollen that we saw emerging from the flowers we'd picked. I looked down and noticed I was still holding a few of those blossoms and a thick layer of the sparkly dust now covered my hands. I dropped the flowers and began rubbing my hands to shake off the dust, which fell away easily. Sarah did the same and then we took turns brushing the dust from one another. After just a few moments we both seemed satisfied that we'd removed the glittery coat of pollen and we headed back along the path that had brought us to this field.

'Well that was certainly interesting', I said as we made our way back to the main trail.

'Those flowers were amazing. Too bad they're so damn messy', Sarah added.

'True, but they are a great source of glitter, if you're into that kinda thing.'

'Ha ha. You're so funny.'

We made it back to the main trail and continued our trek. Soon we arrived at the base of a small hill where at the top we expected to find the trailhead we'd been aiming to reach. We started to walk up the hill when I looked up and could see what appeared to be a clearing ahead. I put my head down and took a few more steps before looking up again. This time I saw a small shack to the left. I could have sworn the shack was not there only seconds before... but now here we are standing in that shack.

'Whaddya think, babe?' my wife asked once more.

I found myself staring at a park ranger who was telling us about the optional trail we could take from here. Something about this guy seemed off to me but I couldn't put my finger on it. This small shack, which seemed to appear out of nowhere, had an engraved sign which read 'Park Ranger Station', so I asked myself why there would be a ranger station sitting out here, in the middle of nowhere?

My wife Sarah and I had fallen in love with taking long adventurous hikes in our early retirement. She was ten years my junior at 52 and as stunningly beautiful as ever. We'd been travelling around the country, seeing the sights, finding great trails and loved to take day-long hikes. It had been an amazing experience and we'd been looking forward to this trip for a few weeks.

Finally here, in her home state of Minnesota, this hike was supposed to take us around several lakes of various dimensions and over a few modest-sized hills. We'd already crested one of those hills, near the ranger station. The map we'd picked up when we arrived this morning indicated that this was where we should find the start of the more challenging trail we were hiking to reach, but there was nothing on it that indicated either a shack or an optional secondary trail, let alone an actual park ranger.

'Let's do it!' said my wife, 'It'll be fun.'

The park ranger gave us a half-smile and I still thought there was something not quite right about the guy. His features were too perfect, his uniform too crisp and clean. He was two hours away from anything and looked like he could be a GQ model getting ready for a photo shoot.

Despite my misgivings, I shrugged and said 'Whatever, sure, if that's what you want.'

My wife grabbed the map from the ranger, thanked him and pulled me toward the door in one single sweeping move that seemed to defy the laws of physics; but that's my wife, she does things like this every day. She is a *tour-de-force* in every way and I'm the lucky SOB who's had the good fortune of spending the last 25 years by her side. There was nothing I wouldn't do for her and right then she was thinking of an adventure out there waiting for us, so off we went.

I scrambled to pull the original map out of my back pocket as we hurried towards the alternative trailhead, which we'd been told sat behind the ranger station. I was eager to compare the original map with a new map which Mr Perfect, Minnesota Park Ranger, had provided. As we circled around the small building, we noticed a sign posted at what must have been the beginning of the trail. It was carved on wood with a thick prop and read 'Dimagenanthia Trail.' I looked around but didn't see any of the flowers we'd noticed earlier.

'Maybe we're gonna see some more of those flowers?' Sarah wondered.

'Yeah maybe', I replied as I turned to look back at the Ranger Station. I was still bothered by its location out there. 'How in the hell. . .' I begin but trailed off as my mind was racing.

'What?' asked my wife with a hint of exasperation. She was still excited about tackling this unexpected trail.

'Where's the ranger's car? For that matter, where's the road! How in god's name does that guy get out here?'

'He probably walks', she responded, as though this should be obvious.

'He walks two hours to get out here to work in that little shack and still manages to look like that?' I asked incredulously.

She tilted her head and with a sly grin said 'He did look good, didn't he?', then chuckled.

I couldn't help but laugh at her. She liked to push my buttons. She had always made me feel so completely loved and secure, so her playful jokes never ignited my jealousy but always brought a smile. So, I laughed, but then quickly added 'But seriously, this doesn't make any sense. How the hell does he get out here?'

'There's probably a bigger station nearby. Stop playing *Much Ado About Nothing* and let's get going.'

'Yeah, OK fine, but I don't see a bigger station on this map. As a matter of fact, I don't see *this* station on this map!'

My begrudging tone did nothing to shake her enthusiasm. 'Whatever, who cares about the map? You can see the station right there.'

She was right, of course, and so was I. It didn't seem to make sense but what did it matter? There was a station sitting there behind us and an unexpected trail before us, so my determined wife was ready to go.

I sighed, 'Lead the way.'

She took my hand and pulled me toward the trail. As I followed her, I tried to orient myself against the original map. Nothing seemed to match up, so I drew the new map from her pocket. Sarah looked back at me but just rolled her eyes and continued along the trail. As I studied the new map, I shook my head in total confusion. I didn't remember seeing any of these landmarks on our original version. I was baffled. I kept tucking one map under my arm so I could check the other. The trailhead for the original path was less than 20 yards from this one, yet the maps seem to be completely different. I shook my head and grunted in frustration.

'What is it?' asked Sarah in a tone that said *I know I'm supposed to ask but I don't really care.*

'The maps, they don't match at all. None of the landmarks on this new map appear on our original map.'

She stopped and turned to look at me. 'Yes, it's a different map'. She said this very slowly as though she needed to do so to make sure her 'challenged' husband could understand.

'I know that! But they both cover a lot of the same territory and they are completely different!'

'Maybe this new map is *a secret map?*'

I saw that twinkle in her eye again and I knew she was pushing my buttons.

Nodding to her and playing along, I replied 'Yes, that must be it. The state of Minnesota has gone to the trouble of creating a secret map so they can surprise people who decide to tackle this trail. It's like, surprise we didn't want anybody to know this was out here, but now that you're here you get the secret map!'

'Exactly!' she said as she smiled at me, then turned and continued along the trail.

What could I do? Her smile had been melting my heart for nearly thirty years, so I shook my head, stuck the maps in my back pocket and followed my best friend along the secret trail.

We walked quietly for the next 20 to 30 minutes as the trail wound through a combination of trees and overgrown fields. It was a beautiful, bright and sunny day but not too hot, perfect weather for this hike and we found the landscape stunningly beautiful. The trail ahead took us toward a decent-sized lake that looked to be about a hundred yards away. I found myself mesmerised by the sun shimmering on the calm surface. Out of the corner of my eye, I thought I saw something rise up out of the water and drop back down. It happened quickly and I thought it might have been a reflection from the sun. Then I saw it again a little farther off to the right.

'Did you see that?' I asked.

'See what?

'I think there's something in the water.'

'Yes, I see the ducks, or I guess they might be geese. It's still too far away for me to tell for sure.'

'No, I mean, in the water or under the water. I could swear I saw something rise out of the water.'

'It's probably fish. These lakes should be loaded with fish.'

I couldn't be sure of what I'd seen but it was far enough away that it would have to be a pretty big fish for me to have spotted it from that distance. I was studying the lake carefully and watching the area where I thought I'd seen... something. I squinted against the bright sun but that was making it hard to see clearly. Then I noticed it again. We were closer now and whatever I saw had to be big. It didn't jump out of the water and splash back in; it slowly rose up out of the water and then gradually sank beneath. I could swear it looked like a head and it was big – and I mean big.

'There it was again.'

'I didn't see anything.'

'It's way over on the right. The ducks or geese, or whatever they are, are on the left but this is over on the right where the sun is reflecting off the water.'

'Maybe it's just the sun playing tricks on you.'

That might have been true but this last sighting was pretty clear to me. 'Just watch for it over there.' I said as I pointed in the direction of my sighting.

'Ok. What do you think it was?'

'I have no idea, but it looked like it was pretty big.'

'I don't see anything.'

'Just keep watching.'

We both watched intently as we continued walking. A few minutes later we reached the part of the trail that opened up to the lake and became a much larger path that appeared to go around, so we had to choose to whether to go right or left.

'Which way should we go?' asked my wife.

'To the left' I answered with far more urgency than I had intended.

'OK, why?', my wife replied with a look that said *what the hell is up with you*?

'Uh, let's just say I have no interest in finding out what that thing was that I saw over there to the right.'

'What is up with you today?' she replied with a smirk. 'You've gone round the bend I think.'

'I don't know. Maybe. Either way I'd like to go left.'

Eyebrows raised, she shrugged at me and shook her head before adding 'Then left it is.'

We started to make our way around the lake, where the views were incredible. There were wildflowers of different colours and varieties surrounding the water. As I marvelled at this kaleidoscope of colour, I recalled the strange glitter-bomb flowers we'd seen earlier and found myself reflecting upon all we'd experienced so far. In addition to those odd flowers we'd come upon a ranger station and a perfectly coiffed ranger in the middle of nowhere. He'd offered us a secret Minnesota trail map, which we'd accepted and we were then making our way around a lake that I'd become convinced was the home to its own Loch Ness Monster. I considered it a serious possibility that we'd entered *The Twilight Zone*.

We reached the other side of the water as I finished my mental recap of all that had happened so far, relieved that we were about to put this lake and its Nessie behind us.

'How long is this trail?' Sarah asked.

Neither of us had thought to consider that before now. 'Good question', I replied as I pulled the 'secret' map from my back pocket. 'It looks like we're gonna go about two or three more miles before the trail starts to turn and work its way back.'

The trail on the map looked a bit like a hot air balloon. It was narrow at the bottom but wide and rounded at the top. We had started on the left-hand side of the trail and the lake represented the narrow base at the bottom.

'It looks like the entire trail is about seven or eight miles long', I finally declared.

'That's not too bad', said my adventurous partner. 'How far do you wanna go before we stop and eat lunch?'

'Let's try to make it halfway. It's 11:45 now and I think it'll probably take us another forty-five minutes to an hour to get to the top.'

'The top of what?' she asked.

'Oh, yeah, sorry, on the map the trail looks like a hot air balloon and the halfway point would be the top of the balloon.'

She chuckled, 'Alrighty then, the top of the balloon it is.'

I tucked the map back in my rear pocket as Sarah led the way and we continued along the trail. We left the lake behind us and were soon walking in a wooded area with trees that appeared to grow ever denser ahead. As they became thicker and thicker, they began to block out the sun. Soon, looming before us, were trees overhung so thickly on both sides that the scene looked like something out of *The Legend of Sleepy Hollow*. It became so dark and felt like we'd entered a spooky tree tunnel. A chill run up my spine and I started hearing *The Twilight Zone* theme tune playing in my head.

I tried to shrug it off and sound calm, 'Well this is kinda cool, huh?'

Still walking ahead of me, Sarah, ever fearless, enthusiastically responded, 'Yes, it is! Very cool!'

I shook my head in disbelief. Nothing, I mean nothing, bothered her. We made our way through the tree-formed tunnel and suddenly emerged into another clearing. I found myself nearly blinded by the bright sunshine. Beyond the trees, we saw tall grass about knee high on both sides of the trail. Ahead we could see the trail begin to bend gradually to the right. We were getting close to the halfway-point, I thought to myself, walking quietly for a few more minutes with the bright sun beating down on us. It wasn't hot but it was also becoming unbearably bright.

I was squinting against the sun when suddenly I saw something out of the corner of my eye. It was above me and to my right, moving at great speed and coming towards my head. In one quick and instinctive motion, I ducked my head in defence and crouched toward the ground. I sensed more than saw the thing as it flashed above me, feeling the breeze as it passed over and along with an almost imperceptible scratching sensation on the right side of my crown. I glanced up and to the left to see something speeding away through the air ever higher and then, suddenly, it was just... gone. I'm not saying it flew away. It just disappeared.

'Holy shit!', I hollered.

Sarah stopped and turned to me, 'What?' she asked as she rushed back. 'Are you okay?'

'Did you see that?' I asked, gasping.

'See what?'

'You've got to be kidding me. You didn't see that? It was huge', I said with exasperation.

'I didn't see anything. What was it? Are you okay?' she asked in rapid succession as she looked me over trying to make sure I wasn't injured. She was a Physician Assistant, a medical professional in trauma, so her first priority in a circumstance like that was to check for injuries.

'I don't know what that was, but it was huge!'

I hadn't seen it long enough to get a good look. What I thought I saw, before it vanished into this air, looked something like a bald eagle or hawk but it was nearly ten times the size of any eagle or hawk I had ever seen.

'It looked kind of like an eagle and it came flying at my head', I finished.

'Well I don't see any injuries. Do you feel alright?' Then, looking at me quizzically, she asked, 'where's your hat?'

I reached up and felt for my hat, which protected my ever-growing bald spot from the sun, only to discover it was gone. I looked around but didn't see it anywhere. I jumped to my feet as I said 'I don't know', as I continued to search. I didn't see the hat anywhere. 'What the hell?'

'Well, at least you don't appear to be hurt.'

'You really didn't see anything?'

'No, I didn't see anything. I did feel a breeze blow through right before you started shouting, but that's all.'

'That breeze you felt almost took off my head! It's like I was attacked by Mothra.'

'What's a Mothra?'

'Oh my god, you don't know Mothra?'

'No, but can you give me a clue?'

'Mothra, you know Mothra, as in Godzilla!'

She stared at me in disbelief. 'So, you were attacked by a movie monster?'

'I'm telling you it was huge and I think it took my hat.'

'So, a giant fictional monster swooped in and attacked you, choosing ultimately to abscond with nothing more than your hat? Where did this beast of prey get off to?'

A sheepish grin came over my face as I realised I hadn't mentioned the fact that it had simply disappeared into thin air. There was no way, given the look she was already giving me, that I was going to tell her that, so I settled for 'Whatever – but I'm telling you something took my damn hat and now my poor bald spot is doomed!'

She started sifting through her backpack as she moved towards me. 'Let me see it.'

'See what?'

'Your bald spot.'

I bent over to show her my bald spot and in one quick motion she drew out a can of sunscreen and blasted the top of my head. 'That oughta do it. You'll be fine. Now can we go?'

I gave her a playful scowl. 'Fine!', I said with a final note of frustration.

As we proceeded along the trail we came to a rather steep hill. By my calculations, the top of this hill would be the mid-point of our journey. We began the climb and we both breathed a bit harder as we exerted ourselves. It wasn't an easy stage but we still managed to reach the top, where we came face to face with a shocking sight. Even on this day of unbelievable experiences, what we discovered there topped them all.

As we arrived on the flat plateau at the top of the hill, we found ourselves surrounded by the sheer face of an enormous mountain. It had to be 8,000 feet or more and appeared to go straight up; but that wasn't the most shocking sight. Nestled in front of the mountain was a small, and apparently abandoned, little town. It looked like something out of the old west. There were small wooden buildings of various sizes with a dusty street running down the centre. I stared in absolute disbelief as my mouth fell open. 'What in the. . .?', I gasped.

'Well now this really is an adventure isn't it?' said Sarah.

I gaped at her as she seemed to be not at all bothered by this shocking development. 'You're kidding, right?'

'No. Why?'

'It's flippin' *Bonanza* in the middle of Minnesota... and do you see that mountain? That mountain simply can't be!'

'*Bonanza*?'

At that moment I was once again reminded that I had robbed the proverbial cradle. She had no idea what *Bonanza* was. 'Forget *Bonanza*! Look at that mountain and that, that, that lodge!' I shouted as I pointed to the biggest shock of all.

There at the centre of the western village, nestled in the Minnesota wilderness, the buildings were divided by a huge swathe of dusty road. The sheer side of the mountain was to our left and on this side there was an opening between the dozen or so buildings. Mesmerised by what we were seeing, we walked to that spot and turned to gaze upon a huge wooden staircase that led to the grand entrance of a... skyscraper? Except the skyscraper was a monstrous wooden lodge that seemed to be built right into the side of the mountain. From what I could tell it looked like the structure rose all the way to the summit. The architecture appeared simply impossible, but there it was.

A carved wooden marquee, that must have been the size of two or three billboards, read 'Dimagenanthia Gateway Lodge' with a surrounding border of the colourful glitter-bomb flowers we'd discovered earlier. The staircase, though wooden, looked like a staircase you'd find at a monument in D.C.

'This isn't happening.' I said as I shook my head in disbelief. 'This can't be real.'

'It certainly looks real', Sarah answered.

'Seriously, this can't be real.'

'Why not?'

'Why not? How in god's name would this not be one of the wonders of the world? Why have we never even heard of this place and, oh, by the way, that mountain has to be at least 8,000 feet high!'

'And?'

'And? Well, you might recall that while we were researching places to hike in Minnesota, we read that the tallest mountain in the state is Eagle Mountain. Eagle Mountain is only 2,300 feet at its peak! This is at least three times higher than that.'

'I see your point. Well, that does make this a bit of a mystery now doesn't it?' she responded in a tone so calm that I almost wanted to jump out of my skin.

In that moment I imagined Stuart Scott covering this escapade on ESPN. During the slow-motion replay of this scene he'd say "... and, just when things got really crazy, there's Sarah, cool as the other side of the pillow."

All I could do was shake my head and surrender. Nothing bad had happened and, at that moment, I thought to myself that this must be a trippy dream. Just relax. You're gonna wake up any minute so just sit back and enjoy the ride. So, I smiled at her and said, 'Yes, it is, isn't it? Shall we take a closer look?'

She beamed back at me, 'Now that's the spirit. I mean this is what we wanted right? A true adventure!'

I chuckled, 'YOU wanted an adventure. I was just looking for a good hike.'

'Well we're getting both! So, let's go.'

We climbed the stairs. I still couldn't imagine how the structure was even possible. We reached the landing, which sat at the top of the 49th stair. There we could finally see the entrance and, given the nature of the day, I was not at all surprised to discover an oversized set of revolving glass doors. Yep, 20th century doors on a 19th century structure. I shook my head in disbelief yet again but continued my surrender. It was just a dream after all.

'Shall we go in?' I asked.

'We have to, right? I mean we're here. We can't turn back now', said Sarah with a look of childlike glee as she gazed at the front doors.

'Of course not', I responded.

It came as no surprise that we couldn't see through the glass doors, making what was to come another complete mystery. Undeterred we pushed our way through and arrived on the other side. Having fully surrendered and joined this dream in earnest, I led the way and, as we stepped from the revolving glass doors into the lobby of the lodge, I saw him immediately. 'You've got to be kidding me?'

Sarah stepped from behind and she too caught his gaze. There, behind the oversized check-in counter of the lodge, which had vases filled with dozens and dozens of the fluorescent hot pink glitter-bomb flowers atop, was the ever-coiffed, park ranger, Mr Perfect. He gave us both a huge smile, displaying his perfect teeth and said 'Welcome to the Dimagenanthia Gateway Lodge. We've been expecting you.'

'What?' I questioned.

'Ah, yes', he added as he reached beneath the counter, 'for you, sir', he went on as he handed me yet another surprise.

'My hat! How...'

He interrupted, 'Yes, I'm afraid Milly gets carried away when it comes to hats. Now, I see your room is ready and that you'll be with us for quite some time.'

'Uh, I don't think so, we won't be staying long at all', I answered.

'Well now, you see, I'm afraid you've arrived in the 7th Dimension and here you can check in any time you like, but you can never leave.'

Great, I thought to myself, we came all the way to Minnesota to check in to the Hotel fucking California.

I looked at my wife and said 'Well, you wanted an adventure!'

FORM

by L. Jay Mozdy

I've been blessed with knowing. Nicolaus Ridic... Ridiculous, as I am to people who know me, or think they know me but for the most part, it's just me and Ma for now, until I can figure out how to make it all right again.

You know how sometimes you can tell when someone's lying to you, or they're being a certain way to get you to do something; not that they're lying, as such, but it amounts to the same thing. So, you know that feeling; well, I have that feeling all the time. Everyone isn't lying; it's just that I know the core to everything. I know what, or who, the world revolves around; and everything people say and do has an air of manipulation.

I lost her, ya' know. Yea, yea, I hear ya', but this was — is different than your average kind of thing. I — we really have something greater than life, greater than a mere existence on this tiny planet and having friends and jobs, or school and wanting more from all this... life. We have love. Yea, yea, yea, happy Valentine's Day, but really, it's not something I can explain and it may seem to you that, well, just go get someone else, right? No, you can't just go find someone else. It's one of those chemical compounds that burst into being and does something completely inexplicable through the laws of physics, or nature, or something and can't be reproduced and never has been; no scientist can tell us how it happened, it just is. That's what we have – but, as I said, I lost her... kind of.

Like, the other day, I went to the fridge in the middle of the night and Ma startles the whole damn room with one flip of the light switch and I'm blinded and rattled and I drop the carton of milk I was drinking out of; it's all over the floor in a puddle at my feet. There I went...

I look up from the beer that Pete re-hands me and I think; what day is this, where is she; and that's always the question; not what do I wear, or am I late, it's where is she? He looks at me, laughing; 'Don't drop this one, okay.' He pats me on the shoulder.

That was Alison's party, the night I left her there, Maggie, I mean, because she didn't want to leave with me. She wanted to party with everyone. I get it, I mean what the hell is life for, right. I wanted to rocket through the stars that night; maybe drive down Butler along the cornfields with the windows down and the radio up as loud as it will go, watch the Moon, full and bright chase us through the sky. I wanted us to get together, alone.

So, like I do, I breathe deep, smelling her perfume even though she isn't near and try to make that happen.

I found out that she had walked home with someone that night, so, I waited around, holding that beer Pete-re gave me, until the party started to simmer, quiet like and stood near the curb where she'd have to go to get home but, this time, I never saw her. I stood there like a jackass while everyone stumbled out of the house and went home. I'll be back, though; next time, I'll just go get her and drag her by the hair, or something.

It's like that, so, I looked at Ma and wiped up the spilled milk, started to go back to bed. 'It's trash day tomorrow, Nicolaus. Take out the trash after, will ya?'

'Yea, sure, Ma, I got it.' Sometimes I think that Ma just comes in to make sure I'm doing something, anything.

How do we have such nasty garbage. It's just the two of us and I don't make that much mess. Oh, yeah, I did make the fish the other night. That's what that smell is; beastly. 'Evening Mister Anderson.'

'You too, ay, they got you out here in the middle of the night to take out the trash?'

'Yes, sir.'

'Why is it always our job to do something with stinking garbage?'

'I don't know, Mister Anderson, I guess we're just built for this kind of thing.'

'Yea, built for garbage. I'm sure that's it.'

I balanced the plastic can with the missing wheel against the curb so it would stay upright and slapped the broken plastic lid on the thing. When I looked up, through the stench of rotting fish and tartare sauce, I saw the light on in her room down the street. 'Hey, Mister Anderson, what day is this?'

'What the hell, boy, it's garbage day.'

'Oh, yea, right.'

'Damn kids, don't even know what day it is on garbage day; garbage in his hand, stink in his nose.'

No, it can't be... I looked up at the night sky full of stars, closed my robe and managed a knot out of a broken and knotted tie-string. My slippers were so thin on the bottoms that I could feel the street against my heels as I shuffled down the sidewalk to see if it was the night I was thinking it was. It was early enough, I thought; probably around nine, or so, judging by how many lights were still on in the neighbourhood, televisions heard through the open windows.

I felt the wet, cool grass her dad had just cut. I could smell it; summertime. I say her dad cut it, 'cos she got so mad that time I walked into her backyard while she was pushing the mower that I didn't want to mention it. She hated cutting the grass and I offered to cut it; she wouldn't let me. I thought she was beautiful, but that's not this day.

I snuck up to her window, looked around behind me to see if anyone was watching; no one. Her perfume mixed with the smell of the cut grass and the glow of the light against her curtain dizzied me with pleasure, like I forgot to breathe for a while, holding it all in. I remember this night; it isn't the night, though. I just got home from working at the theatre putting up the marquee and I was telling her in detail about the movie that I saw for free after work. I sat outside her window in the warm summer breeze, looking up at the night, listening to her laugh and tell me she wished she was there, too. I wanted to tap on the window but I know she would have freaked; how could I have been on the phone and there at the same time?

'I love you, too.' Yea, she said that, I remember what she said. I waited for a couple of minutes and heard her say goodnight to her dad and close her bedroom door behind her. The light went out and I thought that there had been enough time to get to her house after that conversation to surprise her by being there. I could get her attention; tell her I ran all the way to see her. That was a great night, why change anything? It felt so good to be there, to let time pass with her; it was perfect, she was perfect.

It's not really a memory. Memories are just thoughts.

These memories happen in real time but if I try to remember something and be in the memory, it just turns out to be a memory. So I have to pay attention to what day it is, keep asking people, though it sounds weird to ask all the time; be patient and wait for the day she dies to change that day.

'You're up early.'

'Hey, Ma, yea, it is kind'a early.'

'Anything important, today?'

'As always, it will be something.'

'Yes, it will be something. After you get some sleep, go get us some groceries, will you.'

'Sleep, how do you know I didn't just wake up?'

'I know you, Nicolaus, you have things to do in life. All in good time. Don't forget the groceries, okay? Love you, I'll be back later.'

'Okay, love you, Ma.' All in good time, when did she tell me that? I do need sleep. I can't think, right now.

Darkness is the only place where nothing happens. Sleep doesn't really mean that things don't happen, or nothing is there. It's in darkness that I rest. My mind is not going anywhere in darkness; it's not taking me anywhere. If I sleep, I dream and I go everywhere. I have to be careful when I dream.

Static on an old television sheers through a dark and silent moment. I have to ask myself where she is; what day this is. As soon as the static subsides and a clear picture comes to mind, I remember Ma telling me to get groceries.

It's Friday, I remember. I heard a character in a movie say that the Universe smells like rum and tastes like raspberries. Not my universe, my universe smells like her perfume and tastes like lip-gloss; the sweat on her thigh. If I could only stop time right there and breathe the breath we took at that moment, together.

Time never stops, though; I had to open my eyes. Sometimes it's a day I don't remember, or a day that never happened. Maybe, it's a day that I should have had, where I'm sitting on the curb outside her house on a sunny afternoon, waiting for her to come out. She never does, I just sit there picking up little stones and throwing them at nothing in the street. I'm alone with a feeling of insatiable want for her. I go there a lot and it's always the same; empty, uneventful, hopeless, it must be sleep without dreaming. It must be the day after.

I get up and get to the grocery store like Ma asked me to. Cool and calm, the rain felt good the entire way there – and there I was; I'm standing on her front porch with three rose buds in my hand, my stomach in knots, nervous, thinking nothing. Then, she opens the door and smiles like she does. 'I just wanted to give these to you; I hope it's okay.' Seeing her again, her face as bright, her easy manner. I could have stood there studying her face for hours.

'Yeah, it's okay, thank you.' It was another day I wouldn't change. It's been like that lately.

Grey static and loud voices; the television, the radio, a woman's laughter, a commercial about the local bar. 'Get up Honey, you have to work in an hour. Get up, it's time to get up.'

'Okay, Ma, I'm up, I'm up, thanks.' If it wasn't for Ma telling me when I have to work, I wouldn't remember to go at all. It's like she knows. My mind would always drift to where it belongs; with Maggie on any day we shared. I'll be there, Maggie, but I have to go to work, she is usually at work, so I go to work. It doesn't stop me from drifting away but it does get me paid while I drift away with her.

'Thanks for getting the groceries. Here, I made a lunch for you.'

'Thanks, Ma.' Wait, when did Ma make lunch for me? 'Love you, Ma, see you later.'

'Nicolaus, I almost forgot, I talked to the dean and he said it's okay if you sit in on any class you like, as long as you do your cleaning after the class is over.'

'Yeah, I know, it's just difficult sometimes; most of them are obnoxious but I'll sit in if there's something interesting going on. See ya, Ma, thanks for lunch.'

'Ri-dick-u-lous, hey, Ridiculous, nice coveralls; you get them from the warden? You pickin' up trash by the road, after you're done sweeping up here?'

Yea, that's nice, you fucking asshole; swat you like a stickball with this broom handle.

'Good morning, welcome to McDougal's. Have you seen the new McDougal's Merry Morning Muffin Menu? How may I assist you in selecting this morning's breakfast?'

'What? I didn't hear what you said.'

Jesus, man, why are you fucking with him? Keep the line moving.

'Good morning, welcome to McDougal's. Have you seen the new McDougal's Merry Morning Muffin Menu? How may I assist you in selecting this morning's breakfast?'

'No, I haven't seen the Merry Morning Muffin Menu, what's on it?'

'McDougal's Merry Morning Muffin Menu has many Merry Morning Muffin Menu items listed on the Merry Morning Muffin Menu board. Or, I can suggest the Merry Morning Mixed Mash, which has the five McDougal's meats, plus the mashed, hashed and fries on the sides and, of course, our Merry Morning Muffin. It's our most popular Merry Morning Muffin Menu item.'

'Yea, give me the Meats and Mash, or whatever it's called; the number two... and I'll have a shake with that.'

'Thank you for having breakfast with us at McDougal's and choosing from McDougal's Merry Morning Muffin Menu. Please drive through to McDougal's Merry Morning Muffin window number two and have a McDougal's Merry Morning, sir.'

Yea, Merry Morning, what the fuck. Keep the god damned line moving. Poor bastard, he'll never get out from under that stupid hat.

'Here's your McDougal's Merry Morning Mixed Mash from McDougal's Merry Morning Muffin Menu, sir. State law requires us to tell you that this McDougal's Merry Morning Muffin Menu item is hot. If no one from McDougal's home of the Merry Morning Muffin Menu has told you that this McDougal's Merry Morning Muffin Menu item is hot, please notify McDougal's corporate offices at: McDougal's 2222 Merry Morning Muffin Menu Way, The World; like us on Faceit. By buying this Merry Morning Muffin Menu item and coming to McDougal's home of the Merry Morning Muffin

Menu we acknowledge that you have been photographed and your image and/or your likeness will be, or has been, used in McDougal's Merry Morning Muffin Menu advertisements. Thank you for having breakfast with us at McDougal's and choosing from our Merry Morning Muffin Menu. Come again to McDougal's, sir. Have a McDougal's Merry Morning.'

Finally, now go get your number two. Who the hell calls their food a number two? It's a joke, it has to be. Some corporate asses decided to see if they can get people to eat shit and like it. Yea, give me a turd on a sesame seed bun, please. I just love this place. Jesus, they're laughing at us. They sit there and laugh at us.

'Good morning, welcome to McDougal's. Have you seen the new McDougal's Merry Morning Muffin Menu? How may I assist you in selecting this morning's breakfast?'

Why don't they just get a fucking machine? McDougal's Dispensary, bring your own bowl and save a dollar, splat. Thank you. No wonder that guy was fucking with him.

'Sir...'

'What? Are you done? Is that the whole thing? I was waiting for more.'

'Good morning, welcome to McDougal's. Have you seen the new McDougal's Merry Morning Muffin Menu? How may I assist you in selecting this morning's breakfast?'

Ahh, for Christ's sake and who the hell dresses these poor fucking bastards? 'Get a different hat, will ya?'

'Uh... Good morning, welcome to McDougal's — Hey, aren't you Professor Dourum?'

'Yea, okay...' No fucking wonder. 'Get me a coffee.'

'McDougal's has three fine blends of Arabica beans, with a hint of...'

'I don't care. Just coffee...black.'

'Would you like to try our number two?'

'Hell no, I don't eat anything called a number two. Just get me some coffee.'

'Thank you for having breakfast with us at McDougal's and choosing from McDougal's Merry Morning Muffin Menu. Please drive through to McDougal's Merry Morning Muffin window number two and have a McDougal's Merry Morning, Professor Dourum.'

'Yea, thanks.' Damn window number two; place is full of shit.

'Here's your McDougal's Merry Morning coffee from McDougal's Merry Morning Muffin Menu, sir. State law requires us to tell you that this McDougal's Merry Morning Muffin Menu item is hot. If no one from McDougal's home of the Merry Morning Muffin Menu has told you that this McDougal's Merry Morning Muffin Menu item is hot, please notify McDougal's corporate offices at: McDougal's 2222 Merry Morning Muffin Menu Way, The World; like us on Faceit. By buying this Merry Morning Muffin Menu item and coming to McDougal's home of the Merry Morning Muffin Menu we acknowledge that you have been photographed and your image and/or your likeness will be, or has been, used in McDougal's Merry Morning Muffin Menu advertisements. Thank you for having breakfast with us at McDougal's and choosing from our Merry Morning Muffin Menu. Come again to McDougal's, sir. Have a McDougal's Merry Morning.'

'What, can you repeat that, please?'

'Here's your McDougal's Merry Morning coffee...'

'Shut the hell up.'

Of course, lady, drive right into me; I'll wait. Can you make it; turn that thing, there ya' go, turn god damn it. Good, now get the hell out of my way. People can't fucking drive. Where's my wave? Yeah, that's not a wave, is it?

'Alright class... class... we have a new theory. There we go, thank you, class, we have a new theory, which was presented for peer review today and I'd like to share it with you.

It seems that our lives and the lives of our forefathers started with a single cell. Nothing new there, except that this theory of how our species was afforded the grace to come into being was not as a result of some disastrous asteroid like so many of us had believed ricocheted off of Earth and caused a devastation so great as to shut off the sun and freeze out every living thing with a body mass greater than your pet hamster burrowed in two feet of cold, dark soil. Nor is it an image we all know of the squatting ape to standing man we envision when seeing how things evolved. No, this thing that's been found — these tiny fungi had a mind of their own; a way to live unlike anything we had known previously.

About a million and a half years ago, which isn't even a breath in terms of life on Earth, this little bugger started in on whatever life was on the planet, within one tiny area of visible light and conquered all. Found discretely only at the bottom of a 420-foot borehole in the Earth's frozen crust and nowhere else, it's as if this thing splatted to Earth in some spittle a faecal flinging alien spootinged through a rolled down window at the road sign to Earth on the space-highway in passing, then completely disintegrated into nothing, nowhere to be found. Then, twelve thousand years ago it showed up on Earth again in five or six inches of crusty earth. Between a million years ago and twelve thousand years ago it had not existed on Earth, or anywhere else in our discoveries of other planets; an unknown substance that is us.

Yes, we know our planet pretty well. We have gone right to its gooey centre; climbed and stood on its highest points and have stepped off the surface and into the invisible moorage, peering clearly beyond its solar system; and this little sporadic spore has not shown its face for a very long time.

It could have been a Tuesday afternoon that a man named Earnst Gerthund found something in his back yard mingling in something he thought his dog made. It was the same colour, smell and consistency as such material that the old basset has been known to make regularly at five thirty in the evening during its unswerving walks near the neighbour's nearly uprooted mailbox but, this time, it was a little different.

Earnst Gerthund is not the kind of man to sniff and probe every dog shit he finds in his back yard, really he's not. However, since the man is a scientist who studies what is found in the layers of the Earth, he made it his duty to discover what he and his faithful companion could find directly under their feet. As I've said, this coprophilic fungal spore was found within five or six inches of the Earth's surface. Not very deep, is it? We've all been there and stepped in it.

Now, this spore is in a safe place, submerged in a saline solution and has no life energy that we can see. It's dead and will no longer develop in its present state. At first, the scientific community thought that it was just some nocturnal yammerings that went on inside the man's mind; an undigested bit of beef, as it's known to have been said, but Mr. Gerthund insists that this filthy bugger told him how we began on Earth. Yeah, we're not sure about that but what we are sure of is that the budding, adapting mushroom has the ability to cling to anything and survive. It could stick to the bottom of our shoe and replicate its environment and live on like the parasite that it is. Unlike any known parasite, this thing can devour, or sample its host living symbiotically.

One spore (shot out with greater velocity than a shotgun blast) could cling to and grow on anything that needs to be eaten and digested, changing the host or moving on out to become, well, anything. This is one tricky little mother that uses all of everything it finds. We tip our pileus to this mycelium, for it is they who are we.

So, if we consider this as a destroyer of every living thing on Earth, we can see the death of the dinosaur as being not from an asteroid but from this tiny shit-eating son-of-a-bitch that can change itself to become each productive part of the being and congeal with others of its ken to become another organism; anything, anything fitting within the light spectrum as we know it. Then, jump out of the host's visible spectrum and into another; that's just it. It has the ability to see the old host from outside the old host's, or prey's, known spectrum of light; mingling, knowingly, parasitically, predatorily, or not, at its will.

If we can imagine seeing by using the light energy outside our visible spectrum, we would be able to dance with the living, loving bones of the beautiful young lady who sat across the gymnasium, with the pretty white dress and shy smile. Though, we would just see her bones. Perhaps our clothing, then, would be made of metal. We would stand, presenting a flower to fill her senses with the same passion we are trying to convey. Yet, why present an object to do the work; be the flower, rearrange ourselves to be in a single breath she breathes, then grow as passion. Be her passion.

If we crossed a street, so called, we would be able to watch a radio transmission spread throughout the field in front of us, have the music it represents fill our bodies, pass right through and apply themselves to the antennae scattered throughout the valley of radios responding in tune, one first, then the next at the same time, like watching caravans of busses go down the highway all at once.

So, this spore, making itself from any living thing crawling, flying or dying in a guttural gasp, can convert its energy to be anywhere in time, or space; it can be energy of any kind. Is it the reason we eat? Maybe, there is a group of cells, which has congealed into a being as we know and love, formed from every one of us; from everything within this room, notebooks, pencils, computers, from the point under your elbow, above the surface of your desk; that immense space that harbours worlds of things. Or, the other end; between the tip of your left forefinger and the blush of your cheekbone. Maybe, she sits, cross-legged, bright, brown eyed and thinking right here in this room. Could it be the young man in the orange jumpsuit that hangs in our doorway, leaning against that broom? Has anyone developed a rash, of sorts, a patch of flaking skin, an insect bite, perhaps? Is it what we think it is; could it be a few unneeded cells that have been borrowed from one to form another? Has your brown eye had a speck of dust in it lately, today, a moment ago, when you sat down to hear me speak?'

Thank you, class, see you on Wednesday.'

'Professor Dourum, sir.'

'Yes, Miss...'

'How do we know all that from finding one fungal spore?'

'Yea, well, it is mostly from the yammerings, as I've called it, from Mr. Gerthund; but, the community has had some insight into this spore. I don't have the details of that insight, just another footnote in some work done from a former member of the faculty.'

'Wow, which former member?'

'That person was discharged years ago; retired.'

'But, you still believe his findings, right.'

'I don't know, it's interesting. I have to go, excuse me.'

'Professor Dourum...'

'Yes, excuse me.'

'Professor Dourum, a minute of your time, please.'

'Yes, okay, walk to my office.'

'Professor, have you seen this fungal spore; do you know

where it is?'

'No ma'am, I have no – do you drive an old MGB GT by any chance?'

'Yeah, how did you know?'

'You almost fucking crashed into me trying to turn that piece around at McDougal's.'

'Oh, well, sorry about the... expletive... and the finger thing.'

'Right, because me sitting still in the drive-thru lane was a problem for you.'

'Look, I'm sorry, but I need to find that fungus.'

'I'm sure a lot of people want to find the fungus. Who the hell are you?'

'I'm a researcher for a major photochemical producer.'

'Oh, well that explains it. Excuse me, I have work to do.'

'Professor... damn it.'

GAIA

by Casey D. Sloop

His humming was irritating as hell. I almost wished he'd go back to singing but that would mean taking the gag out and I couldn't give him an inch of increased mobility. He was particularly hard to keep captive. I'd told him he'd be free to go soon but, as usual, he thought it was his way or the highway. Being on top of the world all the time really inflated his head and ego. He'd brought up one or two valid issues before I finally gagged him, such as who was going to pilot the sun while he was gone, but I wasn't too concerned. Helios had done a fine job for hundreds of years before Apollo was even born, so I was sure he could handle things for the month or two Apollo was on his forced vacation.

In Apollo's mind, things had got way out of hand. What he had intended to be a little bit of punishment for humanity in the form of a bad cough turned out to be a lot more viral and a lot deadlier than expected. It turned out he was a lot angrier than he thought but that's what happens when you rush into things before a good night's sleep.

Once the death toll climbed over five digits, Apollo had panicked and tried to switch gears back into the friendly healer side of himself. I'm not sure if the change came about because he didn't want to ruin his image or if Zeus gave him a talking to but either way an attempt was made; one that I quickly shut down. Oh, I know the world can't stay like this on a permanent basis but it could go on for a little longer I'm sure. There were a few of us who rather liked this new order of things. Plus, I was more than happy to take a shot at the golden boy's reputation.

Humans were fickle after all. You could literally carry the sun on your shoulders for eons but give a couple people sunburn and you're their mortal enemy. Until of course, they want to go swimming again the next week and then everything's hunky-dory.

Or maybe that was just because Apollo was hot. To be honest, I didn't get the appeal, but some people really like the sun-baked look, I guess. Regardless, it was irrelevant whether humanity condemned or praised him because he wouldn't be leaving here until I decided to let him go. No matter how irritating a hummer he could be. Perhaps I should knock him out just to be on the safe side?

Still, despite being gagged and rumpled, Apollo managed to pull off the façade of a smooth and confident young man, unbothered by anything and drifting casually through life. Only a few small details pointed to the constant stress he'd been under for the last millennia. His bright eyes and smile lines were offset by a worried look and bags that stood out even against the tanned skin. A body that must once have been broad and able started to show signs of weight loss, the type that came about from missing too many meals. Then there was the way he sagged back into the chair, which he tried to pass off as cool swagger but came off more like total exhaustion. I kept him well-bound for backup but, to be honest, I didn't think he could stand up on his own even if he wanted to. God of the sun, medicine, disease, music and poetry. It's no wonder he was so tired.

'I'm going out,' I said. Silence. Sky blue eyes stared at me pleadingly. I might have been moved if it didn't look as though he was pleading to be given some nap time. 'You can stay here for a while more; I'll take care of everything.' My voice reverberated against the cement walls, echoing in the silent room. He'd finally stopped humming. 'Get some rest while I'm gone.'

I flicked off the light as I left, blackening the room. I ensured the door was locked before walking away and I hoped, for his sake, that he followed my advice. Ascending the frigid steps, I steeled myself for work, prepping my bag and getting into the right mind-set. Exiting through the door at the peak of the stairs, I stepped into an empty hallway. I felt the gentle pull in my head directing me toward my job. Like someone had tied a thread around my brain and was tugging on it, leading me where I needed to go.

It took little time for me to hear the low hum of ventilators and the much louder sounds of rapid Italian. Doctors and nurses rushed around. Some looked calm but many were clearly struggling with the stress of the situation. I didn't pay them much mind. Healing had never really been my thing. The pulling sensation directed me toward a room with a prone elderly man struggling for breath. At the centre of his chest a glowing ball, just a little bigger than the average heart, floated surrounded in mist. I reached in and eased the soul out of the man's chest, placing it in my bag with great care. I then left the room to the sounds of doctors and nurses starting an attempt at resuscitation.

As I moved around the hospital in accordance with the pulling in my head, I passed a figure moving steadily from person to person with gentle steady touches. With pale skin and pronounced veins, the figure had a sunken chest and a thin neck, as if they'd been made of plastic that had warped during their creation. In odd contrast to its malformed and ill appearance, the figure moved swiftly throughout the hospital, weaving in and out of groups easily, ensuring that he brushed, at least briefly, against each person whose path he crossed. The crow's wings, forced to remain close to his back in the crowded hallways, gave away his identity. Corvus was apparently hard at work.

He might have been Apollo's creation, but it seemed he didn't have nearly the same level of fondness for humanity that his father did. There was a rather strained relationship there, especially as Corvus didn't seem to care about his father's sudden and prolonged disappearance. If anything, he appeared emboldened, his movements now quicker and more determined. Good for him. Unlike Apollo, I had a certain fondness for the young man. I rather liked his work.

Leaving the over-capacity hospital and the young divinity behind, I entered a town with small streets, made to feel wider by the lack of people travelling through them. A once-lively city looked just this side of abandoned. Usually I would work a while longer before taking a lunch break, but I would rather work a few more consecutive hours later on than miss out on the tranquillity I could get now. I was in a truly beautiful city, one no longer marred by busy bodies and I walked for a while. A long while, way longer than the hour lunch break I'd usually take.

The streets remained, for the most part, empty with only the occasional biker, straggler, or driver breaking the solitude. No one paid me much attention and they stayed plenty far away. Though humans seemed to do that instinctually with me anyway, whether I'm visible or not.

What finally pulled me from my idle wanderings was the steady thumping in my chest. An odd sensation for me as I don't exactly have a beating heart. I soon realised the sensation came about from a heavy base line blaring from a clearing in a nearby park. A base line that didn't seem to be garnering any attention from the nearby population or the cop car rolling down the street. That in itself was a clue as to who was partying in the forest during lockdown. A ways past the tree line, though not quite far enough to fulfil any kind of secrecy precautions, a party full of enthusiastic and drunken nature spirits raged.

Tall, long-limbed dryads, tree spirits, were throwing back shots of an indiscernible substance. Smaller, rounder dryads with stained skin popped in and out of trees, flailing limbs as they went. Naiads streamed from the woods opposite me where I could hear the faint sound of rushing water. Their almost reflective skin shimmered in the midday sun as they joined in with frantic dancing, giving the party a source of ambient lighting. The satyrs danced, drank and hugged trees inappropriately in equal measure, flirting up a storm and enjoying themselves more than they had in ages. Being half goat did terrible things for your manners.

I would have dismissed it all as harmless fun if one satyr in particular hadn't stumbled over and half collapsed on top of me in what I think was an attempt at a hug. 'Thanatos! Look at you, tall, dark and (hiccup) sexy! Did you come to see little old me?' Pan used to be quite nice-looking, even had a bit of a dangerous vibe going on, but over time he'd just become rather sad-looking. He'd shrunk; before we'd been nearly equal in height but now his head didn't even reach my shoulders. His once wickedly-sharp curved horns looked like they'd been inexpertly hacked off, probably quite painfully, and his fair-coloured fur was now a stained and tangled mess. Certainly not someone I was going to let cop a feel. A sharp slap to his hands had him pulling back, bleating shamelessly.

Pan's eyes were hazy with drink, as usual, but also happy. Too happy. Manic would be the best descriptor and very, very desperate. This was probably the best he'd felt in years – and he knew it wouldn't last forever. Probably another deity who wouldn't mind me dragging this out for a while longer. Though we should probably hope Zeus doesn't catch wind of our involvement or we might get into a fair bit of trouble.

Fearless, Pan tugged me into the storm of unhuman forms and shoved a drink at me. I wasn't very fond of the atmosphere, especially as no one here was sober enough to stay away from me. I suppose they wanted to make the most of their freedom for the time they had it.

It was the loud steps characteristic of humans that eventually led to the party's end as there had been no sense of it winding down before. Dryads ran back to their trees and remained motionless within. Satyrs scattered to the winds faster than their drunken state should have allowed and the naiads melted back into the tree line their river was behind, leaving only a low burbling sound in their wake. Pan and I stood in the centre, alone. The steps grew louder and a single average human walked through the clearing. It took them some thirty seconds to cross the space and, throughout, their eyes never so much as flickered in our direction. The human left the empty clearing. There was a soft thump as Pan dropped to the ground. He was looking up to the sky and, following his gaze, it was easy to see why.

Corvus had taken to the sky. In the hospital his disfigured appearance and wings had been disturbing, but he'd clearly been cramped and confined. In the sky he was on full display. His figure was clearly illuminated and his crow's wings were spread wide, finally showing off their impressive length. That in itself would be more than enough to get most gods' attention but even more interesting were the blue vein-like tendrils extending from him and covering all of the visible sky. Those hadn't been on show in the hospital at all. Some of those limbs extended down into the nearby city but not enough to account for even half the number currently infecting the normally picturesque image of the Florence sky. Corvus truly had spread himself farther than any of us could have predicted and in such a short time. All over the world, already.

'Beautiful', Pan murmured. His eyes glistened, as he gripped the grass beneath himself tightly. His fingers wound into it like the hair of a lover. God of the Wild. I may have found him rather sleazy but of all gods he was amongst those who needed this break the most. I sat with him awhile, neither of us talking. Rather unusual behaviour for him. We were there for a long time, just sitting, together. Him lost to thought and me listening to the natural sounds of the park around us. I left when I noticed his breathing even out and become steady. Hopefully he'd sleep off whatever it was he'd drank. Maybe that way he'd manage to avoid the worst of the hangover coming for him. At the end of the day though, he wasn't my problem and I had to get back to work.

So I sank. Downward, or at least what felt like downward, I sank. This transition had never been my favourite, but as the God of Death it was unavoidable. I always felt inkier and slimier whenever I did this, so I had to assume I wasn't solid as of that moment. It took me somewhere around a minute to sink through both the ground and whatever is in between the Mortal World and The Banks. A harsh shiver always goes through my bone structure, presumably as it re-solidifies.

The Banks are always uncomfortably warm, the kind of warm where you'll sweat unendingly if you wear layers, yet you can't walk around with just one on without getting goosebumps. They're also very grey. Grey sand, grey water, grey cave ceiling instead of any proper sky and not a plant in sight. Not on this side anyway. Persephone was the only source of plants in the entirety of the underworld but she didn't like coming to The Banks; always saying she doesn't like how sad everyone is.

I opened my bag. Coloured orbs floated out and found spots around the bank, the mist surrounding them forming into human figures. They'd stay brightly lit in their rainbow of colours for a little while but eventually they'd fade into grey like everyone else stuck on this side of the bank. It's not that Charon, the boatman, wouldn't give them a ride but paying customers went first. He'd been working harder than usual lately so it shouldn't take too long. There were more souls than usual though, more shades of colour reflecting off the walls.

I had trouble swallowing then. At least one of the figures was small and still clutching what vaguely resembled a stitched-together toy kitten. It bothered me. I was apathetic toward humanity as a whole but I'd never before done anything to cause them harm. Not my job really. I just show up in the aftermath. This was the first time I'd ever taken an active role.

Although something had to be done. I may not have started this but I could make it last a little longer for those who needed it. Humanity would be okay in the end, they always were. One month, just one more and then I'd let Apollo out to do his healing magic. I pulled out my report sheet, fully emptying my bag. I didn't much like paperwork, but Hades demanded that I at least record the number of the dead for his records. I dropped the sheet off and left for the day. It might have been a shorter time frame than usual but my numbers were pretty much the same, so I doubt they'd notice; or care.

I wanted to enjoy more of the world in its current state, so I reversed the process that got me down here in the first place – only this time it hurt. It was always worse going up than going down, as going up was always accompanied by pressure, like being pulled through a straw. Thankfully, travelling either way was still quick.

I reformed somewhere in China, to empty streets. Never thought I'd see that again. The sky looked clear, which was also out of place for this area. I felt a twitch in my back and allowed my wings to emerge. Wide, vulture-like wings that would dwarf even Corvus's own beat hard to pull me off the ground. I could breathe easy up here for once, no smog choking the air. Moving past the large city, I eventually ended up flying over greenery. Forests and clearings, vibrant with no human interference.

This, this was all I had wanted. Not suffering or death, just a little bit of peace for a beloved aunt. A couple of weeks where humanity would take a damn break and stop tearing her apart. A time for her to rest and recuperate. I just wanted the best for my Aunt Gaia. Some well-earned sleep for Mother Earth.

ISOLATION

by J. Drew Brumbaugh

I wake up in my wheelchair, groggy from the meds I take now and then to fight the pain in my back. After a few minutes trying to figure out how long I've been asleep, I pick up the remote and turn on the TV. Nothing happens. The little light comes on but there's no picture, no sound. Then I remember, I couldn't pay the cable bill and it was shut off; the internet too. My son, Peter, would probably pay for them if I asked but he's got enough troubles of his own, not the least of which is paying his own bills.

It has been a while since I have been without the cable or internet. In some ways I hardly miss them, preferring to read a good book. My cell phone still works, I think, although the cheap-ass plan I have has glitches that make calling on it a real chore sometimes. Thank God for the landline. The meals-on-wheels person should have been here yesterday, but never showed up, unless they left the food on the porch while I was asleep. Most of the time I don't mind being alone but I was looking forward to their visit. What has happened to the world outside?

I shut off the TV, put down the remote and roll into the kitchen. The counters are spaced far enough apart so even in this darn wheelchair I can easily get around. I open the fridge. Not much in there; milk, a bag of carrots, a couple of eggs, some lunch meat and a loaf of bread. I never have alcohol. I am an alcoholic though I haven't had a drink since I crashed my car and ended up in this chair. That was over twenty years ago. The painful memory never goes away and neither does the regret. I lived, maybe that's my punishment. The woman in the other car did not.

My son Peter takes care of most things around here but I haven't seen him or got a call in a couple of days. When he stops by, he usually stays for a couple of hours, cooks me something frozen, cleans up a little and brings groceries and staples that are above and beyond what social services provide. More than once I've thought of asking him to pay my cable bill but I know he's struggling financially and as long as my social security pays the mortgage and electric, I'll get by.

I do miss Peter and I decide to call him again. It rings but no answer and this time the synthesised voice tells me that Peter's mailbox is full. Hanging up I wonder what the hell is going on. Peter doesn't let his voice messages just sit there. That's not like him at all. There must be something catastrophic going on for his message box to be full. Sunshine streaming through my front window tells me there's nothing wrong with the world. It must be something going on in Peter's life.

I go back to the fridge, grab the bread and luncheon meat and cram together a sandwich of sorts. Something is definitely wrong with Peter but I can't figure out how to get to the bottom of things when I can't get a hold of him. Chewing on a bite of sandwich, I consider going outside. I haven't been outside in several weeks. For a while it was too cold, then as it warmed up it began raining and that went on for several days. Since the rain stopped, nobody has been by and I don't like trying to go out on my own because the screen door wants to shut in my face. If someone holds it open, I can get through easily. It doesn't look like anyone will be coming to open the door.

I finish my sandwich and roll over to it. I open the inner door, which swings in and stays dutifully open. I ease my way right up next to the storm door, turn the handle and shove it open. Bang. It slams shut. I open it again with one hand, leaning out to hold it open with my shoulder and then using my other hand I crank the main wheel on my chair forward and inch through the opening. I bounce down onto the porch.

Once on the porch I let the door slam shut behind me. There, I think, beat you. A warm breeze blows across my face. Sunshine streams down on the yard, grass growing like weeds and the flower beds overrun with... actual weeds. The trees lining the street are summer green, leaves fluttering in the breeze. Scattered puddles dot the yard and I can see wet spots on the pavement. At least it isn't raining now.

Scanning the neighbourhood, I notice that not a single soul is outside. I cock my head, listening. Birds chirping in the trees, a dog barks in the distance, but no cars. Yikes. How can that be? The house is close enough to the Interstate that usually the noise from the constant flow of traffic is a pain. Now even that's gone. For a moment I'm overwhelmed by a sense of isolation. I am used to being alone in my house but today it seems I'm alone, period.

I put that thought out of my mind and settle into a more comfortable spot in the wheelchair. Careful not to go too fast I roll down the wooden ramp my son built for me a couple of years ago. Effortlessly I get onto the sidewalk that leads to the street and still I haven't seen anyone. Using both hands now, I wheel myself out to the main sidewalk and turn right to head for the corner. The little mom-and-pop shop that's there is the one store I get to regularly. They'll know what is going on – and, while I'm there, I'll pick up something else to eat. Except I forgot my wallet. I consider going back inside for it, decide it's too much work and continue toward the corner.

When I reach the store, I am surprised to find the door closed and the windows boarded up. Where are the owners? Why are they closed in the middle of the day? Something's not right. They're always open.

Cautiously, I roll closer to the front door until I can reach it. Trying the handle, it's locked. I pound on the door. 'Hey Rich', I call out. Nobody answers. I hammer on the door again. 'Rich, are you there?' I ask, thinking maybe he's in the back storeroom. Still no answer, no noise of any kind.

I swivel around in the wheelchair and look up and down the street. Not a soul in sight. Hardly any cars either. Usually the driveways on this residential street look like there's some kind of convention going on. Not today. It is beginning to bother me. Where is everyone?

I look over at the dirt dike that runs parallel to the street behind my house and separates the neighbourhood from the canal. I wonder how high the water is on the other side after all the rain. I can't see over the grass-covered mound, so shrug and turn back to the store.

I move as close to the door as I can get. Leaning over, careful not to tip the chair over, I put up one hand to shade my eyes to look in through the glass. Everything looks normal, shelves neatly stocked, fruit bins full of bananas and apples, counters covered with stuff for sale, but the lights are off and it is eerily quiet. The cash register sits ominously silent.

'Rich', I yell again. 'Look, I need a few things. Can you just open up?'

When there's no answer, I give up. Rich must not be there. I roll back out to the sidewalk and turn for home. On the way I notice some serious low, black clouds streaming toward me from the south. A gust of wind rattles the stop sign on the corner and nearly pushes me over. I hang onto my wheelchair with both hands until the air calms down. I look up and watch the dark line of clouds swirling angrily, surging toward me. With an eye on the clouds, I hurry home as fast as I can.

This time I open the storm door, lean over and set the stop so it'll stay open. As the porch is lower, I can reach the catch when I'm outside but not when I'm in the house. With that taken care of, I manage to pop a wheelie and get inside. I yank the inside door shut just as a wind gust rattles the windows. I sit for long minutes in front of my living room window and watch as the wind grows steadily stronger bending the trees that line the street. The sun falls behind an impenetrable bank of clouds. It gets so dark that I have to turn on the lights.

The fridge clicks on and the soft whirr of the motor somehow is comforting. I brew up a pot of coffee and take down the book I've been reading, *War Party*, and sit for a while in the living room, reading and drinking coffee. At some point I fall asleep.

I don't know how much later it is. I wake up as the wind rips my storm door off its hinges and sends it tumbling down the street. I hear the glass in the aluminium door shatter as it bounces across the asphalt. I shouldn't have left that open, I think, but it's too late now. It's dark, my lights are out and even the night light that stays on in the bathroom is out. Power failure, I realise, and wonder when that happened. Outside the wind is howling like a banshee and rain is pounding against my windows with a force that seems destined to break the panes. This is no ordinary thunderstorm.

What the hell is going on, I wonder. I am afraid to move because I can't see anything and I'm afraid to stay near the windows in case they do blow out. I decide to try to get into the hallway that leads back to the bedroom. It'll be tricky because I know somewhere between here and there is a table that I can't see.

Gently I move my wheelchair forward, waiting to bump into the table. Sure enough, I only go a few feet before my footrest hits the damn thing. I don't hit it hard, so no damage to either me or the table. I swivel the chair until I am parallel with the table and can lay one hand on the table top. Using the hand on top of the table as a guide, I inch the wheelchair forward with my other hand until I reach the end of it.

There's a tremendous crash from outside. Followed by a shrill screech and a second crash. I freeze but hear only the howling wind and pelting rain. I get around the table and gently roll toward where I know the hallway is. I bump into the wall, pivot a little to the right, try again and find the opening. With a sigh of relief, I glide into the hallway. Feeling a little more secure between interior walls, I stop and rest, my breath coming in gulps.

I don't know how long I remain huddled in my wheelchair in the hallway. The rain continues to come in waves lashing the house hard enough to make the structure shiver. I begin to think that the dike will soon be breeched if it doesn't stop raining. There's nothing I can do about it. I am getting hungry but don't dare leave the hallway. A damp chill begins to take over the house. Now I wish I had a long-sleeved shirt on but I'm not going to try to find anything in the dark. I am so tired and my back is killing me again. I fumble in my pocket and fish out my pill bottle. In the dark, I manage to get the darn child-proof cap off and shake out one of the painkillers into the palm of my hand. I swallow it dry. It scratches its way down my throat but soon my back pain subsides. After that I finally fall asleep again.

At some point I wake up. It's still raining, maybe even harder than before. The wind howls. I think I hear shingles blowing off my roof. Somewhere toward the front of the house I hear water dripping. Crap, the roof is probably leaking. I wish the sun would come up so at least I could see something. Maybe then I could put a pan under the drip.

Things only get worse. It's still pitch black and though my eyes have had plenty of time to adjust, I can hardly make out anything – and then I hear it, water rushing outside. Not like trickles. This is serious and I realise the dikes have failed. A wall of water slams into the side of the house, nearly knocking it off its foundation. Bad. Even worse is the water that rushes in under the front door, swirling and splashing in the living room and kitchen.

My eyes bulge in fear. How high will the water get? Almost immediately it's a foot deep and rising. I force my way back into the living room against the surge of water coming under the door. As the water continues to spout up like a miniature fountain, my butt realises that it has reached the seat on my chair. I have to get somewhere higher or I'm going to die right here in this wheelchair, but where? I can't open the door and go outside. The water pressure would sweep me away in an instant.

I roll over toward the kitchen counters, bouncing off unseen furniture as I go. Eventually I feel the cupboard handles and stop next to the counter. It's the only spot in the house higher than my chair. I put both hands on the countertop and push up. Fortunately, I have pretty strong arms and manage to drag my useless legs up onto the counter. The water continues to rise. Now what? If it gets too high, I'll drown. There's no place else to go.

Huddled on the counter I say prayers that I forgot I knew. God never figured in my life since the accident. I couldn't understand how any god would let me live and take the woman in the other car. A sense of loneliness consumes me. I long for companionship, an ear to hear my final words. If this was to be my end, I wanted at least to make sure that the Universe knew I was sorry, really sorry. There's no one to tell how I feel.

The water keeps rising until it is lapping an inch over the countertop. It creeps up a little higher and I think again that I'm going to die trapped right here alone. Then it stops rising. I sit for a long time, soggy up to my waist, but alive. Eventually the wind begins to die down and the rain slackens. I am afraid to hope that the worst is over so I remain on the counter for a while and then I wait a little longer. I notice faint light coming in through the windows in the front room. It must be morning. The water drops a little, leaving the countertop damp but no longer underwater. I have fine brown silt all over me. My jeans are definitely ruined. My counters and the sink are now covered in brown paste. I hate to think of the mess that'll need to be cleaned up. Right now, I just breathe a sigh of relief.

It takes a while before I accept that the storm is gone. Leaning over the edge of the countertop I look down. The water has dropped even more and now it appears to be only a foot or so deep in my living room. My wheelchair is on its side laying right below where I'm sitting. Somehow, I need to get it upright and get back in it.

I slither down off the counter, landing in the water with an uncontrolled splash. Sitting in the cold water, feeling the squishy carpet on my butt, I grab the chair with both hands and manage to get it upright. I clamber up into it, turn the wheelchair around and make my way to the front window. Pushing the soggy curtains aside, I am surprised by how heavy waterlogged curtains can be. I look out into the street. It's a mess. There are tree limbs and even a couple of big trees down. The street is a river with water up over the curbs in some spots. Power lines crisscross the pavement like spaghetti. I see an old pickup truck that I don't recognise lying on its side in the neighbour's front yard. I feel like I've survived the apocalypse. Maybe I have. I still don't see a single person.

I check my cell phone. No service. I pick up the landline which fortunately hangs on the wall high enough that it didn't get wet. I smile, listening to the dial tone. I hit redial and listen to the beeps as it dials my son's phone. It rings twice before he answers.

'Hello.'

I recognise Peter's voice immediately. 'Peter', I gasp. 'Where are you? Where is everybody?'

'Dad?' he asks as if he doesn't believe it's me. 'What are you doing at home?'

'Where else would I be?' I realise he's recognised the landline phone number.

'The sheriff told me that you were evacuated with everyone else on the street.'

'Evacuated? I don't know about any evacuation. I do know

it rained really hard here for a while.' I couldn't help wondering if I'd slept through the Sheriff's visit because the drugs had me out cold.

'Oh my God. Dad. You've been at home all this time?'

'Yes; and it hasn't been much fun, I can tell you that.'

'I'm so sorry. You should have called me.'

'I did. Several times. You didn't answer.'

There's a long pause on the other end. 'I forgot my cell phone in my house when they told us to evacuate and I've only just got it back this morning.'

'So, what is this all about? Why were you told to evacuate?'

'Dad, it was a hurricane, hurricane Stephanie. She was a monster. How did they miss you?'

'I have no idea what you're talking about, but can you please come get me in the van. I'm wet, it's cold and I can't even make coffee.'

'Sure Dad, I'll be there in half an hour. I'm so sorry. The Sheriff's office said everyone was evacuated to the arena downtown and I just took their word for it. I was going to go down to the arena to get you this afternoon. Now I'll just come to the house.'

'Fine. I hope you can get through. The street has a lot of junk blocking the way and there are power lines down everywhere.'

'Don't worry, Dad. I'll be careful. Just sit tight until I get there.'

'I'll be here. House is a wreck though. I don't know what I'm going to do.'

'Don't worry about that. FEMA will be getting things back in order soon.'

I laughed. FEMA. They still hadn't finished cleaning up from the hurricane we had four years ago. Oh well, I guess I'll be staying with Peter for a while. Things could be worse.

HOW THE RAVEN MET THE ANGEL

by Jeffrey Caston

August 4, 1974, Winchester Lake, Idaho.

Fourteen-year-old Kurt Giffords struggled to keep the canoe steady. He feared it was a losing battle. After all, he'd never been in a canoe before.

His parents had reluctantly let him go out by himself and he had been improving, becoming more sociable, less temperamental and finally talking to the expensive Seattle psychiatrist hired to help him. So when he asked to 'mess around' at the lakeshore during the last day of their annual summer camping trip, Kurt's parents had bid him have fun.

What he hadn't told them was that he planned to paddle out into the lake in the old abandoned canoe he'd found two days earlier. That, they would not have tolerated; but he needed it as a balance exercise and his parents didn't have to know everything.

'I can't do this. I don't know what to do! I'm GONNA TIP OVER!' Kurt said aloud. To an onlooker, it would have appeared Kurt was talking to himself. Except he wasn't. As the canoe rocked, threatening to dump him into the lake's cold water, Kurt directed his frantic statements to the spectral raven perched on the canoe's bow. The jet-black bird, roughly twice the size of a real raven, stood unfazed by the erratically tipping craft. It stared at Kurt.

'Help me!' Kurt cried out.

'Help yourself', the raven said to him a raspy voice. 'You need to learn balance. You'll never become what you want, what I can help you become, without it.'

Kurt had come to know it as the Spirit Raven. It had claimed to be the original Raven, the celestial spirit that had helped create the world and guide the first people who came to the Pacific Northwest. Kurt had also learned the Spirit Raven had earned a well-deserved reputation as a cunning trickster. Three years previously, when Kurt had sunk to his most desperate low, the Spirit Raven had come to him and proposed an exchange. If Kurt became his protégé and agreed to dedicate his life to protecting the lands and the sea, the Spirit Raven would train and protect him.

The relationship and the lessons had progressed well in the intervening years. Hands that had only been good at rolling gaming dice now had a much stronger grip. Muscles and limbs presently formed a toned, sinewy-strong build. He'd metamorphosed from an awkward, nerdy preteen to a rising star of the school's wrestling squad – and the Spirit Raven had chased away the other voices in his head, so he'd become less reliant on the psychiatrist. This helped him focus, had sharpened his perceptions and improved his grades. He managed everything whilst simultaneously taking an interest in rigorous martial arts training and every other sport the school had offered.

Only the current lesson on balance wasn't progressing well. The small, primitive craft continued to rock. Water splashed in and soaked his pant leg. Kurt sucked in a breath as the cold lake water bit into his knee. He tried to correct it, overcompensated, coming even closer to capsizing.

'Concentrate!' the Spirit Raven said. 'That girl in your judo class threw you last week because you weren't balanced and you weren't concentrating on anything but her pretty blue eyes. Use the gift I taught you.'

The Sight. That was what the Spirit Raven meant. It had promised him the Sight would be a gift that would save his life time and again. It would make him better than almost all of his favourite comic book superheroes. He just couldn't figure out how 'seeing more' would help.

Kurt looked at the Spirit Raven, pleading with his eyes for help.

'Trust me', the Spirit Raven said with a voice that somehow conveyed the paradoxically dual tone of empathy and gritty irritation.

Kurt took a deep calming breath and nodded.

'Close your eyes', the Spirit Raven said. 'Don't rely on those clumsy things in your head. Use the Sight that I have to see everything.'

Kurt complied, his eyelids dropping like curtains over a stage. The canoe still rocked about, but he forced the panic away.

'Let your spirit extend outward. Connect your mind to my Sight.'

Kurt listened but he didn't clearly understand. Spirit? My spirit? What is that supposed to mean? He had no idea. It wasn't like an arm or a leg. It wasn't even something like his own vision or hearing, intangible, yet still sensory.

Lacking direction, Kurt imagined projecting himself outside of his body. That accomplished nothing. He took another tack, imagining his skin growing and expanding in all directions. That just made him snigger at the idea of becoming a human balloon.

Kurt flinched when the Spirit Raven angrily clacked its beak at him.

He tried again, consciously ignoring the sensations coming from his own body until he perceived only his own thoughts. The precariously rocking canoe disappeared. His white-knuckled grip on the canoe eased away. He heard nothing.

He projected his thoughts like a radio signal until it contacted a presence of energy so focused it felt like a boulder in a river. His own energy was that river. Soon Kurt realised the boulder was the Spirit Raven. His thoughts became tactile, psychically creating fingers that felt the Spirit Raven spreading its massive wings. He probed at his patron spirit's presence, feeling the taut strength of its powerful legs, caressing the feathers, the bite of its sharp beak.

Then, finally, its eyes.

Kurt's earthly body gasped as Spirit Raven and pupil, spectre and body, eternal essence and young boy, merged senses.

The Spirit Raven launched itself from the bow. Kurt saw himself from high above. His young body sat, swaying in the small craft. Kurt could see the portside waves pushing at the canoe, trying to capsize it. Return waves from the shore slapped back against the canoe. Kurt saw his arms pulling and pushing on the sides – but not with the waves. Instead, he could now see...

Using the Spirit Raven's Sight.

... that he was exerting erratic force at random.

Unproductively.

Kurt now understood his earlier harried efforts had only worsened the canoe's instability. He watched from above as another wave approached the canoe and timed his reaction, moving with the direction of the lake's water, then easing off and absorbing more of the shock with his other arm as the return wave came.

Soon he steadied the canoe until it rested peacefully on the lake's surface.

Kurt opened his eyes. He could still see the canoe through his own eyes, but simultaneously from above, behind, from the surface of the water and from all around him, as if he had eyes covering every inch of his skin.

He smiled, perfectly balanced and aware of everything.

August 6, 1993, Seattle, Washington.

Amidst the wrecked ruin of his compact armoured vehicle, the Raven faced off against an angel.

Or at least she looked like one of the angels of myth and religion.

The Raven had been chasing a truly evil person, racing behind him on Highway 99. They had dodged through late-night traffic when an inexplicable bolt of lightning struck the Raven's front tire as he reached the northbound lanes of the Aurora bridge, near Seattle's waterfront. The pursuit abruptly ended when he crashed into a guardrail. Another bolt of lightning from behind sheared off the armour-plated hood and fused half of the engine compartment into a smoking block of blackened metal. The front end smashed through a small section of the concrete barrier, bringing his vehicle to an abrupt stop, perilously close to tottering over the edge.

The Spirit Raven circled the area from above. With the Sight, a gift long ago mastered, the Raven saw the Angel, a woman with broad, white wings, fly toward him and land near the vehicle. He grinned as he watched her, outside, gripping the edges of the vehicle's canopy. I designed this thing to smash through barriers, gunfire, you name it, the Raven thought, amused. If you think you can tear it off with your bare hands, you're crazier than I am.

When the struts and bolts creaked with metal-screeching

protest and then gave out, the Angel pulled that smug grin off the Raven's face as well.

He would not allow shock to lead to defeat, however. He jumped into a standing position.

The Raven and the Angel grappled, scrabbling at each other's arms and shifting their weight to gain the advantage. From the awkward way she moved, the Raven discerned that he was the better fighter but her crushing grip dug painfully digging into his arms, even through his body armour, telling him this Angel was far stronger; as did the discarded canopy she had tossed aside like he might have thrown an empty tin can.

The Raven stared into her determined eyes and used the Sight to observe her from every direction and assess her. The Angel was middle-aged Caucasian woman. Her pure white hair gleamed in the moonlight. She wore ordinary functional clothing; nothing ethereal or robe-like, as one might expect. Wings covered with snowy white feathers with gray highlights were attached to the back of her shoulders. They were real and they were part of her. She flexed these powerfully and used them for leverage but with his long hours of martial arts, along with the benefit of the Sight, he anticipated her every manoeuvre and managed to maintain his stance. Twisting slightly, he began to break free of the Angel's iron grip.

'Psychopath', the Angel said through gritted teeth, 'you caused a ten-car pile-up back there! You could have killed someone.'

'I was chasing an evil one, idiot. You let him get away. He would've faced MY justice. I would have ENDED HIM!'

The Angel snarled. 'No', she said, shaking her head. She lifted him up and then slammed him back down. A sharp edge of ripped metal bit into his back. The Raven stifled an exclamation of pain. 'I finally found you! I won't sit by any longer and watch you deal out what you think is right, hurting innocents. I don't care about your crazy motivations, or your insane costume, or your stupid toys! You are DONE!'

The Raven seethed at the Angel's short-sightedness. Even if she were right about causing an accident, modest losses were unavoidable. He could see the bigger picture, the real threats to the lands. He understood the threats posed to the people. He sought to protect the area's inherent goodness. What could she possibly hope to accomplish by worrying about bystanders who had inadvertently got in his way? Now, an evil man who operated a ruthless syndicate of drugs, gambling and piracy had escaped, undoing months of tracking and preparation. What were ten cars compared to that?

The Raven knew none of it would matter to this Angel. She saw only the superficial, the obvious, but her rant sparked his curiosity. Find him? Sit by? What could that mean but that the Angel also lived here? He had never heard of her before. An issue to consider later.

The Angel held a vice-like hand across his throat. If not for the body armour, she might have crushed his windpipe. He twisted his head to ease the pressure. The Raven kneed her in the side and jabbed a talon from his gloved thumb into her elbow. Both blows connected. His knee throbbed, as if he'd struck a brick wall. The sharp bladed talon barely nicked into the skin.

'You like hitting, bird man? You like hurting people? You'll need to try harder than that with me.' Her beautiful and calm face suddenly twisted into a grimace. She splayed her fingers wide in front of his face. Arcs of electricity jumped between her fingertips.

The Raven kicked at one of his vehicle's control panels. It wouldn't do anything, except create a sound, but that was all he needed. The chirps and squawks from a communications device distracted her. She momentarily averted her eyes to the source of the sound.

The Angel was strong but unbalanced, unfocused, and she did not seem to weigh more than a typical female. He shoved up with his legs whilst grasping her hand. The Angel pitched forward. The Raven pushed harder, throwing the Angel off the side of his vehicle and over the edge of the bridge. He stood, fighting against twinges of pain in his neck and back.

The Angel had recovered too. She hovered mid-air, her collar-length white hair tousled by the gentle currents. The moonlight gave her an ominous countenance. Bolts of electricity coursed over her skin and jumped back and forth between her hands.

Seeing her aloft, displaying her own amazing gifts, the solution flashed through the Raven's mind.

Electricity.

Gasses.

Power-generation.

Arcs.

Flash.

Need a conductor?

Screen.

Time the gap.

Escape.

Heat.

Survival?

Knife.

Facing wrong. Need opposite.

The Raven instantly formed a plan, using the other gift the Spirit Raven had provided him with. The Knowledge. In addition to the Sight, the Knowledge provided flashes of inspiration and allowed him to make instantaneous deductive leaps to create plans and tricks when he needed them most.

Like now.

The Raven kicked a small monitor built into the vehicle's console. It broke and sparked for a moment, the tubes inside shattering, releasing the minute amounts of gas within. The Angel flew at him. The Raven shifted stance, preventing the Angel from grappling. She stood in the armoured vehicle cockpit and raised a hand to shoot an electrical bolt at him. Her fingers began to spark.

The Raven drew a knife. The Angel looked at it, contemptuously. The Raven tossed it down, close to the destroyed monitor, then grabbed handholds for the wings built into his suit and jumped back. He extended them and began to glide down. With the Sight, he noted surprise on the Angel's face as she realised his trick.

He hadn't used the knife to attack. As it fell within the vehicle's cockpit, it created a makeshift electrode. The current from her body arced to the discarded knife, creating an electric pathway through the ionized gas. The Raven had reached a safe distance by the time an arc flash started, a burst of energy that would very quickly cause his wrecked vehicle to explode.

The Raven reached the ground. Though obscured by his own eyes, the Sight showed him the Angel fleeing down the road, flying away, trails of her lightning illuminating the distant sky as she fled. From the opposite direction, police vehicles closed in on the scene of their battle.

The Raven laughed silently, the image of the Angel and her escape burned into his memory. She too seemingly feared discovery – something they had in common. The loss of his vehicle was a costly inconvenience but he would manage. He always did.

'Let's call this a draw my lightning-wielding friend', the Raven muttered. 'I suspect we shall see one another again.'

SOMETHING THE MATTER WITH ALPHA CENTAURI

by Anon

Silence and a field of stars, forever.

No... what's this? A small, black square gradually expanding in the centre of that almighty starscape rises to meet us, its four sides widening, closing, blocking the view and just as we're about to be hit... hurtles through our point of view and passes, revealing the star scape behind once again and – ouch! We shade our eyes from powerful laser beams projecting against it from an invisible point in distant space.

The photon backwash takes us and we turn 180 degrees against the pattern of stars. A nudge, we stop and can see the four laser beams pushing a huge, carbon-black and purple, 'sail' in space. There are lines running behind the canvas, hawsers pulling a much smaller habitat fuselage.

The misty, ever-present glow of spent photons is radiating off a shield at the back of the space ship and energising space particulates are seen, which then disperse, cool and fade away.

The solar-sail space ship passes away from us, off into the distance, losing detail again and reducing to a sharp black square scissored out of the Universe.

A simple, compact and tidy habitat, don't you think? The kind of place where you'd want to live, if you were allowed to leave it occasionally. Shall we look around? It contains a flight console area at the forward end with a wrap-around screen-wall above it, then an open walk-through to two rooms behind for sleeping, food generation and storage. Where is everyone? Ah, it seems we've found one of them.

A twentysomething female in a flight-suit. She must be the only crew member, working at a screen, all focussed and intent, then finishing what she's doing, breathes a couple of times as if comprehending the gravity of the moment and look, she's pressed 'submit.'

A calm, computer voice is responding to her, '92 percent'.

'I passed?', she asks it.

'You have completed your programme of education and been granted full access to command the vessel.'

'Wow, twenty four standard years' – and now she's up.

'Correction', the simulated personality replies, 'Your education modules began toward the end of your fourth year of life. Before that, you were uncommunicative.'

'Can do anything I want now? Without you directing me?'

'You can.'

The solo sailor doesn't appear to know what to do. She opens a view to outer space and, quite still, watches absorbed as the stars slide by.

We find her again, days later, drinking clear liquid from a tube, which she finishes. A wipe of the sleeve and she refers to a flight screen, but from here I can't tell you what's on it.

'What's the distance to Alpha Proxima B?' she questions, peering down. 'That's no good. The digits are spinning too fast. Can you convert that to astronomical units?' She seems satisfied with the new reading.

'Open diary. Psychiatric mode. Relative timestamp.'

The calming, computer voice hums 'On', as if it's another Sunday morning cat at the window. She psyches herself up and begins.

'Welcome to my world, diary. We are about to make history. Actually, keep that first line pending approval, in case it doesn't turn out to be that glorious. Ok. You really can lose your mind watching the real-time distance counter. It's compulsive, but I guess I'm conditioned for mental resilience. Drop that, it makes me sound like a stupid cadet but, Diary, it is part of basic training to cope with concepts like, okay, I've travelled 4.24 light years at a quarter of the speed of light. The all-directions information bubble has shown me all the knowledge I need to know, answering my questions whether I asked them or not. I've learned all I can about Alpha Proxima B as well. Ok. Generate auto-questions.'

A new voice emerges, qualified, peaceful and understanding, like an interviewer of librarians. 'How are you alive?', it asks her.

She considers this before answering. 'The AI brought me up and ran the systems which kept me fed and healthy. It compensated on-board conditions to preserve my bone integrity. I suppose other humans don't have that sort of tech in their daily lives, but the space agency and the public invested in me; or more specifically in the four of us on our ways to different destinations.'

'Do you talk to yourself?'

'Yes. Quite often. Is that bad?'

'Describe your waste.'

'My waste, seriously? I am organic, human, so that's regularly shed into space behind my bubble and breaks up in whatever remains of the beams. I'm shielded from seeing those because the system tells me they're much too bright.'

'Are you a pilot?'

'The ship does most of the actual sailing', she concedes. 'A solar-sail passenger then, or live cargo. I am sorry, my diary, I cleared your memory recently and am beginning from first building blocks. To be honest, I've wiped you a few times now because some of the things I recorded were difficult to return to, enough said, but I'm good now. A fresh start. Next question.'

'What do you see when you look at that screen?'

She turns to the screens and relates her impressions in real time. 'The distance counter is accelerating as we come under the gravitational influence of the destination star and out from the edge of the sail I can see the first outer planets of the system appearing. They look kooky. Okay, I can make out the habitable zone on tracking, which the vessel is committed to make for. Stop recording.'

Something is changing. The misty ever-present glow of spent laser energy radiating off the posterior shielding and into the silence of space suddenly switches off. Stars can be seen clearly now in all their terrifying contrast, the white light sharp. It's easier now to see how fast the ship is moving against the reflective bodies of an alien system as it hurls on.

The solar sail which blots out all that's in front has turned saggy. The material tucks itself into a roll, inverts and then expands again, filling the same gap and tightening into position. Stays lock on. The reflective surface is now facing the other way, forward, its circumference curving out like a cup.

A stream of high-energy light sluices by, slightly slower than instant to correspond with the velocity at which the ship is moving. The beam extends to an ice world, or more of an ice-moon orbiting a gas giant world. The beam reflects back in still quite a concentrated path and pushes the solar sail against the direction of travel.

The ship is slowing now, climbing the waterfall.

Back in her habitation, the solo sailor is on edge. 'There's no way an alien civilisation in this system can possibly miss this. It's a massive display of optical engineering.'

The diary voice answers her: 'Are you scared of them?'

She answers with a quote, "There's nothing to be scared of in space, except poor planning.' Mental resilience, see? If you keep reciting that often enough...'

'You seem distrustful of your maker, of their training.'

'Never met them. Never met anyone – and they taught me critical analysis.'

She pauses, before continuing, slightly peeved. 'Look, I have to hope they're not aggressive, but I also hope there is intelligent life out there or I'm wasting my time – wasting our lives in fact.'

'Have you been diagnosed with imaginary friend syndrome?'

'No. Computer? Independent clarification please.'

A calming, ethereal presence rules on the conversation. 'The words 'we', 'our' and 'us' can be taken as references to the supply of first stage hibernated human children in artificially delayed post-natal development. The terms may also refer to the stock of human cells, blank template eggs and genetic sequences for which this crew member is responsible.'

'Thank you, computer. Diary, continue prompting reflection but I don't know whether to talk about those as they might not happen. They're a potential thing, like if I need more crew or colonists to continue the mission. Mission Control are going to bring me home after I complete here and there's not much habitat space, so potential people can stay in their nutrient gel tubes as far as I'm concerned, out of my way.'

'Would you describe yourself as selfish?'

'No. Lower psychiatric intensity setting fifteen percent. Ok, I'd like someone to talk to but it's the resource equation, isn't it? Although all that dribbling does look unnecessary.'

'What are they for?'

'What are they for or what is life for? If the primary intention of my mission is successful and I make contact with an alien species, they're for nothing. The arrested development cycle will not be re-started. If there is no life on the planet I am going to, then we move to the secondary goal: I am to wait to see what the conditions are like before mixing the most appropriate cocktail of genetic adaptations to optimise survival. The gene pool can't be started too small.'

'Could you do that now and then not use them?'

'No. I need data to inform my decisions. The axial tilt of the planet hasn't been measured for a full cycle. How much solar radiation gets through to the surface or in what seasonal patterns, I do not know.'

The diary pries again. 'The post-natal stock may not survive. How would new genetic material be gestated?'

'Naturally, but that work can't all be done by me in case there are complications. The mission's knowledge resource is now a single point of failure. Also me.'

'Is child-birth traumatic?' It's touched a nerve.

'I don't know. I think it might be something like atmospheric entry. They may have withheld some information from me.'

'Do you have implanted memories?'

'Yes. Unreliable ones. Impossible dreams like seeing things alive and running around before they were food. I have a memory where I was staying at someone's home. It was so hot and dusty there and the air wasn't circulating inside. You had to walk through this really gaudy bead curtain when you came in; a horrible sensation of clicking. I remember moving it aside to let the air through and in the evening, they scolded me because the lights were on and the house was full of flies. I remember my tears. I remember putting my hands to my eyes and seeing my hands were a different colour. I had assumed everyone was the same as me on my home world, but that can't be reality. I need to check my messages.'

'Do you do that often?'

'I don't get many, so I've been saving them. For when I'm in the right mood.'

'How do you receive messages?'

'You know solar sails are pushed by laser beams from home? Well, they modulate the beams in very fast binary bursts to include information. As we're now close to the destination world where I have to look for life, home is very far away, so those messages are more than four years old.'

'Can you reply?' the diary asks.

'Barely. The ship can transmit but at this distance the message might never be received. For the same reason, it is really unusual to hear back from the three sister ships going to the other habitable planets; Trappist 1e, HD40307 and Gliese 667C. I'll arrive first but they're travelling faster than us, so we're not on the same temporal coordinate.'

'Are they identical?'

'To me? Not physically, but we have been given an identical education. It's like cloned minds.'

'Are you a good person?' This confuses her.

'I don't know. I have no frame of reference. Maybe it's the way they taught me but I do think it's a good thing to be an inquisitive species, to push the against boundaries of knowledge and make an attempt to find signs of life elsewhere in the Universe. I mean by doing more than just listening, but it has to be a global effort to do it properly. All we've found so far are the building blocks of life; amino acids on comets. A bit expensive but well-meaning.' She doesn't look sure.

'If you fail?', the diary picks at threads again.

'Then we've ruled out one more possibility – and keep going. If there happens to be no life out there at all, we'll know more about what's available to us in the darkness. Let's hope though.'

'You are the mission / The mission is you', the diary resolves for her. 'Does meaningful purpose take priority over your life?'

'I've come a long way; and people have dedicated their lives to less important causes', she affirms, then moves to the screen and starts reading messages.

A few million miles of space float by on the monitors.

'Home seems to be doing much the same. Not that I've ever seen 'home' for real apart from on vid footage. They have mucked up the environment and a lot of people seem to make selfish choices but that isn't news anymore.'

The next message visibly upsets our solo sailor. She toggles to expand the text on screen and it flows across, left to right, reading:

'Alert. An artificial signal has been detected in the system to which you are heading. We have developed more sensitive broadcast reception capability since your mission departed. The signal came from the equatorial region of the fourth planet. Kindly refresh your understanding of contact protocols, engage inertial dampeners and angle the sail by 0.07 and dioptre 1.24 by standard date and time mark...'

She tries to lean back from the edge of panic. 'Oh no, oh zek – that was two standard days ago!'

'Please elaborate.'

'The time mark to make the correction has passed. All this effort and I'm on my way to the wrong planet! Arhhh! Sorry, there's nothing I can do now lads. Send another mission.' Solo Sailor folds her arms, her cross expression foremost, then knocks back at her chair in resignation.

'Have you done anything wrong?', the diary stepped where angels fear to tread.

'You mean whose fault is this shambles? I didn't read the message on time, did I? Okay, staying calm now, mental resilience...' She breathes and composes herself before continuing. 'When the mission began, the inner planet was supposed to have the highest probability of intelligent life. No one planned for side-stepping. It's both our faults; they should have told the AI to do it, not me.'

'Is any method of course deviation available to you?'

'You think I have an engine on my bum? Maybe I should sleep. Close diary.'

Again, she considers wiping these conversations but relents as it's an important cultural record. She wonders if she should redact the word bum, as it's unprofessional.

Solo Sailor is again by the screen, looking annoyed as she receives verbal reports of progress. She pushes aside a tray of food, which resembles Styrofoam building blocks; circles, stars, triangles. The main computer speaks.

'Approaching within remote sensing range of the fourth planet. Seven, six, five... Collecting data.'

'Great. Keep going.'

'Multiple detections.'

'Of what?'

'Heat. Imaging to screen' it informed her as computer graphics invaded the display area.

She looks frustrated. 'Are you detecting any signals?'

'None detected but they may emanate from the far side of the planetary body. Spectral analysis indicates gas emissions consistent with upper Level 1 development. Habitation is isolated on the surface. No species data.'

'They haven't spread throughout the world? That's odd.' Solo Sailor checks the screen and readouts. 'Struggling to survive against an unstable environment perhaps? Are you picking this up too? The oxygen-bearing atmosphere is no longer being protected by the magnetosphere. It's slowly diffusing into space. Those poor creatures. It can't have much of an iron core then.'

The computer voice stays mute for a moment, then adds 'Broadcast detected. Translation error. Contextual probability – a distress call. Instructions?'

'Try to tell them we can't change course. Say... tell them we're sorry, no... Tell them I am sorry.'

'How?'

'Just try! Record everything you can and send a packet broadcast back to the scientists at home.'

'Complete.'

'Let's take stock, shall we?'

'If you wish.'

'The first authentic discovery of intelligent life anywhere in the Universe and there's nothing I or anyone back home can do about it.'

'Correct', the computer replied. 'Planetary entry sequence initiated.'

'So soon?'

The carbon purple solar sail is now a collapsing bloom. It is reconfiguring, forming a much more compact and layered heat shield, then the material folds back over the fuselage of the space ship like a vampire squid turning inside out, cocooning it protectively. The ship now looks like a cocoa pod, then a cocoa pod bursting into flame as the ship starts to pitch into thicker skies.

'Nitrogenous and oxygen-rich atmosphere', the computer updates her. 'Salt and fresh water plentiful. Dense iron core with an active magnetosphere affecting the solar winds. Surface gravity 0.95.'

'That's good. Really good. Spectral analysis?'

'A strong response marker for the chlorophyll compound. Confirming... vegetative cover on all continents – and ice, lots of ice.'

'Broadcasts? Civilisations?'

'None. Entry heat has blinded the sensors', the computer declares as the room bumps sideways. There's a terrific rumble, loud and kinetic.

'What is it?', she asks, needing to know.

'Noise, in an inadvisable acoustic range', the computer verifies.

'I've heard noise. This is new!'

'All of the sound you have heard in your life until now has been modulated to a safe range.'

'Has it? I have to look for those goggles. Everything's going orange in here and I feel heavier!'

Przz, przzzzz, the sound of a communication arriving.

'Great timing! Not now please, not another transmission!'

'Tagged urgent', the disembodied voice insists.

'Sor-rry. T-t-ttoo shaky to read!'

'Would you like to receive it on video and speakers?'

'Ye-ubb, okay. Oh g-ggod, it's the boss.' The message plays, wraps around her:

'This is Mission Control, Proxima Centauri B. Your Mission Director speaking. I hope this message finds you well. In the circumstance that you may still be on course for third planet landfall, we suggest you construct a shelter and follow the guidelines to survive in place. Refer to the database to learn necessary agricultural procedures and endeavour to make a productive fruit and vegetable garden that can sustain you through the first winter. Use the gene bank when you are ready and remember a decade in the slow hibernation pod can narrow any age differences if you wish to have company. Develop some of the male embryos first, recommend generation sequence beginning Alpha.'

'Is that it? Is that the end of the message?' she asks. The shaking is becoming unbearable now. 'They can't just ring off! How l-long? How long 'till you come f-ffor me?'

'I have to level with you, I'm afraid. Retrieval is now more problematic than originally anticipated because we are having an economic and climate situation here which takes priority in the public consciousness. The cost of bringing everyone home is too much to stomach for most people in this, ah, political upheaval. Remember, that planet is your home now. I'm sorry to cut you away but we've discovered over four thousand exoplanets so far with 161 missions outbound, so might have... over done that. Exploration is not so special anymore, it seems, not the focus. You have everything you need, so keep up the mental resilience and do what you can for the children. You only have to keep them alive. When they're old enough, the computer can give them knowledge. Farewell Eve. We're all rooting for you.'

'D-d-diary entry. I think we sh-should call our new home P-paradise.'

The diary hesitates before answering, 'That's irony, is it?'

THE ARRIVAL

by P.L. Tavormina

Bette sat forward in her saddle and urged her mount faster. A trilling wail — something small, perhaps a bird — sounded faintly from the distant scrub. The heath whipped by in faded grays and purples, while above, rough-edged storm clouds stretched from one side of the sky to the next.

'Hai', she called, spurring the gelding. She hoped to make Harald's place before the thin drizzle turned heavy. It wasn't often she left her trading business to visit her man but, when she did, she raced to him and to the promise of full nights. 'Hai!'

The horse pounded harder, trampling fescue and wort-weed.

When she arrived, then on into that night, Harald's strong arms pulled her close. The metal tang from his forge lingered on his skin; and now her skin. With the sounds of pleasure filling their ears, Bette was again whole and happy.

After, with a wild-man gleam in his eyes, he pushed up two-armed above her. 'It's a fine day when you turn up.'

Bette wriggled deeper into the blankets and pushed her hair back toward the braid it had escaped. The bed was warm, no denying, and she brimmed. Words weren't needed, not with Harald.

'How's it you've time to visit?'

He lived in Cross Flats, a burg of twenty, maybe fewer. It was a good place to get a horse shod and a good place to rest, before hauling the cart to the prairie towns with her trading partner Mona. Trading kept them fed, but any fool could do it. Trading roots and herbs? That didn't make Bette special, but Harald, he was another matter. From the first time they'd met, he completed her. Through his lingering looks and gentle words, Harald made Bette feel wanted.

She breathed in the sweaty man-scent of him, filled her lungs with it. 'For you, Harald, I make time.'

He chuckled and ran his finger between her small breasts and down to her stomach. 'More than time, dearie. You make happiness itself, my dark and mysterious Bette.'

Harald was the only one who said such things. She held quiet with a smile playing on her lips. She twined her fingers into his shaggy mane. 'In truth, it's the sickness that made time. Mona's waiting it out in Springville. We've roots and spices but no one to trade with. It's slow. Soon they'll feel better.'

People fell sick every year. This year was a bit worse. Some believed rats carried the malady but Mona said otherwise. Mona said the sickness was a curse from digestive spirits turned evil.

Now Harald's tongue trailed along Bette's body. She sighed in pleasure and he mumbled from somewhere below, 'Boss lady eased up, did she?'

'Mona and me, we're partners. We share it all even.' Bette pushed him off, rolled out and got up. She went to the window and threw the shutters wide. There was an odour in the house, nothing too bothersome, just a slight hint of something from Harald's clothes on the floor. Night air would help. Outside, a small creature rustled near the barn. She turned back to the bed. 'You get a week, love. Then I'm off with Mona to the prairie towns.'

In the flickering candlelight of his little bedroom, Harald's smile was dear. It was a soft thing, half-formed, falling down the side of his face like he tried to keep his happiness inside but some spilled out anyway. It warmed her, that he gave so much of himself and took her visits on her terms, not his.

He came to her and wrapped a quilt around her bare shoulders. 'I'll take the week.'

The odour grew stronger in Harald's hut and now, with the smell of forge smoke washed off, she knew it came from him. The smell seeped from his pores. By the third day a rash had started across Harald's cheeks. Bette put a soup on the fire. 'Keep covered. Here. Eat.'

He grumbled and waved at the window, at the bright light streaming in. She pulled the shutters and kept her breathing shallow. 'You're shaking', she said, pulling his quilt up. She was too, but her trembling came from fear. Harald couldn't be sick. She crawled next to him. 'Rest on me. You mustn't fall from this. Harald, do you hear me?'

Bette was certain she wouldn't take sick. She and Mona had travelled wide, through towns rife with pox, yet stayed hale. They'd taken herbs to appease the digestive spirits.

The house grew fetid and Bette took to sleeping apart from Harald. His breathing came as a pitiful, rattling sound. Her voice choked as she spooned gruel to his lips. 'You mustn't die. Who would insult the horses? Come, Harald. Eat.'

On the seventh day she woke past daybreak to a hut too quiet. Dread overtook her, a sinking weight cold and gray. It filled her with gripping nothingness. She pushed out from under the blankets on the cook-room floor and stole to the bedroom.

She watched from the doorway, waiting for Harald's chest to rise. A howling wind whipped through her mind and a cry tore forth from the gale of her formless thoughts. 'No! You gave me my strength! No, Harald, no! You mustn't — you haven't — I need you! Why did I never tell you?'

His chest did not rise. No sound, no cough, no rattle. She rushed to him and shook his shoulders. She waited for the smallest sign, a gurgle, a burp.

Harald was cold.

Bette fell to the ground, moaning and wracked. 'I loved you. How could you die?' She grabbed at his quilt and ripped her nails along it.

It was a harrowing day of keening disbelief before Bette dragged herself out of the hut to rifle through Harald's smithy. He had a pick and a shovel amongst his other tools. He'd inscribed his initials into both and, as she wrapped her hands on the hafts, she felt his hands, warm and firm around her own.

The first pitch into the soil was the hardest and she cried out again and crumpled to the ground. There, the baying wind called her weak. The sky began to spit upon her. Bette sat in the mud, her shawl falling and her hair straggling.

She pushed up at last, in rain now heavy, and stabbed the ground again. Each strike, there by the barn on Harald's land, each shovelful stood in strange testament to the place he'd wrought, the life he'd built, the fullness he'd given her. She dug deeper but a proper grave was impossible. So, when her shoulders ached and her skirt had grown filthy, when her shawl had long since been discarded and lost, the beginnings of a burial site lay before her. It would have to do.

Bette stumbled back into the hut. The smell, a sickly gluey scent, pushed against her. She lugged the sheet, upon which Harald's body lay, toward the barn. She broke further as the one human being who had completed her fell into a hole in the ground.

After the final shovelful of soil went back onto his body, she slumped into the hut. Coughing, Bette heated a bowl of soup.

Mona threw her gaze to the moor stretching out to the horizon. Bette should have returned days ago. The understanding was Bette would never leave for more than a week and it had been two.

The townsfolk, those not pocked with rash, were buying herbs at last. They wanted gingerroot more than the others. It warded off queasiness. Goods sold; that was the final underscore.

Mona hadn't taken ill, she never did. She knew enough of herbals to keep herself well in the worst of times. No, she thought, standing to her full six feet and giving her chest a thump, she'd never take the sick. 'Turmeric', she called. 'Ginger! Settles the gut.'

A few women ambled over. They said this ailment was the worst they'd seen. Disquieted, Mona cast her eyes up and down the cluttered dirt streets of Springville. No men strode about. A few women, but not many. Odd. Two weeks was long enough for a germ to pass, yet the village stood empty and Bette hadn't returned.

Mona packed up the cart and started west, between hither and yon toward Harald's hut. A day's ride on horseback but two by cart. As she approached his place on the evening of the following day, her heart sank. No smoke billowed from his forge. The shutters had been pulled tight and even the animals, including Bette's horse, seemed absent, save a few rats scuttling near the feed.

Mounded dirt next to the barn filled Mona with unease, presaging a dreadful spirit within, a miasma. She knocked.

After a long, heavy minute, Bette's voice came. 'Sick house.'

Mona's stomach lurched. She'd hoped — had told herself — the mound was nothing, that a horse had fallen, or perhaps a hound. 'Harald took the sick?'

Bette's voice came weak through the door. 'You'll get it Mona. Go.'

'Let me in. It won't take me.'

There was no sound and Mona slumped against the door. Did Bette stand inside? Or had she perhaps fallen? For all Mona knew, Bette may well have crawled away, into Harald's bed, lost to the world. 'Bette', she cried over her shoulder. 'Let me in.'

'You'll catch death.' The voice came in a croaking stutter.

Mona took a long breath against the thought of sprightly Bette falling ill. 'I've been in town', she said, 'and I've seen all comers. My health is good, as strong as ever. Bette, I have need of you. Open up!'

There was no noise, no answer. Nothing but a lonely howl from some animal on the moor. Mona whacked the door with all her might, pounding it against its frame.

The latch lifted and Bette's triangle face appeared through the crack.

Mona gasped despite her best effort. Bette was horribly pocked. Her eyes swollen and red, it was a wonder she could see. Her hair hung in strings, masses of it gone.

What manner of evil was this? Mona pushed the door wide and strode in. She gagged at the smell and threw the windows open. A quick glance told her all; the blanket on the floor was Bette's bed and the cooking room had not been cleaned in days. Flies crawled about a pot. Mona forced cheer into her voice. 'You're eating. See? You're not too bad.'

Bette huddled in the corner, a slip of an already-slight woman. Shaking wracked her. It seemed to Mona, holding herself away from her friend's stench, that a sheen had formed at Bette's hairline. Mona said 'Lie down. I'll make soup.'

Mona nursed Bette but she slipped further into plague. In those moments, when Bette wouldn't talk and didn't eat, Mona abandoned her bravado and went outside to dissolve into a weeping mass. She sobbed in fear that she, too, would fall. She might die and rot, with no one to find her as she'd found Bette. No one to bury her, as Bette had buried Harald; as she would certainly bury Bette. Beating her breast, Mona put herself under a lens, scrutinised every speck within for symptoms... and as often as not convinced herself she'd taken it.

Yet the grief was a blessing of sorts, for after the heaving sobs she found fortitude to return again and wipe her friend's face, her body; undress her and wash her garments, then clothe her dry and warm.

Repeatedly, she strewed sage and rosemary around Bette's bed.

In those first days Mona asked how, if someone as full of the world's own life as Bette could take the plague, how could she, Mona, ward it off?

She ate more herbs.

It was true enough she'd seen ailing friends and strangers alike, but never as sickly as this. None who could not stand, nor lift an arm unaided. Mona stirred the porridge, coughed from the fire and thought again she'd taken ill.

Bette muttered from behind, from the straw pallet on the floor. 'My man ... he was so cold.'

Mona turned and went to Bette's side. She stroked the hair from her forehead. 'What is that? What?' It didn't matter what Bette might say. She was speaking.

'So cold.'

'There, there', Mona said.

'Ground ... so hard.'

It hurt to hear; no possible understanding of the words brought comfort to Mona. Her voice catching on her breath, she said, 'I must check the cart. Sleep. Find strength.'

She held herself tightly until she was outside. Daylight had faded into a bare whisper. Mona cast her gaze wide but there was nothing and loneliness pierced her. Loneliness for a trading partner near death.

The colours on the western horizon, where the last bit of light held, were more gray than gold. She turned from it and shooed rats from the cart. She pulled the cover more firmly over the roots, fixing the corners with twine before checking the horses for fresh fodder and hay.

That night, as she changed the bedding and covered Bette again, in the now-routine of each day's end, Bette roused and looked up. Mona sat back, astonished at Bette's lucid eyes.

'I welcomed the illness', Bette said. 'It muted my grief.'

Then, as easily as Bette had slipped into that moment of coherence, she slipped away again, her eyes rolling back. Shaken, Mona tucked the blanket around her.

One evening, when Mona knew she had not fallen ill and her friend was, at last, on the mend, Bette whispered, 'As much as he and I loved, that very length is the stretch of my pain. Mona. It needs to be said. The words must be given voice. I loved him.'

Silent tears fell on Mona's cheeks.

Bette's rash faded, the pocks leaving a map of cratered scars across the bridge of her nose and down to her chin and neck. She would never again be the unblemished beauty she had been; the beauty Mona had never found the time to tell her she was. Still, Bette's colour returned and she put on a few pounds. Some weeks later, in the middle of a meal, Bette said, 'Harald was the best man I have ever known. When it comes to those we love, there is no place for mystery. He was a very good man.'

Mona paused from chewing a piece of rabbit stew. She studied Bette's face and found it lay at peace. 'That he was.'

Bette said, 'It's wrong to leave him here, with no company. He should not be forgotten.'

Mona wondered if that, in the end, was the bit that had convinced her friend to recover. 'He does not want you bound, Bette. From places wide, you brought the world to him. He wants you going wide, still.'

Bette poked at her stew listlessly.

'He would never want you chained to some hut.' The words felt hollow, for how could Mona possibly know Harald's wishes?; and yet, it felt true enough. In death one should be freed. One would surely grant freedom to those they left. 'Perhaps through knowing him, through honouring the life he lived, we can take Harald with us.'

Bette looked up. 'We could take his tools. We could gift

them to another smith.'

Mona smiled, for sitting before her was the Bette she knew. A brightness had returned to her, the vim that had been missing now filled her face. It was the spark and the life.

Harald's tools. 'Yes. I think Harald would like that.'

Bette grew hale and they prepared to leave. Mona said, 'We must make the prairie towns before the snows. They need our roots and herbs for winter.'

They boarded up the hut and lay a wreath upon Harald's grave, roped his horses to their own and piled his tools, covered with his quilt, onto their cart. They shooed away what vermin they found, worried not about the stragglers and headed toward the prairie towns.

SCARS

by Ville V. Kokko

He was having a confusing nightmare and it took a while to realise he had already woken up. He tried to move but could only writhe; his wrists bound above his head, his ankles also.

He tried to call out but all he managed was a hoarse rasp. The voice that replied was as clear as it was malicious.

'Oh, he's awake now. How are you, boy? Comfortable?'

He looked up and got his first sense that he was in a large, only partly illuminated room. A figure stepped into view from the shadows and he started as he saw its face.

'You?'

'Of course, you stupid little man', came the sneering response. 'Would I let anyone else touch my property?'

Furious anger rose within him at those words but he pulled at his bonds in vain. His enemy grinned a predator's grin and stepped closer.

'And by the way, in just a few moments, I will make you mine forever as well.'

She wasn't the prettiest girl, not really, but there was no question that she was the sweetest. Erdinan could tell they wanted him to marry her and he didn't mind. He soon noticed he wanted it more than anything.

The trip from Tackenvalley to Nale was not one to be undertaken lightly. It was not that far but what the miles lacked in number they made up for in inconvenience and bad terrain – and there was always a danger, if ever so small, of being attacked by roaming barbarians along the way. At least after their invasion of the valley itself, which had been decisively repelled by King Tadron, the tribes had been lying low.

Still, Erdinan liked taking the trip. For one who had grown up within the valley, it felt like escaping the confines of the known world. The horizon on the plains seemed to stretch out to infinity. The kingdom of Nale also looked green and abundant when compared to the austere valley.

Now that he had met Ciela, he could have made the trip any number of times. He probably would have, too, except that now, on his third occasions, she would be coming back with him. They would be married at her family's estate. Erdinan spent most of the trip leaning at the window of his rattling carriage, staring out at the distant horizon and smiling dreamily.

The sil-Martinon estate was a sprawling cluster of buildings built atop a broad hill, all encompassed by old stone walls. It was centuries old, perhaps as old as the castle of the kings of Nale and so large that the family these days only occupied a part of it. The walls and buildings looked ghostly from a distance, light gray shapes that might have been just mirages or mist but they solidified and gained colour as the carriage drew closer. At the same time, the wonderful and frightening prospect of marriage became more real.

Still, Erdinan felt an anxiety, as if it all couldn't be real, or couldn't really be happening. Those last miles seemed to last forever, like a dream where you search all night until you wake up unfulfilled, then when he finally stepped out of the carriage and into the inner courtyard of the main keep, he looked around in a rising inner panic for confirmation that it was all real.

There he had it. His heart jumped. Ciela walked towards him, smiling shyly, clad in a dress of delicate blues. Her eyes just barely dared to look up into his, but when they did, they looked in deep and wouldn't let go.

It took he knew not how long before he even noticed Ciela was not alone. Lord sil-Martinon coughed and stepped in delicately to welcome Erdinan to the estate.

Soon, he was at the reception before the wedding. As custom dictated, Erdinan and Ciela spent most of their time apart, talking to other people. Erdinan took it all in a pleasant yet impatient daze, chatting to various members of the sil-Martinon family. There was Ciela's brother Leon, of course, the lord of the estate, but also his aged father, Keran, whose absent smiles and scattered conversation left no need to explain why he was no longer the head of the family. His wife had passed away years ago and he was, instead, accompanied everywhere by his gentle, silver-bearded healer Doray. There were also Ciela's three sisters, all of them with husbands at least as high-born as Erdinan himself, dressed like him in light ceremonial armour and thin, decorative coats. He felt vaguely proud to be joining their company, but he had little thought for such details next to the pure fact of getting to marry Ciela.

Not many of Erdinan's own family had made it there – mainly a gaggle of aunts he had difficulty keeping straight – but Erdinan was particularly pleased at one late arrival, his sister Sherer, who travelled so much he hadn't been sure she'd receive word about the wedding in time. He hurried to meet her right at the door.

Sherer was adorned as formality required, in a dress with a thin noble's coat like his draped on top of it and she carried the impractical attire with the usual long-suffering regality that others mistook for hauteur. She did wear delicate silk gloves that seemed an extra concession to femininity but he knew she had another reason for that. She was as tall as her brother and looked taller, though, as usual, her almost military bearing reminded him to stand up more straight as well to match her.

They embraced. 'I'm glad you could make it, Sher', he said.

'I know I move around a lot but I wouldn't want to miss this.'

She smiled at him – not too warmly, but then she never did so on formal occasions. He would have hoped that this one would be different, of course, but he also knew she had never even met Ciela and didn't know his happiness.

'Have you been to Nale before?'

'Some years ago.'

He felt a tinge of discomfort, wondering why. He lowered his voice. 'Oh. Is there...?'

'I didn't notice anything wrong. I did hear some rumours that were troubling, about an evil sorceress who had lived here for hundreds of years.' She looked at his face. 'But you're not looking for a report on that. I'm sorry. There's nothing for you to worry about.'

He laughed nervously. 'I'm sure Ciela isn't into dark magic.'

'Probably not', she joked, though he felt a discomfort because she sometimes said such things seriously. They were interrupted by a hearty greeting.

'I see I'm not the only one with a lovely sister around here. You must be Sherer Tenayn. I'm Lord Leon sil-Manon.'

He walked up to them, all smiles, a figure of rugged good looks and self-confidence, Erdinan couldn't help envying just a little every time.

'A pleasure to meet you', Sherer said.

As they shook hands, Erdinan noticed a surprising moment. They froze for a long second, staring into each other's eyes. Then he asked her for a dance and they left Erdinan behind to ponder.

What had that moment been? Surely it would amount to nothing. Leon was engaged, after all, and an honourable man, with Sherer too sensible and morally upright for an inappropriate affair. Even if there had been a moment, it wouldn't be the start of anything.

There was a sense of unease that this thought didn't stop but it was soon swept aside. He could only think of Ciela – and the dream he was living continued as they were soon bound together in front of the gods and the ancestors.

The ceremonies ended soon after the wedding vows, so as not to keep the newlyweds waiting, and they were left alone. In a daze, he walked with her, hand in hand, to the lovely pavilion they were given for this night.

She was shy and demure at first but she melted at his touch and went on to ecstasy, again and again. It was an unforgettable night, even better than he had imagined.

They soon returned home, to his estate in Tackenvalley and marital bliss. Not only he, but everyone else too, loved her and agreed that she was the sweetest wife they could have imagined. She was always kind and caring towards everyone; she was shy but the one thing that drew her out of her shell every time was when someone else was in need of compassion. People would compare her to the sun, or to a precious flower in the forest; and he would ache with love every time, agreeing with them but knowing they could never realise her loveliness in the way he did.

There was one side of her, he knew, that was in shadow and unknown even to him. Her brother had taken him aside on his last visit before the one when they got married and talked to him confidentially. He had been impressed with his earnestness and touched by his trust and concern.

'There's one thing you should know about Ciela', Leon sil-Martinon had said. 'I'm sure a decent man like you won't mind, but you'll notice it when you're her husband. Besides, you should know because it's hard for her and you'll need to be gentle.

'As you see her in a... more intimate connection, you will notice my sister has scars on her body. I'm glad that you're a good man who really loves her, so I know you won't disvalue her for such things. They are not disfiguring by any means but they are visible. Ciela is very sensitive about this. I beg you' – Erdinan had never seen Leon show so much emotion – 'do not speak to her about them. Just show that you find her lovely nevertheless. I'm sure that will come naturally to you.

'Also do not speak to her of from whence the scars came. It was a very frightening experience and she should not go back into it. Years ago, when she was no more than a girl, we let her follow the family men on a hunting expedition. You may find it hard to imagine but she used to be quite headstrong! She rode her horse too close to a ledge and they both fell down. She was badly injured and we didn't find her until a whole two nights had passed. She was barely clinging on to life and she hasn't gone hunting or even ridden a horse since then.

'Still, my sister is a wonderful, loving person and she deserves a husband who is in kind. The only reason she hasn't married yet at past her twentieth year is because we couldn't give her to someone we weren't sure would treat her well enough. I'm so very glad she finally found you.'

Erdinan was moved to tears every time he thought of this. He had seen the scars on their wedding night, as if from several cuts on her body and arms and they did nothing to diminish the wonder and bliss of finally seeing all of her. He never spoke of them to her but he touched those scarred parts of her skin with love and gentleness and her reactions told him it was the right thing to do.

For months, everything was perfect – until her miscarriage.

Erdinan had been told about it discreetly by the maids attending to his wife. They had been reluctant to speak of such things to a man but he was her husband and so they had said she was very upset about it and had shut herself in the bedroom. He knocked gently on the door and got no response, so after a while he just went in.

Ciela was sitting slumped on the bed, her usually lovely curly hair hanging in front of her face like a curtain of seaweed. She didn't respond to his first attempts at calling out.

'Ciela, my love?' he tried again, sitting next to her an putting a comforting arm around her shoulders. 'You must be feeling terrible. But it's all right. We can try again. I'm sure...'

She turned her head with a snap, white eyes glaring from under the curtain of hair. Her movement was so sudden and hostile he almost withdrew his arm.

'That's what you'd like, isn't it? Putting me through that again.'

His heart clenched painfully, not understanding. He embraced her more tightly, knowing his touch always helped.

Except now. 'Get off!' She pushed him away.

'But... what...?'

'It's easy for you to just... plant your seed! Don't you know what I have to go through! Have you even thought about that!'

She continued to glare at him, eyes barely visible in the gloom but seemingly filled with hatred. He was so rattled, feeling so uncanny at this sudden complete change, that he stared for a moment and then all but fled the room. He felt like a coward, but he also thought that it was reasonable to let her be alone for now. She would get better.

Ciela did get better. By the evening, she was herself again and apologised profusely, explaining the miscarriage had been a very traumatising experience because she so wanted to have his children. He soothed her and held her and all was well again.

Until two days later. They had made love and she had seemed to enjoy it as much as always. Then, suddenly, she was angry again and berated him about the same things – and then more.

She apologised for this, too, the next day, but he was left with a nagging feeling of unease; and it soon turned out to be warranted.

It seemed as though a pendulum had been set swinging and there was no more stopping it. Ciela would be her sweet self at one moment, then sullen and explosive the next, complaining about various things that had never been a problem before. There was an unsettling discontinuity between these moments; she would apologise and say completely different things when she was back to herself, then continue attacking from where she left off last time. Just a few instances of this was enough to leave Erdinan feeling like he was teetering on the edge of the abyss, knowing not where to set foot.

A healer visited, found nothing specific wrong with her and left them with some useless platitudes. Finally, what was happening got uncanny enough for Erdinan to call in a priest. It had got to the point where he could believe there was dark magic involved. In her normal mood again, Ciela agreed to be examined; she seemed ill at ease with the idea, but she calmed down when he held her.

'Well?' Erdinan asked, as the priest stepped out of the room where he had visited Ciela.

The old man stroked his coarse woollen beard with long, delicate fingers. His manner told that it was bad news.

'I'm sorry, Lord Tenayn. Your worries are justified. I believe she is possessed by a malign force.'

Erdinan leapt up from his chair.

'What! Are you sure?'

'Yes. There's little doubt. I have used my instruments for seeing the presence of magic. There is a clear strain of enchantment woven inside her and at least part of it is Dark.

It's buried in deep but it's clear. It is in here' – he tapped his temple – 'and that means it affixes to her thoughts, to her soul.

'Judging from what you tell me of her behaviour, I believe it must be an evil spirit that's trying to control her.'

Erdinan collapsed back to his chair, his face pale. The old priest stepped closer to put a hand on his shoulder.

'I'm truly sorry to be the bearer of such news. There's still hope, now that we know what the cause is. It's beyond my skills to exorcise the spirit. Most priests who perform 'exorcisms' have no idea what they're doing but if you hire a powerful wizard from one of the cities, from Allton, who specialises in wrangling spirits, he should be able to help you.'

Erdinan wasted no time, as he wanted Ciela to be freed as soon as possible. Within hours, their carriage, flanked by mounted soldiers, raced out of Tackenvalley.

Ciela sat opposite to him, looking down and not speaking. He felt strangely uncertain and couldn't tell whether things were normal. It seemed as though she was herself, nothing that he could think of gave it away to the contrary, but for some reason he didn't feel as though he could touch her to reassure her as he usually did.

They had sent out messengers, one to her family in Nale and one to seek out Erdinan's sister Sherer. What was surprising was when one of the messengers rode back to them soon after they left the valley – and was followed by another carriage pulled by black horses.

Erdinan pulled his head out of the carriage window.

'Ho, there! What's going on?'

'You sent me to take the message to Lord sil-Martinon, my lord!'

'Yes?'

'I met him on the road. He's here.'

The other carriage stopped and Leon jumped out of it.

'Where's my sister? Is she all right?'

Leon sil-Martinon was accompanied by the family's healer, Doray. They both hurried to the carriage to meet Ciela, who greeted them sweetly, though she seemed timid and listless. The men stepped outside again to talk and the other two listened with concerned expressions as Erdinan recounted what had happened and what the priest had said. When he was finished, they shared a long look that seemed filled with hidden communication. Finally, Leon looked back at Erdinan.

'This is... This confirms fears we had, that we wished were nothing but fears. There's something I haven't told you and now I see that it was a mistake.'

'What? You know of what's wrong with her?'

Leon looked down uncertainly. 'I... yes... and I want to tell you we can help her now. You must come back with us to the estate first. We must hurry before things get even worse.'

'But what is it?'

'I'm sorry. I... can't tell you just now. You will understand. But take heart, at least, in the most important thing: we can fix her now. Please believe me.'

Erdinan acquiesced. It was a long trip, alone in the carriage with his unspeaking wife, not daring to reach out to her. He tried a few times but she was distant and he was never sure whether he had done right; unsure what was going through her mind.

They got to the courtyard of the sil-Martinon estate and hurriedly got out of the carriages. Leon gestured for Erdinan to follow and then...

He was uncertain what had happened. He seemed to remember – had Leon come towards him and done something? The other man now stood there, looking expectant, but he was seeing two of him and everything was swaying...

Erdinan's mind was a blur. He awoke in a dark room, tied to an inclined table of some sort, though he had no clear memory of falling asleep. As he tried to call out hoarsely, a figure stepped out of the shadows.

'Oh, he's awake now. How are you, boy? Comfortable?'

'You?'

'Of course, you stupid little man', Leon sil-Martinon sneered. 'Would I let anyone else touch my property?'

His property? Erdinan guessed it then and anger greater than he had ever felt burned away the fog in his mind. Yet it was not enough – he pulled at his bonds in vain. Leon grinned, showing far too many teeth and stepped closer.

'And by the way? In just a few moments, I will make you mine forever as well.'

'You! You did something to Ciela!'

'Well I had to, didn't I?'

'Why would you curse her?'

Leon stared at him for a while and then laughed horribly. 'Oh, yes! I'll tell you! You're going to love this!'

Another dry laughter cackled from nearby. Erdinan swung his head to see a man who had escaped his notice in the shadows before – Doray, the healer, although he didn't look like one now, in those black robes adorned with blood-red patterns.

'Well, you see', Leon went on, leaning closer with that grin even wider now, 'She was always such a rebellious, headstrong young woman. I did tell you that, once, although I was lying about everything else at the time.'

'About... about her accident?'

'Yes. There was no accident. She got those scars over the years because she was asking for it and I obliged her. She even tried to run away, more than once.'

'You...!'

A backhanded slap cut Erdinan short. Leon had moved so fast that he couldn't even see him.

'Quiet, boy, I want to get to the good part. So, I married off my other sisters, shall we say profitably, but Ciela seemed like a hopeless case. That is, until I met Doray here and we made a deal. Go on... tell the boy what you did to Ciela.'

Doray cackled again. 'I bound her will with a curse. No more rebellion, no more saying 'no'. I made her the sweetest girl you've ever met. The perfect wife.'

Leon looked at Erdinan's expression with delight. 'Yes... and all the time, on the inside, a little part of her knowing what was happening to her.

'Your priest told you she was possessed by dark magic? Well, yes. When she said she loved you, when she delighted in your company, when she melted with your touch and when you made her scream in bed... but when she started going mad, when she got moody and angry for no reason? That was the possession starting to wear off, that was herself beginning to show through.'

'I sensed my enchantment starting to weaken, of course', Doray said. 'That's why we were coming to you.'

'It must have been the miscarriage that triggered it', Leon mused. 'She has some bad memories about her last one. It's too bad if she can't have more children but what was I supposed to do? I'm not a healer and it's not like I felt like being gentle at that point.'

'I'LL KILL YOU!'

But the bonds on his arms and legs still held, even though Erdinan strained against them hard enough to draw blood. Leon laughed contemptuously.

'I'd like to let you try, just so I could get my fists bloody, but I've got other plans. You were easy to fool but you know too much now. What we're going to do is, Doray will perform his spell again, this time on you.'

'What!'

'Yes, we'll make you nice and obedient to us as well. Then we'll have a little lord in Tackenvalley completely under our control. I like the idea.'

'It'll open up... opportunities', Doray said. He held his hands in front of him and his fingers danced together like spider legs.

'Wait. What was that?'

Leon had stopped to listen, his hand on the hilt of the sword on his side.

'What?' Doray said.

'A sound. Is someone at the door?'

They both turned to look and Erdinan's eyes followed them. Though the room was only poorly illuminated by torches on the walls and on stands on the floor, he noticed it seemed to be a large cellar room with various slabs and tables scattered around it. The door was at the top of a flight of stairs by the wall.

'Maybe it's just your guard outside the door...?' Doray said.

'No', Leon hissed. 'That sound was wrong.'

Suddenly, the silence was shattered by a loud bang that left everyone's ears ringing. The thick metal door, its lock blown away, swung inwards and collided against the wall with a loud clang.

'What the...?'

'Guards! Guards!' Doray shouted shakily.

'There are no more guards, when the enemy has got that far!' Leon snarled, drawing his sword. 'Be ready to defend yourself!'

'Erdinan! Are you there?'

Suddenly, it was Erdinan who laughed mirthlessly.

'What?' Doray snapped.

'You're right', Erdinan said, grinning almost as horribly as Leon had done. 'I won't kill you two. She will.'

'What are you...?'

'Focus, Doray!' Leon was closer to the stairs now and staring up, sword drawn.

'Two of them!' Erdinan shouted hoarsely. 'Lord Leon, with sword! Doray, a dark wizard!'

'Shut up!' Doray seemed to pull something from his pocket and throw it at Erdinan, but what hit him was an immaterial bolt of pain that made him writhe and scream. It was intense but it was over in a moment.

Meanwhile, something happened at the door. A dark and silent figure ran in, outlined by torchlight for a moment, took a few steps down the stairs and then suddenly leapt down from them. It rolled on the ground to soften the ten-foot fall, then came to its feet immediately. One second later, Leon was upon it, striking down with his sword.

The lithe figure in dark clothes dodged and then parried the next strike with a sword suddenly in its hands. The two combatants locked blades and stared at each other over them. Leon looked into the steely eyes of the woman and laughed. 'You! I should have known!'

'Your fate was sealed the moment we shook hands and I sensed the taint', Sherer Tenayn said. Her voice was even but cold as ice.

They spun apart. 'Yes, I sensed something too, in that hand of yours.' He made a feint but she stepped aside easily and they continued to circle one another. 'And I found out about you after that: the dreaded witch-hunter. Quite the surprise. I wondered if that would come back to bite me...'

She came in with a fast series of slashes before he could finish talking, momentarily caught him off guard and drove him back, but he soon caught his balance and struck forcefully, then again, taking his sword in both hands and driving her back in turn with superior strength.

He paused for a while, panting and grinning. 'I must say this is –'

She brought forth her off-hand and flung a silvery powder at his face. He screamed and staggered as she stepped forward and pierced his heart with one ferocious thrust.

'He talked too much', she said as she pushed the corpse from her blade with her boot.

'He did, didn't he?'

Doray stood calmly, several yards away from her, holding a wicked-looking decorated staff.

'I wonder what I'll do now', he continued. 'Maybe I should look into making that corpse my puppet. What I know, though, is that you're dead, my lady.'

Sherer straightened up and faced him. 'Is that so.'

'You're a witch-hunter. Isn't it obvious to you? A dark wizard of the power I must obviously have and you, a sitting duck for my spells. All I'm having difficulty with is deciding which agonising death to give you.'

'Decide quickly then', she said, raising her sword and advancing towards him, though at no more than a walking pace.

He raised the staff and shouted words so hoarse they seemed to tear the air apart. A dozen snakes of shimmering green and black energy streamed out towards her, fanged maws open.

She raised her left hand and the magic circle tattooed on her palm glowed with blue energy. The snakes diminished and vanished, sucked into the circle.

She stepped to him and snapped the staff with a swing of her sword.

He staggered. 'But how...?'

She killed him without an answer, but Erdinan knew what she could have said: She was a witch-hunter. Wasn't it obvious? She must know how to fight her chosen prey.

After Sherer freed her brother, they hurried out of the estate before anyone noticed what had happened. They were told that Ciela had already taken a horse and ridden off ahead of them. Sherer said that this must have meant the spell on her had lost its power when Doray died. They caught a glimpse of her, headed the same way as they, until her faster speed left them behind.

Sherer rode with Erdinan in the coach, offering what comfort she could. Though she was much better at killing than comforting, he felt like her presence was what saved him from going insane there and then.

When they got back home, concerned servants hurried to inform Erdinan that his wife had ridden in alone and insisted on getting her hair cut. Too concerned to wonder about the last detail, he asked to meet her right away and was taken to one of her rooms.

Ciela sat there, looking out of the window, her beautiful curls gone, hair short as a boy's. He stopped a few steps away and stood uncertainly. After a while, she turned around to look at him. She looked so different, haggard, careworn, with no warmth in her eyes.

'I never wore my hair like that', she explained, flatly. 'I hated it. It made me look like a doll.'

He didn't know what to say. He had thought so too and he had loved it.

'The spell has been lifted from me. Do you know what it was?'

'Yes. Leon... told me. He and Doray. I'm so sorry.'

'What happened to them?'

'Both are dead. They were... Sherer killed them.'

She smiled wanly, nothing like the way she used to, the hint of teeth a disturbing reminder of her brother. 'Good. That's the one thing that could make me feel good now. Just a little bit.'

An uncomfortable silence, she looking at him dully but expectantly.

'I... can't imagine how you must be feeling...'

'You can't. But thanks.'

His heart clenched intolerably and he stepped closer. She shifted a little.

'I... Ciela... I just want to say...'

'Yes?'

'I'll always be there for you. Always.'

He ached to embrace her, to make it all right. He stepped close and reached out.

'Don't touch me!'

She reacted with violent fear, pushing him away so sharply that he stumbled. He stared in shock as she stormed out of the room and away along the stairs.

When he finally dared to go after her, he found her sitting on a balcony, staring out into the night.

'Ciela? I'm sorry. Whatever I did, I'm sorry.'

'Don't be.' She looked back at him with a pale shadow of the smile he knew. 'You didn't do it. They did it to me, trapping my mind behind a fake smile while my innermost self was screaming where no-one could hear.'

He stepped closer, tears streaming from his eyes. 'It's so terrible. I...'

Her body jerked and she raised a hand to stop him. 'You didn't know but it was you who touched me while I was trapped. I can't... that's what I think of. Please don't come close. I don't know if I'll ever be able to stop feeling it near you.'

He understood, at least well enough that the shock rooted him on the spot and in more terrified tears. 'I'm... I'm so sorry, Ciela...'

'I know it must feel terrible', she said, too flatly. 'I wish I had more sympathy in me to give you. You're a good man and you tried your best. You didn't know and it's not your fault.'

'I... loved you, Ciela.'

'That wasn't me.'

Her words struck like a whip but, after a pause, she spoke in a softer tone again. 'But I know you cared for me. You showed it. You... would have been a good husband.'

He looked up from his tears and understood that her stony staring out into the night came from a place of pain far beyond even that which he felt now. At least he was able to cry. The thought made him stop and his back straightened.

'Ciela... whatever I can do to help now, I will. Whatever you need to get back on your feet. Anything.'

'Thank you.' She nodded at him before returning her stare to the sky. 'I don't know what I can do now. I'll... need time.'

She said no more and didn't turn back to him. He didn't know what to say. Nothing seemed enough or appropriate – or desired. Eventually he just left, letting his tears come back out after he got out of sight.

LIGHT

by Sherri Fulmer Moorer

Colby looked through the small window on the door. Kaya was still sitting at her desk, staring through another window overlooking the hospital grounds. She said she knew how the light fell over the trees outside that window at every point during the day. That's how she was sure it was going to be ok. As long as the sun rose and set every day, she was alright. Not coherent, but calm enough that they didn't have to sedate her to sleep, like everybody else on this ward.

He sighed. That light was her only connection with reality now. Maybe it was the only connection any of them had with reality. Most of the patients on the ward had nothing to do but watch the sun move through the sky outside the windows since they took the televisions away. At least there was a handy excuse for lockdown now.

Colby balanced the dinner tray in one hand and knocked on the door gently with his other hand, a manoeuvre he had mastered since they didn't allow the food staff on the wards. He turned the knob when he saw Kaya nod.

'How are you today?' he asked, setting the dinner tray on the desk in front of Kaya. She looked at the steaming food blankly.

'This is my favourite time of day', Kaya said in her soft voice. 'The light is prettiest in the late afternoon and evening.'

'Yes, it's evening', Colby sat on the small single bed next to the desk. 'Have you had a good day?'

'People are anxious about the lockdown', Kaya said. 'I tried to help as many of them as I could.'

'I'm sure you calmed their nerves', Colby answered.

'We're helping them, aren't we?'

'Of course we are. They need us and we need them.'

Kaya turned her blank stare to Colby. 'For what?'

Colby crossed his arms. 'What do you mean, 'for what?' People live in this community. We heal and support one another, just like we did before all of this happened.'

Kaya turned back to the window, her dark hair framing her

slender face. 'It's not the same.'

'No, it isn't.' Colby ran his hands through his messy blonde hair. 'I'm sure we'll be back to normal soon. We'll be able to treat the patients without having to live here anymore.'

'We can't leave them and we can't go back. Too many people have died.'

Colby looked around the small room, noting that the computer had been removed. 'How do you know that? There's no news coming into the facility.'

'The light talks to me.'

'Who did you talk to today, Kaya?'

'Many people.'

'People outside of the facility?'

Kaya laughed. 'No, that's impossible. We're all stuck in this place. All we have is each other.'

'A community', Colby said.

'It's not a community, it's a prison', she mumbled, staring out the window again. 'Is it Friday? The light looks different on Fridays.'

'It's Thursday. Can't you tell? You have meat loaf for dinner.' Colby shook his head. 'We talked about this, Kaya. You have to look for more signs around you than just the light.'

Kaya stared at the plate. 'I always make meat loaf and mashed potatoes for dinner on Thursdays.'

'Then that's the true sign that it's Thursday. The light couldn't tell you that; I did.' Colby sighed again and stood, smoothing his white coat. 'Enjoy your dinner.'

'I can't eat until Blake gets home.'

Colby glanced at the wedding picture on the desk. 'Blake is sick, remember? He's in the hospital. They can't release him yet.'

Kaya stared at Colby. 'When will my computer be fixed? I need it to make patient notes and I want to send some emails.'

Colby rubbed his nose. 'The IT staff are quarantined, so we can't do anything with it now. We'll get it fixed as soon as possible.'

Kaya turned her stare back to the window. 'I want to watch the evening pass. Maybe the light will tell me more about the new age to come.'

'Maybe', Colby mumbled, closing the door behind him.

'How is she?' Dr Pecori asked, his dark presence stark against the white walls of the corridor.

Colby matched Dr Pecori's pace. 'The same.'

'Is she still mumbling about the light redeeming us from chaos?'

'No chaos this time. Just the light and her husband', Colby said. 'We should tell her the truth. She could heal faster if she had time and space to grieve.'

'No. It would break her if we told her that he's gone.'

Colby snorted. 'This is a mental hospital. She's already broken.'

Dr Pecori stopped and turned to face Colby. 'That's right and we're here to fix her, not break her more. We took her off duty and admitted her as a patient when she refused to believe Blake was sick.'

'How is lying to her about her husband helping?' Colby asked. 'Or pretending like she's still a doctor working with the patients? What purpose does her fantasy serve?'

'You're imaging nefarious motives when there are none. The truth is that she's gone from doctor to patient and we're trying to help her without doing more harm than reality has already done to her.'

'Reality is harming all of us these days. The difference is that we're shielding her and nobody else. You know she won't snap out of this. Something's wrong with her that isn't going away. We need to dig deeper and find out what she needs in order to come back to us.'

'There's no need to dig deeper. Kaya is just in shock. It will wear off. She's better off than every other person on this ward. We have to conserve our resources and there's no justification to take further action on her now.'

'How is she better off than the other patients? Is it because she can keep up with the days of the week? Strike that from your list, Dr Pecori. She thinks today is Friday.'

'We're all getting the days of the week mixed up', Dr Pecori said. 'That's not a sign of anything other than the confusion we're all experiencing.'

'Why aren't you worried that she's lost touch with reality?'

'Haven't we all?' Dr Pecori asked. He put a hand on Colby's

shoulder. 'The lockdown is making everybody anxious. It doesn't mean we all have mental disorders. Yes, Kaya has changed, but so have we. Does that mean anything is wrong?'

'Everything is wrong', Colby replied, 'and you're too comfortable with this lockdown situation. A few months ago, you were testing every patient and adjusting medications repeatedly. All of that stopped when the quarantine was announced but we aren't short on equipment or supplies. Why have you lost interest in finding out what's happening with Kaya?' Colby crossed his arms. 'If she's really in shock, why aren't you concerned that it's lasted for over a month? She should be emerging from it by now, but she isn't.'

Dr Pecori spread his hands. 'Things have changed. We can't make the same assumptions that we were making a month ago. Our treatment shifts with the reality we live in.'

Colby stared at Dr Pecori's blank smile. What was wrong with him? Dr Pecori was the lead doctor now. If he wouldn't help Kaya, nobody would.

He doesn't want to help Kaya. It's beneficial to him if she stays just the way she is.

Colby shuddered, realising that Kaya's illness was giving Dr Pecori just what he wanted: control of the facility, but why? Dr Pecori had never been power hungry before. What changed? Besides everything?

Colby realised that he couldn't win; not today at least. He needed to think about this and consider what Dr Pecori was gaining from keeping Kaya locked in a small room with nothing but the light to keep her company. However, tomorrow was another issue. Maybe Kaya wasn't that badly off and she was just playing the game and biding her time. Or maybe she really was sick. Truth was always hard to discern in this place and the lockdown made it more complicated. Colby needed insight. He needed to think. Maybe Kaya's light would give him some inspiration.

'I'm going to my office to do some research' Colby resumed his march down the hall. 'Kaya's right. This is a prison and we're all inmates. Maybe the light will talk to me next. Maybe it will tell me how to handle this 'new reality."

Dr Pecori smiled, a golden glint flashing in his eyes. 'It will. All you have to do is accept it.'

DIGITAL NOMAD

by Saj Brodie

I was born not far short of twenty eight years ago, not exactly in a cross-fire hurricane, but with the name Sunshine Lovepocket Goodwife, a legacy of a free-spirited commune which has not been an easy thing to forgive, as a man. I have never got around to changing that to something I'd be willing admit to, or shooting my parents, but that was never realistic at a time when little dudes had no money and only a feathered bow and one curved sucker-arrow with their name on.

The circumstances of my birth were as painful and traumatic as I could possibly make them and three minutes after the umbilical cord was cut, I touched the floor, burst through the tent flap, ran away from home and never came back. That is why I am a digital nomad.

Digital nomadcy, if I may introduce the term for all you clakkas, means earning your living through online work and having the freedom to roam wherever you want on this inspirational planet, as long as each infested flop house you end up in has a broadband connection.

Never staying anywhere for more than a couple of months can mean the laptop itself is the nomad's best friend and, I should warn, if you are considering the lifestyle, put some money aside each month because no country will look after you when the work slows down. I've seen so many countries already, such beautiful and memorable places, when staring into the same screen.

My work is simple enough, optimising websites, setting up backlinks, reviewing coffees, proof-reading and posting content on behalf of international bloggers. I'm self-educated and I can do my job anywhere. Freelancing has its peaks and sink-holes but bloggers and site owners pay me to do their work and keep my name out of it, which is all I have ever wanted. Yesterday, I was kicked out of Singapore for chewing gum (what else was I supposed to do with it?) and that's how I got here, putting myself through another airport.

Clearance from airside to the open end of the terminal was a terminal experience, but I'm used to it. When the clakkas saw I only had hand luggage, they thought uh-o, drug mule and held me back. Where was I staying? Not sure – some hotel. Finally they allowed me to go but by then I was the last passenger from the flight to step through into the open hall.

The scene was much as I'd come to expect. Families ticked down boring minutes waiting for reunification, some tour party massed around a leader with a tacky flag and there were the usual chauffeurs sent to collect the business bods.

I skateboarded over the signs and floor stickers to the taxi rank, flipped it up and asked how much it would cost to take me to the city. HOW much? Bloody hell. So I turned around and went back into the arrivals area, looking for backpackers who might want to share a lift and not be a ritefool. Unlucky – all I saw was families.

Standing in the very centre of the entrance way was one of those sniffy chauffer types holding up a card with the logo of some mega hotel, my flight number and the name of Mr Biscotti. A thought stuck its hand up in my mind, saying if I was more or less the last passenger off my flight, this guy might not be coming for his free lift. I could be Mr Biscotti.

It was like one of those dream beaches where you never want to get up. The Hotel Grand Spruzzo Romani was wicked, with its baths, colonnades, palms, sculptures and dining rooms, sometimes all five in one suite. My bedroom was pre-paid and the hotel had been told I could put food and drink on account, but I felt conscious about racking that up too much and being told to pay it back, so asked for my usual cheese sandwich on a *clean* plate. Force of habit.

I do crop and arrange content as a regular gig for flash lifestyle bloggers, so have seen what they see, but I haven't tasted what they've tasted or felt what they felt, rolled with the rattle of a casino or flopped into goose-feather cushions. It was awesome. I soaked and aired my clothes out the window and then I had to get some sleep, clockin' those pillows.

For someone who washes in the sea for nothing, next morning's bath was another level of relaxation. Mango scalp gel, a rubber duck, sixteen towels down to the size of napkins, it was all there. I got into my clothes and remembered breakfast, picked up my board, laptop bag and I was offski.

The strangest thing. I've never opened a door before and found some clakka falling into my knees, bundling around on the floor, reacting in shock and crying out a fine spray that even showed up on the mirrors. This sister was battin' like some Italian-American nervous wreck.

'Mr Biscotti! Spare me! I was not listening at the door. I was finding if you were in there before knocking. Please, please, don't, Mr Biscotti!'

'I'm not going to do anything, missy. Chill out. Are you alright? Let me get you up.'

'I am alright. I was unprepared for you awareness, your reactions like the steel trap when I touched your door. I see in your profession you must know everything to make a killing'

What did she think I was, freakin' Alexa?

When I'd got out of the clakka her name was Clarinetta, second eldest daughter of the Selinunte Family – who were paying my bill – she twitched a bit and began calming down. I tagged with her to breakfast, to see if that helped, although she said we couldn't be long. We both had the mixed fruit cereal, in a rush, which was good, then the mellow green coffee before it went lukewarm, which was good. We talked of this and that and found we got along, which was good.

Clarinetta then wanted me to hurry over the toast and curly sea-shell butter because I had to be in position by 12:00 to murder Antonio Venicioni, which kind of spoiled the morning for me after all. She palmed me a photo of the man, some notorious crime boss, then hid it away in her jacket.

'You are the best! That's why we pay top dollar. You are the man with no home, no identity, no face. Hard to find, harder to catch. You do business then are gone, like a whisper.'

'Am I?', I nodded, taking in this matter of opinion. I found I couldn't run, not after I met her bull-necked cousins waiting patiently for me in the lobby. Nor when their chubby fingers placed me in their flat black car with auto-locking doors.

'Bullet proof – see?' said Lorenzo, with a wave around the windows. I said nothing, through terror, but they took that as professionalism.

'Half the money you received. The rest, when we see the body', Lorenzo told me, which also meant the real Mr Biscotti would be getting all of the money. I didn't want to touch that dodgy cash but wondered if the man I was meant to be might be just as confused about today as I was.

Marco passed me an oblong suitcase, which I opened and then looked over a very serious weapon with a stock, silencer and snap-action coupling that I knew I would have connect together right first time or look stupid.

'The scope with parabolic cancellation, what you asked for. Ammunition?'

'Ammunition? Yes, okay. One please.'

'He only needs one bullet, Marco', Lorenzo noted. 'Not like your clowns.'

'How do you do it without a sighting shot?', Marco asked me. I was about to make something up about peering down the side of the barrel when Clarinetta came to my rescue.

'Marco, you do your job and he does his. *Mi scusi.*' We drove on in deathly silence.

With half an hour to go until 12:00, we had arrived at a municipal building, got out at the rear and headed up a double flight of clanking metal steps. It was quiet, which made the connection in my head that this must be Saturday. Marco and Lorenzo seemed busy pulling crusty pigeon-netting off the brickwork to open my route to the roof, so I said my goodbyes to Clarinetta. I had already decided my shot would miss.

'Don't miss', she said. 'Venicioni will feed your parts to the alligators!'

'Why alligators?'

'He ran out of pigs.'

'Why did he run out of pigs?'

'He had to feed the alligators.'

Clearly a man who took sides, I could see there was only one thing left for me to do; go straight to the police.

'And don't get caught by the police. Detective Habanero has connected your name to many assassinations and you will never see the sun again!' Arse, I summarised to myself, as she pushed a disposable phone into my pocket. 'In case of anything', she ended, smiled tensely and backed away.

It's at times like these, when I find myself sitting on my laptop in the clock tower of a knackered town hall, pointing a weapon of war at a florist shop's doorway that I imagine my mad hippie parents might have got it right after all. I aimed, tried to stop blinking, then someone walked into my circle of glass.

That was when I had trouble. Clarinetta had shared a picture with me of Venicioni's face, but I seemed now to be looking into the back of some chutty's curly head. Was this Venicioni? It was 12:00 and I knew the shot needn't go anywhere, so began to pull the trigger. Then the phone rang.

'Don't pull the trigger!' – It was Clarinetta speaking. 'That is Venicioni's cousin Roberto. He must have sent him to collect the flowers instead. Turn, turn quickly! Venicioni is about to walk up the steps of the bank in the main street, more than half a mile from here. Can you see it? The building like a temple down by the waterway?'

I could make out the building but it was too far from where they had put me. What the goof, I thought, and fired harmlessly into the air.

'He's down! You've got him in the brain! Palermo rat!', cried Clarinetta.

'You are the best, Biscotti, the very best. I said it', Lorenzo called over her. 'Now get him out of this place.'

I have thought about that moment, over and again, trying to understand what really happened. It can't have been me because I fired almost straight up to make certain I couldn't hurt anybody. I can only think that the real Mr Biscotti, who had been paid as promised, decided not to reveal himself to these clakkas and had made his own way to Venicioni without ever hearing about me. Even so, I needed to get to the airport.

I skated in, boarded the internal flight south and flew not a moment too soon by my counting. Name? Profession? Who me? I'm just a digital nomad. The future. Don't bust me up when I'm bustin' up the workplace, clakka.

On the plane, I tried to get back into my webwork and make up for the lost day but could see I wasn't in the best place for thinking. The chutty in the seat next to me asked what I did, so I told her about being a digital nomad and working online. She asked if I had chosen this way of living or if it had been determined for me. I said I wasn't sure.

She said she liked to ask this stuff because she was a philosopher and one of the hardest problems she works on is a thing called free will, which might be an illusion. She said a person with no free will has no moral responsibility and should not be punished for their actions. Wow, I thought, that's a good one. Moral agency, the power to choose, she said, might only happen with complex decisions, not basic survival ones where everyone runs on auto-pilot. What's important in society, she bantered, is our actions, not our judgements and thoughts, so if you decide to do something wrong to someone and then change your mind, that's ok. What the chutty really wanted to study, she said, was a very rare kind of person who doesn't have any auto-pilot and makes their own choices all of the time. They could do anything to society, she said, stuff normal people never do because their brains won't let them.

After clearing customs, I realised I wasn't that much better off than last time. The chauffeurs were back on the concourse, collecting their bodies, and I thought, hey, I have a pretty good moral and ethical code, when I'm not feeling the pinch financially... but again I felt the drifter's choice between eating something today or taking a taxi. Who'd be me?

One of the chauffeurs held up a card welcoming some clakka calling themselves Grand Dragon Quayle, so I walked over, said that's me, got a few funny looks from the other drivers and we're on the way to some stadium as I write this. After all, it should be child's play to fit in as the key speaker at a Swords & Sorcery convention, so I don't think I have much else to worry about this evening.

THE AVIARY

by Thor S. Carlsson

Sometimes a nightmare will end only to welcome the beginning of a wonderful dream. You pray that the good dream will last for a long time, or possibly never end, but all things must end somewhere or sometime and I guess one can only pray and hope that whatever follows will fit nicely into the grooves of past good dreams. You cling to that hope as much as you cling to the hope that a nightmare will get derailed like an express train without brakes, that whatever comes next will be going in the opposite direction and to a warmer place.

You were my warm place, my good dream. The dream that was you, lasting longer than I had dared pray for, but still not long enough. I had never found a pleasant dream with the capacity to ferry me farther through the lake of dreams than the nightmare that had overtaken me, until you came along. You were the rays of the sun that managed to crawl to my outstretched fingertips in confinement. You were the smell of freedom that tickled my olfactory senses while lost in the dark and you were also the strength of a mountainside, able to scoop me up from my pit of despair and raise me towards the light and away from darkness.

Although you came later, it was actually you who saved me from my confinement and taught me to live again. You relinquished a captor's hold on me and gave me my reigns back, the reigns to my own life, where I should be the driver instead of an unwilling passenger.

For the first time since before I met you, I am standing in front of a door that is shut. You made all doors see-through so I could walk through them with confidence. Now I stand before a closed door and I am afraid to open it, let alone walk through it. I know I can leave that door closed forever and set my own tracks for the future but if I do that I will always think back to this moment and whenever I do look back, the door will be waiting for me, closed but not locked, begging me to open it and inevitably walk through.

I don't want to, I don't want to know what's behind that door but it wants me to know and it wants me to open it. I can try and ignore it but it beckons me, calls out to me, not a shout but a whisper, that penetrates and overshadows every other action and thought. I can ignore it for now but I know that I'll have to open that door eventually, open it and take a step through. What happens then, I don't know. I'll hope and pray again, hope and pray that what awaits me beyond the door is a pleasant dream and not another nightmare...

I was a normal little girl. I was boring really, nothing to speak of. My parents were wonderful and we lived a comfortable life. Normal is something I think about all the time now when I think back, back before you; and before him. I guess that when nothing happens that has any real weight to it, whether it's an achievement, a milestone or a tragedy, you tend to slap on a sticker that just says 'Normal'. That can span years or decades for some and they might look back and say that their past was uneventful but, compared to many others, it can so easily be looked upon as a gift because that is what it is. Never take normalcy for granted because you would trade a nightmare for normalcy in a heartbeat, let me tell you that right now. An uneventful life sounds to me like the most beautiful dream I can think of.

I never forget the day I met you, my future husband, in the support group. Mom had been begging me to go for a long time. I didn't see any reason to, what happened to me was in the past and meeting other people that might have a similar story to tell could hardly change the past. If it was set in stone, then what good will it do to hear an account from another person's past, a past I had not lived, a past possibly as horrifying as mine? Would that not give more weight to my own shattered experience and how could it possibly help me move forward?

Is it even remotely possible for good dreams to be born from the combined muck of a collective which focuses only on the violent past and fills in the blanks afterwards? I don't want to talk about it. I know it's in the past, I know he can't get me now and I know it is within my grasp, the normal life I took for granted, but I don't need to be surrounded by people with the same knowledge.

To please Mom I eventually went and sat there, unenthusiastically listening to horrible stories about abusive spouses and even some stories that were similar to mine where people had been abducted and held against their will for long periods of time. Weirdly, I felt like I deserved first prize since my stay with my captor was the longest, at least longest compared to the fifteen or so souls that shared their stories with the group.

The people there knew who I was and I knew that they knew, so because of this I never wanted to share my story and, although I was gently encouraged to share my story, they didn't force me to and I certainly had no interest in doing so. Most people have read all about my abduction and what followed. There was no justice. I was taken because someone wanted me for themselves and when help finally arrived, my captor took his own life. I was simply plucked from my nightmare and placed back home with my parents and the events of the past were kind of left to their own devices. In that sense, my nightmare gradually ended but the good dream one hopes will replace it seemed so far away to me and out of reach.

I was surprised to learn that you were there because of a different kind of trauma, you were there because your mother had been abducted and eventually killed by a man not so different from my captor. I listened to every word you said and it gave me the perspective of the people that get left behind with nothing but anger and unanswerable questions: Why, who, how and why again.

Why were we taken, your mother and I?

Who took us?

How did they take us?

Again, and always again, WHY were we taken?

These are the unanswerable questions that make recovery so very hard. You want there to be rhyme and reason for the actions of people but the sad thing is that sometimes there is no reason, or the reason is so unreasonable to us that we again come to the same question; and that's the reason for that question being asked twice: Why?

You spoke so elegantly and without the constraints of the

near past with its shackles around your limbs. Your tragedy had happened when you were just a boy and now, as a young man, the event was cemented into your past and talking about it became almost a normal thing, therefore making a horrible event just a normal part of life. My wounds were still fresh since my nightmare had ended just a short time ago, compared to yours.

We got to small talk after a few meetings and eventually you asked me out for coffee and that became our thing for a while, we would get coffee after meetings. We never talked about my past, you never asked and I didn't offer it up, until one day. You very carefully asked me what kept me going all those years. I could see that asking me was hard. Not only because of how talking about it might upset me but also how it might upset you. In you I saw my family and everyone left in the dark while I was held in it and in me you saw your mother, the person that was abducted. I instinctively understood that we wanted to ask the other side a question but we were also afraid to know the answers. You looked down into your coffee and you listened to me. I told you then about the aviary, the birds...

When I was sixteen, a man I did not know abducted me. I don't know what happened except that one minute I was walking home from school and the next I wake up on a concrete floor in a windowless room that would serve as my home for the next ten years. During my ten year stay as his captive, he never once uttered a single word. I was raped repeatedly but apart from that there was no violence, unless I struggled and then the only violence was him subduing me, breaking me, making me docile like a lifeless puppet. It really is a blur, a chunk of time I cannot place, peppered with sexual abuse and silence. The silence was louder than the screams of thousands.

When I finally lost track of time, I heard them, the minute I gave up they sang, the birds. When he was having his way with me I focused on them, I imagined their freedom and I visualised them taking flight, going wherever they pleased and singing the whole time. When I turned myself off, I imagined that one day the birds would find me and lead me to their sanctuary, a beautiful aviary with birds of all colours and sizes.

They would flutter around me and protect me, fly me away to wherever I wanted to go, but I wouldn't want to go anywhere. I wanted to be safe with them in the aviary. I imagined going to sleep amongst hummingbirds and swallows. I imagined being gently woken by a family of sparrows and robins, protected by a band of hawks and eagles. I didn't have any knowledge of birds then but they became my favourite thing in the world and apart from you, they remained my only passion.

We got married. I moved into the house you had inherited from your father and on our wedding day you led me into the yard, blindfolded, down the path at the back of the house and there we stopped. You told me that if I ever felt scared or confused I would know that I could always come here and I could wait for you here, amongst the birds. You had built me the most beautiful aviary I could imagine. There were roses everywhere, ones you had planted so they would never go away, and in the middle was a bench for me, for us, to sit on and listen to the bird songs. There were so many birds and each and every one of them sang my favourite song, a song of freedom and security. It was the most wonderful and amazing gift I could ever imagine.

So when I got the news after four years of marriage that you were not coming home, that's where I went, straight to the aviary. You had been sideswiped off the road and apparently killed instantly. You hadn't suffered, they said, but my world collapsed. The only thing that kept me going, just like in the past, was the aviary. Sometimes I would sit in the aviary and I would see you sitting on the bench next to me, with your eyes closed, but smiling and listening to the birds. You would sometimes open your eyes and look at me, smiling, and tell me, without words, that I would never lose you because you would remain with my saviours, the birds, forever.

One day I got a box with your belongings sent from the hospital. Your clothes, watch, wedding ring and your wallet. I opened your wallet and saw a picture of your mother and a picture of the two of us, but then I saw something that turned my world upside down. Sometimes you get news so disturbing that time slows to a crawl and you piece together a mental picture in your head, much like a quilt, but this quilt was not finished and the door I talked about before, the one I now stand before, unsure if I should go through or not, appeared before me and will remain with me until I open it.

With time crawling by at 1/100th the normal speed, I realised that we never once talked about your father; I don't know why. I had assumed he had left you and your mother when you were young. I was too busy healing to even think about it but here before me, in your wallet, behind the picture of your mother, behind the picture of the two of us smiling in the aviary you built for me, there was a picture of you as a child being held by your father.

The thing that rocked me to my core, that made me again long to be nowhere else other than surrounded by the birds, was seeing that picture of you with your father. The man holding you as a child, that man was my captor.

THE MORPHEUS TOWER

by M. L. Roberts

'Remember. There are fates worse than death.' Headmaster Darius stared into Morwenna's hazel eyes.

'Yes, Headmaster, I am aware.' He is trying to frighten me, she thought, and he is doing a right proper job of it, but I won't let him. She had completed her first year at the academy but did not like it there and planned to leave as soon as possible. The only way out would be to sign a contract releasing her at the end of her final year.

'Are you sure?' Headmaster Darius, a skilled illusionist, took pleasure in tormenting his students.

Morwenna nodded. She raised her chin and met his menacing glare with what she hoped was a cool gaze of her own.

'Besides, what will happen if I simply change my mind?'

Headmaster Darius did not reply. They sat in his office located in the uppermost room of the tower, a fire burning in the hearth. The flames behind the screen flared beyond the stone walls and blazed into the room. The drapes and mullioned windows were never opened and the room had become unbearably hot.

'And who told you about these fates worse than death?'

'Many people', Morwenna lied. She knew magical contracts must not be broken; however, rule breakers never lived to tell the tale and rule makers never pointed out the fine print.

'Is that so?' Headmaster Darius gave her a measuring look.

Morwenna tried to ignore the shadowy spiral horns now appearing atop his head and the flames reflecting from his black eyes, but she couldn't. She fanned herself with one hand and tugged rapidly at the collar of her school blouse, pulling it in and out to create a tiny breeze.

'Do you think you have the skill to fight these... fates worse than death?' Headmaster Darius fingered the tip of his dark collar. His forehead remained free of perspiration. Shadows loomed higher and wavered on the walls.

Morwenna dabbed the sweat from her brow. If she were going to reconsider, she'd better do it quickly.

Headmaster Darius watched her. He ran the tip of his tongue over the edge of his upper lip, as if he were drawing a fine line in the sand and daring her to cross it.

Not to worry, she thought. Even if I break the contract, I've never done anything evil — well, really evil. Surely punishment is weighed on a scale of justice, with good deeds on one side and bad deeds on the other?

The Headmaster's thin lips curved up at the corners.

Morwenna paused. Maybe she had better think about it a little more. What if she were put on trial and the magistrate who passed sentence happened to be someone as unfair as Headmaster Darius? Not a chance.

'Thank you for warning me, Headmaster. I've thought about it a long time, you see, and my mind is made up, if you know what I mean.'

'Rest assured.' Headmaster Darius edged the contract across the desk toward her. 'I know exactly what you mean.'

A tremor of fear ran through Morwenna. 'Wait. I'm not of legal age. Pre-graduation age, yes, but I'm still a minor. I need a parent's permission.'

'You do not have a parent.'

'A guardian then. I need a guardian's permission.'

'You do not have a guardian. You are a ward of the court. My ward. However, I sympathise. We will produce a witness to verify your signature.'

The fire flared again and stung Morwenna's eyes. She squeezed them shut and, when she opened them, she saw dark spectres filling the room. Their woeful expressions, their baleful eyes, seemed to plead with her not to do it.

'Not only one witness, a roomful', Headmaster Darius said. 'Whom would you choose to be yours?'

'None of them. I mean, I'm quite all right. I'll sign. I'll take your word for it. No witnesses needed.'

Morwenna picked up the long quill — how heavy it felt. It slipped from her hand and rolled across the desk to where she sat. The wood had bowed, with the lower end of the desk near Darius; the pen should have rolled toward him, not her.

She snapped her fingers once. The pen appeared on her open palm.

'Clever.' Darius reached into his cloak. He withdrew a sharp needle and placed it before her.

'Thank you. That's very... helpful.'

A quick pinprick, a drop of blood, a fine-nib pen. Morwenna put her left hand atop her right to keep it from trembling and wrote her name in small scroll letters. The deed was done.

'Do not forget, Morwenna. A magical contract sealed in blood can never be broken.'

'Yes, Headmaster.'

But Morwenna did forget.

Fifty years passed. One hundred, two. Her numerous lives beyond the crenelated walls did not turn out as expected.

Morwenna stepped close to the window and looked down from the thirty-second floor. Heights made her dizzy. The sight of people below, so small, so normal, going about their personal affairs, made her feel more left out than ever. She would have to be very careful when she jumped. A falling body could easily crush an innocent person.

'Maybe I should wait a day or two.' She paused to reconsider. She had not told anyone what she planned to do, nor had she left a note. There had been no time and besides what would she say? I'm leaving, Edwin, good-bye forever? Her husband Mayor Edwin Barnes had lost his bid for re-election.

'He didn't even campaign', Morwenna said, her resentment spilling over as it had when she had urged him to try harder. All he had done was stare at her as if he didn't know what she meant, then he shrugged and made no effort. The day after election, the results showed a landslide against him, ending his career.

It was not the only thing near ending, Morwenna thought wistfully. She raised her head, stood up straight and tossed her head back. Don't be a ninny. Get on with it.

Yet, her resolve faltered. Even before Edwin's failed re-election, he stopped noticing everything, except for his assistant campaign manager. Morwenna had suspected he might be interested in the young woman — an early mid-life crisis on his part — but when she saw a text, then she was sure. She hadn't really meant to pry — she knew his password — he knew hers. She had merely peeked at his recent messages and found fifty-three of them, all from the same woman, flagged and filed in a special mailbox.

'I should not have looked', Morwenna said savagely. She shoved the chair against the wall. The two legs rose a few inches off the floor and clunked back down. Instead of hurling herself out of the window, she sat on the chair. She could have been a professor at the academy but those prospects had disappeared when she signed the contract granting her freedom at a very heavy price.

How wonderful those happy carefree days had been. Morwenna brightened at the thought. Then, as always happened when she remembered her tweens, the haughty image of Serena Oxblood morphed in front of her. Morwenna closed her eyes as if to wipe the memory away but now all she could think of was Serena. Whatever happened to her?

Curious, Morwenna went to the bookshelf to find her school album. It was not at eye level. She felt along the topmost shelf; nothing there but dust. Morwenna brushed her hands together. At the bottom of the bookcase, a stack of long books lay piled horizontally.

'There it is.' She pulled the school album free from the tomes on top of it. It had been there so long the dust now formed a neat rectangular clear space. The title, 'Yearbook. Class of 1720', stood out in large gold print.

She turned the pages slowly and carefully. Here was Ms Finegold, botany teacher; and there was Mr Chenowith, economics. On the next page, in the musty tower library, Mr Darius sat at his desk, staring into the camera. He had not yet been promoted to headmaster but was the school librarian. His hands were folded in front of him and behind him stood a girl who looked like Serena. Or was it? Morwenna could not be sure. She had not crossed paths with Serena in upper division, going out of her way to avoid her scathing remarks.

Morwenna peered closer. Yes, it was Serena, but she did not look the same. Her hair, which had been dark pink, was shiny blue-black. Her eyes were dark, her face pale, as if all the blood had been drained.

Strange, she thought, turning the page to the class pictures. There, under Serena's name it said, 'Girl most likely to become a...' A blank space had been left. The typesetter must have removed what had been there and forgot to replace it. Morwenna swiped at a small bug on the page, but it didn't move. The bug was a very small word.

I need glasses, Morwenna thought, as she squinted at the mark or speck, whatever it was and read... moroi. Was it possible Serena had become a vampire? What of Headmaster Darius? He certainly looked like a strigoi, a dead vampire, but she had thought his appearance was only so much dramatic excess having to do with his role as an illusionist.

I wonder... She thought back to the day she had signed the contract. She had hurried down the staircase and at the bottom stopped before a suit of armour, the faceplate down.

'Hello, Sir Hugo', she had said.

'Good morning.' His monotone voice had echoed inside. 'How did it go?'

'The interview? Not well.'

'He threatened you, did he?'

'You could say that.'

'And you read the fine print, I take it?'

'Some of it — or, not really.'

Sir Hugo hadn't said anything else and so she had left the tower. Outside, she had accidentally run into Serena, the last person she wanted to see. No way would she tell Serena how badly the interview had gone.

As Morwenna recalled the whole incident, another memory came back of Serena racing across the field calling, 'Devon... Devon.' When he hadn't answered, she turned and called to another boy, 'William... William.' Both of the boys had been too far away to hear Serena's voice, yet even as she had hurried after them, she never called their names more than twice.

'A moroi cannot call a person's name three times', Morwenna whispered. It must be a coincidence, she reasoned, as her pounding heart told her otherwise. She tried to remember if Serena's hair had been yet another colour, an unnatural colour. Not ginger or red but — bright orange. She had seen the same colour recently on Edwin's phone, the small picture of his assistant.

If Morwenna had not already been sitting on the bed, she would have fallen on it. Edwin was having an affair with a moroi. Did he know?

Impossible. Morwenna bolted off the bed. She paced the floor, twisting her hands together. She would have known if there was anything magical, supernatural, or in any way unusual about Edwin. There absolutely was not. It was one of the reasons she had married him; and yet...

The pieces of the puzzle slowly shifted into place — the formerly-focused, energetic Edwin, now morose and indifferent, the vacant look in his eyes, his complete indifference to money — all had come about in the last few months since he had met his assistant.

Morwenna checked the calendar. The date when moroi harvest their victims was April 23 and today was May 5. It was too late. She slumped against the wall. Tonight, while people drank margaritas celebrating Cinco de Mayo, she would be mourning someone as good as dead, or worse.

Stunned, Morwenna staggered to the bed and fell on it. 'The election, the lack of consideration, none of it was his fault', she said into the pillow. 'Serena bewitched him.'

Morwenna lifted her head as another memory bubbled to the surface. Could she still save him? At the turn of the century, St. George's Day had been changed to May 5. The Gregorian calendar had been used for centuries but every century the dates drifted one day apart, making St. George's Day now on May 6. The eve — the night when the strigoi, the moroi and their horrible counterparts, the strigele witches would seize the unwary – was tonight, May 5.

Morwenna ran to the kitchen and searched the cabinets for weapons. Garlic, millet, a knife. She pulled off her tee and turned it inside out. She did not expect to be caught lying down but, if she were unconscious and helpless, her inside-out clothes might fool a vampire lurking nearby.

She threw the chair aside and ran to the window. The chair crashed through the wall and into the next flat. The noise startled her. She stopped, stared and shook her head, then she jumped onto the ledge and leaped.

Her vision blurred; her thoughts fragmented. Echoes of the past surged through her mind and, with them, Serena's mocking voice, Morwenna is going to be sick. She is afraid of heights. Do you need a bag so you won't vomit on yourself? She will never be one of us... never be one of us... never be...

Amid the haze of memory, one solid thought formed. I am not one of them. Wings were not something given or taken away because of violating an agreement. She had not needed someone to bestow them on her. They were inside, waiting to be used, waiting to be summoned, but how? Fear and love, fear and love, they had to work at the same time.

Morwenna felt wrenching pain, sharp quills tearing through her skin. The torture was unbearable. She screamed.

Later, those on the ground who witnessed an object falling would give different versions: cinders drifting from the sky; an eerie light reflecting from billboards, but not one of them saw a raven whose feathers grew in mid-flight. The one constant came from those who tried to capture the image with their phones; they all reported burnt lenses.

Morwenna soared past buildings, over rooftops and out of the city to where houses were set farther apart and lawns were unfenced and overgrown. Gliding over treetops, she saw small objects at a great distance and in great detail.

Where could Serena have taken him?

Not one of us. Morwenna is not one of us.

Then who am I? Her eyes blazed red.

Darius had never told her where she came from. He forbade her to go to the tower library. Once, when she stormed into his office, angry and crying over an unfair bad mark, he had hastily shoved a notebook over a sealed folder. Stamped across the top, 'To Be Destroyed' and underneath, a frayed yellow label, 'Daughter of the Morrigan'.

Daughter of the Morrigan, goddess of war and death, goddess of fate. He knew and he hid it from her. He scoffed at her attempts at magic, called them feeble and unworthy. He knew.

Morwenna's aura glowed red, then white and slowly settled into deepest black.

Your fate is sealed, Headmaster; but first I must find Edwin — and Serena.

The sun lowered near the horizon; the sky faded to purple. Morwenna followed the highway and saw more trees, a winding road and there in the distance a lone car heading east, its lights casting not the solid V-shaped white beam, but a murky vaporous hue invisible to normal eyes.

Morwenna flew lower, trailing the car. In the back seat, a man's head lolled to the side. She could not see the driver.

The raven shrieked. Serena!

Far off the road, a man in a field looked up, shielded his eyes and watched a moment. When he turned, he fell into a ditch that had not been there a moment before. Better a twisted ankle, Morwenna thought, than a fiery raven he could not explain.

A louder shriek rent the air. Serena! Then another, calling her three times. I know you.

The car swerved. Its side wheels lifted off the asphalt and resettled. It sped faster.

Morwenna alit a hundred feet in front of it. The tires squealed; the car slid and stopped. The driver got out and stared at the looming shadow surrounded by fire.

'You finally figured it out?' Serena said in the familiar, mocking voice. 'What do you intend to do about it?'

'I want nothing from you.' Morwenna's voice echoed. 'Let Edwin go and I will release you.'

'Release... me?' Serena shook her head. 'He was only a decoy; he served his purpose.'

'You did this...'

'To get at you, yes.'

'But why?'

'You were in the way; you were his favourite.' Serena paused. 'The headmaster, you fool.'

'But he hated me — and I detested him.'

'Yes, but I am his daughter. The attention he showered on you should have been mine.'

'Serena, he did nothing but berate me, demean me, belittle my every attempt at magic.'

'It was to drive you harder, to get more from you. You were his favoured one.'

'I've had a horrible life — I don't know why — until I met Edwin.'

'What did you expect? You broke your contract the day you signed it.'

Morwenna gaped at her.

'Did you not read the fine print?'

'Yes.'

'You're lying, the same way you did then. The fine print, the secret clause, were different for all of us. Yours said that if you lied to the first person you met you would break the contract.'

'But I told the truth. I met —'

'Sir Hugo. A ghost, not a person; although he still thinks of himself that way.' Serena laughed once. 'Sir Hugo tried to intervene. He was one of the spectres in the room, a possible witness to the signing, or would have been. He wanted to be the first you met because he knew you would tell him the truth, but I was the first real person you met. I asked you the same questions Sir Hugo did and you answered the opposite way. You told him the truth, but not to me.'

'I never knew', Morwenna said in a small voice.

'He's suffered for it, too. It's not easy to torture a ghost, but there are ways. He's locked in the tower now.'

'Sir Hugo.' Morwenna ran her hand through her hair.

'Well, don't feel too badly about it, or him. I broke my contract as well. I couldn't see the fine print either.' Serena shrugged. 'It does not matter now, does it? It's over. I'll tear Edwin apart and —'

Morwenna's aura blistered the air around both of them.

'Yes, well, I supposed in the end we would kill each other', Serena relented.

'Maybe that would be best.' Morwenna, now a more normal size amid her fiery aura, saw through the car to where Edwin lay on the floor in a sad rumpled heap. 'Poor Edwin.'

'Poor, stupid Edwin. Do you know what he talked about? You. Always you. My darkest arts were just not good enough to bring him around. He even called me by your name. How insulting.'

'He did?' Morwenna's red aura dimmed to pale amber. 'I'll take him home... and let you go. I mean, let bygones be bygones. How is that? Serena?'

Before Morwenna's eyes, Serena shrank. She became old and shrivelled, her bright orange hair wispy and shredded. 'You can come with us.'

'Take me home?' Serena rasped.

'Yes.'

'You trust me?'

'No —'

'If you do, you're a bigger fool than I thought.'

'— but you won't try anything. I have millet in my pocket' — She remembered the burnt grains scattering as she flew — 'or I did. Anyway, just for a bit of care, shall we say. Maybe there's a halfway house for vampires.'

Serena breathed deeply. 'No. I don't need anything from you. I'll go my own way.'

'As you wish.' Morwenna waited till Serena's diminishing form vanished amongst the trees, sparing her anymore indignity. Then she took Edwin home. It was not easy breaking the news about the re-election, especially since he did not remember being mayor, but with her care, he recovered.

Morwenna closed the bedroom door where Edwin lay sleeping.

She went to the east window and stared in the direction of Morpheus Tower. Her eyes narrowed; her mouth set in grim line. 'I will find the headmaster. Wherever he is, I will find him.'

WHO SHALL PROFIT

by Carolyn Geduld

It was March 4th. The dean was using two stubby forefingers to tap a keyboard on his mahogany desk in his campus office. Outside the window, students drifted between classes. Many did not wear outer clothing, even though the temperature was frosty. Some wore sandals. It was a sign of what? Indifference? Brashness? Young people were not to be understood.

Every day, his inbox was filled with more emails than he could answer. There were just as many texts and voice messages. He prioritised them into files: Hold, Urgent, Critical. The Critical file was jammed to overflowing. Quickly, he closed it to relax his throbbing throat. It was the Coronavirus. The Administration was in suspended animation, wondering if the campus would be affected, wondering what to do if it was. Much of the correspondence circled around that uncertain subject.

Turning to his voicemails, he noticed one from Larry Anderson. Larry Anderson. Of all people. He pictured the younger Nordic-looking man. Like a Viking. Something stirred. Badly, he wanted to touch himself but that was forbidden. He wasn't gay. Sitting up straighter in his chair with his hands pressed onto the desk, he stared out of the window.

The students. How easy it was for them. Wearing sandals in the snow. Tattoos on every inch of skin. Sexually fluid. Little did they know what it was like to be a Jewish man in his sixties, raised to wear Gold Toe socks and date women.

'Hello, Professor. It's Larry Anderson, the academic ghost-writer who helped you out a while back.'

The familiar voice reminded him of the conversations they used to have about linguistic theory. The dean had hired the ghost-writer to help him with his manuscript, hoping the handsome younger man wouldn't suspect the lustful feelings the dean couldn't reveal. He didn't dare. He couldn't be gay. He had his career to consider. The President of the University was appointed by the very conservative governor of a very conservative red state in the 'Bible Belt.' Everyone on campus knew how intolerant the president could be.

That was not the only secret that made a voice message from Larry Anderson so jolting. What the dean would not want known was that it was the ghost-writer who actually wrote *Similarities in Pronouns in Proto-Linguistic Meta-Families*, the publication leading to the dean's promotion. If it were to come out that he did not do the work entirely himself, he would have a disagreeable time with the Ethics Committee.

The voicemail continued:

'Ghost-writing is only one of the hats I wear, Professor. I am well-connected, having helped out other professionals like yourself in government as well as in academia. That's how I've been able to obtain information about the coronavirus that might be of use to you. Information that hasn't been publicly disclosed yet.'

The dean realised he was probably being set-up by an attractive con-artist, just as he had been when he was having trouble completing, or even starting, his manuscript in the past. He knew he should delete the message and block the caller. Curiosity, he told himself, made him listen to the end.

'I'm calling you before other administrators I know at other colleges.' He named three at rival institutions. 'Get back to me ASAP if you're interested.'

No. He wasn't interested. He wasn't going to be fooled. He should never have allowed himself to get mixed up with someone like Larry Anderson. He could have written that damned book himself. He had only hired the ghost-writer to assist when he was temporarily stuck.

On the other hand, it was unthinkable for the other administrators to have advance information he lacked. No tin-pot college should have a leg-up on a major research university and no small-time dean should have a leg-up on him. It wouldn't hurt just to listen. He could always hang up.

'Professor. So glad you called. How're you holding up?'

'I'm fine. What's this about?' He didn't want to sound friendly.

Larry's spoke softly, as if sharing a secret no one should overhear. This could be flattering, if the dean fell for it.

'I have sources, Professor, in the State Health Department. I hear things. Sometimes before the governor, while it's still developing or when it's held up for political reasons. Someone doesn't want the governor to be unhappy. That sort of thing.'

'Okay. What's your information?' The dean changed the screen on his laptop to *World of Solitaire*. He clicked on 'New Deal'. It would keep his thoughts from straying.

'I want you to believe that I have good sources, so I will tell you two things that will happen tomorrow, March 6th. Neither have been in the news yet. The first confirmed case of the virus in the state will be announced and the governor will declare a state of emergency.'

The dean paused before moving the three of hearts on top of the four of clubs. If what Larry said was true, the university's president would be impressed to hear it from the dean. He might invite the dean into his inner circle, instead of allowing him to languish in a secondary administrative building, perhaps as a penalty for remaining suspiciously unmarried.

'I want you to have confidence in me, Professor, like in the old days when we worked on the linguistics book together. When you discover I've told you the truth, call me. In times like these, information is gold; and I have access to the gold mine.'

The next morning, as soon as he awoke, the dean opened the digital edition of the state paper. In a large font across the top of the screen, the headline read 'First Covid-19 case confirmed; Governor declares State of Emergency.' Larry had told the truth. The dean was both amazed and annoyed that he hadn't believed the ghost-writer in time to alert the president.

Yet, it could have been a coincidence or a lucky guess on Larry's part. He asked him for another prediction, against his better judgement.

'Agreed, Professor. I want you to be satisfied that I'm trustworthy. On March 8th, less than two days from now, the second confirmed case will be announced. It will be man who travelled to Boston for the BioGen Conference, same as the first case. Let's talk on the afternoon of the 8th, if what I am telling you is born out.'

There was a pause. 'By the way, Professor, since we are both interested in the history of linguistics, the expression 'born out' is shortened from 'born out of wedlock.' Meaning illegitimate, but in the modern era, it means the opposite.'

The dean couldn't imagine why the ghost-writer would mention words that reversed their meaning, in the middle of a pandemic that might kill thousands, even millions of people. Was he hinting about something? The dean tried his best to corral the unreasonable thought that Larry was suggesting the dean was in the closet, only appearing to be straight when he was the opposite.

Meanwhile, there would be thirty-six hours of waiting until Larry's second piece of inside information was verified. Nearly two agonising days during which the dean couldn't concentrate on anything else. He was at the point in his career in which influence counted and Larry's intelligence could be a springboard, vaulting him to Provost in spite of his questionable marital status.

The president and his advisors had been trying to determine whether and when to close the university. The dean had heard that the president was spinning his wheels trying to decide. There were all kinds of complexities to consider, from student fees to the fate of overseas programmes. The future of the university might depend on getting this right. Any information about the rate of infection in the state could help. In the absence of testing, foreknowledge would be, as Larry said, gold.

The dean stayed up late on the night on the eighth, reloading the state paper repeatedly until the new edition was posted. The same large font announced the second confirmed case. Just as Larry had predicted, the victim had attended the conference in Boston.

'Do you believe me now?' Larry's triumphant voice was no longer hushed when the dean called him.

'I have to, don't I? You were right both times. What do you want to keep me informed with whatever you find out from your sources?'

The dean didn't want Larry thinking he wasn't on to him. People like the ghost-writer were usually costly. He had paid through the nose for his help with the book, as well as for continued contact with the handsome ghost-writer.

'I have overhead, Professor. I'm glad you understand this will be business deal.'

The ghost-writer named a figure. As the dean anticipated, it was more than he could afford. It would require him to take out a loan.

'Let me think it over.'

'Of course. I'm sure you know that time is of the essence.'

Larry was putting pressure on him. The dean snuck two fingers onto his wrist. His pulse was rapid. He understood. In a changing situation, information that was priceless one day could be valueless the next. If he waited too long, the president would come to a decision and that would be that.

'I'll call you back in an hour', he said.

His thoughts reeled. Who knew how reliable Larry or his sources were. How could he take on such a stomach-dropping loan if the economy was going to tank? What if the pandemic lasted for months, even years and Larry wanted more and more? What if he couldn't pay and Larry dropped him?

There was another side. The dean imagined being helpful. Maybe whatever he could tell the president would swing his decision one way or the other. It was life and death. If the university remained open too long, students in crowded dorms and over-enrolled classes would spread the virus. If it shut too soon, within the next few days, there would be chaos. He pictured being honoured by the president, after the pandemic abated, at a special dinner for his help during the crisis.

'It was only because of the prescience of the dean that the university is in good shape today. He is one of the heroes whose name will go down when the history of this great institution is written.'

'I was just doing my duty', he would answer.

Before the hour was up, he called the ghost-writer back.

The university closed its doors at the beginning of Spring Break, after the dean persuaded the president, correctly, that there would be twenty-four confirmed cases by that date. When he was able to predict a thousand cases by the end of the month and a surge in April, classes were suspended through the end of the semester. The dean claimed to have an anonymous source. This was true. The source was Larry. The dean became the president's new favourite when he predicted a state-wide lockdown beginning on the 25th.

This was when he, with the rest of the university's faculties and staff, began to work from home. Larry arranged a daily morning phone call with updates. Other than that, the dean continued to sort and answer emails in the Critical file.

He had time on his hands, as the campus and all but essential businesses were closed, but he was unable to go to the gym, the library or the opera. Instead, he fantasised about situations in which, for some reason, Larry would be isolated with him. In these imaginings, the young Viking was always the initiator.

'We should comfort each other. Let me hold you.' Larry, handsome Larry, would go to the dean and embrace him. The dean would allow this without responding. He couldn't be gay if he just stood still, no matter what Larry did.

As days passed, his daydreams changed, becoming more reciprocal. Without preamble, Larry grabbed and kissed him. The dean touched himself, imagining it was Larry. He was no longer in control. Larry was. The dean was being forced to respond. It wasn't his fault. Meanings could be the opposite of what they seemed.

Two weeks into the lockdown, Larry made a sly new suggestion during his usual morning phone call.

'My overhead is increasing. I have an idea that could benefit both of us without affecting your financial contribution. Interested?'

The dean held his breath.

'I'm listening.'

'You have connections at the university. Some of your colleagues might be receptive to receiving forecasts.'

'What do you mean?' The dean could guess where this was heading.

'You could convince them to trust you with a couple of correct predictions I will supply. I'm expanding to include sources of secret essential supplies, like gloves and masks. You'd be surprised where they are hidden. There would be many at the university who would want to invest, I bet.'

The dean had a sudden lump in his stomach.

'But that would be illegal! I don't want to get into trouble.'

The ghost-writer spoke in his softest croon.

'Professor. We have our secrets, you and I. It would be terrible if anyone found out.'

What was Larry saying? Which secrets? The ghost-writing? The predictions? Or was the Larry implying he would out him. Maybe he had guessed that the dean was gay from some unwitting gay thing he did or said. He shuddered.

'Are you blackmailing me?'

'I wouldn't put it that way, Professor. I'm simply saying I have to cover my overhead. Now, if you prefer to take another loan...'

The dean had an image of the blond Viking gripping him by the wrists and forcing him down onto the floor. Then rotating him face-downward. He would sob and beat his head on the floor in useless protest.

During the next agonising hours, the dean went back and forth over his choices. Give in to Larry? Or bail and be exposed? Unnerved, he paced restlessly from room to room. Their conversation looped in his head, but suddenly it occurred to the dean that he had as much power over Larry as Larry had over him. Things really could mean the opposite of what they seemed. Even his fantasies of being controlled by Larry were actually controlled by him. Why had he never thought of this before? He called the ghost-writer back.

'Well, Larry, I have 'overhead', as you call it, too. And you have as much to lose as I do if our secrets are revealed.'

The ghost-writer jumped right back. 'I'm not sure that's true, Professor. I'm not the one with an academic career. But I'm not a selfish man. I'm just trying to make a living. Nothing I've done is against the law.'

Was that even correct?

'If you're exposed, you'd be under pressure to reveal your sources. That might make you very unpopular.' The dean won another suit in the solitaire game he played whenever talking to Larry. It was his favourite, spades. 'I suggest a partnership. If I find investors, I get a cut of their fees.'

The dean figured he would be helping others if he gave them the information Larry passed onto him from who-knows-where. It was, after all, accurate information. Not the fake treatments or fraudulent self-testing flooding the internet. Besides, he vowed to give a portion of his profit to charity — fifty percent or maybe five percent. Something.

He would find a reason why meeting with Larry in person was essential business. Although he had more at stake than the ghost-writer, he had the upper hand now. If he were willing to gamble his career, he would have enough power over Larry to be the initiator, if he chose to be. He would decide when the time came.

It was a pandemic. The dean was in the riskier age group. He could die. The president could die. The governor could die. If he were gay and survived, who would care anymore? The world was changing. The coronavirus was freeing him to be who he really was. The spoils would go to those who saw advantages and took them. Sexual advantages, financial advantages, any advantages. He had nothing to lose.

GENEALOGY CLUB

by Faith Jones

Oh wondrous Caliban, glowing with virtues, you have grown mighty indeed, circling your coordinated flurry of successes. Hours, the renewing round of 24 races all there to be won and filling them there's you, so much talk about you, but I sense... washing up, the attributes of a god shrunken to a mere man. Should I relate your montage of pride, or some of the more seedy conquests? Should I expose you before you inevitably expose yourself? Temerity is more your natural vessel than mine but you have become interesting enough for the narrator to... seep through the fourth wall and pick on you. Look at you tonight. All great men turn into parodies of themselves and you have proven to be no different.

Galleries upon galleries of images lie out there, photo archives of those gala awards, entire scripts tapped out only to lure you into them, the lyrics of a song or two sung and then slapped straight back loud in your face across red carpets that could once have been – what? – Moorish tents stamped down by a celebrated stallion? The ruddied pavilions of empires lost, fallen to you, then forgiven and cherished, their hearts and minds stolen with an approachable wave.

Too fanciful a simile, too far East, you're thinking? After all I have witnessed, don't tell me you've become jaded and prosaic when I have not. Can you blame the narrator for dwelling on style when you make such a hero of it? You do often wear the loose-flowing fashion of the Medes and Phoenicians *in videos* but, yes, I can see you have no genuine desire to discover the bones of your unlettered ancestors.

Crowds and fans, nothing new to you, one who encourages sycophants and idolaters. Do you have a home beyond these transient hotel rooms? Oil-paint tubes from where you ordered the lot but forgot to learn, always meant to, time soaked into media headlines and out again to 'do' chat shows and then another broom is out again sweeping mushroom corks off the polish of a parquet floor.

The Dancing House in Prague is your backdrop, or *Jazz* by Henri Matisse, it's all you; another time, another place, no real reason. The components of Jazz pull apart in your mind like acid; the piano keys, the sodium door-light piercing the nightshade of an alley, leaving only the dancing, posing, tissue-paper-thin figure of yourself, the centre of attention even when the musicians have gone.

One trick you learned early, thank God The Artist, was to always draw the eye first. A brush with excess paint flicks and falls into an oblong of blackness as one great artist expires and a new generation hatches out from that tired soul's husk to continue the cycle of rebirth and reimagining.

So there you both sprawl, dissolved in luxury. Legs on a jacket. A gig, the after-party with its candy shop of choices, where you selected by shape but couldn't see into her mind.

'Hello Angel', you ventured, with a practised smile. There are two kinds of angel, Aidan. You didn't see the other women in the room, who instantly coalesced in hatred of her as they faded out of existence. Your fingers, this one's hair.

'So adorable.' So demure. Aidan has an ache.

She's into you but aware of them, the others you've just insulted.

'Let's split', you say.

'Okay. For a coffee?'

'Never coffee after a gig. I have a strange compulsion to get the Space Hoppers out.'

'Are you staying here?', she asks. That was easy. You love her look of nervous innocence which says 'I wouldn't normally be doing this but... as you're so famous... I suppose we *could* do something.' She knows what she's doing.

If you must bless your weary fortune with a vigorous conclusion, we have expectations too. I know you're tired, Aidan, but don't dream. This pretty girl has come a long way to suck up and down your personal area of interest. Theodora, let greatness own her, for she is mean no more!

What do you think a young woman can possibly get out of this act of submission, especially if her prince nods off and flees along the fields of his pride? That's better, you're rising to meet her, a view of that youthful face in the light, sensation awakens into electric frission, the feel of exhilaration under lengthening strokes, an owl-flash of eyes as she looks up into yours – and oops, it's soon over, pulsed into a mop of her silk-soft hair. That's what you wanted. That's what you needed. That's why you act and dance and sing. It's never been about the money or the houses, has it Aidan? Now you can rest, thankful boy, and those loving green eyes of yours are closing.

She looks around. Alone, hesitant, and she's taken it.

There's no mess and you're too far gone to remember when she rolled that sheath along you. Word gets around, doesn't it, that your line of work goes hand in hand with nasty diseases, so perhaps there was some rudimentary intelligence at work after all in this cutie. College girl, is she? You forgot to ask. You've used her and she's really used you. No, she has, you'd never guess there was no spermicide in that carefully commissioned sample collection system.

A pen-light comes on, illuminating a strewn path to the bathroom, then it winks off again. The door from the bedroom opens, the black oblong from *Jazz* again, and into the oblong in essence revealed by distant street lights steps through your little nocturne girl. A criss-cross screen casts fish-net shadows down her legs but she's part of your history now, your fault, your consequences.

She won't switch the main light on, no. Things might get strange and difficult if you were to wake up now. She closes the door silently, opens the clip bag she brought with her and withdraws a plastic test tube with a hinged lid.

Upending her little bag of latex, she pours, squeezing the precious last drop between fingers and the tube is soon filled as the lid clicks decisively shut. Blue fluid from a reservoir hidden in the lid sinks into the sample. At the basin now, she turns the tap to cover any sound this makes and shakes the test tube for five seconds, counting in her mind.

Checking again to see if you're sleeping, nocturne girl takes out from the carry bag what looks like an old fashioned brick telephone – but it isn't. Plastic arms and legs are extracted and locked into position, but again they are not what they seem. Oh, I get it, small propellers and a drone is unfolding. In the centre of the flying, whirling device is a hollow shaft like a coffee cup holder but slim and deep, into which she slides the test tube. Ravens and their twigs.

As a last act, nocturne girl opens the bathroom window, leans beyond, switches on the drone motor to give it life and lets it go, buoyant now, as the cargo floats away and down into the fluorescent tangle that spoils true darkness. A stranger's thumb takes it onward now. Sorry Aidan. You've been had.

'Don't take all night. I'm getting cold in here.'

Unforeseen this, her heart responds and jogs around ribs in realisation. Not the final act then, to clear the massive debt from her brother's treatment. He's called Angelo, by the way, but you weren't to know. She silences the running tap and pauses to control her breathing, retouches the lipstick in seconds and then walks back through the door to the bedroom to play another set in bed, motives and suspicions slipping into infinite blackness behind her.

'Flip a record on, luv.'

'Okay' – but someone else's. She's not your fan. Neither wish I to be your spiritual amanuensis as, believe it or not, I am even more fickle than you are. I choose instead, right here and now, to find a soul who seeks their laurels instead of sitting on them, who fears their imperfections and doesn't huff their future up their nose. I bid you atchoo.

The next day a functional wall-clock unwinds to half past seven and an impenetrable girl restored to her elements of virtue and daylight receives a text: 'Hey, it's Aidan. Let me paint you. You're doing art college or something, right? Paint you in the dark. Yeah, that's totally a challenge.'

She doesn't reply, not to him. Already she's someone else he wouldn't recognise, writing a parking strategy report at the office.

A city at daybreak on another sea-board, with curtains drawn and streets still quiet. The incessant hum of a cycle courier scatters fat pigeons from topiary tubs as this ratting intrusion banks a corner, a kerb, to park outside a modern building, almost blocking the entrance.

Reception is open, strangely for daybreak. The cycle courier approaches the desk and is then intercepted, relieved of the sought after pouch.

'You can't take the bag as well', chips the courier 'and sign'. A small packet, two fingers lifting, the contents removed and the bag handed back to him.

The sound of a lift and a life descending, almost Faustian this. The doors to the chamber tug open and, before the guard can step over the boundary, a poised technician in turn relieves the hand of its burden. The guard doesn't bother getting out, settling instead for the return journey and a saving on shoe-leather. Bloody lab nerds.

At last! *This* is a real laboratory, a business investment. Is it daytime? Who can tell in these underground spaces, no clock, without any signal, where you're not allowed to wear jewellery, trinkets or watches because of potential contamination? A clean room does not always translate to a clean business.

'Aidan Grange', the tube is marked with a permanent felt-tip marker, like a pair of his old school shoes.

It would take you a week to review all of these blinking, plastic-visored facilities, the pins and needles in the intricate process of genetic extraction and sequencing.

Stripped of all pair-bonding baggage, no warmth or scent to the nest, DNA strands alone are being loaded apologetically into bleak containers. He'll soon be a multiple format product, our hapless rock star.

Business staff stand around on the far side of a glass panel, waiting for the technicians to finish; and now they have, securing workstations and putting plastic gowns in their lockers.

'Hello. Are you Brendan Chase?' a new blue suit asks a technician. 'I want to go over the process with you.'

The technician looks bemused at the face, at the tie pin. 'It should all be in your predecessor's notes.'

'My predecessor was dismissed on the spot and wasn't being entirely cooperative, referring me to the gagging order in her contract. I'm having to write procedure notes from scratch. The CEO said he couldn't put anything in writing for me for 'operational reasons' so I should come down here and talk to you. Could you give me a break, please?'

'It's simple, like all good business plans', the tech told him. 'The elevator on the West side of the building opens at floors 1, 3, 4 and 5. The elevator on the East side of the building opens at floors -1 and 2.'

'I'm asking for the process not the architecture.'

'I'll get to that. Floor 5 is the management level, Floor 4 is marketing and distribution of all the test kits to customers, 3 and 1 are the labs that process the public DNA samples, 2 is where we securely archive the reporting data and -1 is here.'

'I don't get minus 1', the suit presses.

'It shouldn't be me explaining this, but if no other bugger wants to take responsibility I suppose I have to. Put it like this: How many other DNA testing companies offer their services to the public, for either full mtDNA sequencing, deep ancestry, disease markers or genealogy?'

The suit counts on his fingers. '23andMe, AncestryDNA, Heritage DNA, AfricanDNA, FTDNA, Argus BioSciences, My Heritage, Cambridge DNA Services, Bioresolve, BritainsDNA, Family Tree DNA, Ethnoancestry... five or six more I've forgotten.'

'Too many, so they're undercutting each other. That tosh is only what we do in our core business, process kits that tell little Sally on her 10th birthday she's distantly related to a sparkly princess – but – to come out ahead in a saturated market you need to have *an angle*.' Brendan pauses, seeing whether the suit needs him to clarify further. It seems he does, so the tech soldiers on.

'In this lab we have compartment 2 of the business. We curate a collection of what you might term A-List genetic samples, with which we provide reproduction options to discerning and wealthy clients.'

'You clone famous people?'

'No, that would be illegal. We provide ideal silent partner genetics for you to make your child.'

'Designer babies?'

'That's one way of describing it. Clients can select a remarkable achiever to contribute chromosomes to the child they've always wanted. The genetics they choose are totally unrestricted by compatibility; male, female, any sexual orientation. We can use real sperm in a few cases for a standard or surrogate pregnancy. Otherwise, we can implant cellular DNA from both parents into voided eggs *in vitro* and then set the fertilised egg either in the client's womb or source a surrogate carrier to take it to term, depending on negotiating a solid financial package.'

'Jesus Christ? Einstein?'

'We don't have either of those assets, I regret to say, as they would be somewhat marketable, but we do have many others of significance banked. The genomes of people who achieved their status from 1980 to 2005 are currently sought after because those able to afford the service at the current point in time often began their careers or businesses in those years. Some have underlying fertility concerns but many are just unattractive super-fans with too much money.'

'Which means there's guaranteed ongoing demand for this?'

'Clearly. Here's what's happening, if you want my opinion. As long as anyone can remember, the most successful actors and singers have flirted with the audience, openly prostituting themselves in many cases, but the audience couldn't touch so were driven crazy by it. The stars didn't know or care who they were seducing at the time, but now the barrier between the intoxicated nut-job fan with unfinished business and the star is breaking down. The new era is here, where a performer in a pretend way openly inviting the viewers to have sex with them will find there are real consequences, as the wealthy obsessed fan can make good on those promises and have their baby.'

'Is that ethical?'

'It's screwed up, but everything is allowed until there's a law stopping you doing it. If that happens, it still isn't the end. We take the whole business into international waters where there's no national jurisdiction and carry on.'

'What about this sample, the film actor-singer Aidan Grange?', the suit wonders.

'Two options for reproduction, this being a live sample of the right kind of cells.'

'The right kind?'

'Freshly donated from the swaggering poser's bollocks', the tech elaborates for the manager without much patience, 'and worth about seven and a half million an ounce.'

'Strewth! Did we pay Grange?'

'I expect he got something nice out of it. This material can be inserted almost naturally by pipetting into the mother's egg, but that option is priced as premium because we would run out of stock. Better still, we've sequenced his code, so can build copies of genetic material to insert into a void egg template whenever we need them.'

'You can do that? Build real DNA from only a data sequence?'

'*We* can do that. Take some responsibility mate. You're a manager – I only work here.'

'But a string is millions of base pairs long!'

'I didn't say it was cheap', the tech chides him.

'When I think of the financial opportunities here... Re-insertion from data alone though, the reconstruction of a man's DNA from a sequence plan, that is something new. When this technology becomes normal, eggs will jump at the chance!' He realises that sounds a little weird.

'It's not just men's genomes I'm talking about', the tech assures him, 'We're working on homogametic fertilisation in addition to heterogametic, so we might soon be able to help women to conceive with their preferred woman and men to do the same, using a surrogate to take that to term.'

Only a little of the material has been destroyed in sequencing, the creation of an identical code which spells Aidan's biology exactly, in every sense except corporeal. The technician walks a glass vial to a refrigeration tray marked 'Strictly confidential', subdivided into 'Intelligence', 'Luminaries' and 'Entertainers'. The sample 'Grange' is archived amongst other tubes with scribbled surfaces that read 'Adams, Anthony, Arquette R, Attenborough, Baldwin, Bardot, Berry, Bowie, Chase, Cheech, Chong, Ciccone, Cleese, Clooney, Connery, Cruise, DiCaprio, Ekland, Ford, Hamill, Hathaway, Murray, Presley, Fiennes, Freud, Feynman, Fox, Houston, Hill, Hutchens, Jagger, Jobs, Jones, Kasparov, Kennedy, Khan, Knightley, Mandela, Marley, Minogue, Musk, Navratilova, Penrose, Perelman, Pfeiffer, Pratchett, Ryder, Sinatra, Smith, Spielberg, Stone & Parker *(mixed due to circumstances of sample collection)*, Windsor, Williams,

Woods' and some presumably cheaper social influencers who only kids and the Chinese state's internet monitoring goons have ever heard of.

'How do you collect these samples?', the suit enquires.

'People chuck away their skin and fluids all the time without thinking about it. We buy used spoons and cups from restaurants then swab them for saliva, take sanitary products from communal waste, hair follicles from hotel pillows and the occasional used prophylactic. Hotels are worth their weight in gold, for genomic collection.

I should advise you that donors won't gift their genetics to every Tom, Dick and Harry who asks, so you will see some high consultancy fees every now and then, to reward our most talented field agents.'

'How many of the donors know this business exists?'

'The genetics are no longer their property, as they've put them in the communal waste. In rare cases, we do hold small quantities of viable sperm like Grange's, for clients who want a natural conception and can pay premium rate. What surprised me is some famous stars make an effort to find us and be sure we have their deposit, Bowie for example.'

'Fuck', exclaims the suit unprofessionally, the implications of it all sinking in.

'We've made that part of the process redundant', the tech replies despondently.

Helsinki. An email arrives on a corporate laptop, squared up at the regulation height for ergonomic working, open and ready for business on a hotel suite desk. The lone occupant, Ms Georgia Farrow CBE has dedicated her life to the business her parents started in the 1970s and one that did well from the original free labour of a hippie community, but it was only under her control that it divested its shoeless friendships and assembled the corporate tonnage it wielded today.

An accountant might tell you Farrow's journey had been close to flawless but, sometimes when you have focussed too hard on reaching the summit of your mountain, you see other mountains and much a bigger picture emerges, a cohesion of awareness about all the other things in life you could have done instead. Priorities - she had achieved them for the firm, that was undeniable, but it had all happened at the expense of everything personal, every human need. She had never allowed herself rewards, personal luxuries, the accoutrements of greed as she considered them anathema to a lifetime's work ethic. She'd never allowed herself pets or cars or men.

Opening and reading the message, Miss Farrow feels a knot forming in her stomach and knows at last that she can have something just for herself. She becomes aware of a new sensation in her body – excitement... is it joy? She feels the chakras opening and the body telling her what it wants, over-ruling the logical mind. Heavens, she realises, she can make a baby with her secret crush Aidan Grange!

Farrow needs to calm down and get control over anything impulsive, so moves over to a tea tray loaded with sachets and makes herself a steady instant hot chocolate, the first in thirty years, and mulls over whether to entrust her egg after lab fertilisation to a surrogate mother or to carry it herself and take a sabbatical. After all, they promised it could be done either way.

It is a huge investment, she knows, but rationalises that not only has she earned the right to treat herself to the best but in the unlikely event that her business did go bankrupt, a natural birth and simple paternity check would ensure Aidan paid serious maintenance money as the father. Was she ruthless enough to do that to him? To anyone else but...

She never made quick decisions in the past and wouldn't do that now, returning instead to the technology, running her fingers along a music station, awakening to the sensation and tingle of something that had been dormant since her twenties. Had she sublimated motherhood?

She finds herself unable to decide what to do. Not about pregnancy, but whether to play one of Aidan's songs or watch either of his magnificent films. No, the documentary. It makes him more real, domestic and close enough to touch. Farrow wriggles under the duvet like she's a teenager and won't sleep tonight for dreaming that Aidan feels the same about her. By midnight she's decided and is transferring currency.

The Genealogy Club in the long, hot summer at Lentwetter's Social Club and Library was somewhere you ended up in Trentsville when you'd reached school leaving age but still weren't allowed to buy drink for a good half a lifetime more. Time passes slowly in this situation, sagebrush slow. Charlie, the club volunteer and amateur student of the comedic tradition, was acutely aware of the dust that accumulated in his own throat by seven each evening and had also seen the effects of tainted home brew on local people who didn't have enough distraction in their lives. It was time to distribute the testing kits.

'Now everyone read the instructions carefully, then I'll go through them on the board'. Were they listening? He supposed so, but their attention might soon be on the drift. 'If you get this wrong, the others will have their results two whole weeks ahead of you.'

Pachu'a was listening intently. Not every male in their 20s would be interested in genealogy and its utility for proving legal relationships, except the few who would discover the power of that particular science at the wrong end of paternity cases, but Pachu'a (who'd changed his name from Jon. His mother had chosen to Americanize him, but when he moved north he found it was slang for the lavatory, so reverting to a Hopi name meant no surprises) had something he wanted to prove, with evidence, not long interruptions.

When the Hopi lands were designated under the ownership of the native community, the people who lived there were ascribed a level of autonomy, by which they could set different rules than the regulations which applied to the lands surrounding them. This suited the Hopi fine, as they maintained a special and sometimes spiritual relationship to certain wild vegetable crops, but it was only with the advent of tax-free gambling that they found their modern niche. Hopi casinos became big business in just a few years and have made their owners wealthy, but to qualify as an owner with a community share of the casino, you had to meet one exceptional qualification: To be a Hopi.

Pachu'a was the first to spit a copious delivery of saliva into his tube. He'd studied this process.

'Hi. I'm Gretchen. Gretchen Clusterbaker.'

'Do your family bake clusters?' replied Pachu'a, with feigned concern.

'Uh, no. Duh. My ancestors maybe did but there's no point doing that now; you'd get undercut by importers. I work in the bowling park. What are you in for?'

'In for? I am establishing my native heritage.'

'Proving it, not running away from it? The employment figures for native Americans are screwy.'

'No, not running. I want to know who I am', said Pachu'a with finality, as an unimpressed Gretchen drooled phlegm into her receptacle.

More voices, more reasons. 'You're doing well Bernie and so are you Tabitha. Do you want to tell everyone your reason for learning more about your heritage?', Charlie asked them.

Tabitha waited to see if Bernie would answer and spoke up when he didn't. 'It's gonna tell me if Dad is really Dad.'

'It will do that', Charlie answered, 'but are you sure you want to know?' Tabitha went quiet but it was too late as she'd already spat and couldn't get a refund. 'Bernie?'

'It's for medical reasons'.

'An inherited condition?', Charlie replied, realising he shouldn't go into such questions. 'If you have markers from both parents... for...?' He really, really shouldn't ask.

'I can't eat chillies.' A laugh breaks the group's reserve.

'Lucas, how about you?'

'The usual. Which part of Africa.' Lucas leans back in his seat, cross-armed, defensive.

'Ruth?'

'Which part of Venus.'

She's funny, thinks Charlie. The practical joke will be so much harder to go through with now because he likes them all. Such good kids. What the hey – comedy must be performed or this town would get boring.

Two weeks later and Floors 5, 3, 2 and 1 were in uproar.

'Oh shit, oh shit.'

'Is that you, CEO Willis? Are you locked in the washroom?'

'Oh shit oh shit screwit, crap dogs!'

'Have you got a dog in there? Is it scratching you?'

'Who is that?', rebounded the most senior voice in the company.

'Tina Heller-Minchkin, Sir. If there's a personal injury in the cubicle, I can be very discreet handling it. I've got cold cream in my bag and might even have some treats.'

'What? Non-ATCG DNA, that's the damn problem! It's FJVR!'

'Sir, they're not even nitrogenous bases. I can assure you there's no such thing as FJVR DNA.'

'Not on this planet, Helluva-Minchkin.'

Back in the olden days long before the internet, when golfers couldn't stop their trousers flapping, a visionary by the name of Carl Sagan received a letter from a provocateur who claimed to have come from another planet and offered to satisfy any test that would evidence it. In reply, Sagan asked to see non-ACTG DNA (all animals and plants on planet Earth are coded from the bases adenine, guanine, cytosine and thymine), which abruptly ended the correspondence.

The thing is, all Earth life has a common ancestor. In addition, all Earthling animals share the same body design of one head at the top (or front if on all fours), a central spinal axis, symmetrical rib cage, four limbs and smaller bones on the end of those. To determine a non-terrestrial animal, you only have to look for a completely different design than the ribcage, head and limb pattern we would be expecting because that's what we know from here.

Of course, if aliens could mimic our bodies, print new ones or decant themselves into a mould, we would be stymied for a visual identification – but – DNA made from *a different set of chemical markers* would be decisive. That's what Sagan asked for. Back to the lab and a flustered technician's meeting:

'It arrived in a batch from a small town called Trentsville in Kansas. The only thing I could find online is it was founded by someone called Trent, when his wagon broke down and he had to stay there and then someone else's waggon broke down and they kind of got acquainted and the place grew on them...'

'Contamination?', asked Willis.

'There's no sign of that – or rather, I don't think it is

possible.'

'Not by a state actor, to discredit us?'

'Not even then. It would be the greatest achievement in scientific history to make a working genome from different chemical bonds and bases. It doesn't even curve clockwise. Probability theory rules this biology must have evolved independently.'

'Is there a legal requirement to inform the Capitol?'

'If you do, sir, we will need enough time to re-label the core samples in the lower lab before they confiscate everything.'

'Authorised. That's re-label, remember, not lose.' The CEO passed into a state of soulful reflection.

'We will never get any more Bowie jiff.'

When you live in a small town in the middle of nowhere in particular and the lazy days of summer don't contain quite the fireworks you had expected, the sing-song sameness of it all can begin to pall. Watch with me now as Lucas appears in the distance, walking home. Pottering along the edge of a wheat field he goes, listening to the natural insect drone of the summer. Not for him, headphones; they give him a rash.

'Hey, Lucas! What did you do?' – and there's Gretchen, leaning out of the window of her parents' car as it passes.

'Huh?'

Gretchen points enthusiastically at a parked black car as she whizzes past it. 'It's the Feds! Run, Lucas, run! Ha-ha-ha.'

'Get lost', he shouts back at her receding bumper.

Taking account of his situation, Lucas registers three parked cars, not one. Knowing in his logical mind he's done nothing wrong, Lucas still feels a minor blink of universal anxiety that he doesn't want to be set up for anything he hasn't. The synchronised opening of car doors tips the balance. Tense, daunted by the attention of strangers, Lucas hurls pell-mell across the field, crunching the baked earth beneath him – and then pulls up short. There are now six cars around the field and a van with lines or bars across the back window. WTF?

'What do we know about the supposed family?' asks a pair of dark glasses.

'There's not much in central records, sir. They've kept a

low profile, paid their taxes on time. A couple of traffic violations and his father unsuccessfully applied to copyright the term Electric Boogaloo in 1981.'

'I knew there was something un-American about that dance.'

'Should I bring him down sir? With the tranquiliser?'

'No, put that thing back in the vehicle. We don't know what it could do to his physiology. We'll walk toward him slowly, showing him open hands.'

'That's not the protocol, sir.'

'The protocol, dumb-ass, was written for humans.'

Fourteen days, that's how long the Federal Biohazard Investigation Team and several shifts of staff from the Bureau detained Lucas. Fourteen days of questioning, sleep deprivation and good cop/bad cop needling.

The first thirteen days had impressed them, how well this species played the part and appeared to the casual onlooker to be completely human, how they never broke or changed their story, how they got the dialect and cultural references spot on, even when thrashing under water, or when subjected to invasive cavity probing. In short, despite a few knocks to hurry things along, Lucas's head didn't crack open and, disappointingly for the federal team, no wiggly tentacles or razor-sharp teeth came out.

Yes, they concluded, this was either awesome resolve or exceptional mimicry through superb training, so they did it to the squealing Gretchen too for good measure because she'd warned him. They sent a tickly robot millipede up her nose.

Bernie and Tabitha checked out and Pachu'a had recently moved to a penthouse on a reserve, which was out of their mandate, untouchable, so every possible accomplice who had supplied a DNA sample to that lab had now been eliminated.

Toward the back end of fourteen, someone eventually thought to re-test Lucas.

'The new test says he's 100 percent human.'

'What? Oh my god. Some bastard mixed the samples up!', the agent raged, struggling to accept that any species could have hoodwinked this whole operation. 'Those kids are gonna sue us.'

'I think they will do that, sir.'

'What about the Electric Boogaloo?'

'Human origin, sir. The President's Office checked with Chaka Khan.'

When Lucas is finally loaded with apologies and allowed to go home on a federally-confiscated Greyhound bus, he limps resentfully back from the Trentsville stop and along a field-side margin that would never again be the same.

Charlie, a former Lentwetter's Social Club and Library volunteer, sits far away on the distant scrub with another of his kind alongside him.

'See what they did? Those monsters?'

'Yes, that is how they would treat us, but worse, so we cannot reveal ourselves to them yet. Humans are not dignified or mature enough a species and who knows how they will behave when they are introduced to the people of Plurp.'

'Agreed.'

'We can see if their maturity has changed after our 21 year each way round trip home. You will stay here, but you must be unnoticed.'

'I understand. I think I've always known they are an odd race but the experiment had to be attempted, the chance to show their worth had to be given.'

'We will do something for the poor boy who was hurt by these fools, but it cannot jeopardise our incremental alignment with their culture.'

'Yes. Alignment is the way, to lessen the shock they will experience. I think I even prefer their language to ours now. I feel strangely self-conscious when I have to revert back to all that clacking and whistling through the ventral and rectal ducts.'

'Anything else?'

'I like dancing, very much. You have no idea, yet, how difficult it is to synchronise movement on two legs with handfuls of toes getting in the way all the time and simultaneously holding the bladder and breathing in and out. When you get those things the wrong way around, it can be devastating.'

'Noted.'

'I find it pleasant here, when they let you alone. Ice cream is of course poisonous and their simulacrum of eee-deees, which they call swans, have no antennae or larval stages *and* they're the wrong way up. I like banjo music very much, but not drums because they hurt me. There's one song called *Lucky Boy* by an Aidan Grange – that's very good. I hope he gets some luck.' He mulled before continuing.

'Have you see those powerful trees called oaks? They have such magnificent shapes and can really hold the soil, which is a boon in case of gravity inversion. I also like ocean sunlight zones, the top 30 feet, and reading novels by unusual minds.

Have you ever seen an octopus in a bottle with one big eye against the glass? I'll never tire of that, so like our entertainers, or when the humans engage in a full-blown Twitter-spat. Remarkable language, economy of emotion.

Jokes are more difficult. I'm writing a thesis on them. I still can't get my mind around puns and suspect they might be the high point of human culture. In England, they have a place called Wareham Down and they tell me that's not a pun but it is funnier than most other jokes I've recorded.'

'Noted. We will monitor the settlement and relocate it off-world if it is a hindrance.'

'You can also tell those podlings printing body vessels for us back on the mothership that they can't just pour our cells into a shape without first checking the literature on internal anatomy. I mean, why is my brain between my legs?'

'Respected literature by one Virginia Woolf states clearly that this location is the origin of male thinking.'

'Tell them not to believe the first source they find on the internet then. Incidentally, livers aren't supposed to broadcast anything – that's not their function at all.'

'Not even your allergies?'

'No, nothing, and ribs are supposed to be connected at both ends, otherwise when you take three good breaths you inflate like a puffer fish and everyone runs away from you. Except kittens. Expansion fascinates kittens for some reason.'

'You've gone native, my pod-sibling.'

'I suppose I must have.'

At a tidy office block, in the leafy business district of a city comfortably far away, photons stream from the sky and an inexplicable hole the diameter of a pencil burns, pierces and pushes through the roof, floors, concrete and girders of a building occupied only by a defenceless genetic heritage testing company. With elegant point-to-point accuracy, the spearlight flickers out and a luminous runny tinkle of plasma which follows vaporises one lab.

A GLORIOUS PIECE OF CHOCOLATE CAKE

Young Adult Sci-Fi by Leticia Toraci

Fatima was at the same time a housewife and a higher dimensional entity. She sat in the passenger's seat while her husband drove. The radio was playing a pop song as she looked outside at the usual landscape. Same old, same old, she was thinking when she was mind-called:

'They have surrounded the planet!' Zarkov, the commander of The Planetary Systems Alliance's fleet told her.

Fatima closed her eyes. Soul travelling was possible with open eyes, which in school had made others think she was quite deranged, but a battle was something for which she would need her whole concentration. She floated out of her body, out of the car and out of Earth to the vacuum of space. To be bodiless was not an unpleasant sensation at all; it was quite liberating.

'I'm here, Commander', she thought. In fact, she had caused waves on the vibrational plane all around her just by being in the higher dimension, so announcing her presence was unnecessary but it was difficult to let human habits go.

Her out-of-body state allowed her to see 360 degrees in all directions, so she immediately realised the situation. A large armada of faster-than-light battle ships and a hollowed out asteroid-ship as big as the moon approached the Earth. So many ships would have enough reptilian soldiers to kill all humans in the planet, but they were not the major problem.

No, the prime enemy was their leader, a huge higher dimensional humanoid dragon pissed off enough to leave its nest inside the asteroid and run towards her through the vacuum of space, moving much faster than his armada. The PSA soldiers called these beings Destroyers because they could destroy an entire fleet with their raging higher dimensional energy. The dragon came towards her with red fierce eyes, prepared to destroy.

Uncountable ships around the planet had become engaged in a colossal battle. Some ships of the people on Earth's side flew away, avoiding the enemy's blasts only thanks to their piloting art, whilst others held their ground, but the Destroyer dragon would eventually tip the scales because it was a lion in a field full of much smaller wild cats. The defenders of Earth had their claws but, in a battle, size mattered.

Fatima flew on towards the Destroyer; meanwhile the dragon broke its run, not expecting its prey to move towards it. She shouted: 'You are invading my planet.' I will die, but so be it, she thought, until she heard something inside telling her she would not die today. The spirit of the Universe felt like an infinite golden sea, full of love and wisdom, where all beings who still had a soul lived. Her connection was still there, even if in her life as a human she had forgotten it existed.

Her spirit was one tiny tendril of the Universe, like a thin paintbrush in the hands of an infinitely gifted artist. Fatima was still herself but also one of the Universe's tools, in the right place to save the planet. A long time ago, in one of her cosmic lives, she had also been a humanoid dragon like her enemy and she could be a humanoid destroyer dragon again if the Universe so desired.

The gigantic destroyer dragon noticed what had happened. 'I'm sorry', it said, then lowered its head fearfully. 'Let's be friends, shall we?' It extended one hand full of claws and a business card toward her. 'I see that you are powerful too. We don't have to fight now' – but Fatima saw beyond its deceptions.

The dragon was nothing but a bully. It attacked only when victory seemed certain, when it saw a rich planet like Earth without enough technology to defend itself. It was only pretending to be friendly to gain time and come back later, with a bigger fleet. She felt not only her own anger at the deception but also something much beyond her, the wrath of thousands of beings enslaved and killed by the empire to which the humanoid dragon belonged.

Fatima closed her clawed fists. 'Coward', she said. 'You didn't want to be friends when you saw only a woman floating in space but you won't fight one of your own. Stand-up and face me with honour or die.'

The dragon lowered its head again. This fake display of humbleness further enraged the being Fatima had turned into. 'Coward!' she roared, extending her right arm and opening her fist. 'Die!'

The humanoid dragon exploded into a thousand particles. When its still numerous fleet saw what had happened, they withdrew in panic and disarray; but Fatima did not go after them.

She preferred enemies who would, for decades to come, tell hushed stories of the higher dimensional dragon who had defended Earth. Besides, the power of the Universe was for defence only.

Her higher dimensional body turned back to its fragile and humble human form while she sighed and left the battlefield. Back to Earth, back to her passenger's seat.

She stretched, then looked at her husband and smiled.

'What are you smiling at?', Fatima's husband asked, frowning at yet another weird thing his wife did. 'Could you at least try to behave normally?'

'OK', she said. 'You know, I think I deserve a glorious piece of chocolate cake.'

Her husband snorted and shook his head. 'Now, where did that come from?'

TIME OUT

by Eileen Moynihan

Meg lifted her head off the pillow and looked at the clock. It was only 5:30 am and the birds were twittering madly outside. It was as if they knew people were acting strangely and the world had suddenly changed. They were relishing having their own space, no people to annoy them, no noisy cars and aeroplanes with noxious fumes. For once they could live the way they wanted to live and were meant to be.

Now the sun was shining through the slats of the window-blind and making patterns on the wall. 'Come on, get up and come out to play', they said cheerily or appeared to be saying.

It was no good, she would have to get up. Meg sat on the side of the bed and stretched out her arms and legs. She threw on a light dressing-gown and made her way downstairs to the kitchen. The first thing on her mind was a cup of tea. She could never function properly until she had had that first cup of tea in the morning. That first sip was always heavenly and had to be savoured.

'Mmm, that's better', Meg said aloud. Next, she made some porridge in the microwave oven and scattered some raspberries on top. She decided she would have her breakfast in the garden, so went outside to sit at the table with her bowl of porridge and cup of tea. Meg felt the warmth of the rising sun on her body and listened to the sounds of nature all around her, feeling at peace for a few minutes, which was very rare these days.

After her breakfast, Meg planned the day in her head. She would get some washing done, clean out a drawer, stop for lunch, do some weeding, shower, read for a while, cook dinner, do a page or two of writing and then watch television. It felt like a good proposition.

Meg managed to get the washing done and hung it out in the sun. She cleaned the drawer and was going to take a coffee break when the doorbell rang. The postman waved through the glass door of the porch and placed a parcel just outside. She waved back, opened the door and picked up the parcel.

Meg took the unexpected package into the kitchen and opened it with the help of a pair of scissors. There was a simple cardboard box inside. She used the scissors again to break the tape that was all around the box, then prised the lid off carefully. It was a jigsaw puzzle!

Before Meg investigated any further she remembered to wash her hands. As she washed them thoroughly, she pondered on who had sent the jigsaw and why there was no picture to follow on the box.

Meg took another look at the jigsaw. There were a lot of dark pieces that looked the same. This puzzle will take me ages, she thought, leaving it on the kitchen table as she prepared a light salad for lunch. Whilst eating her lunch, Meg decided to keep to the plan for the day but every time she ticked off something on her list she would take out a few jigsaw pieces with an outside edge. So, she went about her business and managed to extract quite a few outside pieces from the jigsaw, which she had spread out on the table. That night she decided to give herself more time the next day to really make progress with the jigsaw. The weather forecast was for rain anyway.

The early morning was cloudy so Meg tackled the jigsaw straight after breakfast and became totally absorbed in the task. Before she knew it, it was mid-morning and she still hadn't dressed. Meg had an online meeting at noon so she reluctantly went off to have a shower and find clothes but, as she went out of the kitchen door, she turned back to admire what she had achieved so far and smiled.

After her meeting, Meg made herself a sandwich and started to do the jigsaw again. It was pouring with rain outside and the wind was tossing the trees around. It was a change from the run of hot weather they had been having. This made Meg feel less guilty about just doing the jigsaw and she convinced herself that she would get on with some housework later.

So far she had made the frame of the jigsaw and had started building up a few areas connected to the edges. She had started trying to put the different shades of darkness into groups, hoping that they would match together. By the end of the day, Meg felt she was beginning to make progress.

The jigsaw was becoming an obsession; she found herself dreaming about it and not wanting to be interrupted by her phone, online meet-ups or boring household chores. Every piece fitted was an achievement, every area that was expanded got her excited. The only problem was, she was running out of food and needed to go shopping.

Lately, she had been visiting the local town once a week for a big shop. She was always diligent in taking her homemade mask and disposable plastic gloves. She knew it would be a long wait to get into the supermarket, so stoically took her place in the queue, keeping two metres away from the person in front of her. Meg didn't want to do that today. Then she had a brainwave, she would get her shopping delivered and have her milk brought regularly too. Now that she came to think of it, she was feeling hungry. Instead of cooking, she decided to get a takeaway meal delivered from a local restaurant which had managed to keep going by offering that service. She ordered spaghetti carbonara and made out a shopping list to be ordered in the morning.

Meg really enjoyed not having to cook and the meal was delicious. It also meant there was no washing-up to do, so, as soon as she had eaten, she carried on with the jigsaw. Keeping going at it until the early hours of the morning, she eventually realised that she was tired and reluctantly rolled into bed, where she fell into a deep sleep.

Meg didn't wake up until 10 am the next morning and couldn't believe she had slept in that late. She suddenly thought of the jigsaw and that motivated her to get moving. She slipped on her dressing-gown and went downstairs to make a cup of tea and, once she had the tea in her hand, she was ready to tackle the jigsaw yet again.

The jigsaw was half-finished now and Meg could clearly see that it was going to be a man's face. The chin definitely looked familiar, so she wondered if it was some famous celebrity.

Meg decided to only do the jobs that were necessary around the house and to have a microwave dinner, so she could carry on with the jigsaw. She looked for the pieces for the eyes and nose, to start forming the face, gathering the most likely pieces and placing them together. As she did so, she noticed some very faint small letters on some of the shapes. This whetted her appetite to finish the jigsaw more than ever.

Throughout the day, she would stop on the hour and do any job she needed to do and then went back to the jigsaw, until the next task. The face began to take shape and the letters formed into words as Meg began to see whom the jigsaw portrayed. She stopped and took a deep breath. She felt tears pricking her eyes and her stomach started to do somersaults. Meg forced herself to continue. What would the words say? Who sent the jigsaw? Was he dead or alive?

She knew it was Brendan in the jigsaw. As she discovered each piece of his features and his face began to form, Meg felt a rush of overwhelming love and pain in her heart. The words began to connect and make sense too. She made out the words, YOU, LOVE, ALWAYS, HEART. The words were small and faint as if on purpose, as they seemed to contain a secret message just for her. By nightfall, Meg was exhausted with the emotions with which she was dealing and from the effort to finish the jigsaw. She went to bed fairly early and slept a fitful sleep.

She woke early to the sound of tractors. It was a busy time for the farmers despite most people being unable to work. Meg just knew she had to finish the jigsaw today. She took a deep breath and got up, made her usual cup of tea and forced herself to start... she did want to finish but was half afraid too... what would be the outcome of finishing?

There at last was his beautiful face and she read the words slowly: YOU WILL NEVER LEAVE MY HEART AND I WILL ALWAYS LOVE YOU, MEG. A tear rolled down her cheek followed by another one and another; they dropped in quick succession after that but she smiled and felt loved.

She had believed Brendan to be dead, as he had disappeared one day and she'd never seen or heard from him again. It was as if he had vanished into thin air and there was no reason she could fathom for him to leave her... their hearts had been one. Now she wondered, was someone playing a cruel trick, or were they attempting to be kind? Whatever the reason behind the gift, because indeed she had come to feel it was a gift, she had decided she would have to frame it.

Meg went online to look up frames she could order, as all the local stores were closed except for the supermarkets. She had measured the jigsaw very carefully to make sure she chose the exact frame she needed, when her eyes fell on a beautiful gold frame that was simple but worthy of holding her beloved. She clicked on the purchase button and felt satisfied, then Meg slept soundly that night.

It took three days for the frame to arrive. In the meantime Meg had been trying to catch up with jobs around the house and garden, contacting friends and family. She didn't feel alone anymore and the day the frame came she couldn't wait to get the jigsaw inside and hang it up. She hummed to herself as she carefully slipped the jigsaw from the table onto a piece of cardboard that had been cut to the exact measurements of the frame. She slowly lifted the cardboard along with its precious cargo, gently inserting it into its frame and behind the glass. Ever so slowly she turned it over whilst holding the cardboard and jigsaw in place. Then she turned each little metal tab to hold the whole thing together, taped the back of the frame and then turned the whole thing back over to look. Perfect! Before long, the jigsaw took pride of place on her kitchen wall. She found herself looking at it constantly and smiling.

A couple of days passed and Meg was experiencing a feeling of peace and calmness that she hadn't felt for a long time. She began to write with an intensity and joy, knowing she would create something beautiful; she just felt it. Meg was busily typing away at her intended novella when the doorbell rang. It was the wrong time of the day for the postman and she hadn't ordered anything. Curious, she got up and went to see who it could be.

Standing outside the glass door of the porch was... Brendan! Her hand flew to her mouth as he indicated to her to open the door. Meg opened it with fumbling fingers and, forgetting all about social distancing, threw her arms around him and hugged him tightly. He hugged back and then held her out from him...

'I can explain...', he said.

HELP US

by Jim Hamilton

Krell awoke to the strident sound of the warning klaxon blaring throughout the ship. 'That's not good', he said to himself, as he sat up in his bunk and wiped the sleep from his eyes. A glance at the chronometer told him that it was still the middle of his sleep cycle. He tapped his communicator, 'This is Krell. Will someone please tell me what the drek is going on?'

'We've lost life support, Captain', replied his second in command.

He sighed, 'Turn off the alarm, Rexx. I'll be right there.' After drawing on some pants and deck shoes, he made his way to the bridge. He glanced at the indicators on the status display, 'How come the secondary hasn't kicked in?'

'That is the secondary, Cap'n, remember?'

Krell frowned, 'I thought we ordered a replacement unit about a hundred cycles ago.'

'We did, Cap'n. It's still on back order.'

'So, how long until we can get it fixed?'

Rexx shook his head, 'We can't fix it.' He glanced at the display, 'And, in about thirty ticks from now, it's going to start getting a bit stuffy in here.'

Krell pursed his lips, 'So, we don't have enough atmo to get anywhere before we run out and even on a good day, field support wouldn't get here in time.'

Rexx nodded, 'We've only got the one option, as I see it, Cap'n. We need to land somewhere on the planet.'

Krell tapped his communicator, 'Zarn! If you're not already headed here, would you please come to the bridge?'

Before he even completed the request, his chief technician stepped into the room, 'What's up with the alarm?' He glanced at the status board, 'I warned you that the power diode was going to blow sometime soon.'

'Yes, you did', sighed Krell. 'Now, if we can move past your "I told you so" moment, I need you to figure out the best place to land.'

Zarn took a seat at the navigator's station and connected his link to the on-board network. Several virtual displays were projected into the area above the console. He looked at Krell, 'Any particular parameters? Or just pick some random place where we're not likely to be bothered?'

'Just find an isolated place, for now. The important thing is to get to some breathable atmo as soon as possible.'

Zarn nodded, 'How about the middle of this desert here?' He pointed to one of the displays.

'That's looks as good as any, I suppose', said Krell, sitting down in the pilot's seat. 'If everyone will kindly buckle themselves in, we will be departing this location in one tick from now. Please return your seats to their full upright position.' After they had complied, he accelerated toward the distant planet, their cloaking shield preventing them from being detected by the primitive species that lived there.

Harry woke up as the sun was just peeking over the flat horizon. After relieving his nearly full bladder, he made his way into the kitchen and fired up the coffee maker. He dropped two slices of whole-wheat bread into the toaster and cracked three eggs into a skillet. By the time his toast was ready, he had scrambled the eggs and dumped them onto a plate. Some butter and strawberry jam from the refrigerator completed his preparations and he turned on the flat-screen TV mounted on the wall to see what CNN thought about the world. He idly flipped through other news channels as he sat and ate his breakfast, shaking his head over the current events that were covered.

Breakfast out of the way, Harry left the kitchen area with a cup of coffee and settled into his nest, as he liked to call it. Occupying fully one half of his double-wide trailer, it was a combination studio and research library. A dozen flat screens surrounded his desk upon which were mounted several microphones and cameras. It was from here that he broadcast his video blog to the rest of the world, keeping everyone abreast with the latest discoveries of UFOs.

His YouTube channel had more than two hundred thousand subscribers and had been steadily growing since he first went on the web four years earlier. He logged into his various social media accounts and was pleased to see more than a dozen serious responses since last night. He got thousands of comments a day, but ninety-nine percent of them were of the negative type referring to tinfoil hats and the whatnot. He didn't care. It was like separating the wheat from the chaff. As he viewed the attached photos, two of them caught his eye and he linked them into his vlog display feed. Still five minutes away from airtime, he went back into the kitchen for a refill of his coffee.

As he set his mug down, he noticed a large cockroach on the end of the counter. Moving slowly, he picked up a copy of the *Roswell News* and rolled it into a tube before bringing it down suddenly and decisively on the big insect. Mopping up the mess with a paper towel, he filled his mug and returned to his nest.

Once Krell had the ship on the ground, they opened up the airlock and used the air handlers to recirculate breathable gasses inside the ship.

'Now that we've got things stabilised, what's our next course of action?' he asked his two crewmates.

'We can fix our scrubber module with an off-the-shelf part we can get almost anywhere', said Zarn. Seeing their looks of disbelief, he explained, 'It's a low-tech component that's failed. The rest of the module is fine.'

'Can't we get one from some other circuit we don't need?' asked Rexx.

'Nothing like what's required.'

'So, how do we go about getting one?' asked Krell. 'Can we just use the drones to fetch one?'

Zarn shook his head, 'While we could hunt around for an exception. They are generally kept in places where it would be difficult to remove from the premises and even more difficult to bring it to us.' He smiled, 'It's not like we can just park anywhere that we want to.'

'So, what do we do?' asked Krell.

'We could enlist the help of one of the natives to procure one for us', replied Zarn.

Rexx laughed, 'Just like that!'

'Yes', nodded Zarn, 'Just like that.' He swiped his hand, 'Meet Harry Zingleton.' They watched the holo-feed from their drone as Harry fixed and ate his breakfast, oblivious to the alien presence on his kitchen counter.

'It's part of my job to keep tabs on their technological development, you know. For the past one hundred sols, they've managed to envelop their planet in electromagnetic radiation of all sorts. Starting with only a few dispersed transmitters, they now have one for nearly everyone on the planet. Natives from all walks of life are now interconnected in ways that they've never been before.'

'Is there a point to this?' asked Krell, impatiently.

Zarn smiled, 'Harry, here, sits in front of a microphone and camera every day and talks about UFOs — Unidentified Flying Objects. He claims to have seen one as a child and has never given up hope of being contacted.'

They watched the feed as Harry came back into the room. All three of them gave a slight jump when he suddenly crushed their probe.

'You want this native to help us?' asked Krell, somewhat incredulous.

Zarn started laughing, 'Well, I must say I didn't see that coming!'

Harry finished his one-hour vlog with a reminder to buy his book and a promise that today's video would be available as a podcast sometime this afternoon. He stood up and stretched before taking a bathroom break and getting a refill of his coffee. When he returned to his desk, he stopped and stared at the cockroaches lined up on his notepad. He was fastidiously neat and had never had a problem with roaches before but now it was like he was being invaded or something.

After his initial shock, he realised that they were arranged to spell out HELP US in large letters. He looked around his trailer suspiciously, knowing that he was all alone.

'Help who?' he asked loudly, not expecting a reply. The cockroaches scurried around as more joined them from under his computer. They rearranged themselves to spell out SECRET.

'You want me to keep this secret?' he asked. This time it was a double-wide cockroach font that said YES.

'Okay, I can do that', promised Harry. 'Who are you? Where are you?' He watched as the roaches rearranged themselves again, with more running out from underneath his amplifier to spell out WE ARE ALIENS. After a moment, more joined them and transformed the words into WE NEED YOUR HELP.

'Aliens! I knew it!' exclaimed Harry, a big grin on his face. 'And if anyone finds out, they'll want to capture you and do vivisections on you, right?' Again, the bolded reply of YES. Harry nodded, 'Don't worry, I won't tell a soul. Just tell me what I need to do to help you out.'

The cockroaches rearranged themselves into WE NEED A PART FROM AMAZON. After a few moments, they rearranged themselves into a product number which Harry jotted down on a slip of paper.

'I've got it!' he said, excitedly. The insects scurried off leaving behind enough roaches to spell out THANKS. 'No problem', assured Harry.

With that being said, the rest disappeared from sight. Harry stood there for a few long moments wondering if it had all been a hallucination. The whole interaction had taken less than a minute. He stared at the paper in his hand with the part number and shook his head. 'No', he told himself, 'It was definitely aliens.' He sat down at his computer and logged into his Amazon account, oblivious to the hundreds of eyes that were watching him.

'Well, that was pretty interesting', said Krell. 'How did you know that he would be so cooperative?'

'I've had my eye on him for some time now. He hates humanity and would gladly do anything to protect an innocent alien from the rest of the world', answered Zarn. 'That includes us, of course.'

'So, we should have the part we need in a couple of days?' asked Rexx.

'That's my understanding', said Zarn. 'For a species that's lacking in teleportation technology, they've managed to come up with a fairly decent replacement.'

'How much longer do you give them?' asked Rexx.

Zarn pursed his lips, 'I'm not sure. Maybe five or ten years at most. Right now, they're going through some pretty rough times.'

'It'll be good to get this project wrapped up and go home again', said Krell. 'These primitives have some unique stages in their development that should pique the interest of a lot of our consumers.'

Zarn grinned, 'Oh, I think that this one's going to be a really big hit. We might even get an award for it.'

Krell looked interested, 'An award? Do you honestly think it's that good?'

'I do. At least it will be once they've killed themselves off for good.'

The three of them were sitting around the conference table holding hands. When in a mind-meld session, they could communicate directly from one mind to the other almost instantaneously. Their whole conversation since they had said THANKS to Harry had only taken a fraction of a second. Sharing information and learning new things were both accomplished by direct mind interaction. When they were finished here, the data that they were collecting about this planet Earth would be compressed and packaged for infotainment upload.

'When was the last time that you guys got an update?' asked Zarn.

'I don't know', answered Krell, 'Maybe fifty sols?'

'Same here, I guess', said Rexx.

'I think it's time that you got all caught up. They've made a lot of progress in a very short time.' Seeing their nods of agreement, he said, 'Okay then, standby for update.'

A moment later, Rexx nodded, 'I see what you mean.' He looked at Zarn, 'You really think that they'll last another ten years?'

'At the most.' He shook his head, 'Their technology has far outstripped their social ability to utilise it properly. It's only a matter of time.'

'What a story', commented Krell. 'Ten thousand years to go from a few cave dwellers to destroying the planet with its teeming billions.'

'Like I said, it might get an award', said Zarn. On that note, he relinquished his grasp on Krell and Rexx, effectively ending their meeting.

Harry hadn't heard anything further from the aliens and he eagerly awaited the delivery of their part. He wasn't sure how to contact them but he suspected that it probably wouldn't be necessary. When the small package finally arrived, his suspicions proved to be correct as the cockroaches once more swarmed out from under the equipment on his desk.

OPEN THE BOX commanded the roaches. Harry happily complied and removed a small blister pack with a two-inch square rectifier.

'Now what?' he asked. The insects rearranged themselves, PUT IT OUTSIDE. More roaches ran out and added, THEN STAY INSIDE.

'Okay', said Harry. He opened the door and set the package on the ground and watched as it was swarmed with cockroaches. Closing the door, he walked back to his desk. THANKS HARRY, spelled out the roaches. 'They know my name!' he thought to himself, smiling.

'What do I do now?' he asked. WAIT was the reply and so Harry sat down at his desk and waited. After about ten minutes, he felt a low vibration and his trailer shuddered slightly. The cockroaches rearranged themselves one last time and spelled out GOODBYE before finally scurrying away.

He had promised not to tell anyone, but he had wanted proof that this had happened. Yesterday, he had clipped a webcam to his shelf which afforded a clear view of his desk. It had been running this whole time and he eagerly brought up the video recorder screen and began playing it back. When he got to just before he entered the trailer with the package, the camera was suddenly blocked by a cockroach which had crawled onto the lens. 'Seriously?' he uttered out loud. His entire conversation with the aliens had been effectively neutralised with this simple hack. He shook his head as he realised that the cockroaches must have been watching when he placed the camera. 'Oh, well', he said to himself. Keeping his promise was certainly made easier by this turn of events.

He wondered if anyone else had ever experienced an alien encounter via roaches. He exited his video software and began researching the subject. This would be the focus of tomorrow's vlog and he began to get excited about this angle.

The new part was almost identical to their own part. Zarn ground a bit off one of the spade terminals and it fitted precisely into the recess of the old one. Rexx powered up the life support system and one by one, the green tell-tales lit up.

'Looks like we're good to go', he said.

Krell shook his head, 'How unlikely is it that a primitive race of beings in a remote corner of the galaxy would produce the same identical part?'

Zarn laughed, 'Apparently, the odds are not zero.'

They quickly closed the hatch and prepared for take-off. 'Everyone strapped in?' asked Krell.

'Aye, aye, Cap'n', replied both of his crewmates in unison.

'Okay, then, here we go!'

Before long, they were back in their usual orbit within the asteroid belt. Zarn idly brought up one of the feeds with Harry in it. 'Do you suppose he'll figure out the secret of the cockroaches?'

'You mean that they're of alien origin?' asked Rexx.

'Yes', nodded Zarn. 'He's been looking for aliens for a long time and they're literally right under his feet.'

'Technically, they're bio-engineered creations, but I suppose that you could call them aliens', mused Krell.

Zarn agreed, 'They certainly make mapping a planet exceedingly easy. Just sprinkle a few around and wait until they go forth and multiply.'

Krell nodded, 'Speaking of which, I got a message from the home office that they've located a likely planet for our next assignment. They're already seeding the planet with drones and by the time we're done here, intelligent life should be just starting to emerge.'

'Ten more years, eh?' asked Rexx.

'Or maybe only five', smiled Zarn. 'We'll know soon enough.'

LUNAR ILLUSION

by Julia Davenport

'They're going to burn it down, they're going to burn it down. We don't have much time. You need to let me out. They're going to burn it down. They're going to burn it down. None of us are safe. I can see the demons. The demons are over there. Out there in the car park. They're going to set fire to the hospital. Can't you see them. Why don't you see them? Why don't you believe me!'

Next minute I saw the shouting man running naked towards the main double doors, which had two sets of white bars on them and wide bolts. He launched his body at it, headfirst, throwing himself at the doors. He did this several times with reckless abandonment and each time his body hit the smooth, uncarpeted cream floor with a loud smack. He kept getting back up undeterred and with each attempt he was getting more bruised and bloodied. His face and arms were getting the worst of it.

After his fourth or fifth attempt, a team of medical staff and security guards gathered together. A hurried discussion and much pointing and gesturing followed, then they split into pairs and each pair moved towards him slowly. Then as the doctor was speaking to the man, the group formed a circle by joining hands. Half of the circle was formed in front of the double doors and the other half around the back of where the man and the doctor were standing. Then the group stood still, waiting to see what the doctor wanted to do next.

I overheard one of the doctors saying: 'The demons aren't real, Alex. Only you can see them because you're having paranoid delusions. There aren't any demons in the car park and the hospital is safe. You're having an hallucinatory experience but you're quite safe. Maybe you should sit down and have a rest. Have you been taking your medications Alex?'

'No, I didn't forget to take them. I stopped taking them on purpose because I don't need them anymore. I don't need any more stupid, pointless tablets. They don't work on me. They don't work. Now let me out before this place burns down. Let me out. Let me out. Let me out!', screamed Alex.

I felt sorry for the medical staff. They were being gentle and sympathetic with Alex but it was quite clear he was in fear for his life and the last thing he wanted was to sit down.

Alex was tall, white and very thin. I suppose you could say his body was slight and not what you'd call a masculine build, but the forceful passion with which he threw himself at the doors somehow made me admire him. He was clearly tougher than he looked.

I felt sorrier for Alex. His face was white-knuckled pale, like he'd seen hell or Armageddon. He was the most agitated and panic-stricken person I'd ever witnessed in my life.

At this point I started to feel guilty for staring at him. It was like the time I'd seen that car crash into a moped and the moped driver got tossed into the air and landed headfirst on the road and his blood gushed so fast and full on the dark grey, hard concrete. It was like watching a small, red river running free down that dark hilly road. As sad as the sight made me feel, each time I turned away I felt a magnetic desire to look back.

Eventually Alex's sad scene was brought to a close by the team of medical staff and security guards that had gathered around him. With two people sitting one on each of his legs, two sitting on his arms and one big and burly security guard holding his head down, Alex was successfully restrained. The doctor quickly administered a large needle into his arm. Sedation had saved the day and Alex was swiftly lifted onto a bed, strapped down and wheeled off to the isolation ward; the ward where you get your own room, where the door has so many locks on it that it puts Fort Knox to shame.

Feeling traumatised, I look around the room at the other patients. Most of them have relaxed back into a comfortable sleep. Some hadn't even been disturbed. I was shocked by their lack of response. They were either heavily medicated or just used to and unfazed by Alex and his condition.

The next day I was woken up by a woman with a food trolley asking me what I wanted for breakfast. The choice was limited to either eggs and bacon, or toast with tea or coffee. I opted for tea and toast. A simple and safer option I thought, with less chance of developing food poisoning. By 10:30 a.m., breakfast had finished being served. I fell back asleep. Then an hour later I was woken up by a nurse giving out the morning meds.

My tablets were long and thin but I was in no state to argue, so I swallowed them quickly with water. Later that day, way after lunchtime, think it was about 4 o'clock, anyway whatever time it was I awoke from my afternoon nap feeling refreshed. You could say it was the best sleep I'd had in years.

I stretched and yawned, then looked around the ward. In the bed directly to my left was a young woman called Suzy. She was smiling and looking very absorbed with the book she was reading.

It was *Alice in Wonderland*, one of my all-time favourites. Two beds down from Suzy, an older-looking woman was retching and vomiting, loudly and repeatedly all over her bed covers. As I turned to my right, I could see that the women in the first few beds next to me were sleeping soundly. I began to lie down to get cosy in bed again when my nose caught a whiff of a very rank stench. It smelt like someone had a bad stomach and forgot to flush the toilet. I assumed the nurses would deal with it and the smell would be gone soon.

As time went on, the smell got stronger and stronger, it smelt stronger than dog shit and it filled and burned my nostrils, then the vile stench filled my throat and made me cough. I sat up abruptly, coughing and retching. Out of the corner of my eye I could see nurses milling around the last bed on my right. It was about four beds away from mine, directly under the barred windows.

The nurses were moving fast and were using a large metal shovel to scoop up a series of large brown turds. Apparently, the woman in bed fourteen had been shitting on the floor for the last two hours, as she'd been constipated for three days, had taken powerful laxatives and said she didn't have the energy to go to the toilet.

The sight and smell of her human shit knocked me sick. I sprang out of bed and ran fast to the nearest bathroom, which was only about five seconds away, but just as I got to the outer door, I lost control as my stomach lurched and I vomited my last two meals all over the doors and floor.

I was so embarrassed that I raced into the bathroom, locked the door and sat hiding on the loo for about twenty minutes. I felt dizzy and lightheaded and very guilty for spewing chunks on the floor, making even more work for the overburdened medical staff.

The day after that, the ward was less chaotic. I think it was a Saturday. Something about the weekend made people more relaxed, even in a mental health ward. Maybe it was because the standard of food was better at the weekend.

Later that day I was due to have an interview with a psychiatrist at 3:30 p.m. As she approached the reception area, I could see that she was of average height and weight, with toned skin, dark brown eyes and black curly hair. Sort of Spanish looking and she appeared to be in her late forties, with a smile that made you feel safe.

She led me into a medium sized, rectangular shaped room that was framed with fully stacked wooden bookcases from floor to ceiling. The main part of the room comprised two sections: The left side contained a selection of black leather sofas and armchairs, while the right section was more formal with black wooden desks and each desk had executive chairs, one on either side.

We sat in the desk section as the psychiatrist had some paperwork to fill out for my review.

She gathered together her notebooks, pens and questionnaires and then the questioning began.

'Ok, so let's begin. My name is Dr Lily Bryant. I'm the senior psychiatrist at this hospital and I've been practicing for twenty years this year. I just need to check some basic information with you first. So, I've got you down on my list as Jackie Gilligan and your date of birth is listed as the twenty-first of November nineteen seventy-six is that correct?'

'Yeah', I said.

'And you live in South Manchester in a three-bedroom semi-detached house with your mother and older brother, is that right?'

'Yeah', I said again sheepishly.

'And you've been living there for the last twenty-five years and you're not currently engaged in employment or education? Sorry that was two questions', said Dr Bryant, who was clearly running late with her appointments and finding it hard to disguise that she was rushing my interview.

'Yes to the first question and no to the second one', I said, disappointed with my answers.

'Ok that's section one of the questionnaire completed. Now onto section two.

Four days ago you tried to kill yourself. Anything you want to say about that?'

'No', I said.

'Why did you try to commit suicide, Jackie?'

'I didn't try to kill myself', I said in a raised and agitated voice.

'Jackie, I don't mean to alarm you, but four days ago your mother found you unconscious in your bedroom, you were taken to A & E where you had your stomach pumped and the doctors said you had swallowed over 100 paracetamols and washed them down with a large bottle of vodka. What were you planning to do?' Dr Bryant asked, in a matter of fact way.

'I don't know, I just couldn't take it anymore', I said.

'What circumstances in your life, do you think, brought you to the point of suicide?', said Dr Bryant.

'I don't know, lots of things. Do we have to talk about this now?' I said.

'I think it would be good for your mental health to open up and talk about this. It isn't good to keep things bottled up. Opening up about what happened by talking to someone, or writing it down, will help you to make sense of the situation and help us move forward with your treatment', said Dr Bryant with a passionate and sympathetic tone.

I felt tense and couldn't think of a good reply, so I stayed silent in anxious hesitation.

'Maybe we could backtrack a little with the questions. What do you think Jackie?'

'Yeah, ok', I said.

'Have you ever attempted suicide in the past?', Dr Bryant asked.

'No, not really. I used to think about it a lot though', I said nervously.

'Ok. So, looking at your medical file, it says here that you were diagnosed with Depression in October 2004 and you've been taking antidepressants since then. Later, in August 2015, you were diagnosed with Bipolar Type II and since then you've had antipsychotics added to your list of repeat prescriptions, is that correct?' said Dr Bryant.

'Yes, I take 60 mg of Fluoxetine and 300 mg of Quetiapine daily', I said.

'Have you ever had therapy or counselling for your conditions?'

'Yes, in the past I've seen three counsellors, five psychologists, two psychiatric nurses, two CBT therapists and one other psychiatrist', I replied.

'Have you recently experienced any emotional loss, such as the death of a loved one, or a divorce?' said Dr Bryant.

'Yes. Earlier this year. My nephew passed away in January and my dad passed away in February', I said. Then I started to cry and I couldn't stop. I cried and hyperventilated for just over an hour but it seemed like much longer.

Then Dr Bryant said we would continue the interview another time and she telephoned Security for assistance. The last thing I remember that day is being strapped to a bed, injected with something and a nurse telling me I would be alright once the sedative kicked in, all I needed was a good rest and things would look better tomorrow.

The next day was Sunday and I was in a much better mood.

The night before I had dreamt I was back home in the living room when a healthier and younger version of my dad walked in.

'What are you doing I thought you were dead', I said.

He turned to me and answered 'The life force is energy and, as the scientists say, you can't kill energy; it just transfers to another state. In other words I'm just living in another frequency of existence. Also, please don't kill yourself. Your mother needs you. If you want to be happy you need to change your life, not end it. And you have the power to change your life. I believe in you and so does God!', he said.

Then he hugged me and I woke up with tears running down my cheeks. I felt something cold in my hands, so I looked at them and saw a small angel that had been carved in tigers eye crystal.

I don't know how it got in my hands. Then I realised it was a present from dad. His way of telling me to keep the faith. Then I smiled.

THE FINAL CHAPTER

by Hákon Gunnarsson

I finish rolling the joint – it seems to be the only thing that makes the pain go away these days – and I put it in my mouth. My fingers search slightly trembling for the lighter in my pocket but I can't find it. Frustrated, I pick my green typewriter up and look underneath, then at the balcony floor. It's not there. I slam the typewriter down on the table again.

'Damn.'

I sigh and put the joint back into my shirt pocket as I hear a drone fly by. It's a big one, probably delivering something to a house close by. For a moment I sit and look at the tree branch that almost touches the railing. There is a bird in the tree. I'm not sure what kind but its song is pleasant, which is in an interesting contrast to the sky that is so grey and foreboding. When I had a look earlier at the computer, it said that a storm was approaching and it was going to be a bad one. It's not here yet and I write better outside. Well, I did at one time anyway.

I rub my fingers slowly without looking at them. Seriously, I really need to go inside to look for fire, to calm my body, but I just don't feel like getting up. The house is full of people that I don't really want to talk to right now. No more fucking sympathy, thanks. That's what I want to say to them. I don't, of course, but I've kind of had it with the worried looks.

I hear two of them talking inside the house about something that doesn't interest me. Can't they ever just shut up? I want peace and quiet.

For a moment I glance towards the half open door. The brown paint on it is starting to peel as the whole house is slowly decaying. Just like me. I should give up on it but it's the house my parents built in their thirties and the house I grew up in. They are both gone, so maybe the real reason why I can't give up on this house is the fact that it is the last link to my parents – or perhaps it's simply laziness. Having to move all my books somewhere else would take some major effort. Fixing it up would probably take even a bigger effort, but that is another story and one that I'm not going to write.

I take a look at the paper in the typewriter. Two lines, one long, the other shorter. That's all. The result of three hours of work this morning. Two lines that I will may have to cross out because they are no good. I'm never going to finish this final chapter am I? Not that it matters. After forty two years of writing I've reached the point in my career where no one reads me anymore; and I have no more time to change that.

'Hi, Karl.'

I look up and smile at the familiar face. 'What are you doing here, Linda?'

'Can't I come to visit my favourite writer?'

I smile and look at the paper again. 'You know, I'm always happy to see you. You don't need a reason to come and visit me. Well then, what do you think of this?'

She bends over and reads. Then glances quickly at me, before sitting down in the chair next to mine and I see it in her face.

'Okay, I know, I know. It's shit.' I scratch my beard, pull the sheet out of the typewriter with a swift movement and cross the lines out with a pen. Then turn the paper around and put it back in.

'No, no. It's... Yes, you're right, it's not among your best.'

'I just can't find that final chapter, that ending. It's just... somewhere in outer space I guess along with the rest of my brain.'

'Well, that's...'

'I know there is very little point in writing now but I've done this my whole life and I want to finish my career with something that I can be... end it with something that works at least, you know. You don't have a light do you?'

'Eh, no.'

'Of course you don't. You don't smoke, do you? You're too young. You're not an old and grey shit like me, waiting to dive one last time into the earth.'

She doesn't reply. I stare at the blank page for a moment. It's the scariest thing that a writer can face, a blank, unfillable fucking page. Especially when the mind is as blank as the page is. I know this story. It has resided in my brain for three years, the characters have breathed in there, they've argued, they've made love, they've blundered things, had their victories and their sorrows. Basically lived in there 24/7 for years, but the ending is still in a fog. I give up and look at her.

'This is driving me up the wall. I know the story, but...' I stop mid-sentence. 'What's wrong, Linda?'

'Have you seen my dad lately?'

'Not recently, no. I haven't been able to finish this thing here, so I haven't had any reason to go and see him. Why?'

'I don't know.' She turns quiet and looks away. 'I haven't seen him for a week. I got a text five days ago saying that he was going visit Steina and would be back the same night. Since then, nothing.'

'You've gone to the police?'

A deep inhale, then: 'Yes, they weren't exactly helpful.'

'Well, I suppose they are still dealing with the fallout of the riot.'

'I guess, but they weren't interested at all. I mean, they took down the information, the name, what he does for a living, when I'd seen him last and all that, but I gathered missing persons didn't really make their radar at all.'

'You've been to Steina?'

'Yeah, she hasn't seen him for a month and not heard from him in at least two weeks.'

'Strange, he's always been so reliable.' Linda looks older than she did the last time I saw her, probably hasn't been sleeping. I wish I could help her, I really do.

'Yes, he has. You know, I just thought if anyone would know where he was, it would be you.'

'Sorry.'

She sits for a little while longer, bites her lip for a moment. 'I have to go.'

'You came on the bus?'

'Yeah.'

'I'll walk you there.'

I stand, pick up my typewriter, momentarily the pain stops me in my tracks and I close my eyes, but then walk to the door and Linda follows after she's picked up the stack of paper that was on the table. I put the typewriter down with a thud on the chair next to the door. Linda puts the paper down on top of the typewriter and we walk through the living room. Two people are working on something with computers at the table.

'Have either of you seen my lighter?'

Ahmed looks up, then down on the table and picks something up. 'Yeah, you left it here when you went out.' He throws it to me and I catch.

'Thanks mate.'

Linda and I continue to the front door. I feel like I shouldn't leave the house, not now, maybe never, but I have to. I've known Linda before she was born and it pains me that I can't help her, but at least I can walk with her to the bus stop. We walk in silence out of the driveway, turn and head towards the sea where the bus stop is. When we get there I sit down on the bench and look at the water. The sea wall, that ugly eyesore, is still working. For how many years that's going to last I don't know but I think I won't be here when it fails. I haven't got that much time left.

For a while, the government thought it could build a strong enough sea wall to protect the houses here and they tried, they really did, but of course it was a mistake, a delusion and now we are here. The houses are worthless, some already abandoned, others, like mine, full of people that haven't got the money to choose where they stay and people like me that know they haven't got long enough left to start over somewhere else.

I put the joint in my mouth and light up. Finally a little calm for my bones. I close my eyes and feel my breath coming in through my nose, going out through my nose, coming in, going out, coming in, going out. Linda lets me be for a while, just sits there next to me.

'Let me know if you hear anything, Linda.'

'Sure. You know old man, it would be easier if you came back into the present, from wherever you've been for the last few decades.'

'I'm too old Linda and, besides, I don't like the present very much.'

'Neither do I but I still use the technology that it has to offer.'

'You'll find your dad, Linda. No worries. You'll find him.

He's out there somewhere and you'll find him.'

I close my eyes again, put the joint in my mouth and inhale. Then I sit there with my eyes closed and slip into semi-meditation again. Anything that works, right? Time ticks by. Then she touches my left shoulder. 'Karl, the bus is coming.'

I put out the joint and store what remains of my calm in my shirt pocket. 'I'll see you, Linda.' She says her goodbye and gets on the bus.

I stand there like a rotting tree and watch the bus go away. I feel the wind is picking up a little bit. The bus turns the corner and I look towards the sea. I've never liked that sea wall. It looks wrong. It wasn't like this in my youth. I remember playing by the seaside, on the grey beach, the shells, the seaweed, the birds. It's all changed. Now all that I see is an unfinished sea wall that destroys the sea view and didn't even manage to save the property value.

Slowly I walk back towards the house. I stop at the fence. The street up to my house is almost level but still it feels too steep for me. I stand there for a little while. Don't think about it. Think about something else. That final chapter. I still need the ending even if my publisher and friend has gone walkabout; and I need it sooner than later. I'm not going to finish it through a psychic-medium, am I? While I look around at the houses, I go through the story up until where I had got to. It's a pretty good novel, if I say so myself, but it does need some closure. Oh, that bloody pain. I fish the joint out of my pocket and light up again. I start walking again and eventually I get home. The wind has picked up a little more since I left the bus stop.

When I get inside, I meet Ahmed and the others. Most of them have backpacks, or suitcases.

'We have to go.'

'Why?'

'It was on the news. It's going to bad here tonight.'

'We just pack the essentials and then we're off to the crisis centre. You need to pack your stuff and come with us.'

'No, I don't.'

'What do you mean? Everyone is leaving. It's going to hit again here tonight.'

'Yeah, yeah, I know it's going to. I'm not leaving. I'm not ending up at the crisis centre. That's not my ending. Not what I had in mind. This is my house and you can go if you want to, but I'm staying. Right. Here. And that's the end of it.'

'Okay, if you're going to stupid about it, then stay.'

'I'm not stupid Ahmed, I'm just not going to run off every time something happens around here. I'm tired, you know, I really am tired.'

'Okay, suit yourself. If you change your mind, there's one bus after the one that's coming in a couple of minutes.'

'Yeah, sure, thanks'. They leave one by one. I stand there watching them go, see them walk out of the driveway, then I turn and go in. I go into the kitchen to make myself something to eat, but I can't find anything that I feel like having. Nothing looks that tasty. If there is one thing I miss, it's my appetite. Eventually I take a beer out of the fridge and go into the living room. I find my typewriter and take it to the table. I put it down gently, then sit on the chair and start to type.

I manage one sentence before I stop to look at when I have just written. Now, where is this going? I look at the sentence for a little while, then add another and the third one. I nearly manage to get into the rhythm of writing but I stop after an almost half a page, the longest that I have written in some time. I read it, put my hand over my face and rip the paper out of the machine. I crumple it up and throw it onto the floor. I insert a new sheet of paper into the typewriter, put my hands on the keyboard but can't for the life of me figure out what is going to put an end to this chapter. I can't even find the beginning of the end.

For a moment it crosses my mind that perhaps I don't want to finish this damn thing because it's going to be the last thing I ever write. I think about this and shrug it off. No, I'm really not that deep. No, this is an old fashion writer's block. The thing I thought didn't exist, on top of a list of other problems, I've now got that to deal with. I lay back on the sofa, drinking my beer, listening to the wind pick up and become a storm. The good thing is that there is one house between this house and the open ocean so it never becomes quite as bad here. Nearly, but not quite. I put the beer on the table and fish out a joint. Don't even ask me how many I've had today. Probably far too many, but still not enough to really send the pain flying off into outer space for good.

I sit there in a haze or a daze or something like that. Then all of a sudden I remember reading a while back that smoking this shit can add to one's risk of dementia. Lucky me. That won't be a problem. I put the rest of the joint out in the ashtray and snuggle up on the sofa. I'm just going to close my eyes for a moment. I'm tired. I'm really tired.

A couple of hours later I wake up when something hits the house. For a moment I'm out of it. Trying to focus. Trying to find out where I am. Trying to figure out what woke me up. I push the hair out of my eyes, but that doesn't make much of a difference. It still takes me a couple of moments more to realise where I am, then I stand up and walk to the window. The storm is raging like an angry preacher at the sight of a heretic. I look down and I see it. The sea. It's at the house. Some of it has probably got in on the ground floor. For a moment, my foggy mind gets scared that my books may have been damaged but then I remember that I moved most of them to the second floor years ago, when I moved upstairs. They're safe, I guess. They may be safe but my house isn't, that's for sure. It wasn't in great shape to begin with, so with this...

I sigh, turn away from the window and walk towards the hallway. I'm going to have to take a look at the damage. After all, there is no one else to bear witness to all of this but me. No one to fix it but me. There is wind in the house. A broken window somewhere? Probably. I get to the stairs and see a little water seep under the door downstairs. Standing on the last step I open the door. The light switch. I flick it, but no light. The power seems to have gone out. I take the last step down and into the water. The uncomfortably cold water soaks my socks. I want to tiptoe, but the water is too deep for that to matter. So I walk as normally as anyone could in water, indoors. It's not completely dark, but the shadows are deep and heavy. I go into the room on the ocean side. I feel the wind coming in from there. I know this house, this room, but in the dark the room feels alien to me. It like being in an ocean cave just after the sun has set.

Splashing, I walk all the way to the window. It must have been broken by the wave that apparently hit sometime while I slept. Ouch. I've stepped on glass and cut a toe on my right foot. I limp to the sofa and sit down. There, I pick up my foot to have a look. Take the sock off. It's bleeding a little, but at least there is no glass stuck in the cut. I look around. The flooring is going to be even worse once we manage to get all of the sea out. When we get it out. If we get it out... and the window. How am I going to pay for a new window? Maybe I can board it up? Or get one of the others to do it? If they come back, that is. This house is getting too much for me.

Maybe I can find something in the cellar to board up the window? I get up and limp to the stairs. I forget the sock on the sofa. When I get to the stairs I see what I should have realised already; that the cellar is full of water. Still, I walk down the stairs, down into the water, the cold water, the freezing water and I have to turn around. I get up the stairs again. I'm not going. There is no way I could get all the way down there and back up again. Shivering, I get far enough up the stairs to be completely out of the water and I sit down. The pain. The fucking pain. I reach into the pocket for my joint, my hands wet and trembling. Finally I manage to put the joint in my mouth, but I realise that it's got quite soggy. I try. I find the lighter and aim some fire at the wet paper. It doesn't light up. I try again. It's the same thing. So I sit there with the soggy paper in my mouth and the lighter in my right hand.

I should have gone with them. I know that. That would have been the sane thing to do, but my sanity probably left a long time ago. For a long moment I sit there, occasionally glancing into the water. Finally, I get up, climb the stairs and limp my way into the living room where I crumble down on the sofa. The storm is still raging and I'm still tired. My mind races without knowing where to go and then I get up with a jolt and all of a sudden I see in my head what the last chapter really is. It's just this; and for a moment I'm happy. It's done. I can write the ending at last but I don't want to write it like this. I don't want to be depressing. I don't want any sympathy. I don't want... I don't want this.

As I lay back down on the sofa, I hear the front door open and Ahmed call: 'Are you there Karl?'

ABOUT THE AUTHORS

Hákon Gunnarsson is an Icelandic writer that has taken part in some twenty anthologies in Icelandic and in English. He has also published a little book called *Swimming in Space* which is a collection of flash fiction. Despite that, his dog thinks his only job is to feed and walk it. Hákon's books include: *Swimming in Space*, *31 Days of October Volume II: A Haunting Collection of Hallowe'en Tales*, *Smásögur 2017: Drama*, *Flash Fiction Addiction*, *Ellipsis*, *Chronos: An Anthology of Time Drabbles*, *The Binge-Watching Cure*, *Chaos of Hard Clay: An Anthology of Post-Apocalyptic Fiction*, *Heimur kvikmyndanna*, *Smásögur 2013: Þetta var síðasti dagur lífs míns*, *Hunger: The Best of Brilliant Flash Fiction 2014-2019*, *Carrier Wave: The Inner Circle Writers' Group Comedy Anthology 2018*, *Well Said, O Toothless One*, *Smásögur 2015: Jólasögur*, *Kúreki norðursins: Kvikmyndaskáldið Friðrik Þór Friðriksson*, *Ástarsögur 2018*, *Smásögur 2014: Skuggamyndir*, *Áfangar í Kvikmyndafræðum*; and *Andvaka: smásögur 2019*.

Perry Lake Perry Lake has made up stories about monsters and the supernatural since he was a small child. You would think he'd have grown out of it. Escaping through the flames that consumed the unimaginably boring city of Paradise, California in 2018, Mr Lake was able to save his laptop and most of his fiction. An unpublishable novel written in his teen years was consumed, so the fire did some good. Originally known for his freelance non-fiction and small press comic books (especially the *Cassiopeia The Witch* series), Lake is now delving into terrifying short stories, collected into ten books. These include the upcoming *Legend of Dracula* series, of which *Blood Curse* will be a part – and will probably make more sense if read in that context. His other series include *The Legend of Frankenstein* and *The Krantz Family Chronicles*. Check out www.perrylakeproductions.com for more details.

Sherri Fulmer Moorer writes science fiction and mystery novels in the US. She works full time in professional licensing and is also a book reviewer, social media rambler and church volunteer. The purpose of her writing is to escape reality and experience the adventure of ordinary people dealing with extraordinary circumstances. Sherri's prolific publication list includes: *Progenitor, Metamorphosis, Emergence* and *Trigger A* (The Earthside Series Books I to IV), *Anywhere But Here, Splinter, So You Want to Be a Writer, Quarantine, Blurry, Resonance, Move, The Tanger Falls Mystery Box Set, Battleground Earth: Living by Faith in a Pagan World, Joy on the Journey, Incursion, Shatterpoint, Feathered Frenzy, Convergence, Obsidian, The Experiment, Tips to Navigate National Novel Writing Month, Lost and Found, When a Pet Dies, The Eleventh Hour, Terminal, Hoyle's Carnival, Night Life: Paranormal Short Stories*; and *Short & Happy (or not)*.

Saj Brodie is a former musician and comedian based at Strangeways in Manchester, lucky enough to find himself only a few doors away from a well-stocked library. His concern for the privacy arrangements around Daisy Ridley's home and particularly her bathroom were misunderstood by the British justice system and he hopes this will soon be cleared up at a second hearing, if Natalie Portman's representatives can keep out of it this time. He writes that it is good news that no cases of coronavirus have so far been found in his closed community, although the Governor has said it is likely to be an underestimate and the true figure could be double that. Saj thanks the Editor for giving him this opportunity and for leaving her return postcode on the envelope.

P.L. Tavormina integrates scientific principles into fictional stories to foster discussion of topics such as the climate crisis. The author of *Aerovoyant*, she's currently writing a climate-based trilogy, set on her fictional world of Turaset. When that's finished, P.L. Tavormina plans to write a trilogy focused on disease transmission and epidemiology. *The Arrival* represents the first scribblings toward that future endeavour. You can learn more at www.pltavormina.com

Magnus Stanke writes from Spain: "Unlike my short story *RN40*, my novels never take place in the present. That's because I've been a busy time traveller for as long as I can remember. I started writing fiction relatively late and perhaps I'm trying to make up for lost ground. My detours in getting to this place included song-writing, screenplays and film criticism. I was a banker in Munich, a dishwasher in Tel Aviv, an English teacher in Buenos Aires and a Shiatsu therapist in London; now I help out my wool-selling-wife in Spain, though I try to keep my touch-downs in the present to a minimum. There are never enough hours in the day. *Falling in Death and Love* and *Time Lies* were my first two retro-thrillers. Currently I'm working on an alternative history trilogy."

Ville V. Kokko is a Ph.D student in philosophy living in Turku, Finland who's trying to start a career in writing both fiction and nonfiction, in both English and Finnish. He has short fiction published on the First Fandom Experience website (https://firstfandomexperience.org/the-solar-system-united-and-symphony-of-armageddon/); Varjorikko magazine 1/2018 (https://varjorikko.com/maatilan-tytto/); and in the anthologies *Love 'Em, Shoot 'Em* (Dana Bell, Ed.) and *Nova 2015 antologia* (Pasi Karppanen and Leila Paananen, Eds). His nonfiction articles have been published in Areo, The Latest, Hybris, Sosiologi, Paatos; and Indeksi. His Goodreads author page can be found at https://www.goodreads.com/author/show/17105199.Ville_V_Kokko

Jenny Torniainen teaches English Literature at The British School of Valencia, Spain. A graduate of French from University College London, she came to writing only recently and since then has dedicated every hour she can to honing her craft. Her chosen genre is Literary Fiction, inspired by contemporary writers Ian McEwan, Lionel Shriver, Donna Tartt and William Boyd. In addition to writing, Jenny enjoys singing and performed for over ten years with the London Philharmonic Choir. She has written several short stories and is currently finalising her first novel, *Half Orange*.

Dale E. Lehman is a veteran software developer, amateur astronomer and bonsai artist in training. He writes mystery, science fiction, humour and assorted other stuff. His writing has appeared in *Sky & Telescope* and on Medium.com. With his wife Kathleen, he owns and operates the imprint Red Tales. They have five children, six grandchildren and two feisty cats. At any given time, Dale is at work on several novels and short stories. Visit him at DaleELehman.com. Although also a writer of non-fiction, Dale's fiction books include: *Space Operatic, The Fibonacci Murders, True Death, Ice on the Bay, The Signature of God, Spiritual Telemetry, A Planet with a View, Indies Unlimited 2016 Editors' Choice Flash Fiction Anthology*; and *Indies Unlimited 2017 Editors' Choice Flash Fiction Anthology*.

Kristýna Corres is based on the Isle of Wight in England. *The Trout Ticklers* is Kristýna's second work in print, after a short story in *Mission Chaos - Tales Of Survival*, but she has time to catch up because she is still at school.

Adam Corres, Kristyna's father, is the author of the novels *Raffles & the Match-Fixing Syndicate* and *Lightspeed Frontier; Kicking the Future* (also a computer game), the play *Mamma Pissaro's Miracle Sauce* (BBC Radio 4 Play for Today) and *Aiken Drum* (for stage), scripts *The Alfalfa Guy* and screenplays *Golphinmire* and *The Seasteaders*. A speculative television script of *Mad Language Broadcasting* has recently been submitted to the BBC Comedy 2020 round.

Mike Sherer lives in the Greater Cincinnati area of southwest Ohio. His screenplay *Hamal 18* was produced in Los Angeles and released direct to DVD. Mike's books include a paranormal/suspense novel *A Cold Dish*, horror novella *Under A Raging Moon*, middle-grade readership *Shadytown*, the novella *Uncertain Cat* and around 20 published short stories in *The Society of Misfit Stories Presents... Volume One, The Society of Misfit Stories Presents... No Way At All, Double Feature Magazine: Science Fiction & Horror, Book of Faith Advent Reflections: While We Wait*; and *Exhibits: An*

Anthology by 67 Press. Links to his published works are available on web page https://mikesherer.org where his travel blog 'American Locations' is also posted.

If it wasn't for **L. Jay Mozdy's** luck and ability to write, he would surely be parting a long, scraggly beard and surviving on rattlesnake somewhere in the Mojave Desert instead of Mississippi. If you see him, ask for a copy of *The Last Redhead.* His short fiction can be found on Medium https://medium.com/@ljaymoz and you can read the first few pages of upcoming novel *Forethought* here http://www.thelastredhead.com/

M.L. Roberts writes short stories and novels of fantasy and crime. Her work history is split between legal and corporate environments. She likes sunny weather, the outdoors, a good book and a fresh cup of coffee. She lives in Southern California with her husband and their dogs and cats. Her other publications include the novels *The Wind from The Wall* (two-book series), *The Alchemist, The Promise of Illarion*; and upcoming in Autumn 2020 *One of Us* and *The Boy Who Drew Horses*; together with the short stories The Scary Short Story of Little Max Bruno, The Girl Witness Caroline, Biker Bounty Hunters of Galaxy Thirteen; and The Prisoner of Monte Verde. You can find out more at
https://mlrobertswriter.wordpress.com/
https://twitter.com/mlrobertswriter
https://amazon.com/author/robertsml

Thor S. Carlsson has lived most of his life in Reykjavik, Iceland, except for a five-year stint in Australia. He has travelled to more countries than he ever thought he would. Having set foot in various situations all over the globe, he weirdly enjoys staying inside more than anything. Having been brought up on a cocktail of movies that span all countries, eras and genres, he much prefers to live vicariously through the world of cinema and literature. Thor's books include: *Reverence for the Art, Little Magician's Magic Set*; and *Somnambulist Sonata.*

Casey Sloop is a 16 year-old aspiring author who likes reading, writing, literary analysis and the study of various mythologies. She is excited to see how people like her first published story and hopes everyone enjoys it!

Originally from Seattle, Washington, **Stephen Mills** spent eight years in the United States Navy and enjoys writing short stories, horror, adventure and historical fiction. His family currently make their home near Phoenix, Arizona. *Isleman*, his first title, is a historical fiction novel set in the Scottish Highlands during the reign of Mary, Queen of Scots. *The Devil's Cohort* is the first title in the Vampire's Vault series.

J. Drew Brumbaugh lives in north-east Ohio where he spends his time writing sci-fi, fantasy and suspense novels, teaching and training at the karate dojo he founded, building a Japanese garden in his back yard and taking walks in the local metro parks. He has six novels in print, a collection of short stories and a co-authored children's book. He continues to work on his next book and always seems to have several stories in various stages of completion. His published works are: *War Party, Shepherds, Fall of the Western Kings, Child of Evil, Bula Bridge, Foxworth Termnus, Girls Gone Great*; and *Ten More*. J. Drew Brumbaugh can be reached at www.jdrewbrumbaugh.com or at his Facebook page https://www.facebook.com/jdrewbrumbaugh/

Jeffrey Caston is the author of *Immunity: A Novel of the Horrific Northwest*. He is a Northwest native who currently makes his home in the Puget Sound region. Inspired by reading at a young age, he took up writing by the age of 11. One of his most cherished gifts is a manual typewriter he received for his birthday while still in the fifth grade. Once he got older, he discovered other genres, including horror. He became an instant fan of Anne Rice, Stephen King and Robert McCammon and is now embarking on a new phase with an indie writing career. His writing focuses on horror but includes elements of thrillers, science fiction and fantasy.

Carolyn Geduld, author of *Who Shall Profit*, is a mental health professional in Bloomington, Indiana. Her fiction has appeared in numerous literary journals and anthologies. Her novel *Take Me Out The Back* will be published in 2020 by Black Rose Writers. Carolyn's other works include: *Filmguide To 2001: A Space Odyssey* and *Harbinger Asylum: Winter 2020*.

Eileen Moynihan was born in Essex, England and grew up on the Isle of Wight from the age of three. At the age of 22, she moved permanently to Ireland, where she lived in West Cork and then more recently on the border of Counties Roscommon and Longford in Termonbarry. For most of that time, she was teaching children with Special Needs and raising her three children with her husband. After taking early retirement, Eileen loves to write stories for children. Her children's books include *Rory Gumboots*, *The Reckolahesperus*, *Hattie and Jacques Love London*, *The Dreamsmith*, *Frances Darwin Investigates*; and (just out) *A Posy of Wildflowers*. She has an adult poetry collection *Dipping Into The Font* and a collaborative novella *Let Him Lie* (Longford Writers Group). Eileen's work has appeared in the anthologies *Home Made* (Longford Writers Group), *Ring Around The Moon*, *Midir and Etain*; and *The King at the Back of the Hill*.

Jim Hamilton writes: 'I have been an avid Science Fiction reader for more than half a century and have always wanted to contribute works of my own. While I mostly write for my own amusement and gratification (and to keep me off the streets after dark), I am always pleased when someone else gets a modicum of enjoyment from my musings. Whether you enjoyed reading this story or not, I would appreciate any honest reviews on Amazon or Goodreads. It's the only way that I can get any feedback as to how I'm doing as an author.' Jim's other publications include *The Chaos Series* ("A trilogy of exuberant and lucid tales ..." — Kirkus Reviews), comprising *The Chaos Machine*, *The da Vinci Butterfly*, *Second Contact*, *Mankind 2.0*, *Colony Ship New Hope*, *Goddess of the Gillani*, *The Race at Valli Ha'I*, *Vacation on*

New Haven, *Before the Fall* (a prequel), *After the Fall* (a prequel); and his other works are *Raising Miss Ellie*, *The Conqueror*; and *Stranded in Eloi* (in press, July 2020).

Julia Davenport is a freelance author and poet. Born in Salford in 1977, she now lives in Manchester in the north west of England. Julia holds a BA(Hons) English Language and Literature degree and is currently studying for an MA in Creative Writing with The Open University. Since 2010 her work has been widely published in many anthologies, exhibitions and magazines. In 2017, her first poetry collection *Order & Chaos: a collection of protest poems* was published by Ragiel & Gill Press.

Leticia Toraci is a Brazilian freelance writer and artist who lives with her husband and her two sons in South Germany. She has a degree in Masters of Food Science from the University of Reading, England. As a child, she won an Honourable Mention for two of her short stories in the Sao Paulo Public Servants Contest in 1986. She has also participated in theatre in Campo Mourao, Brazil, where she recited several of her poems; and her drawings and paintings were also featured in an exhibition. She has also had art exhibitions in Regensburg, Aschaffenburg and Munich, Germany. She has lived in many different cities in Brazil, England, and Germany. For this reason she considers herself a traveller, as are many of the characters in her stories.
Website: https://leticiatoraci.wordpress.com/ Goodreads: https://www.goodreads.com/author/show/9665061.Leticia_Toraci Facebook: https://www.facebook.com/LeticiaToraciAuthor/

Faith Jones is an editor of non-fiction publications and the writer of an Australian television serial which is fossilising in pre-production. She is also responsible for the technical field guide *Seldom Completed Walking Tours Across the Sahara*, for which no feedback has ever been recorded.

If you have enjoyed these tales, please leave a comment or rating for us on https://www.goodreads.com/

I know I said I wouldn't do this (bite me) but here's an Easter Egg for Perry Lake fans. A warning might be appropriate for this one, so to distort the mighty Monty Python:

Read on, but only if ye be unshockable, for if you do doubt that, come nay further, for death awaits you all with nasty, big, pointy teeth...

INSURRECTION

by Perry Lake

1. The Wolf Hunt of 1676.

Countess Báthory Erzsébet grasped the battlements of the White Tower of Brasov and looked at the Barsa River, flowing sluggishly through the city. Getting over it would be a problem, should the need arise.

As the bells of St. Maria's rang the midnight hour, the countess propelled herself from the tower. Under the light of a full moon, she transformed into a great bat, allowing her eight-foot wingspan to catch the air and let her drift to the cobblestoned street below.

Her lackeys, Krummel and Sarvarski, watched as the countess transformed back into human guise and landed. Her gown and cloak were jet black, as was her perfectly-coiffed hair. Upon her bosom rested a large, rectangular amulet of gold, embossed with the ramping dragon of the House of Dracula. The men bowed.

'Come', she ordered. 'Our prey must lay without the city, south to the Carpathians. We may not find him this night, but perchance we will spot some spoor or —'

The men only stared as the countess went silent, cocked her head and allowed her ears to grow pointed. Then they as well heard the low, baleful howl.

'A wolf!'

'To the east', said Countess Báthory. 'Good. We need not overly worry about crossing the Barsa. Hurry! To arms! The beast is not far!'

The men left their horses behind, following her on foot as best they could. The sly Krummel carried a stout spear and a short sword hung from his belt. The hefty Sarvarski hoisted his wicked axe and had a dagger in each boot.

Through the winding streets they ran and into the empty market place, heading for Catherine's Gate. Then they heard the howl once again, clearly within the city. The countess, perhaps also the men, were able to pinpoint its nearby source.

'The stockyards', the countess said, pointing. 'Our wolf seeks an easy meal this night.'

Most men would hesitate to face a ravening wolf, even armed as they were, but these men had tasted the blood of Countess Báthory, thus imbuing them with strength, courage and blind obedience.

Inside the stockyard, the cattle lowed uncomfortably as one might expect, finding a predator in their midst. As the undead countess entered the principal pen, the animals only bellowed louder.

As silent as Death, Lady Báthory stepped within. With only gestures of her head and eyes did she indicate that her men should fan out, left and right. They did so.

The countess stood in the centre of the stockyard, a large area for the herding of the animals. Her eyes slowly scanned the perimeter of the stalls. Only the wide eyes of cattle met hers.

'It is fitting that thou are trapped in this place, pup', she said, smirking. An observer might think she spoke only to the cattle or the empty air. That observer would be wrong. 'For weeks we have played this little game, but now thou art trapped. Thy depredations upon my own cattle will now cease. Step forward that thou might grovel and be granted mercy should we so desire.'

'Wrong', came the reply from within an alcove.

The countess's eyes, once blue, now reddened, flicked to the alcove from whence a man now stepped. He was swarthy, well-built and handsome. His dark hair was long and his beard short but both were unkempt. His attire consisted of an open shirt that was once white and pantaloons, ragged and worn. His legs were otherwise bare. Around his neck hung a cord and on this was a silver triangle, possibly an arrowhead.

He also held a pistol in each hand.

These pistols he raised, pointed left and right. He fired one, then the other. Krummel and Sarvarski both cried out and fell, though Krummel had time to hurl his spear, but the man easily avoided the missile.

The stranger finished his thought. 'You are the one trapped, she-fiend.'

The countess laughed. 'Sayest thou? Methinks thou hast no idea of whom thou wouldst trifle. I came hunting a wolf and here I find a wolf — but this I expected. Art thou so well informed?'

'I do say. I have sealed the exits with holy water and the Host. Overhead is strung a net I soaked in garlic. Prepare to die—forever, this time!'

The countess gave pause. She glanced up at the netting— the stench of cow dung had masked the stench of the garlic. This fellow knew exactly what she was and had some idea of how to deal with her. Still, she was more curious than afraid.

'My, but thou art determined, good fellow. Why dost thy heart hold such hatred for I, a simple, harmless noblewoman? Dost thou think I have done thee wrong?'

The man scoffed. 'Harmless! I think not. I know full well that you are Countess Elisabeth Báthory of Hungary, the Tigress of Csethje! You are a killer of women! I know you have returned from the dead to continue your crimes.'

'Indeed? And how dost thou know these things?'

'Kaspar Wolkenstein told me', he said.

Countess Báthory raised an eyebrow, as decades-old memories resurfaced. 'Did he? Wolkenstein was the magistrate who dared to imprison me. I sent a werewolf — like thyself — to kill him; but he failed. Wolkenstein disappeared thereafter.'

The man scoffed.

'Thou art Kaspar Wolkenstein? I never laid eyes on him for I was tried in absentia, yet I think not.'

As the countess spoke, she moved toward him. Barely a step had she taken when he reached behind and from the back of his trousers he pulled a large, silver crucifix. This he displayed boldly.

The vampire countess wheeled away, throwing up her cloak as protection from the accursed icon of Heaven.

'Insolence! Thou darest? Know thee not who I am?! It is given to all lycanthropes to serve the Undead of the line of Dracula! Thy only hope is to serve me, as Zoltan once did. Thou wouldst forsake this?'

'I do. And I am not Kaspar Wolkenstein. My given name is Imre.'

'I know thee not', she said, still recoiling from the sight of the cross. 'Wouldst thou parlay with me? I propose an hour's truce, that thou might tell me thy tale.'

'You deserve no such treaty, but that you might know who has sent you to Hell, I will tell you the story.'

2. From Father to Son.

Kaspar Wolkenstein lay on his deathbed. Attending him was a fourteen-year-old boy, the only family left to him.

'They said I had a sharp mind when I was your age. I studied law and became first a clerk then a magistrate of Gratz. I wish I could have provided you with the education I received. I was able to make a name for myself and, in time, I was attached to the court of King Matthias and the Lord Palatine.'

'Yes, Father', said the boy. 'I know.'

'Ah, but you do not know that it was in this capacity that I tried the case against Countess Elisabeth Báthory. She was a godless woman, capable of the worst cruelties and without repentance. She murdered sixty girls.

'So I ordered the countess to be imprisoned in her primary castle, that of Csethje, for the rest of her life. I felt that was the end of the matter. But when she died, four years later, she came back from the dead as an evil, malignant ghost — what the Hungarians call a vampire. I think the Devil threw her back, for she was too evil even for Hell! The countess had command over lesser demons. One of them she sent for me. His name was Zoltan Windischer — at least when he appeared as a man. In truth, he was a wolf. A werewolf!'

The boy gasped and crossed himself. He had heard his mother speak in hushed tones of such a creature. In retrospect, it seemed she had been warning him.

'Windischer came to me as a wolf. He attacked me. He bit me. Here. But I lived and I stabbed him with my sword. He too lived — long enough to be burned at the stake!'

The former judge began a coughing fit, hard and deep. It was a moment or two before he could continue.

'Somehow', he said, 'the werewolf infected me. As a vampire will do, I became a wolf like him—No! Not like him— different. He was a devil-worshiper. He changed form as he wished, when he wished. I am cursed. I am a werewolf, doomed to become a wolf every time the full moon rises. Then I must kill.'

Kaspar gripped the boy's trembling hand in his own.

'I killed my wife. I killed my son — a half-brother you never knew. I had no control. A demon had taken over my body, pushing my mind away. After that, I fled. I knew not what to do. I thought of killing myself — oh yes, many a time I have thought of that, but I could not. Something, the demon within me I think, prevented it. After five years, years without aging, I found myself in Hungary once more. I spotted a caravan of Gypsies and I knew those people had magic powers. I was desperate, so I went to them for help.'

'At first, the hetman wanted me gone but the tribe's witch-woman, your mother, Dunicha, was a good woman. She implored me to tell her my tale and I did. From her I received sympathy. So we fell in love. Weeks later, Dunicha consulted another, more powerful phuri-dai. Together, they created this — the silver amulet of Cerberus, which I wear around my neck to this day. You see, the amulet is the only thing that prevents me from turning into a monster when the moon is full.

'Even with the Amulet, I do not age as other men. I am not free of all diseases. I am sick and dying. I only hope the Lord will forgive the terrible murders I have committed and allow me to be with my Ilsa and my Dunicha in Heaven. But you, my son, I — I can only... only warn... Ack! Y-you m-must—!'

Kaspar Wolkenstein's heart stopped. The youth sobbed for some moments, then wiped his eyes, trying to be the man he felt his father would want him to be. He buried his father the next day.

Imre soon confirmed his father's words. They may have come from a noble family, albeit a cadet branch, but the other Wolkensteins had foresworn them. The youth was left with no inheritance and no family.

His mother's family was even more hostile. The current shuvani — witch — said that his father's curse now rested on Imre's head. He almost struck her for those words but the men of the camp restrained him, beat him until he was bloody and left him behind as they rode away in their wagons.

For the next few years, Imre wandered from town to town, begging, stealing, sometimes finding work in a stable or chopping wood. He grew taller, stronger. While working at a farm, he found himself admiring one of the milkmaids and she returned his smile. That night, during a rendezvous, the girl screamed and ran as the light of a full moon turned Imre into a monster. It was his first time. He was confused, awkward. The girl escaped, thank God.

He left the farm the next morning and, finding himself in a new village by dusk, he barricaded himself in the church. It did no good. He still took on the form of a wolf-man and escaped from his own prison.

If he had killed anyone, he did not know. His memory blurred while he was changed and he had run far that night. By daylight, in human form, he kept running.

Unlike his father, upon discovering himself cursed, Imre had an idea of where to run. He sought out the Gypsies, hoping to forge a new amulet, but Gypsies leave few traces, so it was a year later that he found another band.

This shuvani, Shashi, would have nothing to do with Imre. She spat at his feet and they all turned their backs to him. They refused to help him, saying he was a half-breed and cursed, but Shashi had a young apprentice, Zelyna. As Imre wandered off, Zelyna followed him. She heard him out and offered to help, as his mother had helped his father.

'I know of a ritual', the girl said. 'I have never tried it before but I think I can do it. The spell will separate your two halves and send them their opposite ways.'

'You can do this?'

'Yes, I think so, but it will be dangerous. The ritual must be cast just as the full moon rises over the hills. That way, as you are both man and wolf-man, I will be able to split you in two and then the wolf half we will kill.'

Imre had doubts but what other hope was there for him?

In a clearing in the woods, Zelyna drew a pentagram with salt and red chalk. In this, Imre lay naked, trembling.

Zelyna performed the ritual over Imre. 'Oh great Lady of the Moon, I ask you to take back that which you have put into this man. I give you an offering of five silver pieces and a bottle of wine. Please grant this wish and separate man and wolf. I thank you, Moon-Lady for freeing Imre of his curse.'

Zelyna's thanks were premature. As the moon became full, Imre cried out suddenly. The novice witch gasped and covered her mouth in horror as Imre writhed and twisted on the ground, obliterating the protective wards. Hair sprouted from his skin. Fangs grew in his mouth.

She ran. So did he.

The werewolf grabbed her by the arm, halting her escape. With a single slash, the wolf-man ripped her blouse away and she screamed. Her scream and the sight of her bare torso excited the man-beast. His organ bulged against his pantaloons. He wanted her.

And he took her, then and there, throwing her down and ripping her skirts open. He plunged his hardened member deep into her. She screamed in pain as her maidenhead was torn asunder. He pounded his shaft into her again and again. The wolf-man howled and ejaculated.

Zelyna collapsed. It had been horrible but it was over in minutes. Before she could think what to do next, the werewolf had her in his powerful grip once more, his claws digging into her bare arms. His fangs went straight for her throat, sinking in, ripping flesh just as his claws had ripped her clothes. She gasped loudly but she couldn't scream.

The monster would have chewed and bit off chunks of her throat and devoured them but he was startled by the sound of approaching men. Her father and other Gypsies arrived, sticks and knives in hand. He had no choice. He dropped the girl and ran. The Gypsies gave chase but he was too fast. The wolf-man escaped, still cursed.

3. Tooth and Claw.

'I kept running. It took me another year, but at last I made my way back to the village where I buried my father. I dug up his skeleton and I took the Amulet of Cerberus. Now, I only become the wolf if I so wish.'

'Interesting', said the countess, feigning interest, but she did note that the silver amulet he wore was not an arrowhead but rather a wolf's head. 'Yet this explains nothing of why thou hast plagued my cattle and horses these last few months.'

'It explains everything, woman. It was thee who started all of this. Once, the Brotherhood of the Wolf was its own thing, devil worshipers maybe, but they killed honestly — as wolves. They never spread their lycanthropy to others.

'But you had to mix your accursed vampire's blood with a werewolf's! You made Zoltan into a new monster, half vampire and half werewolf. Then the curse spread, first to my father, then to me and maybe to that Gypsy girl I bit. I've heard tales of a wild wolf-bitch marauding villages in Moravia and Hungary.'

'And for this thou would persecute me?' the countess asked, fairly astounded. 'Better you should come to me, offer thy services and let me accept thee into my retinue. I would appreciate thee for what thou art.'

Imre scoffed with derision. 'Never. I have learned of your activities after death and I have vowed to hunt you down and kill you for the curse you have brought upon my family. I attacked the cattle you keep so that I would draw you here. Now I shall avenge my father. I only regret it has taken me this long to find you and lay a trap.'

'A trap? Hah! It is I who have trapped thee, foolish pup.'

Imre scoffed. 'You think so?'

'I know so. I sense my blood within thee, Imre Wolkenstein. Thou must answer to me as did thy father. We shall teach thee better.'

He shook his head. 'My father never answered to you and, thanks to this amulet, I now become the wolf only if I so wish.'

Imre grinned at the undead countess with an evil grin. 'And now I do.'

With that, he ripped off the amulet and flung it down. The silver cross he also flung away. Once more, he transformed, growing hair and claws and fangs. Lady Báthory was taken by surprise. The cattle that looked on from their pens were not contented either.

Imre had not become a wolf, like other lycanthropes; the vampire countess now faced a ravening, bestial wolf-man — with no means of controlling him. He ran at her. He lunged!

Countess Báthory changed form as well, even faster. The wolf-man landed not on a woman but on a great black tigress. If the wolf-man was taken aback, it was only a second. He plunged his fangs into her undead neck. The tigress slashed with her claws, leaving three deep cuts across his chest. He let go and they both fell back.

A tiger has an advantage over a wolf due to its size but although Báthory could take the form of a tiger, her mass remained the same. In weight, he had the advantage of perhaps thirty pounds and none of it fat.

The respite lasted but an instant. They met again, slashing, rending flesh. Blood, living and undead, flew in streams. Enraged by blood loss, the wolf-man redoubled his attack and he flung himself at the vampire countess with a flurry of savage blows.

The countess, being undead, could feel no pain. Blood loss only weakened her, forcing her to revert to human form. Her plan to match the wolf-man in combat had failed; now she could not even transform into a bat and fly off. Not that she'd get far, with that garlic net above her.

Nude but for her dragon amulet and a few shreds of black cloth, the countess fell back and landed in the dirt. Over her, the wolf-man flexed his powerful arms, extended his bloody claws and raised his snout to the moon above.

The howl of the wolf-man terrified the cattle, who tried to escape, knocked boards from their pens and woke half the city of Brasov. His triumphant howl also gave the vampiress the time to regroup, pull both legs back, then kick them forward. The blow of her feet caught the wolf-man in the belly, knocking him over.

She was on her feet before him. Cows that had broken down their pens, now shoved aside by their stampeding fellows, threatened to crush the two monsters. Lady Báthory ignored them and lunged at the fallen wolf-man. She had no need to take on the form of an animal to attack like one. Her nails rent his flesh as had the claws of the tigress. He fought back, clawing with equal ferocity.

Then a stampeding cow, shoved by its fellows, stepped on his head. Dazed, the wolf-man's eyes looked in different directions. He tried to claw either of the countesses he saw — and missed both.

Erzsébet Báthory took the wolf-man's head in her clawed hand and slammed it once against the hard-packed earth. The wolf-man fell flat.

The countess raised up, bloodied, weakened, but before she could take further action she heard a curious sound from above. It was the sound of clapping.

She looked up to see Vlad Dracula standing on the roof of the stockyard. He smirked.

'Well done, my beloved', he said. 'Fortune and that cow's hoof are with thee this night.'

'How long hast thou stood there?' she asked, her eyes flashing. 'I might have been killed.'

'How could I help? The lycanthrope has sealed the place well.'

'Thou hast men with thee. They could lift these charms.'

'They travel not so fast as I', he said. 'Ah. Here they are now. I shall instruct them to free thee.'

With that, he disappeared. Lady Báthory only caressed her golden amulet.

Vlad's men removed the Host and other wards, allowing Countess Báthory to walk free. Her own men, both still alive but bleeding freely, begged her to help them. She drank from both of them to regain her strength, then snapped their necks.

The wolf-man was bound with ropes and chains then tossed in the back of a covered wagon. It was a short ride to a castle in the woods; one of many the countess had held in life. Currently, she kept it as a refuge, with extra coffins of Hungarian soil, should she need them.

Dr Faust and Gretchen welcomed them and laughed at the prisoner, now no longer a beast but a man, stripped naked.

Erzsébet Báthory needed no order from Vlad to lay down sentence on he who had defied her. First, Faust and Gretchen held him down. The countess herself took a curved knife and castrated him. If the howl of the wolf-man was loud, it was nothing compared to the scream of Imre Wolkenstein.

Next, she had Vlad's thrall come forward. The Undead, all of them, turned away as the instrument of execution was brought forward. It was the same crucifix which Imre had used against the countess, but now the bottom portion had been sharpened to a point.

The Countess Báthory gave the order and the thrall set the silver blade above the Imre's chest. After his defeat and his unmanning, he made no resistance. Another thrall raised a mallet and in a single blow, drove the silver dagger through Imre's heart. He grunted and died.

The countess had his body taken to a crypt without the castle's walls and over this she had a great slab of granite set, holding him in place.

'I won't have to worry about him ever again', she concluded.

Afterwards, perhaps hoping for a memento, the countess had one of the thralls chisel Imre Wolkenstein's name and dates of birth and death on his sarcophagus. When she looked at the finished work, she saw the dolt had carved one letter incorrectly.

Rather than become angry, she laughed.

THE END

Printed in Poland
by Amazon Fulfillment
Poland Sp. z o.o., Wrocław

61085356R00164